A THREE TEAM TOWN

Blake Fontenay

Published by Fontenay Publishing – Old Hickory, TN
ISBN: 978-0-692-85835-6
Card Catalogue Number: 2017937223
A Three Team Town/ Blake Fontenay
Digital distribution | *Fontenay Publishing,* 2017.
Paperback | *Fontenay Publishing,* 2017

DEDICATION

To Lynnie, whom I proposed to at a Major League
Baseball game.

CHAPTER ONE

For a change, everything was going according to plan.

Raymond Goldfarb, commissioner of Major League Baseball, was putting the wraps on the league's winter meeting. By all accounts, the meeting had been notable only for its total lack of excitement.

Not even baseball's dyed-in-the-wool geeks, the kind of people who religiously followed the so-called "hot stove" of offseason developments, could muster much enthusiasm about what had been discussed so far.

No changes to the instant replay rules. No adjustments to the league's collective bargaining agreement. No changes to the policies concerning performance enhancing drugs. One blogger had dubbed it "the Winter Meeting of Discontent."

It was certainly less than the assembled members of the media had been promised. It was hard for them to complain, though – after all, they had spent the last four days at Puerto Rico's luxurious Hotel Paraiso, a gleaming oceanfront high-rise not far from Old San Juan. And yet, when they returned home, they were going to have to justify their expense accounts.

After all, newspapers and TV stations were shedding expenses right and left. All the bean counters needed was a good excuse to cut back some more on travel. And for reporters who had become accustomed to an annual expenses-paid trip to the tropics, that would never do. They needed some headlines.

They had been led to believe by league sources that something was going to happen at this winter meeting – something very big. Maybe the repeal of the designated hitter rule. Or a new TV revenue sharing agreement that would give the small market teams a fighting chance against the Yankees and the league's other big boys.

So far, they had nothing newsworthy to report. So as the meeting was drawing to a close, they were getting anxious. Which is just how Raymond Goldfarb wanted them to be.

He was giving his closing remarks in the hotel's palatial conference center, doing an admirable job of summarizing a whole lot of nothing. Then, the bombshell.

"I want to thank the good people of San Juan for being such good hosts to us this week," Goldfarb was saying. "Particularly San Juan's mayor, Jaivin Santiago, and Puerto Rico's governor, Osvaldo Colon, who are here with us today. I've really enjoyed coming down here for our winter meetings and I hope you have as well.

"San Juan is such a wonderful city and it's a shame we have only been able to make it down here once a year. I say 'have been' because that's about to change. Ladies and gentlemen, the league's owners and I met this morning in a special session and the owners voted unanimously to add San Juan as Major League Baseball's newest expansion franchise city."

There was a collective gasp from the assembled members of the media. No one had seen this coming. That had been by design. Goldfarb had wanted to keep the decision under wraps until he was ready to make a dramatic announcement. He had personally planted the rumors about the DH rule and revenue sharing in order to keep reporters distracted from the real story that was right under their noses.

After heaping some additional praise on San Juan and Puerto Rico in general, Goldfarb turned the microphone over to Governor Colon. The governor's excitement was palpable as he began to describe what a historic day this was for the commonwealth. The very first Major League franchise off the North American mainland - and it would be coming here.

He was quickly joined at the podium by Mayor Santiago, who was more than a match for the governor in terms of enthusiasm. Together, they donned baseball caps bearing the San Juan Barracudas logo, a giant fish leaping over the city's skyline. They began pumping their fists goofily and leading the crowd in a chant of "Cudas! Cudas! Cudas!" Even some of the bloggers who were part of the media crowd, caught up in the moment, put any concerns about journalistic objectivity aside and joined in the chants. They were looked upon with disdain by their more seasoned colleagues.

Goldfarb surveyed the scene with a placid smile on his face. He supposed politicians were pretty much the same everywhere. Put a microphone in front of them and it was like pulling the string on a wind-up toy. But he had to give Colon and Santiago credit: They had done this the right way.

Rather than launch a petulant media campaign in which they publicly talked about how Major League Baseball owed the city a franchise, they had done their lobbying quietly and behind the scenes. No negotiating through the media. They had spoken frankly and earnestly with Major League Baseball officials behind closed doors. The way it should be.

Yes, with a population of only 400,000, San Juan would be one of the league's smaller cities. Yet the island's population was 3.7 million – and its leaders had successfully made the case that this would be the entire commonwealth's team.

They had reminded Goldfarb and the league owners that the city hosted an opening day game between the Toronto Blue Jays and Texas Rangers in 2001 – a game where 4,000 people had to be turned away because the stadium was filled to capacity.

They also noted the Montreal Expos had played 22 games in San Juan while they were in the transitional period between their move from Canada to Washington D.C. At the time, the Expos had even briefly entertained the idea of staying in San Juan permanently.

Giving a franchise to San Juan made sense on a lot of levels.

It couldn't help but boost baseball's popularity among Hispanics, the United States' largest and fastest-growing minority group. Hispanics were also the nation's youngest ethnic group, with a median age of just under 28.

More than one in four Major League players were Hispanic. And they were continuing the tradition of great players like Roberto Clemente and Orlando Cepeda.

Clearly, this was a demographic group Major League Baseball needed to satisfy if the league was going to be successful in the future.

Plus, this would be a big boost to the Puerto Rican Professional Baseball League. The league's season was during the winter months, so there was no conflict there. More major leaguers might decide to play their winter ball in Puerto Rico after visiting San Juan during the regular season.

Puerto Ricans loved baseball so much that having the sport year-round would be a dream for them. Baseball truly was the national pastime in Puerto Rico, which Goldfarb was not sure he could say for the mainland United States any more.

So yes, this made good business sense. Goldfarb had to keep telling himself that.

He knew plenty about running a business. Before he became commissioner, he had founded and run Ray of Hope, a foundation that raised millions for research into AIDS and other sexually-transmitted diseases. A grandfather and Sunday school teacher, he had a squeaky clean image. Which is why the league lured him out of retirement to clean up baseball in the wake of the steroid scandal.

He could see the big picture. Bringing a franchise to San Juan could be a gateway to help the league establish a foothold in Mexico and throughout Central America. If Mexico City's problems with pollution and drug cartels could be reined in, Goldfarb could see a franchise there at some point in the future.

Who knew? The richest man in the world was Mexican, so maybe he could build Mexico City a domed stadium and provide the necessary security. But that would only happen years down the road. Goldfarb had more immediate concerns.

For example, San Juan would need a new stadium to replace venerable Hiram Bithorn Stadium, which had been built in the early 1960s. Goldfarb had no doubt the people of Puerto Rico would rally and find a way to make that happen.

So this was a good thing, Goldfarb told himself. And even if he was doing a good thing for the wrong reasons, didn't the end justify the means? He wasn't sure he could answer that question. He'd made a terrible mistake – one for which he was beginning to pay today.

On stage, Mayor Santiago and Governor Colon were wrapping up their remarks by high-fiving each other. There would be questions from the media, many of which Goldfarb would dismiss as "premature." Then after giving the reporters time to file their stories, there would be a farewell banquet.

The reporters would partake of a feast that included black bean soup, chicken with rice, Puerto Rican beef stew, plantains, diced potatoes and green peas – all seasoned with the best spices Puerto Rico's Spanish, African and Taino cultures had to offer. Dessert would consist of flan and tropical fruits. And of course, there would be much beer and rum consumed as the party lasted late into the night.

Marisol, a beautiful young singer whose fusion of rock and salsa made her a star in Puerto Rico and moderately successful on the mainland United States, would provide the entertainment. The reporters would leave the island hung over but happy – which greatly increased the probability there would be favorable stories and opinion columns about the new expansion team in San Juan.

Of course, if history was any guide, the chances were excellent that a good portion of the rich food and strong drink from the party would be regurgitated before the assembled media throng headed for home the next morning. For the sake of the hotel's cleaning staff, Goldfarb could only hope most of the over-indulgers would find their way to a toilet, sink or – at worst – one of the many flower pots filled with tropical flora that decorated the hotel's stately interior. Major League Baseball had worn out its welcome at the nearby Hotel Caribe when an inebriated columnist from Cincinnati had left a mess rivaling the BP oil spill in the hotel's outdoor pool a few years ago. Journalism might be changing, but many of its practitioners still clung to the old school ways of carousing.

No matter. Goldfarb had made up his mind that he was going to do his best to enjoy the evening. At least for tonight, everyone around him was happy. He was a hero to the Puerto Ricans. He might even get a street named after him here some day.

So Commissioner Goldfarb took a few deep breaths and savored the moment. Because he knew it wouldn't last.

He knew what awaited him upon his return to the mainland.

CHAPTER TWO

The meeting took place aboard a 40-foot houseboat anchored in a cove on Old Hickory Lake, just northeast of Nashville. The houseboat was usually moored at the lakeside home of one of the meeting's participants in the affluent suburb of Hendersonville.

However, when this group got together, privacy – actually, secrecy - was of paramount importance. While the cove was a popular spot with boaters during the daytime in warm weather months, it was deserted at this time of night.

The six members of the group were the leaders of Nashville's business community: A recording industry executive. The head of a religious publishing house. The owner of a chain of resort hotels. The CEO of a chain of discount department stores. The CEO of a large restaurant chain. And the founder of a giant healthcare firm.

Their meetings were infrequent. They got to get together no more than once or twice a year usually, to discuss matters of mutual interest. Without any irony at all, they referred to themselves as The Cabal.

There were rules when they got together. No cell phones or other personal communications devices of any kind. They had made that rule after the first couple of meetings, when they all tried to show each other how busy they were.

No subordinates were allowed to attend the meetings. All business had to be conducted face-to-face among the principals. Promises made during these meetings were never written into contracts, but they were treated as if they were bound by the force of law.

No notes or meeting minutes were written down, either. Participants were expected to remember what was discussed and decided.

Talking about what was said at the meetings with the outside world was strictly forbidden. Not with employees, friends, family members – and certainly not the media.

They ate dinner first, making what passes for small talk among multimillionaires. Stuffed crab cakes for an appetizer, then filet minion, new potatoes, asparagus spears, iceberg lettuce wedge salad and rolls. Then over cigars and drinks, they got down to business.

The resort chain owner kicked off the discussion: Had everyone heard about the Major League Baseball commissioner's announcement in San Juan, he wanted to know.

Heads around the room nodded. "So what does this mean to us?" someone asked.

It was noted that for scheduling reasons, new major league sports franchises usually came in twos. San Juan was going to get one of them. So which city would get the other?

For years, landing another major league team for Nashville had been a popular topic of discussion for The Cabal. A team which its members would own and profit from. Of course, they were all always looking for new ventures that would add to their fortunes. But this was a chance to do good while doing well. Making millions was fun. Making millions while being hailed as community heroes was even better.

While members of The Cabal were level headed and unemotional when it came to running their own businesses, they were also true believers when it came to Nashville and its civic virtues. They still bristled when outsiders made "Hee Haw" jokes, even though the cornpone TV show had been off the air for decades. They were among the optimistic few who bought into the hype that Vanderbilt's football team was on the verge of turning the corner and becoming a powerhouse in the Southeastern Conference. And while Charlotte was known as a financial headquarters city, Raleigh was known as a research center and Atlanta was known for just about everything, well, Nashville was by gosh the Athens of the South. So of course Nashville should have its own Major League Baseball team.

And they would be hailed as heroes if they were able to pull this off. Bringing a Major League Baseball franchise to Nashville would cement their legacy as community leaders. Who could deny that this was the opportunity they had been waiting for?

But what about the city's minor league team, the Nashville Sounds, someone asked.

What about them, came the reply. No matter how long the Sounds had been fixture on the Nashville sports scene, this was too good of an opportunity to pass up.

Someone wondered aloud why the commissioner hadn't announced two new expansion cities at the same time. Had a decision already been made about where the other franchise would go? Was the commissioner merely waiting to make another dramatic announcement in the selected city?

That was a possibility, they all had to agree. But it was also possible that the site of the second franchise was still in play. Could they afford not to try to land a new team in the Music City?

Of course, this was all conjecture, the pessimist in the room said. Perhaps Major League Baseball wasn't planning to add another team at all. It would be unusual for the league to have an odd number of teams, but not unprecedented.

And what if another franchise was going to be added, but the decision had already been made about where it would go? Members of The Cabal could lose face if they publicly lobbied for a team and Nashville was jilted.

The public wouldn't understand the high-risk, high-reward nature of pursuing a major sports franchise. There would only be disappointment if the effort failed. Members of The Cabal would be blamed, as unfair as that was. And the city's disappointment over losing the franchise might even lead to a backlash against The Cabal's business interests.

Besides the risk, being out in front on an issue like this could be a pain. Members of The Cabal were used to running their businesses without public scrutiny. Trying to land a baseball franchise would open them up to constant scrutiny.

But what if The Cabal had someone to act as a buffer? To be the public face of the campaign to bring a team to Nashville while The Cabal's members remained safely anonymous?

The question then was who could fulfill such a role. It would have to be someone extremely personable and popular. Someone who loved both the city and the sport of baseball. Someone wealthy enough to buy at least a token share of the team's ownership. It would be important for The Cabal's front man to have some skin in the game.

And, of course, it would have to be someone who would do as he was told.

Several names were mentioned and then dismissed for various reasons. Politicians were quickly ruled out. Doubtful that any of them would be willing to put up any of their own money toward the venture. Besides, politicians would be more useful playing another role in the process – and that role involved keeping them at arm's length.

Country music singers were plentiful in Nashville, but the music industry executive ruled out bringing any of them into the fold. That could complicate his other business dealings. There were a few actors and actresses living in Nashville, but one-by-one, they were ruled out as too flighty or too egotistical.

Finally, someone mentioned the name of Wynn Hammerskal.

Hammerskal was a retired professional baseball player who had grown up in Hohenwald, Tennessee, a small town about 80 miles southwest of Nashville. His pitching talents were apparent at a young age – so much so that the St. Louis Cardinals had drafted him at the age of 17.

After a couple of years in the minor leagues, Hammerskal made the Cardinals' roster and immediately made a name for himself. The left-hander won 15 games in his rookie season – the first of seven seasons where he won 15 or more. In two of those seasons, he won 20 or more games, once earning the Cy Young Award for his efforts.

Hammerskal was popular, not just because of his talents, but also his outlandish personality. He believed – or at least professed to believe – that he was the reincarnation of Dizzy Dean, another great Cardinal pitcher who grew up in a small Southern town. Hammerskal was nicknamed "The Jackhammer" – and early in his career, he invented what he called "The Jackhammer Jump."

Whenever he made a key play to end an inning – a strikeout, a pop-out with the bases loaded, a great fielding play from the mound – he would hop back to the dugout with his arms extended, shaking uncontrollably to mimic a jackhammer's vibrations.

Hammerskal's antics drove opposing teams crazy, which made their hitters even less effective against him. And of course the fans began emulating "The Jackhammer Jump" in the stands. After a couple of seasons, the Cardinals institutionalized the practice by staging a stadium-wide "Jackhammer Jump" in the middle of the fifth inning – a higher energy version of the time-honored tradition of the seventh inning stretch.

Stories – some true, some most certainly untrue – were always circulating about The Jackhammer. Like the time he injured his pitching arm and then pitched batting practice to his teammates right-handed for two weeks until his left arm healed. Or the time he had baited an umpire who was calling a tight strike zone into charging the mound and bumping him, prompting the league to fine the ump. Or the time he had found the Philadelphia Phillies mascot costume unattended in the clubhouse at Veterans Stadium. As the story went, The Jackhammer had strapped the mascot's head to the roof of his rental car and drove through the streets of Philadelphia until dawn.

The Jackhammer was still in the prime of his career when the New York Yankees, looking to make a deep postseason run, had traded for him late one season. The Jackhammer wasn't wild about the move, but he had promised to make the most of it. Unfortunately for the Yankees, making the most of it meant challenging a teammate to a bullpen car race at Yankee Stadium late one evening. As that story went, The Jackhammer had been leading the race around the warning track when he turned to taunt his competitor – and slammed into the rolled-up tarp at the edge of the field. The wreck tore up his knee so badly that he never pitched an inning for the Yankees. But he had a guaranteed 5-year, $100 million contract, so his financial future was secure when he left the game behind and returned to Nashville, his adopted hometown.

So yes, members of The Cabal had to agree, Wynn "The Jackhammer" Hammerskal could be a popular front man for their efforts to bring an expansion franchise to Nashville. But could a man of his reputation be trusted? Would he be, to pardon the pun, a team player?

16

There was a heated discussion about this. If the stories were true, Hammerskal might be difficult to control.

On the other hand, there were the media interviews he had given shortly after the bullpen car mishap. When asked about his goals for the future, he had expressed the fervent wish that he could bring an expansion team to Nashville. That, along with his other wish of designing a new baseball video game.

So, one member of The Cabal mused, he wants to be a baseball team owner? Do you think he'd be willing to be a 5 percent team owner? A 5 percent owner who would be the face of the team to the media and the public?

As a possible deal-sweetener, the CEO of the department store chain had some contacts who might be able to help with the video game thing. Who knew? If the game actually got developed, maybe his stores could even make some money selling it.

Yes, the kid was rich. But he was also only 30. Surely he wasn't done making money, was he? And what did he want to do with the rest of his life, sit around boring people with stories about his baseball career? Playing video games?

It was worth pitching the idea to him. They could send their attorney, Julius C. Malfair, to make Mr. Hammerskal an offer. Mr. Malfair could be very persuasive. And if Hammerskal agreed, Malfair could arrange a meeting with the mayor. It would be important to get City Hall's support early in the process. Having Hammerskal aboard would definitely help sell the idea.

After a bit more haggling over the details, it was agreed that was what The Cabal would do. As the meeting was about to adjourn, the head of the religious publishing house posed questions that caught everyone off guard:

Was this just vanity? Were The Cabal's members really doing what was in the city's best interests, or were they just feeding their own egos?

The questions were met with laughter as the men got up to refill their drinks and light fresh cigars.

Meeting adjourned.

CHAPTER THREE

The meeting took place in the mayor's office, overlooking the Cumberland River at the Davidson County Courthouse in downtown Nashville. Mayor Kent Gables sat at his desk, facing his public policy advisor and the two visitors seated in front of him.

Mayor Gables looked every bit the part of who and what he was: Neatly dressed with great posture, a wide smile and a perfect helmet of anchorman hair. He'd begun his career in real estate, starting a small firm and turning it into a large one. His real estate ads were all over town – creating the public profile that had allowed him to run for office. After two terms on the Metro Nashville Council in which he was mostly associated with media-friendly "feel good" legislation, he had won his first term as mayor. He managed to hang around and earn a second term mainly because he had hired or – in some cases, retained – competent City Hall employees who managed to make him look good.

Among those was his public policy advisor, Horton Edison, who had joined him in this meeting. Appearance-wise, Edison presented a striking contrast to his boss. Short, squat and unassuming in appearance, it appeared as if Edison's ill-fitting suit was trying to swallow him. His face showed not a hint of emotion. He was a seasoned veteran of City Hall. He'd started as an intern in the city's planning department and worked his way up to his current position. He had also served as public policy advisor under the previous mayor – and he was one of the holdovers Gables had wisely chosen to keep on staff. Lots of people described

Edison as "dour" or "unsociable." But those were the ones who didn't really know him.

Seated beside him at this meeting was Julius C. Malfair, a tall, thin man with gray hair and half-moon spectacles. His suit was as neatly tailored as the mayor's, but considerably more expensive. His expression was pleasant but intense as he met Mayor Gables' gaze. Lots of people described Malfair as a jerk. And they were right.

The fourth seat in the room was occupied by Wynn "The Jackhammer" Hammerskal. The former Major League pitcher was dressed in jeans and a golf shirt with 'Supermax Country Club' emblazoned on the front pocket. His hair was bleached blonde, with expensive sunglasses perched on top, and he had a deep tan. He was repeatedly tossing a baseball into the air with his left hand while his right hand held a cell phone to his ear. It was the same conversation he was on when he and Malfair had entered the room 10 minutes earlier.

The mayor's smile was unwavering as he and the other two men waited in silence for Hammerskal to finish.

"Oh, man, the graphics have to be sick," Hammerskal was saying. "That's what makes or breaks a video game. Yeah, yeah, yeah, we're gonna make it happen. I know a guy in Seattle. A straight-up nerd, but he knows his stuff. I'll put you in touch with him. Got some other business to take care of before we get around to that, though. In fact, I'm in a meeting right now. I'll hit you back later."

Hammerskal clicked off the phone and stuffed it into his shirt pocket. He continued to toss the ball into the air.

"Mr. Hammerskal, I can't tell you what an honor it is to meet you," Mayor Gables began. "I'm a huge fan of yours. In fact, I had you on my fantasy baseball team that year you, well, when that little accident happened.

Sorta wrecked my team's season. Not that I blame you of course..."

"Uh, Mr. Mayor, I just met you, but I have one rule they should have told you about beforehand," Hammerskal said, rising slowly to his feet. "Nobody – not even the mayor of Nashville – mentions 'the accident' to me. Not unless they're looking for a fastball aimed at their chin."

"Now, Wynn..." Malfair was saying, his hands outstretched in protest.

With alarming quickness, Hammerskal wound up in his pitching delivery and whipped his left hand toward the mayor. However, he released the ball before bringing his arm forward, allowing it to drop behind his back, where he caught it with his right hand.

The sudden series of movements caused all three seated men to flinch.

"Man, I'm just playing with you!" Hammerskal said, laughing loudly. "It's nice to meet you, too! And hey, I'm really sorry about that little accident, too. You see, I'm a competitor – and sometimes things like that happen in the heat of competition."

"Yes, well, I guess I understand," Mayor Gables said, trying to repaint the smile back on his face. "You're trying to give your best, whether you're playing baseball, or racing...well, whatever it was that you were doing that night."

"Mayor, thank you so much for agreeing to see us on such short notice," Malfair said, trying to end the awkwardness and steer the meeting back on track. "Mr. Hammerskal has a proposal that we think might be of interest to you. And, by extension, the citizens of Nashville."

"Well, of course, I'm all ears," Gables said. "We're so happy to have Mr. Hammerskal back in Middle Tennessee. You could live anywhere you want, so we're glad you've chosen Nashville as your home. Are you here because you want to do a public service announcement for the city? Maybe something about our new program aimed at discouraging jaywalking? It's called 'The Crosswalk Lines are Just Fine.'"

"Crosswalks?" Hammerskal asked quizzically. "Those little base paths they put in intersections?"

"Mr. Mayor, I think a public service announcement is something we could probably talk about some other time," Malfair said. "We've got something a little bit more important to discuss. Wynn, why don't you tell him what's on your mind?"

"Mayor," Hammerskal said earnestly. "Do you know what it's like to feel you're on the verge of something really great?"

"Like that three-hitter you threw against the Braves your second-to-last season?" Gables said.

"That really should have been a two-hitter," Hammerskal said. "That scorekeeper wouldn't know an error if one took a bad hop off the infield dirt and nailed him right in the..."

"Wynn, I'm sure the mayor's a very busy man," Malfair said. "Why don't you tell him why we're here?"

"Right," Hammerskal said. "Mayor Gables, Nashville needs its own Major League team. And I want to be the owner of it. Well, at least one of them, anyway."

"I don't know what to say," Gables said. Which was rare. The mayor was seldom at a loss for words.

"You don't have to say anything," Malfair said. "A Major League team is just what this city needs. The city already has a National Football League franchise and a National Hockey League franchise. Adding a Major League baseball team would put the city in another league, so to speak. We'd be a three-team town. Just like Atlanta, which has a Major League baseball team, a National Basketball Association team and a National Football League team. Doesn't that sound great?"

"It would establish Nashville's rightful place in the universe," Hammerskal said proudly.

"Do you really think you can bring a team here?" Gables asked.

"We do," Malfair said. "As you may know, Mayor, the commissioner of Major League Baseball recently announced that San Juan, Puerto Rico will be getting an expansion franchise. The speculation – the very strong speculation – is that the league will add another team to add balance to its scheduling. We believe Nashville should get that team."

"So what do you need from us?" This was Edison, speaking for the first time since the meeting began.

"Well, we'd like your political support, of course," Malfair replied. "We would like for the mayor to join Mr. Hammerskal at a press conference in the next couple of days when we announce our bid for the franchise."

"And what else?" Edison asked.

"What do you mean, what else?" Malfair said.

"What else do you need, besides political support?" Edison said.

"Well, I..." Hammerskal said.

"Please, Wynn, let me handle this," Malfair said. "Mr. Edison, I don't recall us asking for anything else."

"Where will the team play?" Edison asked.

"Well, of course we'll need a new stadium," Malfair said. "But we'll take care of that. What we really need from you right now is your help in galvanizing the community behind our effort. A little cheerleading, that's all. You know the mayor's seal of approval would be a great help to us."

"No financial support from the city?" Edison said. "No subsidies? No tax breaks? Nothing at all from the city?"

"Did we say that?" Malfair said. "We've got to make a case to Major League Baseball and the world that Nashville deserves that new franchise. It would just be nice to have the support of the mayor and the city's other political, business and community leaders. That's what we're asking for."

"And who would be the team's other owners, besides Mr. Hammerskal?" Edison said.

"We can get into all that later," Malfair said. "This is really more of a get-acquainted session. The details we can hash out down the road."

Edison fell silent again.

"Well, I think we've said our piece," Malfair said, patting his knees as he rose from his chair. "Wynn, I think it's time to give Mayor Gables and Mr. Edison some time to talk this over."

"Right, right," Hammerskal said, popping quickly out of his seat. "Mayor, sorry about pranking you earlier. Here, please take this autographed baseball as a sign of, well, let's just call it a gift between buds."

With that, Hammerskal picked up a pen off the mayor's desk, scribbled "The Jackhammer" on the ball, and gently tossed it to the mayor.

"Thank you, Wynn, I appreciate that," Gables said as the four men exchanged handshakes. "I must say, given your reputation, I wasn't sure what to expect out of this meeting."

"Well, I could still set some furniture on fire or something if you'd like," Hammerskal said.

"I don't think that will be necessary," Gables said. "But no Jackhammer Jump?"

On that cue, Hammerskal thrust his arms out at his sides.

"Let's save that for the news conference," Malfair quickly interjected.

"All right," Gables said. "My staff will work out the details on that. We'll be in touch soon."

"Well, holding a news conference is certainly something we can talk about," Edison hedged.

Hammerskal and Malfair made their exit. When Gables and Edison were alone, they sat in silence for a few seconds. Gables pressed his hands together just below his nose. Finally, he spoke.

"I'd love to have your thoughts, Horton."

"It's an interesting proposal," Edison said slowly.

"That's what I thought!" Gables said. "Just imagine – we could be a three-team town! A three-team town! Just like Atlanta! Nashville is always getting compared to Atlanta - and not in a good way. We're not as big. We're not as sophisticated. We don't have the kind of economic growth that they do. They get all the corporate headquarters and fancy shops and restaurants that we don't. They've got their own "The Real Housewives of..." show. Well, all that may be true. And maybe we'll never catch up to them in some areas. But major league sports, well, that's something that people really look at when they're evaluating what makes a city a major city."

"I don't know," Edison said.

"What's not to know?" Gables replied. "They said all they needed from us was political support. It's pretty easy for me to be the pro-baseball mayor, isn't it? That's about like supporting mom, hot dogs and apple pie. Isn't it?"

"It is."

"And it doesn't hurt that this drive for a new team is being led by the guy who is arguably the most popular athlete in the city, does it?

"No, it doesn't," Edison admitted. "Although in addition to arguably being the most popular, Wynn Hammerskal is also unarguably the city's quirkiest athlete. As we saw evidence of today."

"And the media eats that sort of stuff up. They'll love him. They already do love him. So tell me, Horton, what's the problem?"

"Well, for starters, we just spent $65 million of public money to build a new stadium for the Sounds in Germantown less than five years ago."

"Right."

"Right. And a lot of people might think it would be a little wasteful to turn around and spend money on a Major League team after we just made that kind of investment."

"It can't be helped, Horton. For cities that are serious about having major league sports, those kinds of expenses are just the cost of doing business."

"That's a pretty heavy cost, Mr. Mayor."

"But don't you think it's worth it, Horton? Think about what we'd be getting – and giving up almost nothing in return!"

Edison hesitated. A person couldn't survive City Hall politics as long as he had without knowing the difference when it was time to be honest with his boss and when it was time to shut up.

"I don't know, Mayor, I don't know," Edison said finally. "I just get a strange feeling about this one."

CHAPTER FOUR

Horton Edison took a bite out of his lunch and winced.

He was eating hot chicken, one of the trendy foods the city of Nashville had adopted somewhere during its journey from being a sleepy Southern backwater to an up-and-coming urban center. Legend had it that the dish was invented by a woman seeking revenge against a cheating boyfriend – which Edison thought was believable.

At one time, hot chicken was only served in a couple of seedy places in the city's less desirable neighborhoods, but now you could get it everywhere. Edison was sitting in a place called Lavamouths, located in Hillsboro Village, a cute neighborhood near the Vanderbilt University campus. Edison wasn't sure why he was here. Hillsboro Village was a bit of a drive from downtown, particularly since he wasn't meeting anyone here. And Edison wasn't a particular fan of hot chicken.

He loved spicy foods – Mexican, Indian, Korean, Thai and all the rest – but he liked foods that were spicy and flavorful. To his way of thinking, hot chicken was just spicy. The peppers and other seasonings were great for searing tongues, lips, gums and stomach linings, but they overpowered the taste of the chicken.

Edison was wondering why he had chosen Lavamouths when he suddenly felt a strong hand clap on his shoulder. He turned and looked up into the grinning face of "Big Paul" Castellano, the owner of the Nashville Sounds Minor League team.

Big Paul was a forgotten legend around Nashville. He was a legend because he had brought professional sports back to the city after a long absence. He had built a baseball park, Greer Stadium, in an industrial area beside a rail yard south of downtown.

It wasn't exactly a destination location, but Big Paul had made it work. He was a great salesman for his product. He held all the usual promotions – free bats or balls to the first customers to arrive on certain nights – but he did much more than that. He became the face of Nashville's minor league franchise, hosting burger cookouts before games and awarding prizes to the fans who could eat the most. In fact, he had to stop participating in the contests after the first couple of years because he was capable of downing a massive number of the rubbery burgers in a short period of time. But in addition to all that, he never missed a chance to promote his team – and his city – in the media or anywhere else.

So for a while he was a legend, then he became forgotten when Nashville grew up and got itself a couple of major sports franchises. With an NFL and an NHL team in town, the Sounds quickly found themselves playing third fiddle. Even though the baseball season didn't overlap with the other two franchises, going to a Sounds game didn't have the same allure that it once did.

Still, Big Paul persevered. With cheap food, ice cream served in tiny batting helmets and cheap beer, Sounds baseball was still a decent summertime option for many Nashvillians.

In fact, the Sounds seemed on the verge of making a major comeback when the city had agreed, after years of intense negotiations with Big Paul and his lawyers, to build a brand new stadium in Germantown, a historic neighborhood just north of downtown that was in the middle of a major revitalization.

With the new stadium open, Big Paul had little reason to be upset with Edison, his boss or anyone else at City Hall.

"Horton!" Big Paul exclaimed. "I didn't think they ever let you out of City Hall."

"Hey, Big Paul. They do let me out to eat a little lunch now and then."

"Glad to hear it!" Big Paul said. "This is one of my favorite places."

Somewhere in the back of his mind, Edison remembered that. Maybe that explained why he was here.

"Do you have a minute to sit down, Big Paul? Have you already ordered?"

"Ordered and eaten," Big Paul said, patting his heavy belly as he plopped down facing Edison. "How's yours, by the way?"

"It's, um, hot," Edison said. In fact, his eyes were watering and he was starting to sweat profusely, even after only a couple of bites.

"Yeah, you know, the hottest chicken they serve on the menu isn't even the hottest chicken they can make?" Big Paul said. "Once I was kidding around, telling one of the cooks: 'Is that all you've got?' Well, he went back into the kitchen and made some chicken that was so hot that I was sick for days afterward. I think I actually lost a couple of pounds because I couldn't eat anything else for the first 48 hours afterward. All I could do was drink water. I say all that to say – don't challenge the cooks here. You'll pay for it."

"Good tip, Big Paul. Although I wasn't planning on doing that. What I have here is plenty hot for me."

"You're a wise man, Horton. I don't care what anybody else says about you. So what brings you out this way today, anyway?"

"You know, Big Paul, I'm not really sure."

"Well, I'm glad you made it out this way. I just want to thank you and your boss for helping make that new stadium happen."

"Well, it was a long time coming. And you've earned it, Big Paul. You and the Sounds have been great corporate citizens. You've given the people of this town great family entertainment for nearly 40 years."

"Ah, Horton, you're nice to say so. To tell you the truth, though, without that new stadium, I don't know how much longer we could have made it. You know, things have changed a lot over the years, Horton. It used to be that people were content to sit out in the bleachers, eat a bag of peanuts and watch a little baseball for three hours. Now that's not enough. People want 'amenities.' Specialty foods. Comfy seats. An entertaining scoreboard show. Between-innings entertainment. You know, it's all like a big arms race. Memphis built that new stadium downtown a few years ago and suddenly nobody in Nashville was satisfied with old Greer Stadium any more. I mean, nobody in Nashville wants to compare unfavorably to Memphis in anything."

"That's true," Edison said. "So are you satisfied with the new stadium? Everything working out OK there?"

"Absolutely! No complaints at all! You've pretty much guaranteed that the Sounds are going to be around and successful for another 40 years."

With that, Edison's indigestion was mixed with a pang of guilt.

"So, Mayor Gables hasn't been in touch with you today, Big Paul?"

"No, he hasn't. Why would he?"

Horton Edison took a deep breath. He really wanted to come clean with Big Paul, to tell him that the city was about to launch a pursuit of a Major League team that, if successful, would render the Sounds obsolete.

So long, Big Paul. Thanks for all you've done, but your time has passed. Horton decided he just couldn't do it. He was the mayor's chief of staff, which meant he had to take care of many of the tasks the mayor didn't want to handle personally.

But not this time. If Mayor Gables wanted to pursue a Major League team, he should be the one to break the news to Big Paul. Big Paul deserved to hear that from the city's chief executive, not someone who worked for him. After all this time, Big Paul was owed that much. And Horton hoped Mayor Gables would recognize that and do the right thing.

"No reason," Edison said, rising from his seat. "It's been good talking to you, Big Paul. And if you want the rest of my chicken, you're welcome to it."

"Good to see you, too, Horton. And if you're done with it, I will take that chicken off your hands. You're a good man."

Horton shook Big Paul's hand and walked out of Lavamouths, feeling guiltier than he had in a long, long time.

CHAPTER FIVE

Hunt Blazen slipped the disc into his computer and waited for it to download.

He was sitting in his second-floor office overlooking the showroom of Blazen Motorcars, a highly successful car dealership located just off the interstate ramp on Broadway. There were few better locations in Nashville's Midtown neighborhood. The dealership was just a few short blocks from Lower Broadway's famed entertainment district. And from the front lot, one could see the spot where Broadway merged with West End, the major artery connecting downtown with some of the city's most affluent neighborhoods.

When the rotating arrow on Blazen's computer screen disappeared, he clicked his mouse to start the video of his latest commercial.

"It's wintertime," the video version of himself was saying. *"It's a time when cabin fever causes a lot of people to go a little bit craaazy."* In the video, Blazen appeared to be standing in a driving snowstorm. In fact, the production crew was emptying buckets of shaved ice in front of a giant fan just off camera. It hadn't been a particularly fun scene to shoot.

"Well, with some of the blazin' hot deals we've got here at Blazen Motorcars, folks may think we've gone a little crazy, too. They wonder how we can offer outrageous prices like these!"

The video cut to another scene. Blazen was sitting behind the wheel of an SUV, with the camera filming him through the open driver's side door.

"Global warming? Sure doesn't seem like it this winter, does it? And when it snows, you know you need one of these terrific SUVs to help you get around. It's craaazy to go out in bad weather without one!"

Never mind that, on average, Nashville got about a half a foot of snow each winter, spread out over a few light dustings. Blazen knew customers would pay a premium for an SUV based on a couple of bad days a year. Even though the city's schools and many of its businesses and other institutions shut down for almost any measurable accumulation of snow and driving was therefore unnecessary.

Another scene cut. Blazen was standing in front of one of the dealership's newest hybrid models. A few steps away was a static electricity ball like the kind often found in science museums.

"Of course, it's not just the weather that's wacko! High gas prices are enough to make you go nuts! So give your driving experience a jolt with one of these good-looking, high-mileage hybrids!"

In the video, Blazen walked over and put his hands on the static electricity ball. His hair stood on end and he convulsed as if he were being electrocuted.

"Ah-yah-yah-yah-yah! Oh, I'm just kidding." He stopped shaking. *"But I must say, our deals on these hybrids are electrifying! Get it? Get it? Electrifying!"*

Watching in his office, Blazen winced. OK, that part hadn't seemed quite as stupid when he read the script. But seeing it on video was a different experience. Oh well. This was almost over. Blazen was slamming shut the sliding back door on a minivan.

"Parents, you love 'em, but you know your kids will sometimes drive you craaazy, too! That's why you need a spiffy minivan like this one, with the optional DVD players mounted in the seats to give your young ones something to do besides yell: 'Are we there yet?'"

They'd actually tried a couple of takes with the minivan loaded with children, but when Blazen had slammed the door shut, it conjured up images of him sending them off to reform school. So in the end, a decision was made to keep the van empty.

"We'll offer you all these models, and more, with dealership financing and the lowest sticker prices you'll find anywhere in Middle Tennessee."

Last scene. Blazen, standing in front of the dealership, the sign visible directly overhead.

"Yes, the deals we're offering are so good that some people might even say we're a little crazy. So what do you think? Are we crazy? Are...we...craaazy?"

On cue, a red convertible with the top down screeched to a halt in front of Blazen. The driver, a platinum blonde in a tube top, delivered her line:

"Crazy – crazy like the fox!"

The video monitor went blank. The production company that filmed the spot would add the graphics – prices, loan terms and conditions, disclaimers, information about the dealership – after Blazen had given final sign-off on the video footage.

Blazen thought about the last scene in particular. Crazy like *the* fox. Not crazy like *a* fox. For what they were paying her, why couldn't the actress get that one line right? They had tried eight different takes with her scene. In two of those, she had nearly run over Blazen's feet as she drove on camera. In the end, Blazen had decided that the take he had just watched was good enough, especially if it meant he'd be able to walk away from the shoot without casts or crutches.

Oh well. Maybe the mistake was something that would stick with people. Years of experience had taught Blazen that the most grating ads were often the most memorable ones. And who was he kidding, anyway? *Craaaazy!* His own lines in the commercial were like nails on a chalkboard. After one of the takes, he'd caught a couple of members of the production crew laughing up their sleeves at him.

Hunt Blazen had no illusions about who he was or how people looked upon him. He was a third generation car salesman. He and his kind were regarded about as highly as lawyers and telephone solicitors. When he told people at cocktail parties what he did for a living, it was not unusual for their eyes to start darting about the room, looking for someone to rescue them from the conversation. What did they expect him to do – lure them into some small overheated room and discuss the merits of rustproof undercoating?

Hunt Blazen provided a service that people needed – or at least they thought they did. Why did customers feel like they had to trade for a new car every couple of years? If they didn't, the world wouldn't need as many car salesmen. Hunt Blazen didn't make the world the way it was; he just lived in it.

And he was good at what he did – he knew that. Yes, he had inherited his chain of dealerships from his grandfather and father. And yes, he wasn't exactly what you would call 'book smart.' But he had not only managed to keep the family business afloat, but he had modernized it, brought it into the 21st Century. In addition to the Midtown location, Blazen had opened dealerships in MetroCenter and Cool Springs, two of the city's other hot spots where car lots clustered together, as well as the fast-growing bedroom communities of Murfreesboro and Clarksville. There was no question that Blazen Motorcars had grown into an extremely profitable enterprise.

Not that Hunt Blazen got an appropriate amount of admiration for what he had done, at least not to his way of thinking. He had plenty of money, most of which he had invested wisely, but he wasn't regarded as a pillar of the community.

When he took his lunch breaks at the restaurants along West End, he sometimes eavesdropped on the conversations of the professors, doctors and researchers from nearby Vanderbilt University and the hospitals that made up the city's Medical Center. Those were the people society held in high regard. If only he'd done better in sciences classes in school. Biology was one subject that had particularly interested him, but interest hadn't translated into good grades.

Hunt Blazen glanced down at the map spread across his desk again. Outlined in red ink was a small parcel of property located along the bank of the Cumberland River in downtown Nashville. Blazen had put aside a substantial amount of his savings to purchase that five-acre hunk of land from an industrial scrap yard.

Waterfront property in Nashville was expensive and hard to find. There were two large lakes on the east side of town – Old Hickory and Percy Priest. The Corps of Engineers owned all the land around Percy Priest Lake and the land around Old Hickory Lake was covered with residential development. The city had originally been built along the Cumberland River, so that meant there was very little riverfront property that didn't already have some type of commercial or residential buildings on it. Convincing the scrap yard to part with some of its land hadn't been easy, but Hunt Blazen was a deal-closer. And he had a special interest in this particular piece of land, anyway.

Soon, the property would be used to fulfill his dream: Hunt Blazen would open a charter high school on the site - a school catering to students with an interest in biology or other natural sciences. Like almost all land along the Cumberland, part of Blazen's property was located in the floodplain and therefore undevelopable. That was the beauty of it, though. The bottomlands along the riverbank were teeming with wildlife that could be found nowhere else in the middle of a bustling city. Migratory birds followed the path of the river like a highway as they moved south in the winter and north in the summer. Blazen knew that firsthand since bird watching was a hobby of his. He'd spent many of his free hours hiking along the riverbank, studying waterfowl. Even though doing so now made him a little sad.

The new school would be a perfect place for the students to practice hands-on learning. That would help students like he had been – kids who had learning potential but didn't always thrive in traditional classroom settings. And the kids who were academically gifted could develop those gifts to their fullest potential in a nontraditional setting. Blazen's two daughters, who were both science whizzes and just a couple of years away from high school themselves, would be among the first classes to graduate. Some fathers dreamed of seeing their daughters in wedding gowns. Hunt Blazen visualized his in lab coats.

The mental image made Blazen smile. He would turn one of the saddest places in his world into something good. He stood and walked to the window of his office, overlooking the showroom floor. For a winter day, business was good. Four of his salespeople were currently occupied with 'ups.' Salespeople used the term 'ups' to describe customers – as in, 'A customer just walked in. You're up.'

From their body language, Blazen could tell that three of the four customers appeared serious. They weren't trying to brush off his sales representatives; they were chatting amiably with them. The fourth customer seemed a bit sketchier. He was fidgeting and appeared to be trying to avoid eye contact with the salesman as he circled the same model convertible that blonde in the commercial had been driving. In fact, he was circling the car as he attempted to move away from the salesman.

Wait a minute – did he actually just kick one of the tires? Blazen thought to himself as he watched the uncomfortable scene unfold. *Do people really do that anymore?*

Not a minute later, the 'up' was headed for the door, waiving off the salesman's offer of a business card. A 'be-back.' More slang for customers who always promised that they would 'be back.' Although few of them actually returned.

After the customer had completed his retreat, the salesman looked up and caught his boss' eye. With a smile and a shrug, the salesman mouthed the word 'bogus.' Blazen couldn't argue that point. He answered with a shrug of his own and returned to his desk.

Bogus prospects came with the territory in the car business. So did 'quality ups,' which Blazen Motorcars was attracting more than its fair share of. 'Quality ups' kept the lights at the dealerships on. And they also provided the extra capital Blazen knew he would need to get his charter school launched.

A decent winter of sales, followed by a good spring and summer. Then Blazen's version of the American Dream would roar to life.

CHAPTER SIX

"Please don't do this, Mr. Mayor."

"Hmmm. What's that?" Mayor Gables looked up from his computer screen and across the desk at Horton Edison. For the last half hour, Gables had been working on a staff memo about the proper etiquette for refrigerator use in the City Hall break rooms. Normally, the mundane duty of churning out staff memos would have fallen to the city's human resources director, but Gables liked to write such memos because, frankly, he usually had enough time on his hands to handle them personally. His administrative staff did such a great job of overseeing the various city departments that the mayor was rarely required to intercede. So other than ceremonial duties like presiding over ribbon cuttings and entertaining visitors to his office, Mayor Gables often found himself at loose ends.

His project today was laying down a few ground rules for thoughtless employees who treated the contents of the refrigerators like personal buffets, snacking on whatever unguarded food they found there. The mayor's diatribe against this form of unruly conduct was already well into its second page, although he was winding it down. He wanted to make one more point about items left too long in the freezers – a nod to the complaint he had received about the bag of mixed vegetables that had been in the freezer in the public works department's break room for more than a year. But Horton Edison wasn't going to allow him to properly focus on freezer burn.

"I said, please don't go through with this, Mr. Mayor," Edison said. Although his expression rarely changed, Edison's eyebrows were slightly raised and his mouth was pulling slightly to one side – which Mayor Gables recognized as a sign of his employee's extreme agitation.

"What are you talking about, Edison?"

"I'm talking about the news conference you're supposed to be attending in a few minutes," Edison replied. "I think this is one you need to pass up."

"The baseball thing?" Gables said, a perplexed look passing his handsome face. "Why would I want to back out of that?"

"As I tried to tell you before, Mr. Mayor, I've got a bad feeling about this one."

Mayor Gables laughed, in what he hoped was a reassuring way. "You did tell me before, Horton, but you never really explained your reasons for feeling that way."

"Mayor, I've been doing this a long time," Edison said. He often offered up that reminder of his longevity when he was trying to emphasize an important point. "And I can't quite put my finger on it, but something doesn't seem right here."

"Horton, you know how much I respect your political instincts," Gables said. "That's why I kept you on my staff after the election, if you'll remember. But I think your instincts must be failing you on this one. Wynn Hammerskal walked into this office a couple of days ago and delivered us with a tremendous opportunity. The man, whom we previously discussed, is pretty much a local legend in this state. And he wants to lead a group that wants to bring Major League Baseball to our city. And, as he and his lawyer Mr. Malfair told us, they're really not looking for anything in return from the city except for a little moral support."

"And what if this group is unsuccessful? If they can't actually bring a franchise to the city? There hasn't even been an official announcement that the league is interested in adding another team. It's all just speculation at this point."

"Oh, I'd say it's a little more than speculation, Horton. Have you been following the sports programs on cable and the Internet? From what they've been saying, the commissioner of baseball is primed to announce plans for another franchise any day now."

"And what makes you think Nashville will be the one to get it?"

"Come on, Horton! Try to think positive for a change! Thirty years ago – actually, twenty years ago – no one could have ever imagined that Nashville would have professional sports. Now we've got an NFL and an NHL team! We're on a roll! It used to be that the big cities in the Northeast and Midwest got all the teams. Then California, the Southwest, the Pacific Northwest and eventually Florida. Now, those parts of the country are all played out. The South, if you'll pardon the pun, is hot! As we say in the real estate business, we're in a hot neighborhood. I mean, where else could they consider putting this franchise? Salt Lake City? How much beer do you think they'd sell at a stadium in Mormon country? "

"There are no sure things when it comes to landing pro sports franchises..."

"The only sure things are death and taxes. And you know, politicians don't usually fare very well when they talk about either of those things. Baseball, on the other hand, is our national pastime."

"Which explains why there are so many more game-watching parties planned around the World Series than the Super Bowl."

"Spare me the sarcasm, Horton. This is a no-lose deal. If Hammerskal and his partners land a franchise, then we'll look good for having been in on this from the ground floor. Which reminds me, make sure we've got a photographer at the news conference today so I'll have some shots I can use for my next campaign brochures. And if it doesn't happen, for whatever reason, then I'll still be seen as the mayor who got into the batter's box and took his swings."

Edison was about to reply when the mayor's secretary stuck her head in the door and interrupted the conversation.

"Mr. Mayor, they're ready for you now. Mr. Hammerskal and Mr. Malfair are waiting for you down on the courthouse steps. And the media is all set up and waiting for you."

Mayor Gables straightened his tie, slipped on his jacket and headed downstairs with Edison at his side. He shook hands with Malfair, high-fived Hammerskal and then strode to the podium covered with microphones to make his opening remarks. Edison stood off to the side, far enough away not to appear in the background shots on the TV news that night. Edison made it a point to avoid any kind of media attention, whenever possible.

Mayor Gables did his usual excellent job of building up the announcement that was to come. He reminded the reporters that Nashville was known as the Athens of the South for good reasons. He listed some of them – the thriving business climate, the cultural amenities, the hospitality and can-do spirit of its inhabitants – then delivered his set-up pitch.

"Yes, ladies and gentlemen, Nashville has accomplished great things, particularly over the last few years," Mayor Gables intoned. "We've grown faster than kudzu in a pasture. But we're not done yet! Nashville's future will continue to sparkle like those stars who record country hits on Music Row! And now I'd like to introduce a star of another sort, Wynn Hammerskal, whom some of you know as "The Jackhammer." He's been warming up in the bullpen and I believe what he's going to tell you will really shake you up!"

Hammerskal strode to the podium with the same confident gait he'd displayed so many times as he took the pitching mound during his baseball career. Malfair stood a few steps away, nodding encouragement as Hammerskal began to speak.

"Thank you, Mayor Gables," Hammerskal said. "Those of you who followed my career know I'm a man of few words – unless I'm dealing with umpires who don't know how to call strikes."

The reporters laughed at the joke, even though what he had said was absolutely untrue. Hammerskal was, as they said in the news business, 'a quote machine.' He could give a half-hour's worth of analysis about a game that had been rained out.

He spent the next several minutes spouting metaphors about how Nashville needed to "get in the game" and "step up to the plate." Then he delivered his news about the plans to pursue a Major League franchise like a 100 mile-per-hour fastball.

He talked in generalities, avoiding the details about the proposed ownership group or the steps that would need to be taken to land the franchise. The main point, he repeated several times, was that Nashville couldn't afford to pass up an opportunity like this.

"After all, baseball is our national pastime," Hammerskal said while Edison rolled his eyes just out of view of the cameras. "And does Nashville need a baseball franchise? I would say it's time. In fact, I would say it's past time!"

It was obvious that Hammerskal had received better coaching for the news conference than he probably got as a player. That closing line was a sound bite that was sure to make its way into all of the coverage of the event. Most of the questions that followed were predictable. Reporters pressed Hammerskal for details on the how, when, where and why of his group's plans. Hammerskal fielded most of them deftly and with his characteristic snippets of humor. Whenever he received a question that might have prompted a revealing answer, Malfair cleared his throat. That was apparently a signal they had worked out ahead of time to keep Hammerskal from saying more than he should.

Only one part of the news conference came as a surprise to Gables and Edison.

Hammerskal had been parrying most of the questions, including the details about the new stadium that everyone seemed to accept as a prerequisite for getting a team. He made a crack about the need for a stadium with wider-than-average lanes for bullpen carts, which drew more laughter. Hammerskal decided the time was right to play to the crowd a little bit, so he gave them a few seconds of "The Jackhammer Jump."

Then a reporter from one of the city's most popular blog sites asked the question that everyone else had politely been avoiding.

"If there's going to be a new stadium built, how will it be paid for?"

Hammerskal stopped bouncing and shaking and turned serious for a moment.

"We're going to build a stadium that will make Nashvillians proud," he said, then paused when Malfair nudged him and whispered something into his ear.

"As for what it would cost, the people of Nashville don't need to worry about that. This stadium will pay for itself."

A few more questions followed, most of which Hammerskal deflected with promises to reveal more at future news conferences. After the reporters began to disperse to head back to their offices to file their stories, Malfair went over to glad-hand Mayor Gables and thank him profusely for his support. Edison took the opportunity to pull Hammerskal aside.

"What did you mean by that comment, 'The stadium will pay for itself'?" Edison asked. "Do you even know what that means?"

"No," Hammerskal admitted. "I was hoping you or someone else would. Mr. Malfair just reminded me to make that point. He was telling me on the way over here about how sales tax revenues from the stadium could help pay for the construction costs. I assumed he had cleared that with you and the mayor."

"I can assure you that he did not," Edison said. "Other than planning the logistics for this news conference, the only conversation we've had about this project was the meeting you and Mr. Malfair had with the mayor and I when you first told us about your plans. And I remember that we didn't talk about stadium financing, particularly financing that involved the use of public money."

"Well, I, let me get Mr. Malfair to help me out with this," Hammerskal said. He called out to the lawyer, who was saying goodbye to the mayor as Gables headed up the steps back to his office.

"Sales tax revenues, Julius?" Edison said, after checking to make sure he was out of earshot of the mayor and any remaining reporters. "Did I miss a meeting where the use of sales tax revenues was discussed?"

"Sales tax revenues?" Malfair said. "Who said anything about sales tax revenues?"

"Mr. Hammerskal just did," Edison replied. "Said you two had a conversation about how that would be the way the stadium 'pays for itself.'"

Malfair hesitated and took a deep breath. He shot a glance at Hammerskal that suggested they might need to have a talk later.

"Well, that's certainly one of the options we think would be worth discussing," Malfair said. "Is there a problem with that?"

"A problem? Why should it be a problem when you're committing taxpayer revenues without clearing it with us?"

"Unless we were listening to different news conferences, I don't recall any taxpayer revenues being committed to anything."

"Yet," Edison countered, his voice rising slightly. "But the way your guy left that line about the stadium 'paying for itself' hanging, I know it's just a matter of time before you start lobbying for that."

"Well, let's think about this," Malfair replied calmly. "We're not talking about increasing property taxes, which I know would probably set some of your boss' constituents into a tizzy. We're talking about sales taxes on tickets and concession sales. That's hardly the same thing."

"Sales tax revenues are still public money," Edison countered. "And since the mayor and I are public servants and you're not, it's best for us to be the ones who make decisions about how public money is spent."

"You're overreacting, Horton," Malfair said. "First of all, Wynn didn't specifically say we'd be using sales tax revenues..."

"No, but when you say a stadium is going to pay for itself, that implies that you'll be using public funds. Unless your owners are willing to finance 100 percent of the stadium construction out of the cut of the revenues they are going to receive."

"And they may," Malfair said. "That's all subject to negotiation, of course. But the second point I was trying to make before you interrupted me was that sales taxes generated at the stadium are a relatively painless way to pay for something like this. After all, the fans who attend games aren't going to complain if some of the money they spend helps pay for the ballpark they're enjoying. It's not even really a tax; it's more like a user fee."

"And do you have any idea how much money these user fees, as you call them, might generate?" Edison asked. "Do you know what the stadium's cost is going to be?"

"Yet to be determined, I would say to both questions," Malfair said.

"Yet to be determined," Edison repeated. "Well, unless your owners are wishing to pay all the construction costs up front – and it's apparent from this conversation that they aren't – then it sounds like you'll need in to sell bonds to finance the stadium. And investors aren't going to want buy those bonds unless they know how the money will be raised to repay them."

"Again, those are details we probably need to talk about later. But I have to say that these stadium sales tax revenues we're talking about are revenues that wouldn't exist if no stadium were built. So it's not like the city would be asked to give up revenues it already has. Since the stadium generates the revenues, I don't think it's an unreasonable position for the owners to ask that some of those revenues be used to support the project. Don't you agree, Wynn?"

"Revenues," repeated Hammerskal, who appeared startled at being brought back into the conversation.

"Don't you think the mayor should be the one who decides what is reasonable and what isn't when it comes to distribution of sales tax revenues, regardless of the source?" Edison asked.

"OK, so ask him if it's reasonable," Malfair said curtly. With that, he patted Hammerskal on the shoulder as a sign that it was time to leave.

Edison silently watched as the two men walked across the courthouse lawn in the direction of Malfair's office a few blocks away.

Maybe it was time for Edison to have a conversation with his boss about what was reasonable with regards to this project. Past time, in fact.

Nashville to Major League Baseball:
"Put Me In, Coach!"
By Gilbert Wise, Sports Columnist

Batter up!

Forgive me, but that just had to be said. What else could be said, really, in the wake of yesterday's announcement that a team of investors led by former Major League great Wynn "The Jackhammer" Hammerskal is planning to bring a baseball team to our fair city? Oh, sure. We've already got a minor league team. AAA league. Which conjures up images of a broken-down vehicle that needs to be towed away from the side of the road. The Jackhammer is promising us so much more - a shiny new sports car that will replace that old beater. Oh, sure. We've already got a National Football League team and a National Hockey League team parked in the driveway. But those are only drivable during the fall and winter months. We need something we can use to cruise, top down and radio blasting, through those dog days of summer.

As he's known to do, Hammerskal threw his best pitch for a new franchise at myself and other assembled members of the media during a news conference on the Davidson County Courthouse steps. My call? A strike, right down the middle. OK, there are a few obstacles blocking the base paths right now. Like the fact that Major League Baseball's commissioner hasn't yet officially announced plans to add another franchise to join San Juan. But sources tell me that's going to be happening any day now. And yes, there may be other cities that would like to snare that franchise, too.

Maybe Charlotte, our rivals to the east. But let's get real. Major League Baseball isn't going to put a team in a city where they don't need streetlights downtown because nothing ever happens after 5 p.m.

Oklahoma City? What would they do? Sing "The Surrey with a Fringe on Top" during the seventh-inning stretch?

Omaha? That's in Nebraska, isn't it? The players' union might rise up in revolt if other teams had to take road trips there.

Plus, no matter who shuffles out of the woodwork, we were here first. Thanks to Mr. Hammerskal, we've staked our claim. And that claim is being backed by our mayor, Kent Gables, who – to his everlasting credit – has managed not to run the city into a ditch during his tenure in office. Let's give a politician his due. Mayor Gables knows what's needed to take Nashville to the next level as a civic powerhouse.

So clearly, this is Nashville's team to lose. Not that there's any indication we will. With his characteristic gusto, The Jackhammer promised a franchise that would be first-rate. He didn't get into a lot of specifics, but he didn't have to. I can already imagine the sound of organ music and the smell of hot dogs grilling on Opening Day.

Who will emerge as our franchise's top rival on the field of play? Atlanta? St. Louis? Cincinnati? How many years will it take to become a pennant contender? Will The Jackhammer become the league's first owner/manager?

Questions like these are enough to make any red-blooded Nashvillian giddy. Yeah, we'll need a new stadium, but as The Jackhammer noted, it should pay for itself. What more do you need to know?

Oh, there will be naysayers. Any time anyone dares to suggest that Nashville needs a new concert venue, theme park or sports team, the curmudgeons crawl out from under their rocks and whine about how the time and energy devoted to making the city a more fun place to live could be better spent planning for better schools, roads or whatever.

To those people, I ask: When's the last time 15,000 people came out on a Tuesday night to attend a town hall meeting about a new road-widening project?

I rest my case. Not to say all of this will happen overnight. Unlike the situation with San Juan, which seemed to get a franchise delivered to it like a Jimmy Johns sandwich, there will be lots of hoops Nashville will have to jump through to make this happen. But those are just details.

As surely as the mighty Cumberland River winds its way through our town, Major League Baseball is coming to Nashville. For that, I commend Mayor Gables, Wynn Hammerskal and his as-yet-unidentified partners.

I say they made a Wise choice.

CHAPTER SEVEN

Devin Underwood took the phone call his secretary relayed from Horton Edison on the second ring. Underwood's firm, Underwood & Drake, was a private company that served under contract as the city's financial advisor. So Edison usually had no trouble getting through to Underwood when he needed to.

"Mr. Edison, what a pleasant surprise," Underwood said. And he was being sincere. A call from the mayor's public policy advisor almost always resulted in a spike in the firm's billable hours. "What can I do for you today?"

"I have a special assignment for your folks, Devin." While Edison's speaking voice was always a bit raspy and unpleasant, Underwood detected a bit more edge to it than usual. "The mayor needs to get some projections on sales tax revenue."

Edison spit out the last three words through gritted teeth. He'd made his argument about sales tax revenues to Mayor Gables and lost. The mayor had been in a bad mood anyway after spending most of the morning being bawled out by the owner of Nashville's AAA minor league team, who called the pursuit of a Major League team a breach of a partnership that had served the community well for more than three decades. Which, in Edison's opinion, the mayor deserved. He should have reached out to Big Paul personally rather than letting him hear about the pursuit of the Major League team through the media. There were just some things that needed to be handled in a certain way.

Despite Edison's objections, Gables hadn't seemed bothered in the least by the proposed Major League ownership group's arrogance in discussing sales tax revenues as a financing method without getting approval from City Hall first. The mayor thought Malfair had made a valid point when he noted that the sales tax revenues would never exist if there were no stadium. "Just check it out, Horton," the mayor had said curtly. So that's why Edison had called Underwood.

"Well, sure, we can help with that," Underwood said. "What are you trying to find out? How much more money a sales tax increase would generate? We can get that to you in no time at all."

"No, this request is a bit more specialized. We need to know how much sales tax revenue a Major League Baseball stadium could generate for the city."

"Ahhh!" Underwood said. The mayor's news conference had been publicized on every TV station, blog site and newspaper in the city over the last 24 hours. "What an exciting project this will be! I'm really hoping we get a team! Do you think it will really happen, Horton?"

"Too early to say."

"Be the best thing ever to happen to Nashville," Underwood said, not sensing that his enthusiasm was not shared on the other end of the phone line. "I mean, football and hockey are great. But baseball, well, you know it's our national..."

"So, anyway, here's what we'll need," Edison interjected. "We want you to run some hypothetical scenarios – worst case, best case, mid-range – for what type of sales tax revenues we might expect a major league baseball team to generate in Nashville."

"Absolutely! Are we talking about revenues at the existing sales tax rate or are we looking at a possible sales tax increase?" Underwood loved the feeling of being 'in the know' when changes in the city's finances might be happening.

"Existing sales tax rate. No tax increase. For the love of God, please don't even mention tax increases in this context."

"Sure, Horton, whatever you say. I'm sure a team would bring in more than enough money to make it worth having."

"I don't want you to be sure," Edison said. "I want you and your people to be skeptical. Double- and triple-check all of your assumptions. And play the numbers straight down the middle."

"Straight down the middle?"

"That's what I said."

Underwood paused for a minute to process what Edison had been saying. He knew politics well enough to understand that sometimes 'yes' meant 'no,' 'up' meant 'down' and 'give it your honest assessment' sometimes meant exactly the opposite. And anyone who did any kind of professional consulting – financial or otherwise - understood that it was hard to go broke by telling clients exactly what they wanted to hear.

"Well, of course, we'll play it straight down the middle, Horton. You can assure the mayor that the projections we'll send you are based on sound economic principles. I'll assemble a team of my top staffers as soon as we get off the phone."

"You do that," Edison said, clicking off the phone.

Within a half hour, Underwood had gathered his staff in the firm's training room to discuss what he had decided to call Project Diamond. Underwood & Drake's offices were on the fifth floor of a high-rise just a few blocks from City Hall. The firm's training room looked very much like a school classroom, with desks facing a whiteboard that doubled as a projector screen.

Iris Moon wasn't particularly early for the meeting, but she was nevertheless able to secure a seat on the front row. Just like church parishioners, Underwood & Drake employees preferred to sit toward the back of the room. That had become even more true since Dr. Moon joined the firm a couple of years before. Since she liked to sit up front, it made easier for her male colleagues to discreetly leer at her.

Dr. Moon was a real rarity – a Nashville native who had attended Vanderbilt University, the city's largest and most prestigious private college. In fact, she had earned her undergraduate degree, a masters in business administration and a doctorate in economics from Vandy. She was brilliant and, in sharp contrast to the stereotype of brilliant people, also quite beautiful. Which meant her male colleagues regarded her with a powerful mixture of lust and envy. "The Pinup with the Pocket Protector," they called her behind her back.

Underwood quickly outlined the assignment that Horton Edison had described to him. And he somehow managed to do so without wetting his pants with excitement.

"This is big, people," Underwood said. "This may be the biggest assignment in this firm's history. Most of the time, nobody knows who the city's financial advisors are unless something gets royally screwed up. But when this project gets rolling, it has the potential to keep us in the media every day – and in a good way. So let's talk about what we'll need. First of all, we'll need the sales tax rate."

"The city's share only or the city and state rate?" Dr. Moon asked. She wasn't shy about asking questions, particularly when she was trying to understand the nature of an assignment.

"Not sure yet," Underwood said. "So let's run the numbers both ways. With only the city's share of sales taxes and with both the city and state's share. Because surely the state is going to end up contributing something to this project to help Nashville get a team.

Moving on, we'll need to find out the average per-game attendance for Major League Baseball teams to use as our baseline for revenue assumptions."

Dr. Moon cleared her throat slightly as she looked down at her notepad.

"You disagree, Dr. Moon?" Underwood asked.

"Well, I know absolutely nothing about baseball," Dr. Moon said. In point of fact, she knew a little about baseball and what she did know was that it seemed incredibly boring. Whenever she stumbled across baseball while surfing through TV channels, it appeared to her that the games mostly involved a pitcher and batter staring at each other and spitting. "However, if Nashville is going to start a new franchise, I would assume some of the same rules would apply that you'd typically see with other types of business franchises."

Someone muttered an unintelligible comment from the back of the room, which drew a few giggles. Dr. Moon wasn't fazed. She knew that some of her more immature colleagues could find a double meaning with sexual undertones in just about everything she said.

"So, assuming we're to treat a Nashville baseball franchise like any other type of start-up business, wouldn't it be safer to assume that it might take a while to build up attendance numbers?" she asked.

"Actually, I would have to disagree with that," Underwood said. "Since this franchise will be brand new, it should generate more interest and enthusiasm than teams that have been around for a while. Especially teams that haven't been winning. So let's start with the average Major League attendance – and then add another five, no, 10 percent to that assumption."

"Does that take into account the possibility that the franchise might see an initial spike in attendance, then a drop off after the novelty has worn off? Particularly if Nashville's team isn't one of the league's winning teams?

Isn't that a bit of a gamble?" Iris Moon could hold her own in economic debates with anybody. Even the guy who signed her paychecks.

"Maybe," Underwood admitted. "But let's remember what we're doing here. We're going to come up with low-end, high-end and mid-range numbers for the city. So let's set the average attendance-plus 10 percent as our mid-range. The city will have the low-end numbers, too, so they'll certainly be able to take them into consideration if they want to."

It seemed illogical to Dr. Moon, but that was a political argument, not an economic one. And she tried to avoid politics as much as possible.

"Now, moving past the attendance numbers, we're going to need to get the average ticket price for Major League Baseball."

"Should we assume that Nashville's team will jack up that price, to account for the pent-up demand you described?" Moon was persistent. The phrase 'pent-up demand' prompted a few more titters from the peanut gallery. No mystery why most of her colleagues, even those in their 30s and 40s, remained unmarried. Moon felt the inside of her nose beginning to tingle. She tended to sneeze when she was aggravated.

"No, we're going to assume the average ticket price is what the team will actually be charging." Underwood knew projections based on higher-than-average ticket prices would look terrible from a public relations standpoint. And he knew there was more of a public relations component to consulting than many of his holier-than-thou colleagues were willing to admit.

"So, working with those variables, we should be able to get a good handle on the sales tax revenues that will be generated by ticket sales," Underwood continued. "So we'll need to do the same thing for sales of food, drinks and souvenirs. Again, let's take the league averages and increase them by a factor of 10 percent. Because we all know Nashvillians like to eat, drink and be merry, right?"

A joke by the boss always brought an obligatory chuckle or two. Although not from Moon, of course.

Underwood asked if there were any further questions and there were. Mostly details like how the projections should be formatted, how much supporting documentation should be included in their report, what their deadlines were, and so forth and so on.

When Underwood asked who was interested in writing a first draft of the report, Moon was the only one who volunteered. It was conventional corporate wisdom that it was much easier to critique a report than to actually author one. Besides, as Underwood had noted, this was going to be a high profile project. If it went south for whatever reason, nobody else wanted to be caught in the glare of the media spotlight. And since Dr. Moon's socially-challenged male colleagues lusted after her but didn't dare to ask her out for fear of getting shot down, throwing rocks at her work was about the most titillating experience they could hope to have with her.

Of course, Dr. Moon knew what to expect. She'd been working in that type of environment since her first group science project in junior high school. She also knew she was willing to put up with all the aggravation, the patronizing comments and the half-baked criticisms of her work in order to be part of this.

She hadn't agreed with many of the things her boss had said about his so-called Project Diamond, but she knew he was right about how important this project was going to be to the city, for better or worse. And she truly loved the place. With advanced degrees from Vanderbilt, after graduation she could have moved lots of places where she could have earned substantially more money and probably more respect.

Yet Nashville was home to her. Always had been, always would be. She was a believer in the expression, 'bloom where you're planted.'

She couldn't control what would happen with the pursuit of the baseball franchise. She had no illusions like that. Although she followed neither sports nor politics regularly, she knew things in those arenas often didn't work out the way logic dictated that they should.

But she could do her job. Which, as she saw it, was to make sure the city's leaders and the citizens they were supposed to serve arrived at whatever decision they would ultimately make with their eyes wide open.

CHAPTER EIGHT

Horton Edison and Kent Gables watched Major League Baseball Commissioner Raymond Goldfarb's news conference live on ESPN from the mayor's office. For a change, the experts had called it correctly: Major League Baseball would be adding a second expansion team to join the San Juan franchise.

With the addition of the two new franchises, both the American and National leagues would have the same number of teams. Goldfarb noted that would bring balance to the leagues for scheduling purposes. And he noted that no decisions had been made about which city would land the second franchise. Goldfarb spoke about how this represented a great opportunity for another up-and-coming North American city to join the community of Major League Baseball.

It was the news that Mayor Gables had been hoping to hear, but Edison's thoughts ran in a slightly different direction. He couldn't help noticing how uncomfortable Goldfarb appeared to be while making what was supposed to be a "good news" announcement. Goldfarb had seemed to be beaming as he had broken the news about the San Juan franchise just a few days ago. Today, he appeared dispassionate – glum, even. Edison tried to determine what that body language could mean for those cities that would be in pursuit of the new franchise. Would their jobs be easier? Harder? Of course, maybe Golbfarb's demeanor had nothing to do with what he was saying at all. Perhaps Major League Baseball's commissioner had just had some bad clams for lunch. By his own admission, Edison did have a tendency to over-think things sometimes.

Gables and Edison turned to each other as the news conference ended, preparing to discuss their next move in the pursuit of that new franchise. But the commercial that followed the broadcast brought their attention back to the screen. The video was a series of cutaways to scenes from Orlando. Theme parks. Resort properties with lush golf courses and pristine tennis courts. People enjoying the bars and restaurants along Orange Avenue downtown. Then a smiling man in slacks and a polo shirt, standing on a grassy plain near the shore of a beautiful lake.

"Hello. I'm Orlando Mayor Skip Goodman," the man on the screen said. Back in Nashville, Mayor Kent Gables jolted bolt upright, as if someone had goosed him with a cattle prod. Edison shot him a puzzled look. *"First of all, I want to congratulate the city of San Juan and the commonwealth of Puerto Rico for landing a Major League team. I know that the new franchise there will be a tremendous success. I also want to congratulate Commissioner Raymond Goldfarb and the rest of the league officials for making such a courageous choice. Baseball isn't just the national pastime for the mainland United States – it's the national pastime for all our states and territories."*

Edison rolled his eyes. If he were at his favorite bar instead of work, he could have come up with a pretty good drinking game involving the number of times the phrase 'national pastime' was used in these types of public pronouncements about baseball.

"We also congratulate the league for its wisdom in adding another franchise to join San Juan," Mayor Goodman was saying. *"And we hope and expect that Orlando will get that franchise. Thanks to the generosity of one of our leading citizens, Landon Overstreet, we believe we will put together a proposal that Major League Baseball will find irresistible. Please tell the viewers what you have in mind, Mr. Overstreet."*

The camera panned slightly to the right, bringing another man dressed in an expensive suit into the frame.

"Hello, everyone, I'm Landon Overstreet," the other man said. *"For years, I've been investing in and developing property in the Orlando area. To be quite candid, that's made my family and I very prosperous. So now I want to give something back to the community I love so much. You see, I own this property where Mayor Goodman and I are standing. And it's here, on the shores of Lake Manatee that we plan to build a stadium to accommodate Orlando's new team. And we'll do it without placing a burden on the community's taxpayers. Right, Mayor?"*

"That's right, Mr. Overstreet. And here's how we'll do it. This land is presently undeveloped, so it's taxed at a lower rate than developed property would be. When the stadium is built, the property value will go up, so the amount of taxes owed will go up, too. But instead of putting that extra tax money into the city's coffers, we'll use it to finance the stadium's construction costs. So the development of the stadium will pay for itself, with no extra cost to our taxpayers. We'll be sharing more details of our plans later, but we wanted to let the viewers of this program across the country know how serious we are about landing this franchise. Very soon, we hope you'll be watching baseball games telecast from this very site. And those of you around the country who haven't yet had a chance to visit Orlando will see why we call our hometown the City Beautiful. Anything else you'd like to add, Mr. Overstreet?"

"PLAY BALL!" Overstreet said, as the commercial ended. Gables and Edison sat in stunned silence for a few seconds. Finally, Gables spoke.

"Skip Goodman," Gables said, the words dripping with acid. "Why did it have to be Skip Goodman?"

"I'm not sure I follow, Mayor," Edison said. He waited for an explanation, but Gables didn't offer one.

"Why did it have to be Orlando, of all places?" Gables said.

"Well, I think we had to expect that other cities would be interested," Edison replied. "These franchises don't get awarded without a healthy competition first."

"We can't lose to Orlando, Horton," Gables said firmly. "I wanted this before, but I want it even more now. Orlando only has one major pro team now – the National Basketball Association's Magic. But if they get a baseball franchise, they'll have two major teams – just like that. So instead of catching up to Atlanta, we'll be dragged down to Orlando's level if we're not successful."

"They also have a Major League Soccer team, " Edison pointed out.

"Yeah, but soccer isn't really considered a major league sport," Gables said.

"The rest of the world might disagree with you there."

"Well, this isn't the rest of the world. And in the United States, there are four major sports leagues – the National Football League, the National Basketball Association, Major League Baseball and the National Hockey League. Probably in that order. So we can't let Orlando pull even with us."

"Some might say Orlando's already even with Nashville in many areas," Edison said cautiously. "Better in some areas, some might say."

"All the more reason we have to stay ahead of them in the sports franchise department," Gables said. "So let's focus on the task before us. How did they manage to get that commercial buy on the day of Goldfarb's announcement? How could they have known what he was going to say?"

"Several existing baseball franchises have their spring training facilities in or near Orlando," Edison said. "My guess would be your friend Mayor Goodman or Mr. Overstreet got a tip from one of them."

"Skip Goodman is not my friend," Gables snapped. "So what did you think of their commercial?"

"It was interesting," Edison said. "I can't believe they managed to explain tax increment financing in a commercial sound byte."

"That thing they were talking about with taxes – that's what tax increment financing is?" Gables asked.

"Yes, you didn't know that?"

"No, I used to hear the term from time to time as a councilman and then a lot more when I was campaigning for mayor."

"And you didn't ask anyone what it meant?"

"I didn't want to look dumb," Gables admitted.

"So what did you say when you were asked about it on the campaign trail?"

"Oh, the usual. I'd just say that I took issues related to taxation very seriously and tax increment financing is something I'd have to study further before I could comment on it."

"Well played," Edison said. Maybe he did underestimate his boss' political skills from time to time.

"So what they were talking about – this tax increment financing – is it a legitimate way to pay for a stadium?"

"It could be," Edison said. "It depends on the difference between what the city is collecting on the undeveloped property and what it could collect on the stadium property. If that amount is equal to or greater than the debt service on the stadium's construction costs, then yeah, it could work."

"So why aren't we doing that?"

"I thought you wanted to use the sales tax revenues from the stadium to pay the construction costs."

"And I thought you told me that could be an iffy proposition," Gables countered.

"That's why we've got Underwood & Drake preparing some estimates on that."

"Right, right. And we still need them to do that. But I'm thinking, what if they come back to us with a report that says the sales tax revenues alone won't be enough? It sounds to me like Orlando already has a leg up on us with a proposed site and a financing plan. And if our financing plan doesn't pan out, then we'd be even further behind Orlando."

"So what are you suggesting, Mayor?"

"Well, don't you think we need to get Underwood & Drake to run some numbers on tax increment financing, too? I mean, what could it hurt? Whether it's sales tax revenues generated by the stadium, property tax revenues from the site or a combination of both, it's still not costing taxpayers anything."

"That's one way to look at it, I suppose."

"What do you mean, Horton?"

"Are you familiar with the 'opportunity cost' theory? It says that by dedicating all revenues from sales or property taxes collected on the site to that one purpose of paying for construction, you would deny the city the tax revenues that would be generated there if something else were developed instead. So none of those tax revenues end up paying for city services. It's like saying to a homeowner, 'we're going to charge you property taxes, but then we'll give you back what we collect so you can spend it on your own property.' Which sort of defeats the purpose of charging taxes in the first place."

"Hadn't heard that theory," Gables said. "But have you heard the 'bird in hand is worth two in the bush' theory? It says that we have no idea if the property Mr. Hammerskal's ownership group wants to use would ever be developed for anything else. So we might not be losing anything in revenues, anyway."

"How do we know it wouldn't be developed with something else if we don't even know what site they want to use for a stadium?"

"Exactly," Gables said. "So I need you to get in touch with Hammerskal or Julius Malfair or whoever and find out where our stadium is going to be built."

"And then ask Underwood & Drake to calculate the difference between the property value now and the property value after a hypothetical stadium is constructed?"

"Yep. Although I wish you wouldn't use the word 'hypothetical' to describe our stadium. This is going to happen, Edison. And it's going to happen on my watch."

Edison nodded and got up to leave. He knew there was no sense arguing with Mayor Kent Gables about this. Not right now, at least.

But Gables wasn't quite finished.

"You know, I wish you could muster a little more enthusiasm for this, Horton," Gables called out after him. "We're talking about spending money we wouldn't otherwise have to pay for something we wouldn't otherwise get. This is the perfect project – one where everybody wins and nobody gets hurt!"

The Nashville Bulletin, Dec. 10, 2017

Nashville's Major League Competition? Don't Sweat It
By Gilbert Wise, Sports Columnist

In Nashville's quest to get a Major League Baseball franchise, we have met the enemy. And it's a town that claims to be home to "the happiest place on Earth."
No sooner had league commissioner Raymond Goldfarb announced that some lucky city would be getting a new franchise than Orlando tossed its baseball cap onto the diamond. Metaphorically speaking, of course.

To which I can only say: Don't worry, Nashville. We've got this.

Going head-to-head against Orlando for a baseball team is like challenging Pippa Middleton to a barbecue-eating contest. She may look great and wear all the right clothes, but you can look at her and tell that she's just not equipped to stuff 100 hot wings down her gullet in 10 minutes or less.

Oh, get ready. You know the Orlandoans are going to bash us. I expect my counterparts in the Orlando media to dust off their shopworn collection of "Hee Haw" jokes, even though that program has been off the air for about 30 years. We could retaliate by making fun of a popular TV show set in Orlando, but – oh, that's right – they don't have one!

Anyway, those so-called journalists from way down South have no idea what a hotbed Middle Tennessee has become for health care businesses, auto and auto parts manufacturers and lots of other industries that don't have any connection to country music.

Yes, we still have country music, too. It's a creative industry that produces a ton of wealth for our community.

So what's Orlando got? Well, before a certain theme park got built in the 1960s, there were more oranges than people there. That pretty much tells you all you need to know about the community's history and cultural heritage.

The Orlando economy depends almost entirely on people who think Bermuda shorts, socks and sandals make an effective fashion ensemble. Capped with a t-shirt featuring some goofy cartoon character, of course.

The members of Orlando's creative class? Nobody that people who don't subscribe to Teen Dream magazine would recognize.

Really, if you take away tourism, what's Orlando's biggest claim to fame? It's the largest city in Florida that's nowhere near a beach. In a state with about 4 billion miles of coastline, that's saying something. Not that they'll mention that in their tourist brochures.

Then there's the weather. Step outdoors in Orlando 10 months out of the year and within five minutes you'll look like somebody clobbered you with a water balloon. Miami's basketball franchise is called the Heat. In the unlikely event that Orlando gets this baseball franchise, it should be called the Humidity.

Of course, if Orlando were a great sports town, that might make up for some of its other shortcomings. And granted, way back when Shaquille O'Neal was better known for his basketball skills than his TV commercials, the Orlando Magic once went to the NBA Finals. Where they promptly pulled a disappearing act and lost to Houston in four straight games.

Since then, Orlando's greatest sporting claim to fame is being the site of various cheerleading championships and the hometown of ESPN college football analyst Lee Corso. Who, if pressed to put his prognostication skills to work, would surely pick Nashville over Orlando in this contest.

Look, towns in Florida always get a lot of buzz when major sports leagues talk about expanding. That craze peaked in the 1980s and 1990s, leaving the state with new franchises from Miami to Jacksonville. That turned out to be an economic boon to companies that make giant tarps since so many of Florida's stadiums are covered in them to mask their dearth of fans.

Riddle: What do you say to a fan at a professional sporting event in Florida?
Answer: How was your flight down from New York? (Or Green Bay, Boston, Dallas or…well, you get the idea.) I'm not saying Orlando is completely without redeeming qualities. If you want the same kind of skin tone you'd get by falling asleep in a tanning bed, then by all means hop a plane there.

If you want to live in a place where they actually frown upon jaywalking and spitting on the sidewalks, Orlando may be the place for you.

If you want to be exposed to so much cartoon music that you go insane and end up terrorizing motorists with a deer rifle from the top of a highway overpass, then Orlando's your spot.

But if you want to pick a place where Major League Baseball is going to thrive, Nashville is your best bet.

I know league commissioner Goldfarb will make the Wise choice.

CHAPTER NINE

Hunt Blazen knocked twice on the door of the battered construction trailer, then entered after hearing a welcoming grunt from inside.

"Hello there!" Blazen said as he entered Grover James' office. James and his family had owned the metal scrap yard on the bank of the Cumberland River for generations. James' office was a cramped space with filing cabinets bursting at the seams with car titles, bills of sale, tax documents and other assorted paperwork.

His thin wood-paneled walls had several "before and after" photos of cars that had visited the yard's compactor. There was a poster of two bikini-clad, sledgehammer-wielding women poised to lay waste to a mint condition Mercedes Gull Wing above the caption, "You Trash 'Em, We Smash 'Em!" There was another poster with a photo from "National Lampoon's Family Vacation" that showed Chevy Chase and Anthony Michael Hall staring forlornly at the smashed car they were forced to trade for the Family Truckster in the movie. Two illegible autographs were scrawled on the poster, which could have been put there by the actors or almost anyone else capable of holding a pen.

On the filing cabinet nearest James' desk was an ancient coffeemaker that churned out coffee that, even when freshly brewed, tasted like it had been sitting on a warmer in a convenience store for a week or more. Maybe because James never bothered to clean said coffeemaker. ("Why wash something that's got water running through it all the time?" he reasoned.)

When Blazen arrived, James was sitting at his metal desk, sipping some of the grey-colored coffee from a

Styrofoam cup and snacking on strips of beef jerky directly from the bag. He seemed oblivious to the sights and sounds of cars being pulverized right outside the small, grimy window over his left shoulder.

"Whooooa! It's the craaaaazy deals man!" James said, his standard greeting for Blazen. "How's the car business these days?"

"You ought to know," Blazen replied as he shook James' outstretched hand and took a seat in one of the two metal folding chairs facing the desk. "I think I saw about 10 of my cars flattened into pancakes out there in your yard on my way in."

"Welcome," James said, fluttering his arm and dipping his head in a flowery bow, "to the International House of Pancakes."

"If those are the pancakes, I'd hate to see what the omelets look like," Blazen quipped.

"That's not a bad thing – all those cars getting smashed up - now, is it?" James said. "I mean, if you didn't sell them, they wouldn't eventually make their way here, would they? In fact, if your manufacturers wouldn't make them so well, those cars might wear out faster so I could crush them up quicker."

"I'll bring that up at our next dealers' meeting," Blazen said with a chuckle. "They might actually like that idea. More crushed cars for you means more people lining up at our dealerships to buy new cars."

"Our businesses are like two sides of the same coin," James said. "Can I get you a cup of coffee?"

"No thanks," Blazen said. He'd visited James enough times over the years to know better. In fact, Blazen's father had warned his son long ago that it would be safer and tastier to drink the used oil out of one the dealership service bays than to take a chance on James' coffee.

"Some jerky?"

"I think I'll pass on that, too. I've got an early lunch appointment. So, Mr. Grover, why did you want to meet with me today?" Blazen always addressed James as 'Mr. Grover.' Even though they had become colleagues and friends, Blazen still considered the older man a mentor and a father figure.

"Yeah, why I wanted to meet with you," James said with a sigh. "I've got some news."

"Uh-oh. What's up?"

"Well, I got a call from Horton Edison over at City Hall yesterday afternoon," James said. "You know Edison, right?"

Blazen nodded. Any smart businessman in the city knew who Edison was.

"OK, Hunt, have you heard about the city's plans to get a Major League baseball franchise?"

"Of course. Who hasn't?"

"Here's the thing: Horton says the group that plans to own the franchise has picked out a site where it wants to build a new baseball stadium. This site."

"This site?" Blazen took a second to process what he was hearing.

"Correct," James continued. "The ownership group wants a stadium located downtown on the riverbank. That doesn't leave them very many options. So the city has offered to buy my land."

"All of it?"

"All of it. They're particularly interested in the chunk you wanted to buy, Hunt. They want the stadium to be so close to the water that home runs could land in the river. Sort of the same way San Francisco's ballpark sits right next to the edge of the bay."

"And you're going to sell?" Blazen asked. He was no longer the brash, loud-talking persona people recognized from his TV commercials. In fact, it was all he could do to keep from stuttering.

"Looks that way. My options are pretty limited, too."

"What are they offering to pay you, Mr. Grover?"

"By law, the city can't pay me any more than the appraised market value of the property. Before they can close the sale, they have to get three separate appraisals. And I'm led to believe that if I agree to sell, those appraisals will be pretty darned generous."

"What if you don't agree to sell?"

"Not really much of a choice there," James said. "If I don't willingly sell out to the city, they can use a legal process called eminent domain to take the land from me. They'll say my property represents 'urban blight' and the ballpark is needed for economic development. I can fight it in court, but I'm not likely to win. Then a judge will decide what's fair compensation for me. And it might or might not be as generous as the city's initial offer."

"But we had a deal," Blazen said. "I had an option to buy that parcel by the river."

"Yes, I know we did, Hunt. And I know how much that property means to you. But you know the expression about how you can't fight City Hall? That's true here. The problem is that you haven't already exercised your option to buy yet. And now that the city has expressed interest, they might not look too kindly on me if I closed a deal with you. And I'm not looking for trouble here."

"But what if you did go ahead and sell to me? What would happen then?"

"I don't think it would change a thing in the end, Hunt. They could do the same thing to you – with the eminent domain thing – that they would end up doing to me. You still wouldn't get to keep the property – and you might end up getting compensated less than you were planning to pay me. You could end up taking a loss on land you'd own for only a few months, tops."

"I can't believe this. Do you know how much time and money I've invested in planning for a charter school on that site? And you know how much that particular site means to me."

"I know, Hunt, I know. But I hope you can see this from my perspective. I'm 77 years old. Ever since downtown became trendy again, people have been trying to pressure me to move my little scrap yard somewhere else. I've fought and I've fought. But now I'm tired of fighting. For half the money they'll pay me, I could buy another site in Whites Creek, Joelton or anywhere in north Nashville, really. Of course, I wouldn't be welcome in west or south Nashville where all the fancy neighborhoods are. And now that East Nashville has been taken over by hipsters, I probably couldn't go there, either. But somewhere up north, they'll let me go there. Particularly if I cooperate instead of fighting this in court. Mr. Edison suggested that if I played ball with the city, so to speak, then he could probably help steer any zoning changes I might need through the City Council with a minimal amount of fuss. Or I might just take the money from the land sale, sell off all my equipment and retire. Let somebody else have the fun of smashing up cars for a while."

"I don't know what to say," Blazen said, his hands trembling. "You've been talking about letting me have that land for years. Ever since..."

"Yeah, I know, son."

"What did you call me?"

"Sorry, Hunt. It's just a figure of speech. I know why that land is so important to you and why you wanted to do something special there. But there are other places you could go. And the meaning would still be the same."

"That's not the only consideration here. If you let the city do this, you're going to set my plans back two years, at least. I'll have to start from the beginning on site selection. And the way people are filing applications to open charter schools, the market could be saturated before I'm able to get off the ground."

"I understand, Hunt, I really do. Your family and mine go back a long ways. I know this school is a big deal for you. But this baseball thing, it's bigger than both of us."

"But as I understand this, Nashville doesn't even have a guarantee that it'll get a team," Blazen said. "Why does the city need to acquire the land right now?"

"Just the way it works, I guess. Cities competing for these franchises have to make a show of how much they want them by making commitments. Like building stadiums."

"On spec? The city is going to build a new baseball stadium before it knows for sure if it will get a team or not?"

"Sure looks that way."

"So what happens if Nashville doesn't get the franchise?"

"In that case, your kids and my great grandkids probably will have an awesome Little League stadium to play in. Or, I don't know, a place to hold monster truck competitions. Wouldn't that be something? They get rid of the scrap yard, then end up with monster trucks crushing cars in a fancy new stadium on the same spot?"

"Can't say I appreciate the irony there. This just isn't right."

"I get that. What's right to you and me doesn't count for much here. But there's no point in getting upset with me about this. I'm not the one driving this train."

"I know, Mr. Grover. It's not your fault."

The two men stared at each other for a couple of moments. The conversation was pretty much over, but neither of them knew exactly how to end it.

"Listen, Hunt, I hate this for you. I know this charter school thing has been a dream of yours for a long time. But you're making good money selling cars. Even if the school never opens its doors, you've had a business career that most men would envy. Your family will always be proud of you, no matter what. Don't let this baseball thing get you down. If we get a team, people all over town are going to love it. It's just going to make life a little more difficult for a few folks like you and me. But you don't want to be the one of the few complaining about it, either. There are always some malcontents who'll come out against a project like this, but there are barely enough of them to fit into this office. I'm old, so nobody cares what I say or do, but you've got a lot of your career still ahead of you. If you kick up a fuss, you'll be called a 'naysayer' or worse. Sportswriters like Gilbert Wise will eat you up. A lot of your business contacts – the people who you think are your friends – will freeze you out. And you think you'll be doing any more fleet deals on vehicles with the city? It's a no-win proposition for you, Hunt. Because criticizing baseball is about as popular as criticizing mom or apple pie."

Blazen sat for another minute, breathing raggedly and clenching and unclenching his fists.

"What you're saying is right," he said finally. "I know all of it is right. But I also know this: Mom and apple pie aren't making a grab for my land. Baseball is."

CHAPTER TEN

The conference room at Underwood & Drake was set up for visitors. In particular, it was ready for this day's visitors, who were Julius Malfair and Wynn "The Jackhammer" Hammerskal, representing the would-be baseball franchise ownership group, and Horton Edison from the mayor's office.

Two of the conference room's walls were covered with charts and graphs related to the presentation that was about to be given. The third wall was decorated with posters of athletes performing various feats of skill – dunking a basketball, driving a golf ball and of course hitting a baseball – captioned with motivational slogans like "Begin to Win," "Can't Doesn't Conjugate Here" and "Perfection Doesn't Care About Monday Mornings." The fourth wall was made up of plexiglass windows looking out over the office towers of downtown, the Cumberland River, the Tennessee Titans' football stadium and, beyond that, the gentrified hipster neighborhood of East Nashville.

Devin Underwood and Iris Moon welcomed their guests to seats around the glass-covered mahogany conference table, where stacks of paper were laid out in front of each seat. After a receptionist had provided everyone with coffee, water or iced tea, Devin Underwood kicked off the meeting.

"Mr. Malfair, Mr. Hammerskal, welcome to Underwood & Drake. And Mr. Edison, welcome back."

Malfair and Edison nodded their greetings. Hammerskal gestured with his thumb and forefinger as if simulating a pistol shot. Hammerskal's attention toggled back and forth between the people in the room and his cell phone, where he was either checking his messages or playing some sort of video game.

"On behalf of myself and my partner, I want to thank you for the confidence you have shown in selecting our firm for this work," Underwood continued. "We are very excited about the prospects for Major League Baseball in Nashville. We know that if – I should say when – the city is selected for the new franchise, it will have a tremendous economic impact."

Moon winced slightly and shuffled some of the papers before her, but said nothing.

"Mr. Hammerskal, we are particularly thankful that you and the other members of your ownership group have taken the initiative to do what you're doing," Underwood said. "And Mr. Edison, please pass along our thanks to the mayor for his involvement."

"I certainly will," Edison said, not unpleasantly but with a tone that suggested it was time to get down to business. "Now, if you wouldn't mind, please tell us what you found."

"Well, I'm going to turn that part of our presentation over to Dr. Iris Moon," Underwood said. "She's one of the brightest minds in our firm."

"Nice to meet you, Doctor," Hammerskal said with a certain lilt in his voice. The gleam in Hammerskal's eyes announced to her – and everyone else in the room, for that matter – that he now realized he was in the presence of an attractive woman. "The last doctor I saw spent so much time cutting into my knee that I couldn't walk for a month. If I'm able to leave this meeting without crutches, I'll consider myself ahead of the game."

Since Moon couldn't think of a comeback that wouldn't have been insulting, she smiled slightly and began her rehearsed pitch.

"Gentlemen, you asked us to develop projections for two different types of revenue streams," Moon said. "One was the amount of sales tax revenue that could be generated by a hypothetical baseball team at a hypothetical baseball park. The other was the amount of property tax revenues the hypothetical park could hypothetically use to repay the debt on its construction costs."

Underwood grunted slightly. He wished she weren't using the word 'hypothetical' so much. Underwood just hoped Hammerskal, Malfair and Edison would understand that was the way economists talked. He gestured for Moon to continue.

"Let me start with the sales taxes first," she said. "For this portion of the project, I decided to work backwards. Instead of calculating how much sales tax money a new stadium would generate, I decided to focus instead on how much sales tax money would be needed to cover the stadium's debt service. I hope that approach is OK because it makes this easier to explain."

Another nodding of the heads from the visitors, except Hammerskal, whose head was bent toward his phone again.

"OK, so let's start with the cost numbers," Moon said. "These assumptions will also hold true for the property tax revenues, when we get to that. Anyway, I did some research on construction costs for baseball stadiums that have been built since 2008. The costs ranged from Target Field in Minnesota, built five years ago for $522 million, on the low end to the new Yankee stadium built in New York six years ago for $1.5 billion."

Edison grimaced, Hammerskal let out a low whistle and Malfair remained expressionless. Underwood watched their reactions carefully. He honestly had no idea how this presentation would be received, which is why he asked Moon to deliver it. If things didn't go well, she'd make an easy scapegoat.

"So we're looking at a median construction cost of about $1 billion?" Edison asked.

"Oh, no, not necessarily," Underwood said. "After all, Nashville is not New York. It's not even Minneapolis. I'm sure we can build a state-of-the-art stadium for much less than that. Assuming that's what Mr. Hammerskal and his group wants, of course." His eyes drifted expectantly toward the former baseball player.

"Well, a billion here and a billion there and suddenly you're talking about real money," Hammerskal said. The joke, if it was intended as one, fell flat.

"Let's get into the specifics of the construction costs later," Malfair said.

"I thought you might want to wait on that," Moon said. "So I went ahead and assumed Nashville's construction costs would be on the low end of the scale. In fact, at Mr. Underwood's suggestion, I rounded the projected cost down to $500 million."

"Which can be done with good old Nashville value engineering," Underwood said brightly.

"And that would still be over $200 million more than the combined cost of our football stadium and hockey arena," Edison said.

"True, but those arenas were both built in the mid-1990s," Moon observed. "In today's dollars, they would have cost about $430 million. And inflation adds to the cost every year."

"Still a big jump," Edison observed.

"But below what other Major League Baseball cities have been investing," Malfair countered.

"OK, so let's start with the premise that the city would be adding $500 million in new debt," Moon said. "Typically, municipal bonds would be issued to pay for such a project. And typically, those bonds would be repaid over a 20-year period. Now, let's assume that the city could sell these bonds with a 2 percent interest rate. That would be a 40-year low for interest rates on municipal bonds, which I personally think may be overly optimistic..."

"But let's just call it aggressive," Underwood said. "Two percent is theoretically possible."

"Yes, theoretically," Moon said, pausing to scratch her nose for a second. "So, we're looking at $500 million to be repaid over 20 years with 2 percent interest. That translates into an annual debt payment for the city of $30,353,040. Again, that's a very favorable assumption in terms of actual construction costs and the interest rate."

"Couldn't the loan be repaid over a longer period of time, say, 30 years instead of 20?" Hammerskal asked. "Sort of like financing a car over five years instead of three or four?"

So Hammerskal was paying attention.

"Hypothetically, yes," Moon said. "But in order to sell bonds to investors, they have to be convinced of the city's ability to pay. And since investors are accustomed to 20-year notes on municipal bonds, a longer repayment period would probably signal some doubts about the city's ability to repay. That means the investors would consider the bonds higher risk, which would translate into higher interest rates. So the annual payment probably wouldn't end up changing much, if at all. And the city would end up absorbing an extra 10 years of interest costs."

"Let's keep the assumptions at 20 years, then," Edison said.

"Right," Moon said. "So the combined city and state sales tax rate for metro Nashville is 9.25 percent on each dollar of goods or services purchased. So assuming the city were able to use all of its share of the sales tax money and the state's share too –"

"And we're going to assume the state would be willing to forego its share for the sake of economic development," Underwood interjected.

"Yes, that's a political calculation, not an economic one. But assuming that's the case, then the new stadium would need to generate an average of $328.1 million in sales every year for 20 years to produce enough sales tax revenue to cover the debt payments," Moon said. "So, let me break that down a little further: The average attendance for Major League Baseball games last year was 30,895 fans per game - "

"And we're going to assume Nashville's average will be at least 10 percent higher," Underwood said. "Because we'll have the greatest fans in the world."

"Yes, so we'll figure an average of 34,790 of those greatest fans in the world will attend every game in Nashville over the next 20 years," Moon said. "So in order to generate the amount of sales tax revenues needed over an 81-game home schedule, every man, woman and child who attends a game would have to spend at least $116.76 per visit."

"That's a lot of beer and hot dogs," Hammerskal said. At least he wasn't looking at his phone as much any more.

"Indeed," Moon said. "I'll leave it to you, Mr. Malfair and your partners to figure out how much you would need to charge for tickets, parking, concessions and the like in order to meet those numbers."

"Are those numbers sustainable?" Edison asked.

"That's a business decision," Moon said. "But if you want my opinion – "

"Let's steer clear of that kind of speculation, Dr. Moon," Underwood said. "Why don't you move on to the property tax revenues?"

Moon stopped to rub her nose vigorously again for several seconds before continuing. She appeared to be on the verge of sneezing, but caught herself.

"OK, it's my understanding that you're also considering tax increment financing as a method for financing the construction of this stadium. So we'll keep all of our earlier assumptions about construction and interest costs the same. You're still looking at

$30,353,040 in annual payments. Now, with tax increment financing, you take the assessed value of the property after it's been improved – in this case, by building a new stadium – and subtract the value of the property before its improvements. The difference in those two values is the amount that can be taxed under this method of financing."

Hammerskal waived one hand over his head.

"OK, let's keep this as simple – and as optimistic - as possible. Let's say the land the city gets for this stadium is completely worthless, at least for tax purposes. It isn't likely to happen that way, but it will make the math simpler. So after the new stadium is built, let's assume its assessed property value is the same as the cost of construction, $500 million."

"So property taxes on $500 million should be able to cover $500 million worth of debt, right?" Hammerskal asked.

"Well, let's look at that," Moon said. "In Tennessee, property isn't taxed at its full value. Residential properties are only taxed at one-fourth of their assessed value. For commercial property - which is what this stadium would be classified as - taxes are levied on 40 percent of the value. That's $200 million. Now, in metro Nashville, the property tax rate is $4.64 per $100 of assessed value. So property taxes on $200 million worth of commercial property would get you about $9.28 million per year, which is less than one-third of your annual debt service payment. Is all this making sense so far?"

"Those are some hard numbers you've given us," Edison said, breaking a short silence.

"Actually, they're not hard numbers, they're only estimates," Underwood said.

"I meant, they are difficult numbers," Edison replied.

"I'm not sure that I follow you, Horton," Malfair said.

"What I mean," Edison said with a scowl, "is that according to these projections, even if every penny of property taxes collected from a new stadium were set aside to repay the stadium's construction costs, then it still wouldn't be enough to cover the debt payments. Not nearly enough."

"Well – " Malfair began, but Edison cut him off with a wave of his hand.

"And in order for the sales tax revenues to cover that debt, your average family of four would have to spend close to $500 per game every time it visited the ballpark. And that family – and a lot of others like it – would have to keep doing that, game in and game out, season in and season out, for a full 20 years. And again, that's assuming not one cent of that sales tax money would be used for anything else except the stadium debt."

"Of course, the projections we've shown you have a number of variables in them," Underwood said. "The papers in front of you show a range of possibilities based on different scenarios."

"Yes, and if I understood Dr. Moon's presentation correctly – and I believe I did – the financial realities might be even more daunting than what we've seen laid out here. A 2 percent interest rate doesn't seem likely, unless our economy is in such a sad state that lenders are willing to offer rock bottom rates as incentive to get capital flowing again. And, while $500 million seems like an obscene amount of money to spend on a patch of grass surrounded by some bleachers – "

"As you well know, Horton, modern sports facilities have a lot more amenities – " Malfair said.

"Yes, I'd hope so. Otherwise, I'd have to wonder if those bleachers were plated in gold," Edison said. "But the true cost could be more than $500 million, given what Dr. Moon has told us how much has been spent other stadiums during the last few years and accounting for inflation. And I'm also skeptical of Nashville's ability to pull attendance numbers 10 percent above the league average for two decades, unless the team is going to be playing in the World Series every year."

"That's not a bad goal to shoot for," Hammerskal said before glancing down at his phone again.

"Horton, I can assure you that the team owners will be properly motivated to ensure that attendance is as high as it possibly can be," Malfair added. "They'll take care of the marketing and promotion to make sure their investment is protected."

"Well, that's the other thing," Edison said. "Based on what we've heard here today, I'm not exactly sure what investment the owners would be making. The scenarios we've discussed today assume that the stadium would be 100 percent publicly financed. No contribution at all from the team owners, who would stand to directly benefit from the stadium construction."

"As you said, they're just scenarios," Malfair said. "I still think we've got a lot of details we'll need to work out."

"Are you saying the owners will be willing to pay some portion of the construction costs themselves?" Edison asked.

"I think that's a conversation for another day," Malfair said. "We'll need to talk to you and your boss about what everyone can expect to get out of this."

"So you can't give me a yes or no answer to my question?" Edison said.

"Not here," Malfair said, shooting a glance in the director of Underwood and Moon. "Not now."

An awkward silence followed. Finally, Hammerskal broke it.

"I wish I could have gotten my coaches to stay this quiet during my playing days."

CHAPTER ELEVEN

Autumn Sunshine could barely contain her excitement. She was heading east on Interstate 40 in her Volkswagen Thing with her cassette of Bee Gees' greatest hits blaring and her mind racing. Her three young passengers – twenty something guys she'd met in an East Nashville bar a couple of days before – were in good spirits as well, although Autumn couldn't tell whether that was due to the mission at hand or the reefer they had been sharing. At a minimum, she hoped it was a little of both.

Autumn certainly hoped her recruits understood the importance of what they were about to do. If it went well – and Autumn had every reason to believe it would – then it would be the launch of a great political movement. Which is what she had waited for her whole life.

By a cruel twist of fate, she had been born in Bell Buckle, a tiny rural community a couple of hours southeast of Nashville, on New Year's Day, 1980. It was a cruel twist of fate because she should have been born a child of the 1960s or '70s.

Her father had been a sociology professor at Middle Tennessee State University in nearby Murfreesboro and her mother had worked as a veterinary assistant in the same town. They had given her a very average middle class upbringing and had hopes that she would follow in their footsteps, landing a job in a respectable profession and raising a family.

Predictably, Autumn had rebelled against her parents' goals for her. She had always been fascinated by the hippie lifestyle and resented her parents for choosing not to embrace it. Autumn had tried to be hippie enough to compensate for her parents by becoming active in various trendy causes from an early age. Starting around age 9, she'd been part of letter-writing campaigns to save the whales. Marches to end apartheid. Fundraising drives to support AIDS research.

While she had a great work ethic and was as zealous about the causes she championed as any of the people she worked with, she never really fit in completely with any of them. Maybe she was too zealous. But this, this would be different.

No longer would she be the follower. These kids were *her* recruits. The first of many, she hoped – no, expected. She'd met them at an East Nashville bar near the art gallery where she worked part time. Two of them worked as bartenders at other places in the neighborhood and the other was a clerk at an organic foods store. The three of them had formed a band called Drunk Thirty that performed Southern rock cover tunes in local clubs. After a night of good conversation and Pabst Blue Ribbon, they were ready to endorse Autumn's newest cause – the legalization of marijuana in Tennessee. They were committed to become her acolytes as she launched a petition drive to get a constitutional amendment on the ballot statewide.

They knew their work would be cut out for them. In the last few years, several states had voted to legalize marijuana use for medicinal purposes – which was really just an incremental step toward the ultimate goal. Some forward-thinking states had actually achieved that ultimate goal of decriminalizing the recreational use of weed. But this was Tennessee, in the buckle of the Bible Belt. Winning hearts and minds here to the virtues of a baked lifestyle wouldn't be easy.

As the first few chords of "Tragedy" began to play on her cassette, Autumn launched into her pep talk.

"Guys, I don't have to tell you how important this day is," she said, glancing in the rearview mirror at the boys in her backseat and then at the boy seated next to her. "This could be a day we remember the rest of our lives!"

"Or *don't* remember," the one in the back holding the doobie said. All three of them chuckled.

"Oh, we're going to remember this. And so will the squares who want to keep the whole world from lighting up!" Autumn said, a gleam of fierce intensity in her blue eyes. She was an extremely pretty woman, with strawberry blond hair and pink lips that required no makeup. In fact, her good looks were what had enticed her young disciples to come over and talk to her that night in the bar. None of them were politically active or even politically aware, although their interests happened to align with Autumn's on this particular issue.

"The powers that be like the status quo," Autumn said. "And because they control the media, they're able to keep their modern day version of Prohibition in place. But they can't fight forever against what's free and natural."

"I hate to tell you this, but this weed was not free," the backseat toker countered. An even bigger chuckle. Autumn knew she needed to get her charges focused.

Her eyebrows lowered and her nose crinkled, highlighting the freckles that stretched across her face from cheekbone to cheekbone. In high school, a date had once referred to her freckles as "the rusted ends of her iron nerves." She'd never forgotten that expression, even though she was certain the dude had only said it in an unsuccessful attempt to get into her pants.

"OK, everybody, we're almost there," Autumn said. "We need to get our game faces on."

"I'm not sure I can still feel my face," the other boy in the back seat said, touching his face with his fingertips to underscore his joke. The laughs were getting bigger by the minute. Hack comedians dreamed of performing in front of audiences filled with kids like these.

Autumn sighed as she pulled off the exit ramp near their destination. OK, maybe she had expected too much out of these guys. But surely they could help her pull this off. After all, this wasn't like breaking into Fort Knox or anything.

She turned the car into the entrance for Nashville Shores, the popular water park next to Percy Priest Lake. It was Dec. 21, the official first day of winter, and Nashville Shores was sponsoring a polar bear swim.

The event had been concocted by one of Nashville Shores' PR people as a way to get the water park some media attention during the offseason. The flack had correctly judged that anything with the potential to generate good video would attract the local TV stations, particularly since they had long ago run out of ideas for stories about the Christmas shopping season.

If the motivations of the water park's officials and the members of the media were obvious, those of the people choosing to strip down to swimsuits and jump in a lake during 40-degree weather were less so. Most were young and looked as if a plunge into the lake was just one of the legs in a triathlon. Most wore regular swimming suits, with or without t-shirts. A couple were wearing long john underwear. One older guy wore a Hobbit costume over an old-fashioned set of long white-and-black striped bathing trunks that left no skin exposed above mid-calf. A handful of participants wore wetsuits, which earned them scornful looks from their fellow participants.

Autumn eased her VW Thing into a parking space on a hill near the ramp and took in the scene. Although the entire park sat along the lake's edge, the waterfront property was normally off limits to visitors. And for good reason: If park visitors thought too much about the fact that there were numerous beaches and recreational areas within a short driving distance where they could swim in the lake for free, then they might be less inclined to shell out big bucks on Nashville Shores' wave pool, water slides and other attractions.

But for this event, the Nashville Shores staff had set up an area that looked like the starting line for a marathon, with a wooden archway topped by a decorative Santa and his reindeer display. Rows of Christmas trees decked out in lights lined a ramp descending toward the water. Beyond the tree lines on each side of the ramp, there were two huge machines blowing dry ice flakes into the air to simulate snowfall. Christmas music blared from the speakers set up between the trees.

Autumn's eyes scanned the crowd. There appeared to be about three dozen people who were prepared to abandon good sense by leaping into the chilly water and at least twice as many who were there to watch the show. Autumn's mood brightened as she saw the TV crews in the crowd. At least three stations were there, including one intrepid crew that had rented two kayaks so both the reporter and the cameraman could capture the moment from beyond the water's edge.

That was what Autumn was looking for. She fully expected to be the lead story on all of their newscasts this evening, talking about how she had transformed this boring old polar bear swim into "A Dip for Dope."

A Nashville Shores executive decked out in a Santa suit was addressing the crowd now. The polar bear swimmers were hopping up and down in an effort to stay warm. Sensing his audience's discomfort, the executive appeared to be wrapping up his remarks. It would just be a few more moments before he cut them loose.

Autumn and her trio of cohorts passed around the joint for one last hit as the pulsing notes of the Bee Gees' "You Should Be Dancing" played on the cassette.

Her head buzzing with excitement, Autumn turned and held the gaze of each boy for just an instant.

On the ramp a few short yards away, they heard a collective yell as the swimmers charged down the ramp. The yell dissolved into a series of shrieks as they bounded into the water.

"OK, boys!" Autumn said as she peeled off her halter top. "Let's go skinny dipping!"

The boys, accustomed to more difficulty in getting women to disrobe, appeared momentarily taken aback, but they quickly recovered and began tearing away their clothing.

"Oh, this is so worth it," one of them muttered as he struggled to get his shirt over his head.

In a few seconds, they were all four out of the car and running down the ramp naked except for their shoes, with Autumn and the boy who'd been riding shotgun in the lead and the other two trailing just behind.

"WHOO! LET'S DIP FOR DOPE! DIP FOR DOPE!" Autumn shouted as she ran. She found the cold air and soft pelting of the dry ice against her skin to be exhilarating. The boys seemed to be having a good time streaking with the crazy naked lady, too, at least until a strong gust of wind caught them just before they reached the water.

"Awww, no, man," one of the kids in the back said as he pulled up short. "That water's gonna cause shrinkage. Massive shrinkage."

His buddy who had been running beside him also stopped, pondering that warning.

The guy who was running alongside Autumn – Kayle or Kyle, she thought his name was – wasn't going to lose face by chickening out in front of a hottie, even one with a little bit of age on her. As Autumn dashed into the water, he was matching her stride for stride. It took a few moments for the stinging sensation brought about by the near-freezing water to register with his pot-inhibited central nervous system, which gave him enough time to submerge himself all the way up to his waist. When his brain finally caught on to what was happening, it brought a shock of pain to a particularly sensitive area of his body.

He intended to shout out a vulgar term for the word 'excrement,' followed by the words 'cold lake,' but in his stoned state, it came out as "SH-LAKE!" That was all he was about to say before doubling over in response to the frigid assault on his private parts.

Up until that point, the streakers had mostly gone unnoticed since they were bringing up the rear of the group and everyone else in the crowd was shouting, too. But the word "snake" – or a near approximation of it – caught the other swimmers' attention. A couple of the swimmers closest to Kayle/Kyle turned at the sound of his scream, saw his hunched-over posture and reached the same conclusion.

"SNAKE!" one of them yelled. "THAT GUY JUST GOT BITTEN BY A SNAKE!"

Had there been a herpetologist in the group, it might have been calmly pointed out that a snake would be unlikely to be swimming in water so cold and even less likely that it would be able to move fast enough to bite anyone. As it was, though, the screams about snakes awakened a primal fear shared by the group.

"LET'S GET OUT OF HERE!" someone shouted – and suddenly the stampede was on.

The water quickly began to froth and churn as the swimmers scrambled out of the lake as quickly as their numbed limbs would take them. The reporter and cameraman in the kayaks, who had paddled into the center of the mass of swimmers to get on-the-spot interviews, were suddenly caught in choppy waves they were unprepared to handle. Both kayaks capsized.

The swimmers stumbled over each other as they exited the water and swarmed toward higher ground.

The guy in the Hobbit costume tried to look back at the lake as he ran up the ramp, which caused him to plow headfirst into one of the artificial trees. The Hobbit and the tree both went down, triggering a chain reaction that caused the trees in the row to fall like dominos.

On the other side of the ramp, a fleeing swimmer clipped one of the fake snow machines, which redirected its blast directly into the face of another of the TV reporters who was trying to document the madness around her. She screamed an obscenity that rendered her footage useless for the evening news, although it would be extremely popular on the video of bloopers and outtakes played at the station's staff New Year's Eve party a few days later.

The members of Drunk Thirty decided to join the herd in beating a retreat from the lake. Autumn watched their skinny behinds sprinting toward her car and decided it was time to cut her losses and join them. The "Dip for Dope" appeared to be a lost cause, at least for today.

As the streakers approached the Volkswagen, a couple of security guards emerged from the crowd of onlookers in an attempt to cut them off. They zeroed in on Autumn, apparently more interested in tackling her than three naked stoner dudes. They brought Autumn down to the ground and secured her hands behind her back with a pair of plastic cuffs. Since there were TV cameras present, they did so with a minimal amount of unnecessary groping of her body.

From her vantage point, Autumn looked up to see what had become of her companions. They were piling into her car now, with Kayle/Kyle landing awkwardly in the driver's seat. Autumn had left the keys in the ignition, as she frequently did in the spirit of communal living. Autumn saw the car lurch forward as the kid popped the emergency brake and appeared to be trying to start the car.

For a brief instant, Autumn thought back to when she had bought the car. She'd had her heart set on a 1960s or 1970s Volkswagen bus, the signature ride of the counterculture movement, but she hadn't had any luck finding one. She settled on the boxy and battered old Thing she saw at one of the many used car lots along Gallatin Road, consoling herself that she had at least bought a Volkswagen. She was less consoled later when she found out the Thing was a model that had been used by the German army during World War II – making it the very antithesis of everything she thought the Volkswagen buses symbolized.

Now the Thing was rolling downhill toward the ramp, without the reassuring sound of the engine puttering. Autumn could see through the windshield that Kayle/Kyle looked rigid behind the wheel and she immediately understood what was happening. The kid, who obviously hadn't driven a stick shift before, had panicked and slammed his foot against the clutch, believing it to be the brake.

The car picked up speed as it approached the ramp, causing swimmers and onlookers to scatter. As Autumn groaned in horror, the car struck one side of the entryway arch, causing it to collapse. As the arch came down, it brought with it the decorative Santa, along with his sleigh and reindeer. Rudolph, the lead reindeer, plunged headfirst into one of the speakers, putting a squawking end to Bing Crosby's rendition of "White Christmas." Not that anyone was still listening, anyway.

The car continued forward, bringing down the other row of trees and pushing them into the lake. The Drunk Thirty crew bailed just before the Thing hit the water, where the car bobbed up and down like a giant yellow cork amid the faux green vegetation.

Autumn slowly lowered her face into the yellow dried-out bed of grass where she lay.

God, she thought to herself, *I really could use a smoke.*

CHAPTER TWELVE

Mayor Kent Gables was suffering from a serious case of writer's block when his office intercom buzzed. He'd spent the last half hour trying to craft a memo outlining some dress code rules for casual Fridays. Clearly, jeans were OK. And equally clear – in his mind, if not the minds of all his employees – pajama bottoms were not. But where to draw the line between what was acceptable and what wasn't? He was so flummoxed by that question that the drone of the intercom actually came as a relief.

"Yes, ma'am?" Mayor Gables replied to his receptionist.

"Mr. Hunt Blazen is here to see you, sir."

"Send him in please." Gables rose to shake hands with Blazen as he entered the office. "Hello, Hunt. This is a pleasant surprise."

At Gables' invitation, Hunt took a seat across from the mayor's desk. With his carefully-styled hair and bright white teeth, Blazen could have passed for a blonder, slightly younger version of the city's chief executive officer.

"So, Hunt, how's the car business?" Gables asked. "A lot of husbands with guilty consciences buying last-minute Christmas gifts for their wives?"

"As always," Blazen replied. "You know, I could probably make a few hundred dollars here and there if the manufacturers would just let me sell some of those giant bows you see on car roofs in a lot of commercials this time of year."

"Yeah, what happens to all those bows the rest of the year?" Gables mused. "Do they end up in a giant attic somewhere?"

Blazen tried to laugh, but it didn't suit his mood. His smile came across as more of a grimace. Gables took that as a sign the time for chit-chat was over.

"So what can I do for you, Hunt? You look troubled."

"I am, Mayor. I'm sorry to say it, but I am."

"What's on your mind?"

"It's about the plans for the baseball expansion franchise."

"Very big plans!" Gables said. "So what do you need? You'd like to talk to the team owners about some kind of sponsorship deal? Maybe some kind of promotion where you raffle off a free car to a lucky season ticket holder?"

"Well, that's not exactly what I..."

"Oh, I know. I know. You can't just give away free cars all the time. Maybe that's something you'd want to save for the team's first playoff appearance or something. But listen to me: It's easy for me to spend someone else's money, isn't it? It's not like my real estate company is likely to be giving away houses, I'll admit. But I do hope the dealership will at least get a luxury box. You and I could waste many a summer Sunday afternoon at a place like that, you know."

"I'm sure we could, Mr. Mayor. But that's not really why I'm here."

"Oh. Then why are you here?"

"It's about the site you've picked out for the stadium, Mayor. I've got a problem with it."

"Oh?" Gables was genuinely surprised. He didn't know the stadium site had gone public yet.

"Yes. I know you're interested in putting it where the scrap yard is on the riverfront."

"OK, I'm not sure where you heard that, but you're right, Hunt. A great location, don't you think?"

"It is a great location. It's such a great location that I have an option to buy part of that property. I want to put a charter school there."

"A charter school? I had no idea."

"I've been working on this for a while. It's actually been my dream for years. You know, I love the car business – well, sometimes I love it – and I'm grateful that my family got me set up in it. I want to keep that business going for a long time, but I also want to branch out. To do something that I would build from the ground up, not just inherit and maintain. Plus, I've got a...sentimental attachment to that site."

"That's quite an idea, Hunt."

"You must understand what I'm talking about, Mayor. You built your real estate business up that way. But to me, this would be more than a business. I didn't do really well in school – and maybe part of that is my fault. Maybe a lot of it is my fault. But I think this school could help reach students who are like I was, who need a little extra help to reach their potential. And it would be a place where students with special skills could build on those skills, the way they might not get a chance to do at a regular school."

"All that sounds great, Hunt. But couldn't you put a school like that a lot of places?"

"No, not really, Mayor. Like I said, I have sentimental reasons for wanting that site. Plus, I want the school to have a special emphasis for kids who want to study natural sciences. And the kind of nature study that's available on a campus near the river isn't available in those other places. And I've got a couple of years of time and money plowed into the planning for this site. If I have to start all over, I'll fall behind other charter school applicants. Maybe forever. The window of opportunity to make this happen is actually pretty small."

Mayor Gables nodded and stared at the ceiling for a couple of seconds. Now he wished writing that dress code memo was the toughest thing he had to do today.

"I sympathize with you, Hunt, I really do. But I'm not the one driving this train. The people who want the franchise in Nashville, well, that site is the one they want."

"So why can't you just tell *them* to consider another site?"

"I would if I could, but that could mess up the whole deal. Who knows? Wynn Hammerskal and these other owners, they've got money enough to do what they want, where they want. And that means they could just as easily pick another city."

Blazen raised his hands to his head and ran his fingers through his hair violently.

"But Mayor, what about me and my business? We've been part of this city for three generations. Don't we count for anything?"

"Of course you do, Hunt! And I'm going to see if I can do something to make this right by you. To make sure that even after the stadium is built, the people of this city will understand the sacrifice you're making. Hold on just a minute. Let me make a quick call."

Gables started to rifle through the cards in his Rolodex, looking for Wynn Hammerskal's number. Then he realized he didn't have it, just an autographed baseball, so he found Julius Malfair's instead. After a brief conversation with Malfair's secretary, he was patched through. He clicked on the speakerphone so Hunt Blazen could listen in.

"Hey, Julius. Mayor Gables here. I'm sitting here with Hunt Blazen. You know him, right?

"Oh, sure," Malfair said. "I think I bought a car from his father once, a few years ago. How are you doing, Mr. Blazen?"

"Just fine," Blazen said, although that couldn't have been further from the truth.

"OK, Julius, here's the situation: Mr. Blazen has a pretty interesting idea. He wants to put a charter school in downtown Nashville. But the problem is that the site he had all picked out for his school is the same one your clients need for the baseball stadium. So here's what I'm thinking. Since he won't be able to put the school where he wants it, the city ought to do something to show that we appreciate the sacrifice he'll be making for the greater good. So why don't we name the stadium after him? The Hunt Blazen Ballpark has a nice ring to it, don't you think?"

Gables winked at Blazen, whose face was a blank mask of shock. There was a long silence on the other end of the line before Malfair finally spoke.

"Well, Mayor, Mr. Blazen, I can appreciate what you're trying to do here. But I just don't think that will work."

"Why not?" Gables said. Blazen remained speechless.

"I believe – well, actually I'm quite sure – that Mr. Hammerskal and the other owners will want to leave the stadium name open for the time being. You see, there's a great opportunity to sell the naming rights to a corporate sponsor. Naming rights deals can be worth millions of dollars. Tens of millions, in some cases."

"Hmmm, OK. Well, I guess I can understand that. But what about naming one of the roads around the stadium after Mr. Blazen? That would fit, since he owns car dealerships and all."

"There again, there's naming rights money to be made with stadium property. I'm sorry, but I just don't think the owners are going to be willing to give away for free something that they could sell."

Gables glanced at Blazen, whose expression was darkening. He thought about switching off the speakerphone and picking up the receiver, but decided it was probably too late for that.

"OK, but there must be something. The media room? The concourses? The locker rooms? Surely, the owners aren't planning to sell the naming rights to all of those, are they?"

Another pause.

"Actually, yes," Malfair said.

"So what might be available, to show a small gesture of good will to Mr. Blazen and his family, who I might remind you have been excellent corporate citizens of this city for a long time?"

"Probably nobody will want their name on the bathrooms," Malfair said. "That's about all I can think of, offhand."

Without saying another word, Blazen sprang up from his chair and exited the mayor's office.

"Hunt, wait!" Gables called after him, but Blazen didn't stop. "Julius, this didn't go as well as I'd hoped. I'm going to have to get back to you."

With that, Gables ended the call. He started to get up and go after Blazen, then sank back in his chair. He started to get up again, then sat back. After drumming his fingers on his desk for a few seconds, he did what he usually did when he was in a jam. He buzzed Horton Edison on the intercom.

Edison shuffled into the office a minute later, closing the door behind him and taking a seat. He waited until the mayor spoke.

"Horton, do you ever feel like you can do no right?"

"Constantly," Edison replied. "Something specific troubling you?"

"Just this deal with the baseball franchise. Here I am, doing something that ought to have me being hailed as a hero from Bordeaux to Beale Meade. But instead of that, I've got the owner of the local minor league franchise mad at me because he thinks a major league franchise would shut him down."

"He's right about that."

"Well, yeah, I expected that. But that's not all. I've got a couple of neighborhood groups that are upset, too. They're saying I'm focusing too much attention on developing downtown at the expense of the outlying residential neighborhoods that could use some help."

"You've heard that criticism before."

"Right, right. But now Hunt Blazen's mad at me, too. He and his family are among this town's leading corporate citizens. The city's been doing business with Blazen dealerships on fleet vehicles for decades. That family and I go back a long way personally, too. My real estate firm even brokered the deal on the Blazen dealership property at Cool Springs."

"I understand. But you knew when you went into politics that you couldn't make everybody happy, Mayor. Particularly on something this big."

"You're right, Horton. Of course you're right. But here's the thing: We're jumping through hoops, trying to figure out how to pay for a stadium with sales taxes, property taxes or whatever. And we don't even know what the stadium owners – the guys who would benefit the most directly from this project – are willing to contribute to the effort."

"With the exception of Mr. Hammerskal, you don't even know who those owners are."

"Right again! So what do you suggest?"

"Well, regardless of your personal feelings about having a baseball franchise, I think you should remember that this is still a deal. A deal involving politics and business. A lot of politics and a lot of business, more than likely."

"So, what does that mean?"

"That means you've got to start treating it like one. In the real estate business, when you know you've got someone who's willing to sell a piece of property and someone who's willing to buy it, what do you do?"

"Draw up the paperwork?"

"Eventually, Mr. Mayor. But before that, you've got to negotiate a deal. And that's what you need to do here. You need to find out what the team owners – let's still call them 'potential team owners' for now – what do they want and what are they willing to contribute to help get a team to Nashville. Then you have to decide if that's something you're willing to live with. And what the city is willing to give up in return."

Kent Gables stared at the ceiling before responding.

"OK, so set it up, Horton. I want you to set up a meeting with Wynn Hammerskal, Julius Malfair and whoever his other mystery clients are and see what's what."

"I'll get right on that."

"Horton, you know I trust you more than anyone else in city government. I need you to be my eyes, my ears and most importantly, my mouthpiece on this one. I need you to go out there and drive the hardest bargain you can. For you, for me, for the city and its taxpayers. Can you handle that?"

"I can handle it."

"Any questions? Any comments?"

"No questions, Mayor. And my only comment is that it's about time."

"Where's Your Resolve for the New Year, Mr. Mayor?"
By Gilbert Wise, Sports Columnist

As we usher in a new year here at the Wise family compound, Orlando Mayor Skip Goodman is one old acquaintance we'd like to forget.

Imagine our surprise yesterday – the day of the year all but dedicated by national decree to college football – when Goodman managed to divert everyone's attention to baseball.

He did so during a nationally televised interview at halftime of the Citrus Bowl, the annual football game featuring the runner-up teams from the Southeastern and Big 10 conferences. The interview with the host city's mayor usually features a predictable bit of banter about the virtues of balmy weather, orange juice and artificial tourist attractions.

But what I heard yesterday made me want to spit my Mimosa out on the floor. Mayor Goodman was telling a national TV audience about his city's fully formed plans to build a Major League Baseball stadium with 45,000 seats and 50 luxury boxes. All financed with the city's hotel and motel tax revenues.

Mayor Goodman has already demonstrated his flair for the dramatic once before in this pursuit of a team. His infomercial following the coverage of Major League Baseball's announcement about the new franchise was a stroke of sheer marketing genius.

Baseball Commissioner Raymond Goldfarb surely has to be paying attention. Not that he's had many distractions to contend with here in Nashville lately. Sure, our mayor, Kent Gables, held a news conference in which he basically declared that Nashville would, um, really like to go out with Major League Baseball. But almost a month has passed since then and Hizzoner doesn't seem to have taken the first steps toward actually picking up the phone and asking for a date.

Yes, I know that a month ago, I wrote that Mayor Gables deserved credit for not screwing up anything too badly in our city. That could be about to change.
Maybe Orlando does have an advantage with the hotel and motel tax revenues it receives. With the millions of visitors who blow through Central Florida every year, it's like the town almost has its own money printing press.
But we're not without our own resources here. When the city wanted a National Football League team, we found a way to build a stadium. When we wanted a National Hockey League team, we found a way to build an arena for them, too.

So why is this different? What has Mayor Gables been doing this last month while his counterpart in Orlando has been pushing approval for a financing deal through the city council there? Oh, I'd like to think that Mayor Gables has been feverishly working behind the scenes to come up with a deal for Nashville that will blow Orlando's out of the water. Experience leads me to believe otherwise.

Politicians like Mayor Gables love the "feel good" news conferences. They announce plans for something big and shiny and new, like a Major League Baseball franchise. Everyone ooohs and aaahs. Pundits comment about how good Mayor Gables looks in a suit. They speculate about how maybe he should consider running for governor some day.

Then when the big plans don't pan out, everybody forgets. Well, I could be wrong, but this time I don't think people will forget. They'll be reminded every time they turn on the TV and see a new baseball team playing in Orlando uniforms.

Mayor Gables staked Nashville's claim for the new franchise first – no doubt about it. Then Orlando actually presented a vision for what a team could expect if it were located there.

Our vision? Who the heck knows? Does Nashville have a plan if we're able to land this team? Surely our esteemed mayor doesn't think the team will use Greer Stadium, our minor league team's relic from the 1970s. What's Mayor Gables thinking? That every home game could be a 1970s retro night, with throwback uniforms, ushers in bell bottom pants and disco music over the PA system?

The mayor's lack of action is frustrating. It's like the other team ran out to take the field at the start of the game and our team is still sitting in the dugout.

It's also feeding the stereotype people from other parts of the country have about Nashville: We're unimaginative. Slow. Maybe even a little slack-jawed.

Can we turn things around? Maybe. In this pursuit of a new franchise, are we in the first inning or the ninth? When Major League Baseball is involved, it's hard to know for sure. This much is clear: It's high time for Mayor Gables to pick up a bat and start swinging. If he doesn't, then the business and community leaders of this town – our de facto team managers – need to start looking down the bench for a pinch

hitter. From where I sit, that looks like
the only Wise choice.

CHAPTER THIRTEEN

Horton Edison read the column through a second time, then shook his head and tossed the newspaper onto his desk in disgust.

No doubt about it, Edison thought, *Gilbert Wise is an idiot.*

Couldn't he understand what was going on here? Yes, Nashville was in competition with Orlando for the baseball franchise. And yes, it mattered what each city offered to the potential franchise owners and when.

Not just a competition, but a high stakes competition. Now that the mayor had publicly committed himself to bringing a team to Nashville, the failure to do so would result in a political loss of face. And in Mayor Gables' world, that was the loss that mattered most.

Defeat would affect public perception of the city and the mayor's office, not just locally but on a national level. The national media, not anxious to be shaken from its comfort zone, would crow about how Nashville remained the Little City that Couldn't – cute, quaint, but not on the same level as real cities like New York, Los Angeles and Chicago. Having a new city join the established metropolitan behemoths wasn't something the national pundits could easily get their minds around. As much as they claimed to celebrate what was new and different in the world, those pundits clung to that which they found consistent and familiar.

Even worse would be the impact the failure to get a franchise would have on the collective psyche of Nashvillians. They would think to themselves: *We're not quite good enough. Why aren't we good enough? We should be good enough.* And that would eventually lead to the most dangerous thought of all: *Maybe it's all the mayor's fault.*

Edison wondered if his boss had considered the stakes when he'd thrown Nashville into the middle of this. It was hard to talk rationally to Mayor Kent Gables about baseball. His devotion to fantasy baseball had always bordered on obsession. And the way he was talking about landing this team crossed that border and kept on going.

Whenever Edison tried to engage Gables about the details of landing a team, the real work that lay ahead, the mayor steered the conversation toward the romance and wonder of baseball.

What other sport has a great tradition like the seventh-inning stretch? Gables would ask. *A chance for fans to stretch their legs before the final innings and join in the singing of "Take Me Out to the Ballgame."*

Well, whoopee. To Edison's way of thinking, the really amazing thing about the seventh-inning stretch was that fans retook their seats and watched the rest of the game after it was over, instead of heading for the exits.

It wasn't that Edison hated baseball. He just had a hard time figuring out what all the fuss was about. In his younger days, he had road-tripped with friends to Atlanta Braves games. Paired with the right amount of beer, the game could be tolerable. Edison probably still had a foam tomahawk somewhere in his closet that was left over from the days he joined the crowds at Braves' games in doing "The Chop."

But stripped of the game day atmosphere, the sport itself could be tedious. The pace was far too slow for Edison's liking. Too much time was wasted between pitches. Edison thought the game could be improved if pitchers were on a shot clock, just like basketball, where they had to throw the ball within 20 seconds or so. The same with batters. Those who took inordinate amounts of time spitting and adjusting themselves should be penalized.

Then there was the length of the schedule. Major League Baseball teams played 162 games a year, which made it difficult to get too emotionally invested in the outcome in any of those games, at least not until the season entered its final days.

And that was a practical concern for Edison. If Nashville did land a team, that would mean 81 home games per year, played during the time of year when the city's weather was at its best. Were there enough people living in and around the city to consistently support a team over that stretch of time?

It was one thing to sell out the Tennessee Titans' football games. There were only eight of them played in Nashville each year. With the hockey team, there were 41 home games per year – a lot, but still only half as many as a baseball team would bring.

Plus, there was the economic question. Did Nashvillians, as a group, have enough disposable income to support a football team, a hockey team and a baseball team? Mayor Gables loved to throw around the expression, "a three-team town," but was he really aware of all that would require?

Then again, it was too late for Edison to second guess the mayor's decision. Nashville was going after a team and there would be no backing out now. As the mayor liked to say from time to time: *We're in this to win this.*

If Nashville did win, Edison knew there would be benefits, chief among them the intangible value of image enhancement. If Major League Baseball chose Nashville over Orlando, it would make a statement about how the league perceived each city's future. Even the national media would have to acknowledge as much. Later, if the franchise performed poorly financially, the media would take the opportunity to return to the Little City that Couldn't theme. But at least initially, the pundits would have to eat some crow and admit maybe Nashville wasn't such a backwater place after all.

Would that lead to more economic development? New businesses relocating to the city and existing businesses expanding their operations there? Edison wasn't so sure about that. Chamber of commerce types liked to talk about how sports franchises were amenities that helped make communities more attractive to businesses.

But if that were true, then why was Wal-Mart, the nation's largest retailer, headquartered in Bentonville, Arkansas? Edison suspected big businesses were far more interested in extracting whatever financial incentives they could from government to enhance their own bottom lines. If the company executives got to sit in luxury sky boxes and sip overpriced drinks at ball games, that was probably a nice bonus for them, but not the factor on which relocation and expansion decisions were based.

And after all, wasn't a major league team just like any other big business in its pursuit of government incentives? With the possible difference being that a furniture distribution center or prosthetic limb manufacturer didn't inspire columnists like Gilbert Wise to try to whip the public into a frenzy and place political considerations ahead of good government policy...

Edison's thoughts were interrupted when his intercom buzzed, announcing the arrival of Julius Malfair. In spite of the mayor's suggestion, Edison had decided to meet Malfair alone rather than with the somewhat manic Wynn Hammerskal. After all, Edison and Malfair had known each other a long time and might get more accomplished in a one-on-one session.

Edison knew Malfair back when he insisted on being called Julius C. Malfair. Malfair had thought using his middle initial had made him seem more important. But he became less insistent about its use after a newspaper profile had revealed that the 'C' stood for 'Cletus' and not 'Caesar,' as he'd led some people to believe.

"I see that you've already seen this morning's paper," Malfair said as he entered, nodding toward Edison's desk and taking a seat across from him. "So this baseball team looks like a real political winner for you and your boss. Gilbert Wise is practically salivating over the team's arrival."

"And if we get a team, he'll be the first one complaining about how difficult it is to make his deadlines when games run late," Edison replied.

"So true," Malfair said with a pleasant chuckle. "So how have things been with you, Horton? Are you still playing in that band?"

That band was a group called "The Chronies," which consisted of Edison, two downtown lawyers and an accountant. They played popular Southern rock tunes at small joints around town, partly out of enjoyment and partly to show people that they weren't as dweeby as their professions might suggest.

"Doing just fine," Edison said. "We've been playing a few times a month at Capital Indiscretions." That was the name of a place on Printer's Alley, not far from City Hall, where Edison occasionally went after work to unwind.

"Well, I'd like to come listen to you play sometime."

"You should."

"I will. So anyway, Horton, you called this meeting. What would you like to talk about?"

"Well, the mayor and I think it's time we got down to brass tacks about this baseball franchise. So we can sort out what the team owners are willing to contribute to this project and what they're going to be asking from the city."

"What the owners are going to contribute? Well, let's see," Malfair tipped back in his chair a bit as if he was thinking of an answer to a question he never expected to be asked. "I believe they'll be investing millions of their hard-earned wealth to pay the franchise fee and support the ongoing operations of an enterprise that will bring happiness to millions of Nashvillians for years to come. So you're welcome for that."

"And they might make a few more millions along the way, too, right? So it's not exactly a charitable contribution, is it?

"I think they would say they're being very charitable. They've already got millions."

"Funny thing I've observed about millionaires is that they always seem interested in making more money. Except for lottery winners, who have great fortune thrown in their laps with no real effort on their part, wealthy people never seem to think they're wealthy enough."

"The last time I checked, that wasn't a crime. In fact, there are some people who call that the American Dream, Horton."

"I'd venture to say that those people don't have to deal with millionaires coming to them with their hands out, requesting special considerations to help them get richer."

"What considerations?"

"You tell me, Julius. Because there's still the issue of how we would pay for the stadium a new team would need."

"When you say 'we,' are you speaking of the city?"

"I was speaking of you, me and all the people we're representing here."

"Oh. Well, Horton, we – and by 'we' I mean myself and the team owners – think it's the city's responsibility to build the stadium."

"WHAT?" Edison rose from his chair slightly before re-seating himself. "What happened to what you and Mr. Hammerskal said at our first meeting about this project? About the owners not needing anything but the mayor's political support?"

"You read it yourself, Horton. The city of Orlando is willing to build a publicly financed stadium to support its bid. If Nashville doesn't agree to do the same, then our city will be at a disadvantage. Maybe a fatal disadvantage."

"Orlando is planning to pay for the thing with hotel and motel taxes. I don't know if you've noticed, Julius, but we don't have a theme park on every corner to draw enough tourists to generate that kind of money."

"We have plenty of tourists. Your boss, Mayor Gables, talks about that in his speeches all the time."

"We also have plenty of commitments on our hotel and motel tax revenue. You may remember that we just built a brand new convention center. In case you've forgotten, it's that big building next to the hockey arena. And believe it or not, the Tooth Fairy didn't give us the money to build that. We're paying off our construction debt with hotel and motel tax revenues – and we will be for a long time."

"As the expression goes, there are other ways to skin a cat, Horton. You've already identified a couple of other possible funding sources – sales taxes and tax increment financing."

"And we've shared the projections we have for those. Tax increment financing wouldn't produce anywhere near the amount of money we'd need to cover the construction debt. And even with the most optimistic assumptions, it's not reasonable to expect that stadium to generate enough sales revenues to cover the cost of building it."

"Time to start thinking bigger then," Malfair said with a slight smile, as if the conversation had finally steered into the direction he had wanted to go all along. Because it had.

"What do you mean by that?"

"Don't think of just the sales taxes that would be generated at the stadium itself. You could use sales taxes at properties in the area around the stadium, too. Restaurants, shops, that sort of thing."

"Over how big of an area?"

"As big as it needs to be. Just figure out what your construction debt payments are going to be. Then get the data on sales tax collections for the surrounding properties. Figure out how many properties you'd need to support those debt payments. Those properties would become part of what you governmental types refer to as a 'tourism development zone.'"

"In tourism development zones, the law only allows you to use the growth in sales tax revenues created by a new development – in this case, the stadium – not all the sales taxes collected."

"So? Like I said, you'll be the ones wielding the pencil when the zone boundaries get drawn. Make them as wide as they need to be to support the debt. It's as simple as that."

"It's never that simple when you're talking about taking tax money collected by a bunch of businesses and redirecting it to support one single business. Politically, that creates quite a challenge."

"So? Leave the part about the political support to us, Horton."

"I don't want to leave that part to you. And we have no idea whether the economics of a tourism development zone would work. We don't know what the sales tax growth generated by a stadium might be."

"And that's why you've hired some very good bean counters, to help you work through those types of issues. So, why don't you guys do your homework on that and get back to us?" With that, Malfair stood to leave.

"DO OUR HOMEWORK?" Edison ignored Malfair's outstretched hand. "You come in here and tell us we have to build a stadium for your team, all by ourselves with no help from you, and then you even tell us how we should pay for it?"

"Oh, calm down, Edison. Don't be such a drama queen. We're just trying to help you out by suggesting some options. I'm sure you and Mayor Gables will figure out which of those options is best. Let's talk again after you've had a chance to confer with him about all this."

Malfair walked to the door, then paused and looked back.

"I really am looking forward to hearing your band again, Horton. Living in the South, you just don't get that many chances to hear someone play 'Smoke on the Water.'"

Edison fumed as he stared at the empty doorway after Malfair had departed. At that moment, there seemed to be nothing the least bit poetic or romantic about baseball.

CHAPTER FOURTEEN

Iris Moon's second assignment from City Hall was significantly harder than her first.

It hadn't taken her very long at all to come up with the sales and property tax projections for the new stadium because there were based on straightforward assumptions. If someone built a baseball on a vacant piece of property, it was fairly easy to calculate how that would impact the property's value and therefore the expected tax revenues. And if sales tax revenues from the stadium were needed to pay off the stadium's debt, it was easy to figure out how high sales needed to be.

But this request was different. She'd be asked to estimate how much sales taxes might be expected to grow in the area *around* the stadium, not just for the stadium itself. More than that, she was supposed to estimate how much faster those sales tax revenues would grow in the area around the stadium than they did, percentage-wise, for the entire county.

That brought a lot of variables into play that weren't easily quantified. First of all, there was that assumption that sales tax revenue would grow faster within the district around the stadium. Maybe that would be true, maybe it wouldn't. If metro Nashville saw its sales taxes grow from one year to the next by 3 percent, was it safe to say the sales taxes within the stadium district would be 4 percent higher during the same time period? Five percent?

And her clients at City Hall hadn't given her much guidance about how big the stadium district should be in the first place. Should it be only the stadium and the properties directly adjacent to it? Or all those properties

121

in a 10-block radius? Or a 20-block radius? None of that had been made clear to her. So she was left to try to guess which businesses near the stadium might see higher sales if a stadium were built.

But a lot of factors could affect retail sales. Businesses could close. New businesses could open. Businesses could offer specials that improved their bottom lines. Downtown restaurants and bars might experience changes in sales due to concerts or other special events that had absolutely nothing to do with the baseball team.

Trying to figure out sales tax growth for the whole county – the baseline against which stadium district sales were supposed to be measured – was even trickier. There were thousands of businesses in metro Nashville, each of which had its own story.

Then there was the time issue. Dr. Moon had been asked to offer projections about sales taxes over the length of time it would take to repay the stadium debt. Investors drove themselves crazy trying to predict which direction the economy would be moving in the next three months. Trying to say with any certainty what would happen over the next 20 years was practically impossible.

It was such a dilemma that Dr. Moon was relieved when Devin Underwood summoned her into his office. He gestured toward the flat screen TV that took up most of one of the walls in his office. A news conference was just beginning and Wynn Hammerskal, that baseball player she'd met when she gave her presentation on the sales and property tax revenues, was speaking to a group of reporters.

"Good afternoon, ladies and gents. Glad so many of you could make it out here today. When I was pitching and had this many people gathered around me for a meeting, it usually meant I was going to have to hand one of them the ball and head for the showers."

The reference went over Iris Moon's head, although several of the reporters laughed. Her nose started to tingle.

"Anyway, I've got some good news to share with you about my ownership team's plans to bring a Major League baseball team to the city. We've been negotiating with city officials and we think that, working together, we've identified a way to build a new stadium that would pay for itself."

Hammerskal paused for a second while reporters shouted questions calling for specifics.

"Now, before I get into this, remember that in my previous job I never had to count more than three strikes or four balls, so numbers aren't my thing. But I understand that there's a way we can use money from sales taxes collected at the stadium and other nearby businesses to pay for this whole project."

From where Iris sat, that proposition seemed much more of an open question.

"Yes, there's no question about it. Sales taxes collected in and around the stadium are the way to go. That way, people who pay property taxes but don't attend baseball games – and I certainly hope there aren't a lot of them out there – those people don't have to pay anything to support the stadium. People who buy stuff in other parts of town don't even have to pay sales taxes to help support the stadium. The only people who would be paying for the stadium would be the people who attend games and then eat and shop at places near the stadium before and after the games."

At the news conference, reporters were starting to pepper Hammerskal with technical questions about how the sales tax financing plan would work. He let them go on for a minute before he held his arms to his face, as if shielding himself from a line drive.

"Now, I'm not the expert on all of the details, just like I don't understand the physics of what makes a curve ball

curve. I just know if you throw it right, it works. And from what I'm told, this will work, too."

Iris Moon turned to her boss and shook her head. "Well," she said. "I'm not sure why we're needed. It sounds like that jock has this all figured out." After making that pronouncement, she sneezed explosively on her boss.

In another office a few books away, Thor Jantsen, executive director of the city's convention and visitors bureau, was watching the same news conference. And he, too, was shaking his head in disbelief.

So it had already been decided that sales tax revenues collected from businesses around the stadium were going to be used to pay for the stadium itself. Which meant that they wouldn't be available to pay for other improvements the downtown entertainment district needed to stay competitive with other peer cities – things like streetlights, landscaping, upgrades to the city's decrepit water and sewer system.

Wasn't that always the way? The big projects not only drew all the headlines, but they came at the expense of investments in public amenities that benefitted the entire downtown area. Which, of course, benefitted the entire community at-large. Downtown's prosperity was like the proverbial rising tide that lifted all boats.

When downtown businesses succeeded, everybody in Nashville succeeded. But without proper capital investment to keep it all going, the whole thing could crumble like a house of cards. And why? Because the city was about to pour all the sales tax money collected downtown into one place. To Jantsen, the strategy Hammerskal had just outlined to the media made as much sense as buying a new car while the rent and the electric bill were due.

"Somebody needs to talk some sense into Mayor Gables," he muttered under his breath.

A couple of miles across the river, in a modest bungalow just beyond the outskirts of East Nashville's gentrified Five Points neighborhood, Melvin and Ingrid Swift were also watching the news conference. They were the co-founders of Clean and Green, a nonprofit organization that advocated for strong and sustainable neighborhoods.

"Well, here we go again," Melvin said to his wife. "Once again, the city is planning to invest hundreds of millions of dollars to support downtown, even though downtown is already thriving. Everywhere you look downtown, there are gleaming new office buildings, gleaming new storefronts, gleaming new restaurants, gleaming new condominiums. Meanwhile, weeds grow in abandoned lots in Bordeaux and sidewalks crumble in South Nashville. The city's codes department pursues action against run-down properties with the speed of a geriatric glacier recovering from knee surgery. Downtown keeps getting richer, while our residential neighborhoods are always an afterthought to the politicians at City Hall."

"Right, honey, here we go again," Ingrid replied. "We've had this conversation a million times before. That's just the way things are. The way they've always been. And the way they always will be."

Melvin snorted. They had had this conversation a million times before. And Melvin knew Ingrid was right. *Unless...*

"Maybe not always and forever," Melvin said in a faraway voice. "Maybe the time has come for someone to rise up and make a statement."

Horton Edison was watching the news conference in his office, too. He silently fumed as the news conference wrapped up with Hammerskal deflecting most of the tough questions with folksy anecdotes about his baseball career.

It was only the day before yesterday that Edison had his meeting with Julius Malfair. And even though Hammerskal was doing all the talking at the news conference, the words he spoke were clearly Malfair's.

In his own loopy way, Hammerskal had presented the case Malfair had made to Edison – only Hammerskal's audience at the news conference seemed receptive to the point of fawning. It was obvious from the way those reporters had reacted that they were going to present their stories just the way Hammerskal, Malfair and their unseen cohorts wanted.

If he or the mayor or anyone at City Hall seemed resistant to Hammerskal's proposal, they would be the ones on the defensive, trying to explain why they were against a proposal that made so much sense. After all, Hammerskal had made it all sound so simple. Why would these city bureaucrats want to complicate things?

Well, so much for negotiating in good faith. So much for keeping politics out of the process. If there was any doubt before, there wasn't any now. The team owners – would-be team owners, Edison kept reminding himself – were trying to use the court of public opinion to force the city's hand.

Now is when it starts to get interesting, Edison thought to himself.

"Get Your Wet Blankets! Get Your Wet Blankets Right Here!"
By Gilbert Wise, Sports Columnist

OK, let me say this right off the bat: I love our readers. You're the people who pay the bills that keep the lights on and the presses running here at the Bulletin. Thanks to you, a certain loveable columnist gets a paycheck deposited into his account every other week.
So, let it never be said that I take you for granted. I'm always grateful for those of you who provide me with feedback about the columns I write. I read your e-mails and the comments you provide at the bottom of my online columns each week.

And I respect your opinions – I really do.
Well, almost all of your opinions. But I take issue with the e-mail I found waiting in my inbox this morning about some of my recent columns concerning Nashville's pursuit of a Major League Baseball franchise.

This one particular reader – who shall remain anonymous, mainly because he or she didn't sign the e-mail – apparently believes that Nashville is on fool's errand. Which, by extension, would make me a fool.
This individual told me, in no uncertain terms, that pursuit of this franchise carries too high of a cost. The stadium would be too expensive. Public money spent to help cover that expense would be better used for other purposes. There are so many better ways Nashville could improve its civic image besides recruiting another sports franchise. Blah, blah, blah, blah, blah.

You know, I should have expected this. Any time there's talk about bringing a new sports team to the city, a small group of naysayers comes out of the woodwork and starts chirping about how everyone involved is wasting their time.

Oh, it all sounds so high minded: Sports aren't as important as schools, or safe streets or good jobs, or all the other wonderful things that cities provide to their residents. Well, maybe not. But that's a simplistic way to look at civic life.

Cities – at least the successful ones – are able to walk and chew gum at the same time. It's not a question of having great schools or having a baseball team. It's not a question of building a stadium or paving the potholes on city streets.
It's not a question of hiring people to take tickets and sell hotdogs or hiring police officers to patrol our neighborhoods.

And let me just say this, too: Sports *are* important. It was important for the city to get a National Football League franchise. It was important to get a National Hockey League franchise. And for the same reasons, it's important to get a Major League Baseball franchise, too.

Sports teams are amenities that make cities more desirable places to live, just like libraries or museums or concert halls. They also create jobs. Not only for those ticket takers and hotdog salesmen at the lower end of the pay scale, but also for multimillionaire players and front office executives who can pump major tax revenues into the city's coffers. And let's don't forget all the people who attend games and spend money in our community.

This e-mailer who contacted me just didn't understand that. Or didn't want to understand.

He (or she) ranted about how sports franchises get special treatment that isn't offered to other types of businesses that come to the city. Hardware stores and groceries don't get tax incentives or other forms of public assistance.

Here's a quick economics lesson: It's all about supply and demand. The city doesn't need to offer incentives to lure those types of businesses here. They come anyway. Do people in their right minds think the same is true of a baseball franchise? If Nashville isn't willing to go to bat for a franchise, other cities will. Orlando, I'm looking at you.

As a matter of fact, I'm not entirely convinced this anonymous e-mailer isn't someone involved with Orlando's effort to get a team. That sure would make it easier for Orlando if Nashville decided not to play the game, wouldn't it?

The end of this e-mail I received took on a rather ominous tone. The e-mailer talked about starting a new group called the Anti-Arena Agitators. It listed a web site for this group, which I won't legitimize by sharing the address on these pages.

The Anti-Arena Agitators. AAA. Just like the minor league baseball team we have now. The same old team we've had for more than 30 years. Which makes perfect sense, in a way. This "group" would hold back this city's progress and keep everything stuck in the past. Maybe while they're at it, the Anti-Arena Agitators can even bring back bell-bottoms and disco music, too.

That's not what this columnist thinks we should do, of course. Giving the Anti-Arena

Agitators any credibility whatsoever isn't
a Wise choice.

CHAPTER FIFTEEN

Raymond Goldfarb watched the interview from his hotel suite in downtown Las Vegas. He'd come back to his room after his business meeting and shed his coat and tie, but he was anything but relaxed.

He paced back and forth in front of the wall-mounted flat screen television as the program called "Clubhouse Chatter" began.

Hosted by Wanda Fong, an attractive Asian-American woman who was one of the rising stars in the field of sports journalism, "Clubhouse Chatter" was among cable television's top-rated shows. And the program was followed closely by virtually everyone who had more than a passing interest in baseball.

Fong's interview subject on this particular night was Orlando Mayor Skip Goodman. They were seated across from each other with a small coffee table between them and a faux locker room set in the background. Based on what Goldfarb knew about this interview, he was prepared for the worst.

"Good evening, everyone. And welcome to another session of 'Clubhouse Chatter.' I'm your host, Wanda Fong, and tonight our guest is Skip Goodman, the mayor of Orlando. As you know, Orlando has declared its interest – in very unabashed fashion, I might add – in being the home of Major League Baseball's newest franchise. And to improve its chances of landing that franchise, the city has taken a very unusual step. In fact, it may be unprecedented. So welcome to the program, Mayor Goodman."

"Thank you, Wanda. I'm delighted to be here."

"Now, Mayor Goodman, tell us a little bit about the action that you recommended – and the Orlando City Council approved – just this week."

"Well, Wanda, as you know, we already have a team owner who is committed to bringing the franchise to our city. And he most generously offered the land that will be used as the site for a new stadium. So this week, the Orlando City Council approved a contract with a well-respected construction and engineering firm to begin work on the design of our new stadium."

"Now, if I could, let me stop you right there, Mr. Mayor. There are a couple of things that make what you've done so out of the ordinary. For one, isn't it customary for cities that hope to land new franchises to actually get commitments from the league before they begin building new stadiums?"

"That may be the case, may have been the case in other situations in which cities were competing for franchises. But we wanted to make a statement with our bid. We wanted to show the league just how serious we were about getting this new team. So we decided one way to do that would be to begin building a new stadium while the league is still in the evaluation process. I think that sets us apart from other cities that might have an interest in this team."

"But isn't that an incredible risk? The city building a stadium to house a team it's not even sure that it will get?"

Goodman laughed and took a sip of water before continuing. "Well, Wanda, we believe it's a risk well worth taking. We're confident that Major League Baseball is going to see Orlando represents the best market for a new team. And the league won't have to rely on promises we'll make about how we'll build a new stadium. They will actually be able to monitor our progress on the stadium's construction while they are making their decision."

"Mayor Goodman, this seems like a real high-stakes gamble. A new stadium would cost hundreds of millions of dollars to build. Do you have an estimate on what the total cost would be?"

"No, not yet. That's something we will negotiate with the firm that's going to be designing and building the stadium."

"And that brings me to the other aspect of this that seems truly remarkable, Mayor. In most stadium projects that I'm aware of, there's usually a competitive bidding process used to select the firm or firms that will be used to oversee design and construction. That process normally requires several weeks to advertise that a contract is available for bids, then often several more weeks to evaluate those bids. Your council voted to select a firm without going through that process. Is that unusual?"

"We're not aware of whether it's been done on a stadium project before, but there are alternatives to competitive bidding that are used on other types of city contracts for goods and services. In this case, we were able to do what's known as 'piggybacking' – that is, extending the terms of a contract previously put out to bid so the firm that was originally selected through competitive bidding can work on the new project without going through that process again. In this case, we're using the same firm that handled the design and construction work on renovations we did for the Citrus Bowl, the city-owned football stadium."

"Mayor, tell me if I'm wrong, but isn't renovating a football stadium quite a bit different than building a baseball stadium?"

"In many ways, yes. But there are only a handful of firms around the country that specialize in sports stadium construction. Whether it's a baseball stadium or a football stadium, you're going to have the same firms looking for the work. They certainly have people on their staffs who specialize in one type of stadium or another, but it's the same small fraternity of companies in this line of work."

"Doesn't competitive bidding help ensure that you get the best possible price, though?"

"Not really, in this case. Since the design and construction costs are negotiated with the firm, that process would remain the same no matter which firm we were dealing with."

"Interesting. Now, I mentioned at the top of the show that what you're doing might be unprecedented. You say you're not aware of another city following the path you're taking. We're not, either. So what about this? Do you think you're setting an example that other cities seeking franchises will try to follow in the future?"

"I don't know about that. As mayor of Orlando, all I can do is run my city the best way I know how. But what I think is that the process of getting a new franchise is getting more competitive all the time. Major League Baseball already has a lot of great franchises in a lot of great cities. If we want to join that group, we know that we've got to do everything we can to set ourselves apart from other cities that would also like to have that franchise."

"Thank you for sharing this with our audience, Mayor. I suspect there are a lot of people out there who have listened to what you had to say with great interest. I'm thinking in particular of those who live in Nashville, which is seen as your primary competition for this franchise. Do you have anything you wish to say to the people of Nashville, Mayor?"

"Thanks for watching tonight."

With that, Fong threw back her head and giggled, then reached out to pat Goodman on the knee.

"Thanks again for coming on the program. This has been an exclusive interview with Orlando Mayor Skip Goodman, who's trying to pioneer a new way to land a

Major League Team. Next up, the pursuit of that new Major League Baseball franchise took an interesting turn this week when a sports columnist in Nashville called attention to a web site protesting the construction of a new arena. A video posted on that web site has quickly gone viral. We'll show you that video and talk about why it's creating such a stir..."

Goldfarb wanted to listen to that segment, but his cell phone was chirping. He answered the call from his communications director, who wanted to draft a statement to the media in response to Goodman's comments.

"There are a few points we need to stress," Goldfarb said into the phone. He'd already given those points quite a bit of thought. "First of all, let's make it very clear that I, as baseball's commissioner, or Major League Baseball, as an institution, doesn't have any legal authority to tell a mayor or a city council of any city how to spend its constituents' money. We don't have any legal authority to stop them from building a baseball stadium, any more than we have the authority to stop them from building a new library or police precinct."

Goldfarb paused to let his communications director catch up in his note taking.

"OK, now having said that, neither the league nor I is offering an opinion about whether what Orlando is doing is a good idea or a bad idea. Mayor Goodman contacted me and told me what he hoped to do and I told him the same thing. We don't have an opinion, pro or con, but we also can't prevent the city from moving forward with his plans."

Goldfarb winced. His stomach was starting to hurt again, just as it had when he'd been talking to Goodman about this. He walked toward the suite's bathroom in search of his bottle of Maalox.

"Finally, we need to make it clear that we are not prejudging Orlando's bid – or the bids of any other prospective franchisees – based on this new development. Orlando and its competitors are all going to be judged on a combination of factors to determine which city is the most suitable for the new franchise."

He took a deep breath and swigged from the Maalox bottle. He thought about heading for the mini-bar, then remembered why that would be a bad idea. No good answers there.

"OK, do you have all that? Good. Now please draft a statement and call me back so we can go over it. OK? Thank you."

With that, Goldfarb clicked off the phone and sat on the edge of his bed. He took a deep breath as he stared at his opulent surroundings. The suite was decked out with the most modern furnishings and the most hip decorations that casino money could buy.

Goldfarb really hated these business trips, which had become far too frequent for his liking. And he hated what he had just seen on television. It would be the cause of yet another sleepless night for him.

Soon, this will all be over, he thought to himself. *Soon, but not soon enough.*

He lay back on the bed and closed his eyes, trying to stave off the beginning of a headache. It was still hard to believe that his life had taken this particular turn. He knew *why* it had, but that still didn't make any of this easier.

Still, he had to admit that as much as it pained him, everything was going exactly according to plan.

CHAPTER SIXTEEN

Autumn Sunshine stared at the blank computer screen, trying to process what she had just seen.

Since the failure of her "Dip for Dope" demonstration, she had been trying to plot her next move without a whole lot of success.

The legal consequences of her actions hadn't amounted to much. Sure, she had been arrested. And predictably, the district attorney's office had tried to pile up enough charges to adequately reflect the mayhem that had ensued at Nashville Shores that day. Several counts of disturbing the peace. Indecent exposure. Lewd and lascivious conduct. And, of course, resisting arrest. (From her past experiences with civil disobedience, she was convinced that the only way to avoid resisting arrest charges would be to actually apply the handcuffs to her wrists herself.)

She'd spent the weekend in jail, then had an arraignment hearing along with her partners in crime – the members of Drunk Thirty – the following Monday. The Drunk Thirty kids hadn't turned out to be terribly loyal to their new friend. In hopes of receiving lighter sentences, they implicated Autumn as the ringleader of the ill-fated operation.

In truth, they need not have bothered. Since they were all first-time offenders, the judge sentenced them to diversion – essentially promising to wipe away their arrest records if they stayed out of trouble for a year.

Autumn was not a first-time offender. She had racked up several arrests over the years for similar types of incidents, which she wore like a badge of honor. In this case, her lawyer was able to convince the prosecutor to accept a plea deal for a single count of disturbing the peace. The judge accepted the deal and sentenced Autumn to the two days she'd already served in jail.

It was a common outcome for a nonviolent criminal case of that kind in a city the size of Nashville. The prosecutor could claim the conviction as a win and the public defender assigned to Autumn could consider the case closed, allowing him to lighten his workload ever so slightly.

Plus, after the breathless news coverage the incident had received, everyone in officialdom was happy to have the whole matter settled as quickly and quietly as possible.

The news coverage had Autumn Sunshine upset for a different reason. Sure, there had been plenty of stories about what had gone awry at the Polar Bear Plunge. Some of them had included footage of her and her young cohorts, with certain body parts disguised by pixilated dots when necessary. But the reportage was, well, whimsical. The reporters who covered the story had all made a big joke out of it. And there was not one word in broadcast or print about what the "Dip for Dope" was all about. The stories had portrayed Autumn and the members of Drunk Thirty as some polar bear swimmers who had just gotten a little bit overzealous.

After getting out of jail, Autumn went back to work at the art gallery. Her arrest didn't result in her firing. If anything, employing a protestor with a rap sheet gave the gallery an edginess that the owners, counterculture artists and customers all liked. She was a minor hero to those few who knew that she was "that crazy chick skinny dipping on the evening news."

She knew fame – particularly that sort of fame – was fleeting, though. The stars of one news cycle were forgotten in the next. Within 24 hours, the incident at Nashville Shores was upstaged in media reports by someone in Antioch who'd taught his dog how to bark a rough approximation of "The Star Spangled Banner." And Autumn's big idea of legalizing marijuana seemed to be getting no traction at all.

It wasn't that there weren't plenty of recreational tokers in the state of Tennessee. But most seemed to recognize that legalizing their drug of choice was a political nonstarter. As it stood, it was relatively easy to acquire and partake of marijuana the way things were. With hard-core drugs like meth and coke destroying lives across the state, law enforcement officials weren't going to waste time and resources chasing down a barely-hidden army of potheads. Most stoners weren't looking for legal recognition, anyway. They were content to pursue their vice underground. It even made smoking weed a little cooler. Joining a legalization movement would just be a way of calling attention to themselves – which was exactly what they didn't want.

It took Autumn a while to figure all that out, but she finally had. So her latest cause – like all her previous causes – had left her disillusioned. She needed a new direction in which to channel her energies, but where? In her long career as an activist, she'd worked on a lot of causes, but none of which she felt truly meshed with her passions and talents.

But she couldn't just sit idle, either. She didn't want to become one of those people so apathetic that they couldn't be bothered to get off the couch even to protect their own self-interests.

So the You Tube video she had just watched had been a revelation. It had everyone in the activist community talking – and her thinking. For the fifth time, the mouse clicked on the arrow inside the circle on her computer screen to start the video clip again.

The video spun for a few seconds as the video loaded. Then, the title page: "A Public Fleecing."

Followed by the credits page: "A video by Shepherd's Crook Productions."

Then a page designed to look like an ancient scroll, covered in the old-fashioned script popular in fairy tale books: "Once upon a time, there was a baseball commissioner who ruled his domain from a big palace in New York City..."

Another scroll page, with the same type of script: "He promised his subjects that they could have a great, great treasure – a Major League baseball team! But where, oh where, to put it?"

Yet another scroll page: "Of course, this created quite a stirring in the kingdom. While some cities already had Major League franchises, there were still some that did not. And among those that did not, a few were willing to do almost anything to get a team!"

Organ music played in the background as the next page appeared. It contained a different kind of script, the kind used in old silent movies: "A rich man in Orlando said, 'I'll give you a team if you build me a new stadium! If the City Council will just approve it!' And the City Council said..."

The screen filled with an image of a group of men and women, dressed in business suits and seated around a meeting dias, with sheep heads photo shopped where their faces should have been. Bleating sounds replaced the organ music.

Then a cut to another silent movie page: "Then a baseball pitcher in Nashville decided he wanted that team, too. And he wanted a stadium, too. So he asked the city officials there and they said..."

The screen cut back to the photo-shopped sheep again, with the bleating audio.

Then another silent movie screen: "So how will this story end? What's the only possible way it could end for the citizens of those fine cities?"

Another cut to video of actual sheep being fleeced in a pen. Then after a few seconds, a fade to black.

A new image appeared on Autumn's computer screen, this one of a man, dressed in a suit and wearing a sheep's mask. He began to speak.

"Does this fairy tale sound familiar? It should, because we've all seen and heard it many times before. A major sports league tells us it wants to expand to new cities. And it promises those cities the whole world: New jobs, more money, quality entertainment. Sports teams don't dump toxic waste and they don't produce products coated in lead. So we've got to love them, right?

"Cities go after these teams like they're the Holy Grail! Team owners get offered free land, free stadiums, whatever they need. Or whatever they think they need. Tax incentives? Sure, why not? Tax breaks? Of course. It's a competition, usually with only one or two winners and many, many losers. Winning a team, we're led to believe, is like winning the lottery. Because these cities are sheep! BAAAAH! BAAAAAH!

"And, of course, losing a team is even worse than losing the lottery. When you lose the lottery, you toss your tickets in the trash can and don't give it another thought. No one thinks the less of you for having played and lost, mainly because most people never knew you were playing in the first place.

"But losing out in the race to get a pro sports franchise...oh, that's different! The world – or at least the whole country – knows that City X got a franchise and City Y did not. Ooh! So there must be something terribly wrong with City Y. Why aren't they better than City X? Or even worse, didn't City Y TRY hard enough? Were their leaders a bunch of bumblers who let a golden goose slip through their fingertips?

"But what about these so-called 'winners'? Are they really winners? Sure, they get teams, at least for a while. Those teams get special privileges not available to other types of businesses in their cities. They charge people exorbitant sums of money to attend their games. And

when those games are over, then what? Somebody won, somebody lost. We know this because records are kept. But those teams don't manufacture, produce, sell or distribute anything. Their 'product' evaporates into thin air the moment the games are over.

"But people in those 'winning' cities spend their money on overpriced tickets and overpriced beer and hot dogs. Because those people are sheep, too! BAAAH! BAAAH!

"And if they don't spend enough money – and it seems they can never spend enough – or the fancy playgrounds that are built for these teams lose their shine, then quite often the team owners will decide to move on. And the losers of the previous rounds of competition are all too eager to court the teams again. City Y gets another chance to feel good about itself – if its citizens are willing to pay the price. Which keeps going up and up and up."

On the video, the image of the man in the sheep's mask went from a mid-distance shot to a close up. His voice sounded more urgent.

"You know this is true. Look at what happened in Seattle in 2008. The National Basketball Association approved a deal which allowed the Seattle Supersonics franchise to break its arena lease with the city – I'll say it again – break a legally binding lease with the city of Seattle, so that franchise could move to Oklahoma City! If you're a pro sports fan living anywhere, that should send a chill down your spine. Because there's not a dime's worth of difference between the National Basketball Association, the National Football League, the National Hockey League or Major League Baseball. The only difference between the major sports leagues is the size of their balls!

"People, we don't need to keep getting played like this. Depending on which cities we live in, we may think we're winners or losers in this game. But in reality, we're all like gamblers in a casino. We may win a few hands of blackjack or we may lose, but in the end, in the very end, *it's the casino operators who are the ones who really come out ahead. And in this case, ladies and gentlemen, the casino owners are the team owners and league officials who make money no matter which cities win or lose.*

"So let's put a stop to this! We don't have to be sheep! We don't need to make big promises to these team owners. We can let our cities stand on their own merits! If teams want to locate there, well, fine. And if they don't, it's not some great cause for civic shame. I'm founding a group called Anti-Arena Agitators, which you will learn more about in the days and weeks ahead. I hope you'll join me because we are not sheep. We...are...not...sheep! WE...ARE...NOT...SHEEP!"

The image of the man in the sheep's mask faded and was replaced by some footage of some actual sheep being fleeced in a barn somewhere. Then a fade-out to a black screen with a web address: www.dontgetfleeced.com

The video ended with more bleating noises as the computer screen went completely dark.

Autumn sat in silence for a few seconds, taking deep breaths. She put her hand to her chest and realized her heart was racing.

The man in the sheep's mask had delivered a good speech. A great speech, in fact. He had used air quotes a couple of times, but he could have used his hands a little bit more to emphasize his points, in Autumn's estimation. That was just nitpicking, though. With the right coaching, the sheep man could be Martin Luther King, Jr. with wool.

The production value of the video was pretty good, too. Whoever this guy was, he knew what he was doing. But could he use help? It looked like he could use some help, Autumn decided. Successful movements were the product of the ideas and input of many people.

There was little doubt the man in the sheep's mask deserved help. After all, here was a man of conviction, a man with a cause. A man who was willing to speak his mind. And hopefully, a man who was willing to put his words into action.

On top of that, although it was hard to say for sure, Autumn Sunshine thought he looked pretty darned good in that suit.

"Hello, lover," she murmured quietly to her blank computer screen.

CHAPTER SEVENTEEN

It had been a tough morning for Mayor Kent Gables, but he was determined to make his afternoon better. Instead of going to the ribbon cutting he was scheduled to attend after lunch, he sent Horton Edison and headed out to the batting cages.

Gables figured he owed himself a mental health day – or at least half of one – to help him clear his head and focus his thinking. After all, it was mid-January, which meant pro baseball's pitchers and catchers would be reporting for spring training in a month. That meant his fantasy baseball league draft was right around the corner. And with all the distractions of running a major metropolitan city, he hadn't had nearly enough time to think about his potential draft picks.

Gables was a regular visitor to the batting cages at the golf course in the northeast part of the city, near the dam on Old Hickory Lake. Since the temperatures were in the 40s, the batting cages would normally be closed on a day like this. Particularly a day in the middle of the work week. But Gables knew the owner and called ahead for some cage time. Being mayor did have its perks.

With Edison covering for him, Gables figured he could be gone at least a couple of hours before he would be missed at City Hall. He planned to spend as much of that time as possible swatting baseballs in a state of bliss.

It was a perfect plan, but it hadn't worked out perfectly. On the drive out to the cages, he'd received a call on his cell phone from Rowan Atwell, president of the city's chamber of commerce. (Not that it was called the Metro Nashville Chamber of Commerce any more – although that had been the group's name for the better part of four decades. A few years ago, people who worked at chambers of commerce around the country decided it was no longer trendy or cool to be called 'chambers of commerce" and they all decided they needed to rebrand themselves. So after his organization had shelled out about $50,000 from its members' dues to pay for marketing consulting fees, Atwell found himself president of One Nashville! Exclamation point included.)

Atwell was cryptic about the purpose of his call, but he sounded upset enough that Gables had agreed to meet him at the batting cages. A lesson learned: Next time, Gables would shut his phone off when he decided to play hooky.

Gables planned to get as many swings as he could while Atwell was making the drive from downtown. Feeling his oats, Nashville's chief executive had plunked his first dollar's worth of quarters into a pitching machine that served up baseballs at speeds around 60 miles an hour.

Gables didn't have much to show for the 30 swings he got for his dollar. He only made contact three times, all of them weak foul tips that never made it past home plate. For his next dollar, Gables switched to the fast pitch softball machine. With a knee-high swing, he managed to hit a few weak grounders. But the softballs were the size and weight of mock oranges and they arrived at speeds of 45 miles per hour or so. After making contact a couple of times, Gables' arms were already stinging from the wrists to the elbows in the mid-January weather.

By the time Atwell got there, Gables had switched to the slow pitch softball machine, which allowed him to smack a few line drives without feeling like his forearms

146

were going to explode. And he loved the happy pinging sound the aluminum bat made as it met the ball.

"Hello, Mayor," Atwell said. He was a pudgy man, with narrow, close-set eyes and a tiny nose that made his fat face look even fatter. The top of his head was bald, encircled by well-groomed gray hair on the sides and back. In his neatly tailored suit, he couldn't have looked more out of place at a batting cage.

"Hey, Rowan," Gables replied without taking his eyes off the pitching machine. The machine lobbed another softball that seemed like it hung in the air forever. When it finally made its descent, Gables got a piece of it. *Ping!* In an actual softball game, it would have been a routine ground ball to the shortstop. "So what can I do for you? You sounded like you've got something serious on your mind."

"I do, Mayor. And I think you should, too."

The conversation halted as the machine served up another pitch and Gables took his next swing. *Ping!* The ball went to almost the same spot as the previous hit.

"OK, so tell me, Rowan. What's the chamber, er, One Nashville! up to these days?"

"Mayor, our folks have been talking. And there's a lot of concern about what's happening with this Major League Baseball franchise."

Ping! Same spot. Atwell thought about suggesting that the mayor uppercut his swing a little more, but he didn't want the mayor any more distracted from the conversation than he already seemed to be.

"Why's that, Rowan? Have you heard something I haven't heard?"

"I don't think so. But a lot of us in the business community are very concerned about how this is playing out."

Ping! Same spot.

"Not sure I follow what you mean. We're in there, taking our swings for this franchise, just like I am right now." Gables smiled, seemingly pleased with his metaphor.

"Are we? It seems like we're running behind Orlando in this game. They've already got a stadium site, they've already got a team at work on the stadium design and they've already got a plan to pay for the stadium's construction."

Ping! If there were a shortstop shagging grounders in the batting cage, he would be exhausted by now.

"You know, Rowan, it's not always the fastest horse that wins the race."

"Actually, I think it pretty much *is* the fastest horse that wins the race, Mayor. That's what racing is. And your counterpart down in Orlando, Skip Goodman, is starting to look like a freaking genius."

Gables missed the next pitch, swinging so violently that he spun himself around and almost fell. Gables turned and glared.

"Never mention that name to me again, Atwell."

"OK, OK, I won't. But Mayor X seems to have his ducks in a row down there. While you're dealing with some problems here."

Another swing and a miss. Gables' batting technique seemed to have suddenly regressed to elementary school level.

"We've got a site. Wynn Hammerskal and the rest of the owners have identified a site they like by the river."

"Yes, but he's also got a lot of the downtown business owners upset because he's basically said he wants any sales tax revenue collected down there to help pay for this new stadium. If you're going to give businesses a say in how the city spends the tax money it collects from them, those businesses have a few ideas of their own about how they'd like that money spent."

Gables' next swing missed so badly that he almost came out of his wingtip shoes. Mercifully, the green light atop the pitching machine clicked off, indicating that

Gables had exhausted his supply of quarters. Gables stared at the machine as if he expected it to change its mind and start throwing more pitches.

"I would think the downtown business owners would be happy about this. This team will help them most of all."

"Well, some of them are very happy – and some of them aren't. Plus, it seems like the opposition to the team is getting organized. Some of the neighborhood groups are starting to fuss about how downtown always gets the big public spending dollars and they get next to nothing. And then there's Triple-A..."

Gables spun to face Atwell. "AAA? The auto club has come out against us? I pay platinum level membership dues to them for years and then they stick their noses into something like this?"

"Not the auto club, Mayor. This group, the Anti-Arena Agitators. People are starting to call them AAA for short."

"Wait, people are actually *talking* about that group? I didn't even know it was a real group. I thought it was just some kook in a sheep's mask."

"They've got a following. Nobody knows for sure if it's a big one or a little one. But it's out there. The Internet gives anybody with an idea – no matter how crazy it is – the chance to broadcast it to the world. And every once in a while, the world listens."

"How can all these people be against baseball? Don't they know it's America's pastime?"

"It is amazing, Mayor. This country is completely sports crazy. Baseball, football, whatever. If we didn't have sports, who knows what people would talk about all day? I mean, let's face it: Most of our lives are pretty darned boring."

Mayor Gables shot Atwell a puzzled look.

"Well, not everybody's lives are boring. Not the mayors of cities like Nashville. But certainly, for a lot of people, sports provide an escape from a reality that looks pretty much the same from one day to the next. Kids start out playing sports when they're young – and then after they get too old to play, they spend the rest of their lives obsessing over games other people are playing. And Major League Baseball, well, that's the highest level of the sport there is. Bring in the fanciest opera or Broadway show you can think of to town and on its best night, it wouldn't draw 10 percent of the crowd any old Major League Baseball game would bring."

"You're sort of preaching to the choir, Rowan," Gables said, nodding to the bat he was still holding.

"No doubt baseball's got great entertainment value. But there's a lot more to it than that. I just don't think people really understand the economic benefits. These teams create jobs when they move to a city. Ticket-taking jobs. Concessions jobs. Front office jobs. And then of course there are the players, many of whom have millions in disposable income, who live in the city for more than half the year. All of those people who work for the teams spend money in the community. And the fans spend more money in the community because the teams are there."

"Again, no argument here, Rowan."

"And the benefits go far beyond that, even. I mean, my main job at One Nashville! is to sell businesses on the idea that they should expand or relocate their operations here. Do you know how much easier that selling job is in a town with major league sports? It's a sign that your city is going places. Plus, the games are broadcast around the country. That's free advertising beyond anything we could afford to spend to lure those businesses here."

"Exactly what I've been telling people. We need to be a 'three team town.' We've got two major league sports franchises now, but so do a lot of cities. The top tier cities – your New Yorks, Chicagos, Los Angeleses,

Philadelphias – they've already got three teams. Or more. We need to get on their level."

"OK, I can see we're on the same page on this. But a lot of us who want to see Nashville get a baseball team are worried about how things stand now. They want to see more progress toward a stadium deal. Orlando's making us look bad."

"Rowan, I understand where you're coming from. But you've already hit on the problem: We've got some opposition out there. Start with the people out there who don't think government should spend a penny more than it's already spending – and probably needs to cut back on the expenses we already have. Even if a team generates sales tax revenue that we wouldn't have otherwise, those people see this as growing the size of government. Then you've got all the bleeding hearts out there who don't think the city is spending enough on social services, neighborhoods or whatever it is. In their minds, any money spent on a sports franchise is money that could have helped to pay for their pet causes. Even if that's a totally false choice. Then you've got these 'sheepheads' out there who just can't stand the idea of team owners and players making money, even if they're doing it by providing an entertainment option that most people in this city really want."

Gables paused to fish around in his pockets to see if he had enough quarters for another session in the cage. He brought out two quarters, a nickel and a bunch of pennies. Not enough.

"So what's the plan, Mayor? If most people in the city really want baseball, when do you plan to take a stadium plan to the City Council?"

"Here's the thing about that, Rowan: These people who are against having a team may not make up the majority, but they could become a very vocal minority. And you know what? Vocal minorities can put the fear of God into some politicians, particularly those who aren't cagey enough to know the difference between a vocal minority and a majority. There are 40 politicians serving on the Metro Nashville Council. And some of them, quite frankly, are cowards. If I took them a proposal today, I'm not sure I would have the votes to get it passed. And getting it passed isn't the only issue, anyway."

"I'm not sure I follow, Mayor."

"Well, we're in a competition here. Say we put a stadium plan up to a vote and it passes – but it passes in a close vote, say 25-15. But Major League Baseball, they're measuring Nashville's commitment against Orlando's. And if the Orlando City Council is in lockstep support of this and Nashville appears not to be...well, all things being equal, then the league might choose the city where a team's not controversial at all. So we could win the battle on the stadium vote, but lose the war to get a team. See what I mean?"

"So we need to make sure we've got public opinion on our side, right? Or at least make those council members think we've got public opinion on our side. So they'll be inclined to vote right."

Gables laughed and shook his head. "If there's one thing I've learned on this job, Rowan, it's that doing what you just said is often easier said than done."

"It wouldn't be if people really understood those benefits of having a team that we were just talking about. We've already got the sports fans. They'd probably be willing to give up their houses and work on a collective farm if that's what it took to get a team here. But to win over the skeptics, they need to understand the economic benefits. They need to understand that having a team benefits them, too, even if they never set foot in the stadium. Everybody wants to feel like there's something in it for them."

Rowan clapped once and rubbed his hands together. "So we need a marketing campaign. That's something we at One Nashville! can certainly help with."

"Excellent! Glad to hear it! And we can help you to help us, Rowan. We've already got a firm working for us on some of the financial numbers involved with this project. I'll just ask them to do a study on the economic benefits for us, too."

"That's a great idea! People love numbers. Big numbers. Even if they don't really understand where those numbers come from. If you get a study that says a baseball team is going to have a one billion dollar impact on Nashville, then the naysayers will have a hard time arguing against that. And it'll help those 40 council members to find the courage they need to do the right thing."

"I'll get our people to work on it as soon as I get back to City Hall."

Atwell grinned and extended a meaty paw to shake hands with the mayor. "I must say, Mayor, I feel a lot better now than I did when we started talking today."

"Any day I can make the head of One Nashville! feel better is a good day for me, too."

Atwell turned to head back to his car.

"But there is one favor I'd like to ask, Rowan." Atwell turned back to face Gables.

"Yes, Mayor?"

"You wouldn't happen to have a couple of extra quarters on you, would you?"

CHAPTER EIGHTEEN

The meeting of The Cabal took place at the home of the department store CEO on a large farm near Franklin, about an hour south of downtown Nashville. The CEO was renowned for the annual Christmas parties he held there, but tonight the mood was anything but festive.

The group had gathered to talk about the progress – or lack thereof – in bringing a Major League Baseball franchise to Nashville. And the consensus was that there was much more of the latter than the former.

Julius Malfair had delivered admirably on the first phase of the plan, which was to recruit Wynn Hammerskal into the fold, and phase two, which was to lock up the support of the mayor's office.

Since then, things hadn't gone so well. As expected, Nashville wasn't alone in bidding for the team. Orlando had also staked its claim. But the trouble was that Orlando's efforts to land the franchise seemed to be moving full speed ahead while Nashville's were stuck in the mud.

Orlando had already come up with a plan to pay for its stadium – and even fast-tracked the process for developing the construction plans for that stadium. All without any significant political opposition. At least none that had been reported by the local or national media. To the contrary, Orlando's mayor, Skip Goodman, was earning national acclaim as a fixer – a guy who could "get things done." There were rumors that he might soon be featured in a Sports Illustrated cover story – heady recognition for a non-athlete on the pages of a sports magazine.

In contrast, Nashville's mayor, Kent Gables, seemed to have hit a wall. He and Hammerskal had made a big splash with the media when they went public with Nashville's interest in the team.

Hammerskal, despite The Cabal's initial reservations about recruiting him, had proved to be everything they could have hoped for and more. He not only got all the talking points right, but he expressed them in such a way that the media always came away from interviews wanting more.

Gables was another story. He was a popular mayor, by all accounts. But he didn't seem willing to risk any of his political capital in pursuit of the franchise. Not enough of it, anyway. He was reportedly tossing around a number of options to finance a stadium, but nothing was set in concrete.

From Malfair, The Cabal's members knew the mayor's right hand man, Horton Edison, was not the unabashed supporter of the project that his boss was. And that was a problem. Although not the only problem.

The business community, which tended to share the same values as The Cabal, was divided on the stadium issue. Some thought that the investment needed to attract a team could be better spent elsewhere. Of course, The Cabal members considered that the least of their worries. With the right combination of lobbying and outright arm-twisting, they could bring their colleagues in the business community to heel.

But there was also opposition from neighborhood groups, whose default position was to oppose anything that represented progress for the community. Where would any of those neighborhoods be without the benefits that had been bestowed upon them by the business community?

And there was that stupid video by the guy in the sheep's mask. Before the Internet era, his views would have never seen the light of day. And in truth, no one

156

really knew if his views were shared by many or only a few. But clearly, his ideas were getting out there. That video had been seen by who knew how many people on the Internet. Worse still, the national media were giving the video credibility by paying attention to it.

Could that make a difference in Major League Baseball's decision about where to put a franchise? Maybe. Maybe not. It was hard to say what the league would ultimately decide what was important and what wasn't. But to the members of The Cabal, it didn't look like the odds were running in Nashville's favor.

So what to do, one of them asked.

The question was met with a long silence.

Shaping public opinion was certainly a key, going forward, someone said.

No argument there. But how to get public opinion on their side? Shouldn't that be easy? Why weren't the people of this town clamoring for baseball? Not just clamoring for it, but shouting down the naysayers?

Those people who made up the general public, they were a bunch of ingrates. This team would represent free entertainment to them. Jobs for those that needed them. Prestige. Bragging rights whenever the team took the field on national television. And they were risking nothing. Just some tax money that they would never have to pay if the team didn't come to town.

By contrast, the members of The Cabal saw themselves as risking considerably more. If this franchise didn't turn out to be successful, they could end up losing millions. That they could afford to lose millions on a venture like this was beside the point.

Multimillionaires who stopped caring about a few business losses here and there didn't stay multimillionaires for long. That's what the general public would never understand. The Cabal was risking much. And the whole community would benefit from the risks its members were taking.

But there had to be a way to get the general public invested in this project. The people of Nashville had to feel that this was their team, too, even if they weren't investing the big bucks needed to make it happen.

So what could The Cabal give up to get the public emotionally invested? Certainly not any of the revenues a team would generate. The Cabal's members would need every dollar they could mine from this enterprise to justify their investment.

Then what? Naming the stadium, naming the locker rooms and other facilities on the property, those were all commodities that could be sold. They couldn't be given away for free.

But what about the name of the team itself? The franchise would need a name. And that probably couldn't be sold. Even in the world of professional sports, a team named after a corporate sponsor would be unseemly. At least in this day and age. Perhaps someday, America would be ready for the Nashville Express or the Nashville Blue Lighters, but the country wasn't quite that crass yet. Just close.

So what about a naming contest? The public votes on the name for Nashville's franchise. We pick a list of five names to choose from, then put them up for a vote on the Internet? What could be more democratic? And even allowing a write-in option, the members of The Cabal would still pick the top five names from which the winner would be chosen.

People would love the gesture. Particularly those who voted for the winning name. But everyone who participated would feel like they had a stake in the process. It would be hard to vote for a team name and then turn around and oppose the idea of bringing a team to the city.

Members of The Cabal agreed that would be a great idea. The discussion turned to what the possible names for a team might be. Many ideas were tossed around over the next three hours, some silly and some serious. The recording industry executive was adamant that at least one of the possible names had to reflect the city's musical heritage.

After all, country music had put Nashville on the map, long before other industries had seen the benefits of setting up shop there. The other two major sports franchises, the Titans and the Predators, had names that had absolutely nothing to do with that heritage – or anything that outsiders would even remotely relate to the city.

None of the other Cabal members were quite so adamant. They were willing to consider other names that reflected the city's history, its geography, its indigenous animals or whatever else might sound cool.

With such a collection of egos, it took time to get down to a short list of five potential nicknames for a team. But finally, they arrived on a list that they could all agree upon, however reluctantly. When they had their list, they agreed to contact Malfair.

CHAPTER NINETEEN

They sat around the table in the mayor's conference room in an awkward silence. They had exchanged greetings and the usual pleasantries, but they had been seeing too much of each other lately to make casual conversation easy.

Horton Edison, who had called the meeting, was there, along with Julius Malfair and Iris Moon. But they were waiting, as usual, for the arrival of Wynn Hammerskal.

Moon was seething a bit, anticipating that she had been summoned to City Hall for a premature report on her research. She was making progress in her efforts to effectively define a downtown district that would benefit from stadium revenues, but she wasn't quite there yet. She didn't like to issue preliminary reports because she knew that they often led to conclusions that were not preliminary. Plus, waiting for that jock, Wynn Hammerskal, was starting to make her nose itch again.

Edison sat perfectly silent and perfectly still, a trait he had learned from many years of enduring time lost to delayed meetings like this one. Malfair drummed his fingers gently on the table to pass the time. Finally, because lawyers were not particularly adept at remaining quiet for long periods of time, he gave conversation another try.

"You know, Horton, I wasn't kidding the other day about wanting to hear your band play," he said.

"Oh, really?" Edison said. "Because I could have sworn I detected a note of sarcasm in your voice."

"Oh, not at all, not at all. The name of your band is The Chronies, right? And you play at that bar called Capital Indiscretions. I've been in there a few times."

Hardly a revelation to Edison. Most of the city's power brokers visited Capital Indiscretions at one time or another in the course of doing business. It was a regular stop for networking.

"Well, if I know you're in the crowd, Julius, I'll make sure we don't play 'Smoke on the Water.' I got the distinct impression that isn't one of your favorites."

Malfair laughed. "As I said, I was only kidding. You know, in my years of doing what I do, I've learned it's not really smart to fight City Hall. So why would I want to make Mayor Gables' head honcho upset with me?"

"I couldn't tell you that, Julius. Maybe you just seemed a little too full of yourself that day. Like maybe you felt like your multimillionaire clients were the ones running the city."

Moon squirmed in her chair, partly out of discomfort and partly to remind Malfair and Edison that they weren't alone in the room.

"Believe you me, Horton, that is the very last thing my clients would like. They are quite comfortable doing what they do."

Horton was getting ready to respond when the door opened and Wynn "The Jackhammer" Hammerskal entered. He was on the phone again.

"I know, right?" he was saying in a voice at least twice as loud as necessary. "Yeah. Yeah, yeah, yeah. We'll get to all that. But right now, I've got a meeting with some people. I'll talk to you later."

Hammerskal clicked the phone off, twirled it in his hand like a gunslinger, then tucked it into his shirt pocket as he took a seat.

"Well, you're probably all wondering why I called you here today," he said, drawing puzzled glances from the others in the room. "Kidding! Kidding! So what's up? I assume the mayor wanted us to talk about something."

"He did," Edison replied. "Mayor Gables is concerned that we haven't really built the case in the public's eye for why a baseball team is necessary."

"Necessary? Necessary?" Hammerskal said, ignoring a warning glance from Malfair. "How could a baseball team not be necessary?"

"I'm going to have to assume that's a rhetorical question," Edison said. "But the mayor's point is that we've already started talking about how we might finance a baseball stadium – with public dollars – when we haven't yet explained to the citizens of Nashville how that type of project would benefit them."

"Now, Horton, I think we've talked about your definition of public dollars before..." Malfair said.

"Yes, we have," Edison said. "So we don't need to have that circular argument again. But regardless of what you might think is 'public' or I might think is 'public,' the fact of the matter is that the city will have to invest a considerable amount of time and resources to make this project happen."

"My clients are investing quite a bit of their time and resources, too," Malfair quickly added.

"Not to put too fine a point on it, though, your clients need the help of *my* client, the city, in order to make this happen. With all due respect, if Mr. Hammerskal and his friends – whom we still haven't met yet – had the financial and political wherewithal to get a team on their own, then there wouldn't be a need for this meeting."

"I guess now we need to have a talk about what constitutes 'wherewithal' and what doesn't," Malfair said.

"No, we really don't," Edison replied smoothly. "Your clients can chew that word over at their next meeting. What we need to discuss at *this* meeting is how we can win over public support for this project. And luckily for everyone in this room, Mayor Gables has an idea for how we can do that."

"I'm all ears," Malfair said, throwing his arms open wide. Maybe he wasn't a courtroom attorney, but he had some of the theatrical gestures down pat.

"The mayor has asked Dr. Moon and her firm to shift gears a little bit. He wants an economic impact study that should – hopefully – convince the public of the value that a team would bring to the city. Is that something you could do, Dr. Moon?"

All eyes turned to Moon, who hesitated and cleared her throat before speaking.

"Well, I can do an economic impact study," she said carefully. "But I'm not so sure you won't be disappointed with the results."

"Oh?" Malfair said. "How so?"

"First of all, it's important to understand what economic impact studies of this sort measure. Typically, you want to look at both direct and indirect spending. Direct spending is, as the term suggests, the amount of spending the team itself does. So we'd be looking at the number of jobs the team actually brings to the city. Which is really a pretty small number, in comparison to other types of businesses."

Moon wasn't a baseball fan, but she had been doing her research. Edison nodded and gestured for her to continue.

"Of course, you've got the players. Twenty-five, I think, is the standard number on a Major League roster. When they're in town, they spend money, of course, which contributes something to the economy. However, during a season, the players are on the road half the time, so they're spending money in some other city. And during the offseason, a large number of them may decide to live in places other than Nashville. Mr.

Hammerskal, did you live in any of the towns where you played during the offseason?"

"No," Hammerskal admitted. "I lived here in Tennessee."

"Right," Moon continued. "So your players – the biggest part of a Major League team's payroll – have a fairly limited impact on the local economy."

"What about the team's front office staff and the like?" Malfair said.

"That accounts for maybe another two dozen employees or so. Maybe a couple of top executives – who, again, may or may not decide to actually live in Nashville – make big salaries. The rest of those employees are paid fairly modestly. Then you have some seasonal jobs – ticket takers, concessionaires, ushers and the like. Those tend to be part time only and they tend to be minimum wage or something close to it. So, all in all, your average Major League team is going to have less of a direct economic impact on your community than, say, a mid-sized discount department store."

"For which we certainly wouldn't be giving lavish incentives," Edison noted wryly.

"No, probably not," Moon said. "If you tried to give incentives for every business that brought 50 full-time jobs to the community, the city would go bankrupt fairly quickly."

"But what about all the other spending that's generated as a result of having a team in town?" Malfair said. "All those people who attend games and spend money there have to count for something."

"Sure they do," Moon said. "That's your indirect spending – the money that's spent at the stadium and in bars, restaurants and retail stores around the stadium on game days. But that comes with a caveat."

"Oh," Edison said, leaning forward in his chair a little bit. "Please explain."

"To create a big economic impact, you need businesses that bring a lot of new spending into the community, money that wouldn't be spent there otherwise."

"Which is what a team would do," Malfair said.

"Yes and no," Moon said. "To the extent that people come from outside the community to see games, then that's new money coming into Nashville. But that's not a significant percentage of the people who attend Major League games. Oh, you get a few people who might drive from an hour or two outside the city to watch a game every now and then. And you'll have a handful of journalists who follow the visiting teams. Plus the visiting teams' players. But for the most part, the people in the stands would be people who live in Nashville or its suburbs."

"So?" Hammerskal said. "Doesn't their money count, too?"

"It's not new spending," Moon said. "If those people weren't spending money at a Major League baseball game, they would be spending it at the movies, bowling, nightclubs or wherever else in the city. So new money isn't really coming into the community at all. It's just being spent in and around the stadium as opposed to being spread throughout the community. So really, if you think about it, a baseball team isn't bringing a whole lot of new money into the community. It's taking away money from other businesses that are already here and would be in competition for people's entertainment dollars."

No one said anything for a few seconds.

"Talk about a buzz kill," Hammerskal finally said. Moon's nose started to tingle. *Guess we won't see any jackhammer jumping today,* she thought to herself.

"So if I'm understanding you correctly, doing an economic impact study might not be such a good idea," Edison said.

166

"No, I think you should do one because a project of this sort does have some measurable benefits and the public has a right to know what they are," Moon said. "I just want you to be aware that the numbers probably aren't going to be as gaudy as you might have expected."

"Why am I already reading about economic impact studies done for other major league teams that put the total impact in the high millions or even billions?" Malfair said.

"Because, just like you said, those studies are usually done for the teams or groups that are strongly interested in having teams relocate to their cities," Moon said. "So the numbers tend to show what team supporters want them to show."

"Seems like we may have asked the wrong person to do our study," Malfair said.

"You might have," Moon said. "And you're always free to find someone else to do a study that would have findings more to your liking. But if you're going to have me to a study, then I'm going to play it straight down the middle. And I'm informing you of that on the front end, so no one is surprised later."

"Dr. Moon, the mayor and I aren't interested in any analysis that isn't, in your words, straight down the middle. And since I haven't heard Mr. Malfair or Mr. Hammerskal offer to pay for their own study, the city will be quite pleased to hire you and accept whatever your findings are. Do you have an estimate for what this type of study might cost?"

"I'll work up an estimate based on the time I think we'll need to complete the study and send an invoice to your office," Moon said.

With that, the meeting ended. As Moon gathered her things and prepared to leave, she wondered for a brief moment if Devin Underwood would have approved of the way she handled questions about the economic impact study.

She cracked a slight smile. *No,* she thought to herself. *Probably not.*

"What's in a Naming Contest? Too Much Silliness"
By Gilbert Wise, Sports Columnist

There are times when I have great faith in humankind as a species. And then there are days like these.

I've just been online, checking the poll results from the contest to name Nashville's soon-to-be Major League baseball franchise. (I just won't write 'potential' franchise again on these pages. I won't. I won't. The power of positive thinking and all that.)

And, first of all, before I get into my rant, I want to point out what a great thing it is that the team owners would give fans an opportunity to vote on the team's name. I mean, what other owners of a multi-million dollar business would do that? Do you think if anyone except the Walton family had been doing the naming, that Wal-Mart would have ended up being called Wal-Mart?

Fans didn't have to pay the cost of a personal seat license, a ticket or even a postage stamp to participate, either. The owners set the whole thing up online, so anybody with access to a computer could participate. The eight-year-old penny baseball card collector had the same access to the voting process as the Internet executive with the fancy mansion who can afford to buy tickets behind home plate. And as well intentioned as that concept must have seemed to the owners, it has proven to be their downfall. But more on that in a minute.
The owners did narrow the field of choices down to a short list of candidates. Which was pretty smart. Otherwise, they probably would have gotten a half a million

different suggestions and the "winning" choice might have received a few dozen votes.

And the choices they came up with weren't horrible. Would they have been mine or yours? Maybe not. But again, decisions had to be made to avoid having half a million answers and no clear consensus.

Hey, in presidential elections, we basically have two real choices that don't involve throwing our votes away. So anyway, I like the Water Moccasins. While most of the really fearsome animal nicknames have already been taken by other pro sports franchises, snakes generally don't get a whole lot of love. But moccasins are lethal and fairly common around Tennessee's waterways – so, all in all, not a bad choice. And think of the rivalry potential with the Arizona Diamondbacks.

As a secondary choice, I like the River Rats OK. After all, the Cumberland River runs through the city and were it not here, the city of Nashville probably wouldn't be, either. Then again, if you look at the geography of most major cities in the United States – in fact, the world – you'll realize that most of them are located along a river or port. So River Rats would be an apt nickname, but not terribly original.

My third choice would be a tie between either the Statesmen or the Athenians. Statesmen, as we know, is just a fancy word for politicians. And yes, as a state capital, Nashville has its share of politicians, er, statesmen. But it's a bit hard to get worked up about rooting for a team called the Statesmen. (I get some disagreement on this point from one of our copy editors here at the Bulletin, who fervently hopes to write a "Statesmen Negotiate Surrender" headline. It's the kind of thing we talk about to pass time around here.)

And I get the Athenians nickname, too. I really do. After all, we're the Athens of the South. It's a historic nickname for Nashville and sounds classy. Maybe a little too classy. If we were the Sparta of the South, that would be awesome. But don't expect a team nicknamed the Athenians to strike fear into the hearts of opposing players. An Athenian is a guy who simultaneously amazes and bores you with his knowledge of philosophy. An Athenian is not a guy who smashes baseballs out of ballparks.

So four of the five nicknames in the contest – the Water Moccasins, the River Rats, the Statesmen and the Athenians – all have their pros and cons. I have my favorites, which I've outlined to you, and you probably have yours.

But it's the fifth potential nickname (and I do hope this is only a 'potential' nickname) that has the most potential for trouble. It was inevitable, I suppose, that we had to have a potential nickname that paid homage to the city's rich musical heritage. We're the Music City. Were it not for the foundation built by country music, Nashville would not be the thriving economically diversified metropolis that it is today.

But why, oh why, did the owners have to pick the Pickers as their fifth and final name choice? OK, if you've lived in Nashville for more than five minutes, you know that a 'picker' is music industry shorthand for a 'guitar picker.' You may have been able to figure that out even if you didn't live here, but that's not a sure thing.
If you are from a rural area, you might think of a 'picker' as someone who harvests

crops. If you stopped maturing sometime around the fifth grade - as it seems like a substantial portion of the country's adult population did - then the term 'pickers' can be used in the punch line of just about any kind of gross joke you can imagine.

Which is why I was so dismayed to see the results of the team owners' online poll. With just a couple of days left to go in the voting, about 80 percent of the ballots have been cast for the Pickers as the team's nickname - with the remaining 20 percent of the vote fairly evenly spread among the other four choices.

If it seems to you that the game has been rigged, then your instincts are correct. A group called the Anti-Arena Agitators, condemned by me in previous columns, has waged an aggressive Internet campaign to convince people to vote for the Pickers' nickname. And their efforts appear to have paid off. The campaign, like the now-infamous sheep head video, went viral and the votes for the Pickers have been steadily rolling in since the voting began. Unfair? You bet. Do we have any idea how many people voting in this naming contest live in Nashville? Or even within a 100-mile radius of Nashville? My guess is not very many. In fact, I strongly suspect that the Anti-Arena Agitators aren't even based here, either.

One-man (or woman), one vote? There's no way that concept is being applied here. This process has been hijacked by a bunch of yahoos who have nothing better to do with their time than repeatedly vote for a nickname that would make Nashville a national laughingstock. Don't get me wrong: I love our country and the democratic principles it stands for. Except this one time.

The owners, who are holding all the cards anyway, ought to act as benevolent dictators and choose a nickname that won't leave Nashville at the mercy of every sports commentator with a flair for the juvenile. Which, I'm sad to say, is most of us. So come on, team owners. Make the Wise choice.

CHAPTER TWENTY

Autumn Sunshine yawned, rubbed her eyes and looked at her watch. Two in the morning. She turned back to her computer to continue the online conversation she had begun six hours ago with the chatter she knew by the instant messaging handle, "Sheepshead."

Autumn: Are you still with me?

Sheepshead: Yeah.

Autumn: It still doesn't feel real, does it?

Sheepshead: To be honest, I can't really say how I feel yet. I'm still numb.

Autumn: Yeah, but in a good way, right? (Smiley face)

Sheepshead: Un-freaking-believable.

Autumn: It's all verifiable. Or as much as anything on the Internet can be. I know because I tried to vote again a few minutes after midnight. The balloting is officially closed.

Sheepshead: I still can't believe we did it. We actually did it!

Autumn: It's right there on the One Nashville! web site. The Pickers is the people's choice for the team's nickname. With 77 percent of the vote.

Sheepshead: I didn't believe you when you told me we could do it.

Autumn: But we did! The Internet is a powerful medium for those who know how to use it. And now your group, the Anti-Arena Agitators, is an Internet legend.

Sheepshead: LOL. Well, you know, the power of the Internet can be fleeting. And people and groups that are legendary today are soon forgotten.

Autumn: Whoa, a little more optimism is needed here. People will remember you if you want to stay remembered. Most people are happy to have their 15 minutes of Internet fame – make that 15 seconds – and then they're content to give way to the next round of videos about water skiing squirrels. But if you work at it, you can leverage that fame.

Sheepshead: And join the legions of bloggers sitting around in their pajamas, working to convince everyone they're like the Wizard of Oz, wise and all powerful.

Autumn: With one important difference: Most of those bloggers don't have anything of substance to say. People follow them because they're entertaining. Those bloggers are so snarky and callous about the world around them that people actually feel better about themselves because they know that even though they, too, are snarky and callous, at least they're not THAT snarky and callous.

Sheepshead: Leading an Internet campaign to create a baseball nickname that's going to provide 20 years' worth of material for Comedy Central writers seems pretty snarky and callous to me.

Autumn: Awww, feeling a little guilty, are we? So if Nashville gets a Major League Baseball team, it will be called the Pickers. The Nashville Pickers. It's funny. It's entertaining. But you're not the same as those pajama bloggers, my friend. And the difference is that you've got a higher purpose for what you do. You're trying to achieve a greater good.

Sheepshead: I'm still not sure about that.

Autumn: But you are. You can't lose sight of that. The end, in this case, justified the means. But there's something else you should know.

Sheepshead: And what's that?

Autumn: This doesn't have to be the end. In fact, it should just be the beginning.

Sheepshead: I'm not sure I follow. We launched the campaign and we won. It's time to declare victory and call it a day.

Autumn: I don't think so. Not by a long shot. We've been through this a million times. When I saw your You Tube video about the dangers of professional sports, the insidious corrupting effect that they have on people – no, not just people – but whole cities, I was blown away. You've got a message people need to hear. A lot of them have already heard, but it hasn't completely sunk in yet. To a lot of them, you're still entertainment. But if you stick with this, you can be a lot more than just entertainment. You can open people's eyes and help them see the truth that's been right in front of them for a long time.

Sheepshead: Maybe you should make your own You Tube video.

Autumn: LOL! I just might. If you think it'll help your cause. Our cause. But there's a lot more that we need to do besides make You Tube videos and wage Internet voting campaigns. I want to be your partner, Sheepshead. What you said in that video touched me. You gave me something to believe in at a time when I was beginning to think there wasn't really anything in the world worth believing in. I want to help you. We can accomplish great things together. If you'll trust me.

(A long pause followed. So long that Autumn thought maybe Sheepshead had logged off or fallen asleep at his computer keyboard. Then finally, the answer.)

Sheepshead: OK, Autumn. So what do you have in mind?

CHAPTER TWENTY-ONE

Horton Edison and Mayor Kent Gables were watching TV in the living room of Gables' home in an exquisite south Nashville neighborhood. As a real estate executive, Gables had secured an excellent deal during a bear market on the spacious house on Lakeview Drive, just a block from the Radnor Lake wilderness area, one of Nashville's urban treasures.

With three bedrooms and two and a half baths, the place was just about right when Gables' wife and two children were living with him. Since the divorce, though, Gables felt very alone in such a cavernous space. So he was glad to have Edison's company from time to time, even on occasions that were at least semi-work-related.

Visitors to Radnor Lake – and there were many – often rhapsodized about how the natural surroundings could have a calming effect on the most tightly-wound city dwellers. Yet neither Edison nor Gables were enjoying themselves much on this particular night.

They occasionally met outside City Hall on the theory that some of the most productive meetings were held outside the workplace. They had ordered a Greek takeout dinner – gyros, salad and potatoes – and were washing it down with Fat Tire beer as they watched a Metro Council meeting on the local public television station.

The council had a long list of zoning cases on the agenda, but at the moment its members were bogged down in a discussion about the merits of allowing bike taxis to operate on downtown streets.

Although they had important matters to discuss, Edison and Gables could read each other's body language well enough to know that it would be best to take a few minutes to unwind before getting down to business. As was his practice, Edison waited until his boss initiated their conversation.

"So how was your meeting with Julius Malfair?" Gables asked.

"Oh, you know Julius," Edison replied. "He's always Mr. Personality."

"Did he tell you what the team owners said about the Internet poll on the team's name?"

"He was sort of cryptic about that," Edison said. "I gather that there may be some disagreement among them about whether to accept the poll results or just select a name that might be a little less..."

"Less laughable?"

"Right. Although remember that the Pickers was one of the names they selected for that short list. So at least one of them must have liked it."

Gables sighed. "Unbelievable. So now we're bogged down on what to call the team?"

"For the moment, it appears so," Edison said. "And I don't have to tell you how much fun the media has had with its coverage of the poll results. For many of the media pundits, the results confirm everything they have long assumed to be true about Nashville."

"That we're a bunch of rednecks who don't have the sense to realize that everyone else in the country is laughing at us, not with us."

"Pretty much. So, for now at least, it looks like we'll have to add the team name to our list of issues to be worked out at a later date."

"Why can't anything about this be simple?" Gables said, cracking his knuckles and bowing his head as if in prayer. "Why does it have to be that hard to come up with a decent team name? Out of all the things we could be spending energy on, that should be near the bottom of the list."

"I can't disagree with you there, Kent," Edison paused, not really wanting to ask the next question he had for the mayor. "So what's the latest from Orlando?"

Gables abruptly sat up from his spot on the couch, briefly coughing on a sliver of lamb meat as he did. He tapped a few keys on the laptop on his coffee table, then turned the screen so Edison could see it.

"The latest from the Orlando newspaper," Gables said. "While we're in a tizzy about a team name here, they've already got one down there. The city announced today that the new franchise would be called the Orlando Scorpions. And the stadium they'll play in will be called the Scorpions' Den."

"Scorpions? Do they even have scorpions in Orlando?"

"Trust me, they do. A friend of mine in the real estate business down there once had to sell homes in a new subdivision they'd plowed out of a heavily wooded area. And for the first two or three years, they had plenty of complaints from homebuyers that the scorpions who had nested in that wooded area hadn't exactly taken the hint to relocate when the bulldozers arrived. A couple of people went to the hospital with scorpion stings."

"OK, I didn't know that," Edison said. "Not the most obvious choice for the nickname of a team in a state almost completely surrounded by the ocean."

"No, but most of the good nicknames are already taken: The Buccaneers, the Dolphins, the Rays, the Sharks. Squids are pretty formidable seafaring creatures, but that's a nickname that would generate almost as many jokes as..."

"The Pickers."

"So, all in all, the Scorpions isn't a bad name. It's original. And it kind of fits."

"You've got to give Skip Goodman, Orlando's mayor, a little bit of credit."

"No, I don't," Gables said. "And I've told you repeatedly not to mention his name around me."

"And someday you'll have to tell me why."

"Right." Gables took another swig of beer, anxious to redirect the conversation. "So, just to recap, we're behind Orlando on site selection, stadium financing and now the team name."

Edison said nothing.

"Feel free to jump in and tell me where I'm wrong," Gables said.

"No, Mayor. I believe – hope, anyway – that one of the greatest assets I bring to your administration is my ability to tell the truth, no matter how bad the truth may be."

"So, in your estimation, is there any part of the truth that wouldn't make me want to throw up Greek potato balls all over my shoes?"

"I think a little perspective is in order," Edison said. "We'll sort out the issues with site selection and stadium financing. Devin Underwood's firm is working on an economic impact study that should help us win popular support and grease the political skids to get done what we need to get done."

"Are you confident about that? From what you told me about your meeting with Dr. Moon, it didn't sound like she was going to sing the praises of professional sports from the highest mountaintop."

"If she's got a cheerleader uniform, I think she'll probably be keeping it in the closet," Edison said. "But I think she'll be fair. And just having some numbers to quantify the benefit of a Major League Baseball team should help us in the court of public opinion. An economic impact of $1 million doesn't sound half bad, especially if you don't know there might have been some other hacks out there willing to say the economic impact would actually be $1 billion."

Gables laughed. "Man. Your world view skews a little bit toward the cynical, doesn't it, Horton?"

"A little cynicism has served me well during my career at City Hall."

"OK, OK. So we'll get the stadium financing back on track. But what do you know about this group that sabotaged the Internet naming poll? The Anti-Arena Agitators? I can't turn around lately without seeing or hearing something about them in the media."

"I don't know a whole lot, other than what's been in the media," Edison admitted. "The group has become something of an Internet sensation, though. And part of the mystique is that nobody knows much about it."

"So can we find out anything about them? Surely, if they're using computers to stir up people against a baseball team and vote for a perfectly crappy nickname, then there must be a way to track them down."

"Maybe," Edison said. "We've got some people in the city's information systems division who might be able to make a little headway toward that end. Would you like for me to have them snoop around and see what they can find out?"

"Of course I do," Gables replied. "What higher priorities do you think they should have right now?"

Edison took a big bite of salad, allowing himself time while chewing to choose his response carefully.

"I think the mayor of Nashville sets the priorities for all of us who work for city government," Edison said. "And if you say trying to track down the Anti-Arena Agitators online is a priority, then it is, in fact, a priority."

"The top priority."

Edison killed the last of his beer before answering. The alcohol at these meetings away from City Hall was definitely welcomed. "If you say so, Mayor, then that's the way it is."

CHAPTER TWENTY-TWO

Julius Malfair was on a hot streak. He was at a blackjack table where the minimum bet was $25 per hand. And at lunchtime on a winter weekday, he was alone there.

The dealer dealt him two cards, a seven and a ten. The dealer's face card was a three. Malfair stuck. The dealer flipped his hole card to reveal a jack. He took one card, a nine, then threw two more $25 chips over to Malfair as he cleared the cards from the table.

Malfair picked the chips up and added them to the four half-foot high stacks he had amassed in the hour since he had arrived in Metropolis. He bet the two $25 chips he had on the table from the previous hand.

"Hello, Julius."

Malfair looked up and smiled a greeting to Rowan Atwell, the head pooh-bah of One Nashville! Atwell stood awkwardly next to the table, not wanting to sit down and be forced into losing some of his hard-earned money.

"Hi, Rowan," Malfair said. "No offense, but you look a little like a fish out of water."

Other than casino staff members, Atwell was the only one in the room filled with blue-collar workers and retirees who was wearing a suit.

"I thought people got dressed up when they went to casinos," Atwell said.

Malfair gazed around the room theatrically. "I think you must have seen too many Rat Pack movies, Rowan. This is Metropolis, Illinois – not Las Vegas."

At one time when casinos were concentrated in places like Las Vegas and Atlantic City, they were in fact associated with glitz and glamour. But as states across the country had legalized gambling, there were more and more places like Metropolis.

The small casino looked like a lot of its smaller brethren around the country – a few blackjack tables, a couple of craps and roulette tables and rows and rows and rows of noisy slot machines surrounding a small bar in the center of the room.

No showgirls or A-list singers in sight.

"So why are we in Metropolis?" Atwell asked. It was a fair question, since Metropolis was about two and a half hours northwest of Nashville by interstate, just across the Ohio River from Paducah, Kentucky.

"Maybe I thought you just needed to get out of Nashville for a while, Rowan."

"I'd be touched by your concern for me, Julius, if I thought you had any. But you know, I'm the head of the Nashville chamber of commerce, so it's a little bit unusual for me to be driving across Kentucky for a business meeting. Which I hope that's what this is."

"Oh, most definitely it is." Malfair had played three more hands since Atwell had arrived, winning one and losing two. "But I have a client who would prefer that you and I not been seen together. It might raise some political questions my client would prefer not to answer right now. And you and I both know we're unlikely to run into anyone we know up here."

That was true. Men in Nashville of their station could afford to fly to Las Vegas whenever they wanted. They didn't need to road trip it to Metropolis or Tunica, Mississippi like the working stiffs.

"Wow, that sounds very cloak-and-dagger, Julius. So who's this mystery client of yours?" As if he didn't already know.

"I'm sure that by now you've heard something about the efforts to lure a Major League Baseball franchise to Nashville. Well, I'm representing the ownership group."

"Oh, really? Your clients want to bring a baseball team to Nashville?"

"That's right. And that's a mission I would think you and the rest of your friends at One Nashville! would enthusiastically support."

"We probably would," Atwell said coyly, "if any of your clients had ever approached our group to ask for our support."

"Aw, Rowan, I'm sorry about that. Would it help if I sent each member of your board of directors a Whitman Sampler?"

"Actually, that might be a good starting point."

"Alright, Rowan. Let's stop kidding ourselves here. We both know that if we took a poll of One Nashville! members right this minute, they'd tell you they would rather have a Major League baseball team in Nashville than a month of sex with their wives. For some of the members, probably a year's worth."

"Some would be willing to forego sex forever. Look, I'll agree that most of our members support what you're doing. In fact, I'm one of them. But that's not a unanimous sentiment. There are some downtown businesses that think you're taking money out of their pockets to help finance the stadium's construction."

"Technically, the city will be taking the money out of their pockets. And besides, it's tax revenue. Not money those businesses would have had to spend themselves anyway."

"Ah, but they could have made a strong case that those tax dollars should have been used for other projects that would benefit downtown and, by extension, their own bottom lines. But then your guys came along and sucked all the air out of the debate about how downtown tax dollars should be spent."

"Surely, that view isn't representative of a significant portion of your membership. Surely, most of your folks understand that the benefits of having a Major League team far outweigh any concerns they have about how much money the city is going to spend on streetlights downtown. The skies will be plenty bright when they're bathed in light from our stadium on game nights, that's for sure."

"Like I said, your clients also hurt some feelings by not talking to us. I mean, for God's sake, you went to Mayor Gables first. We're supposed to be the ones you go to if you want someone to help you get the mayor's support."

"But, Rowan, we already do have the mayor's support. And I know for a fact that in spite of all this posturing you're doing today, we have your support, too."

The conversation was apparently having a detrimental effect on Malfair's blackjack game. After winning three in a row, he had lost the last five.

"I already told you that I'm in support of what you're doing. I'm just telling you, as a representative of One Nashville!, it would have been nice if your clients had come to us."

"As a representative of *my* clients, I'm just telling you that we're coming to you now."

"For help?"

"Yes. Unless you want to spend the rest of your life watching Orlando Scorpions games on TV and wondering what might have been."

"OK, so what do you need, Julius?"

"The mayor has hired Devin Underwood's firm to do an economic impact study on the benefits of having a team here."

"Really?" Atwell said, feigning surprise. No need mentioning his recent conversation with the mayor if it wasn't necessary. "So what's the problem? An economic impact study can help you win over public support, including the doubters within my organization. If the numbers are right on a study like that, then your downtown business owners will be starting up collections to pay for streetlights to benefit the team."

"That's the thing, Rowan. Based on what I've heard, the numbers might not be right. Or at least not as right as they could be."

"A lowball estimate?"

"It seems possible, Rowan."

"I thought Devin Underwood was a team player. I thought the mayor was a team player. So to speak."

"I think both of them are, too. But they're delegators. And in this case, I think the people they have delegated this assignment to don't fully comprehend the concept of the end justifying the means. If you follow me."

The dealer had dealt Malfair two tens, so he split the cards and doubled his bet. The dealer put a three on top of one ten and a four on top of the other. Since the dealer had a three-card showing, Malfair stuck. The dealer flipped his hole card to reveal a jack, then took a seven. Two more losses for Malfair.

"So what I think you're saying, Julius, is that you would like to have a study that's a little more aggressive, a little more forward-leaning?"

"Don't you think that would be best, Rowan?"

"I do."

"And the chamber – I'm sorry, One Nashville! – has some experience working with firms that do this sort of work?"

"We do."

"So how soon could you find the sort of economist we need to do the kind of study we need?"

"I don't know. How much time do you have?"

"Not long. I'm in a position to slow down Devin Underwood's study a little bit by raising technical questions here and there – that's what we lawyers do – but we really need some good PR on this project soon,

Rowan. So far, it's been one problem after another. Is two weeks doable?"

"I think anything's doable for the right amount of money. Which I assume your clients will be willing to pay."

"They will. We'll make this worth their while. But, Rowan, as you surely know, it's probably best for us not to have an official legal contract that someone could come across until after the team's unpacking its stuff in the new stadium. If that soon, even."

"We'll take you on faith, Julius. And you know I don't often say that."

Malfair stood and the two men shook hands.

"But there's one more thing, Julius. How will it look if my travel expenses for this trip show up on One Nashville!'s expenses? Since we get public money, the media has a right to review our books. Which they sometimes do."

Malfair frowned, then shoved his much-diminished pile of chips in Atwell's direction.

"I think this should cover you, Rowan," Malfair said. "On my clients' expense account, which doesn't get the same media scrutiny that yours does. But one bit of advice: If I were you, I'd pick another table. This dealer's gotten hot ever since you showed up."

CHAPTER TWENTY-THREE

"Well, Horton, it looks like we've got ourselves a public relations winner here."

Horton Edison was standing next to Julius Malfair, surveying the preparations that were being made for another news conference outside City Hall.

A raised stage had been set up in the courtyard. Mayor Kent Gables and Wynn "The Jackhammer" Hammerskal were onstage, quietly talking to each other at a safe distance from the microphones that had been set up at center stage. Off on one side of the stage were a group of beautiful women in skimpy rhinestone dresses and cowboy boots, an organist with a small portable organ and a character in a costume that resembled a giant starburst. At a discreet distance at the back of the stage stood a uniformed Metro police officer, a courthouse bailiff who also served as Mayor Gables' driver and bodyguard at public events.

Edison and Malfair were standing in front of the stage, along with assembled members of the media. The organist was warming up the crowd by playing popular ballpark tunes in a tinny pitch.

"You think so, Julius?" Edison replied.

Malfair chuckled. "You know, Horton, I just love your unrelenting optimism about everything related to this project. This is a classic case of turning lemons to lemonade. The results of the fans' poll of potential team names could have turned into a potential fiasco. But, thanks to my clients, a potentially embarrassing crisis has been averted."

"I have to admit, things seem brighter than they did a few days ago."

"Bright, like a star? A Nashville Star? It has a nice ring to it, no?"

"The Nashville Stars is a much better nickname than the Nashville Pickers."

"Aww, that must have hurt to say, Horton. But you've got to admit that it was a great compromise. I don't think I'm violating attorney-client privilege in telling you that one of the team owners really, really wanted that Pickers nickname. He felt it was absolutely essential to have a team name that reflected the city's musical heritage. But the Stars does that because we're home to so many country music stars."

"Which explains the cheerleaders in the rhinestone getups."

"Right! See? You do get it. We're calling them the Nashville Starlettes."

"So why aren't there any dudes out there in matching cowboy outfits or whatever?"

Malfair shot Edison a disgusted look. "Come on, Horton. I know you're not that naive."

"And they can do a lot of cheerleading moves in those skimpy outfits?"

"Horton, they're really more hostesses than cheerleaders. You must understand the importance hospitality plays in the fan experience at ballparks."

"OK, well, what about the mascot? He looks like that guy from the Jimmy Dean sausage commercials. Won't people think the nickname refers to the kind of stars found up in the sky?"

"It'll keep people guessing about what the nickname actually means. Which is good. It adds to the intrigue."

"Of course, people who actually live here in Nashville might think it refers to the Nashville Star commuter train that runs between here and the eastern suburbs."

"Again, I love the optimism, Horton. Anyway, it's the first good news we've had in a while. Not that you and your folks at City Hall aren't trying as hard as you can,

192

I'm sure. So let's just enjoy this. I think they're getting ready to start."

And they were. Mayor Gables and Wynn Hammerskal were at their microphones now, asking for everyone's attention as the organist wound down the last few notes of "Take Me Out to the Ballgame."

"Wow!" Mayor Gables said. "What an exciting day! Who's ready to play some ball?"

His remark was met by enthusiastic cheers from some of the city employees who were standing behind the media members, and a few of the media members as well.

"We have an exciting announcement to make today. Nashville's new Major League Baseball franchise – and it will be Nashville's Major League Baseball franchise – has a name!"

Some applause.

"A much better name," Gables continued, "than some insect name chosen by some city in Florida that I don't want to say out loud!"

More applause.

"So now, for the official announcement about Nashville's team name, I want to turn this over to someone you all know well, former Major League great Wynn "The Jackhammer" Hammerskal."

Hammerskal bounced up to his microphone with his characteristic enthusiasm.

"Hey, everybody! Are you ready to fill out the top of the lineup card?"

An assorted shouts of 'yes' filled the air.

"OK, well here it is: the official team name of Nashville's Major League Baseball franchise is…"

A murmur in the crowd interrupted Hammerskal's speech. Someone had pushed his way through the crowd and leapt onstage. He was wearing a sheep mask over his face.

Everyone laughed. Surely this was just part of the dog-and-pony show that had been planned for this media event. Both Hammerskal and Gables reacted with a start – but surely that was part of the act.

The man in the sheep mask ran toward center stage, directly in front of Gables and Hammerskal.

"DON'T BE SHEEEEEP!" he screamed to the assembled media. Nervous laughter followed.

Then in one quick motion, the man in the mask withdrew a canister from his pocket and opened it, aiming in the direction of Hammerskal and Gables.

"SSSSPLOP!" the canister exploded, covering the city's mayor and its most famous athlete in a pink, gooey substance. Silly String.

"Taking money from hard-working taxpayers to subsidize billionaire businessmen? THAT'S PINKO COMMUNISM!" the man in the sheep's mask shouted. Then he turned to run.

Like everyone else at the news conference Gables' bailiff/bodyguard had stood paralyzed as this was happening. Neither courthouse duty nor the mayor's security detail typically attracted the police force's best and brightest. Neither assignment generated much action, so the officers who served in those capacities were usually one step removed from desk duty.

Still, a cop was a cop, and the mayor's assigned protector overcame his shock and got his feet moving. If the man in the sheep's mask hadn't stopped to make his political statement, he would have escaped with ease.

As it was, he had to jump out of the way at the last minute as the bodyguard lunged to tackle him. The bodyguard didn't fall, but staggered across the stage, trying to regain his balance and pick up the chase.

Unfortunately, the Nashville Starlettes and the Starburst mascot were in his way and he collided with four of them before falling face down near the far end of the stage. The mascot got the worst of it, taking a hit that sent him tumbling like a starfish in the spin cycle of a washing machine. One of the Starlettes was knocked off the front of the stage, falling into the lap of a balding, diminutive sports columnist by the name of Gilbert Wise. Another Starlette was hurled into the organ player and his organ, sending the player and his instrument both toppling over the edge of the stage. The organ plinked in protest as it hit the ground. The third Starlette was more or less undercut at the knees by the cop as he completed his fall, which meant she landed on top of him.

The assembled members of the media took no action to apprehend the man in the sheep's mask, although most of them were furiously scribbling notes or shooting video. Gilbert Wise lay perfectly still under the Starlette, either unable or unwilling to move.

The cop was gamely trying to struggle to his feet with a buxom deadweight on his back, but it was too late.

The man in the sheep's mask had sprinted the few yards across the courthouse square to the street, where a white Nissan Altima was waiting.

"How's that for some pie in the face?" the man shouted. "Shepherd's pie, of course!"

With that parting shot, he jumped into the passenger side of the car and the driver, whose face was obscured by a hat with a wide, floppy brim, sped away.

The car had a temporary tag on it, but only one side was secured to the license plate holder so the paper flapped in the breeze, making it impossible to read.

The media were in a full frenzy now, chattering amongst themselves and frantically calling their newsrooms. Every reporter there wanted to be the first to post or broadcast this story. This was viral news at its best.

The city employees who had been enlisted to serve as a planted cheering session for the news conference were confused about what to do next. Report back to their workstations or wait here for further instructions?

While most of those on stage struggled to regain their feet and their bearings, Gables and Hammerskal stood pretty much as they had as the Silly String attack was unfolding. It appeared that there was at least one way to render Hammerskal speechless.

Down in the front row, Julius C. Malfair turned to Horton Edison and muttered a curse word. He, too, seemed to be having trouble processing what had just happened.

"Communists?" he finally said quietly to Edison. "Communists? He'd never say that if he saw my clients' tax returns."

Edison mustered every ounce of professionalism he had in order to suppress a smile.

"AAA's Silly String Attack Was a Perfect Metaphor"
By Gilbert Wise, Sports Columnist

It should have been one of the most glorious days in our city's history – the day it was announced that our new Major League baseball franchise would be called the Nashville Stars. Leave it to the Anti-Arena Agitators to ruin the moment with a childish act. Really? Silly String? Sprayed all over our city's most beloved athlete and our mayor. Yes, that really happened. Right before the eyes of an incredulous press corps.

Naturally, I have several observations to make. First of all, who left Barney Fife in charge of the mayor's security detail? Nashville's not some cow town any more. It's a major metropolitan city. And in major metropolitan cities, the mayor ought to be adequately protected. And when I say 'adequately protected,' what I mean is that if somebody jumps out of a crowd to pull a stupid stunt like the one AAA pulled, then there ought to be a crowd of cops to swarm all over that somebody, Secret Service-style. Check that: Better than Secret Service-style.

While I'm on the subject of the police, how could they not find the getaway car AAA used? Taxpayers pay so our city can employ thousands of cops. With any kind of decent description of a vehicle used to commit a crime, the cops are usually able to find the car within a matter of hours. You stick up a liquor store on Dickerson Pike, they'll catch you before you get a mile down the road. But in this case, a case of assault against one of our highest profile citizens and our mayor, the car seems to have simply disappeared.

Hey, two dozen people saw that car before it sped away. I was one of them, although I was a little distracted at the time. The description given by those witnesses was pretty clear: A white mid-1990s Nissan Altima with some damage on the right front fender. Several people even got the first three numbers on the car's temporary tag: A44. That really should be enough for the cops to go on. Yes, I understand that Altimas are manufactured 15 miles down the road in Smyrna. And yes, I know that means that many Tennesseans, including most of the factory workers, drive that type of car. But the fender damage? The partial tag number? That should really narrow down the choices.

You'd expect the car to be ditched in an alley somewhere. Or one of our local car lots could provide some information about people who bought cars recently with tags that began with A44. But despite a citywide dragnet, nobody has found the car. And no car lots have a record of any such tag number being issued. Which leads me to my theory: This was an outside job. A Nashvillian wouldn't do this. The evidence suggests a Nashvillian didn't do this. So why would an out-of-towner commit such a heinous crime? Well, let's look at motive. Which city stands to gain the most if Nashville's bid for the team is sabotaged? That's right. Mickey Mouse town.

I bet if police could have set up roadblocks along Interstate 24 or Interstate 75, they could have caught the perpetrators before they made it back to Orlando. You want to find that car? I bet it's cruising down International Drive right now. So our cops screwed up and let the sheep guy slip through their fingers. But we shouldn't lose sight of what's happening here. AAA is a group that claims to be in it for the taxpayers and all that, but it's all really a smokescreen. Hurting

198

Nashville's bid helps Orlando's bid. It's that simple.

You're welcome, Nashville Police Department. Glad I could give you a lead that will help you catch these guys. Just don't count on a lot of help from your counterparts on the Orlando Police Department.

One final observation: KellyeAnn, the Nashville Starlette who landed in my lap near the end of that disastrous press conference, is a rising star in the entertainment business. Remember the name.
I say all that, even though I'm still flossing rhinestones out of my teeth. And KellyeAnn, if you're free a week from now, I'd love to take you out for Valentine's Day. If you say 'yes,' that would be a wise choice.

CHAPTER TWENTY-FOUR

The snowstorm took Nashville completely by surprise. The forecast called for snow and freezing rain an hour north, along the Kentucky state line. Nashville was expected to get no more than a cold rain – and probably not a whole lot of that.

Mother Nature had other ideas. The low pressure system dipped further south than meteorologists had expected, which dropped temperatures a few degrees below freezing in the Nashville metro area. The snow began falling Valentine's Day evening, while much of the population was out celebrating the holiday. Few of them had time to make a mad scramble to grocery stores – the usual response from Nashvillians in response to any threat of snow.

By the next morning, the city of Nashville was covered in a couple of inches of wet snow. In northern parts of the country, they would call it a typical Monday morning. In Nashville, though, it was clearly time to hit the panic button.

The next morning, the city's emergency operations center was fully mobilized. Personnel from various departments scurried about, dealing as best they could with the chaos that Nashville roads became with even the slightest bit of precipitation.

Mayor Kent Gables stood uncomfortably in the midst of it all. He was totally in his comfort zone while writing memos about break room etiquette or dress code rules. Or presiding over ribbon cuttings. Or any of the other largely ceremonial duties he performed as mayor. But this was different.

Police were responding to numerous traffic accidents. Utility workers were checking to make sure no power lines were down. The fire department was responding to a couple of fires likely caused by faulty space heaters. The roads department was trying to get salt and brine onto the roads as quickly as possible.

It was at times like this that Mayor Gables was thankful that he had good people on his staff. His biggest job would be to take the information his lieutenants provided to him and relay it to the media at a mid-morning news conference.

Horton Edison could sense his boss' mood as he approached, but there were some things that couldn't wait.

"Hey, Horton," Gables said as he watched his staff scurrying all around him.

"Hey, Mayor," Edison replied. "I've got some bad news."

"Oh, no!" Gables exclaimed. "More snow is on the way?"

"Nothing like that," Edison said. "In fact, I understand there's supposed to be a warming trend this afternoon. Up to around 50 degrees or so. Most of this snow should be long gone within the next 24 hours."

"Well, that's a relief. Nashville just isn't equipped for this type of weather."

"No doubt. I imagine there will be a run on SUV sales at local car dealerships after this storm has passed."

"Speaking of cars, still nothing on the getaway car used when...when..."

"When that guy nailed you with the Silly String?"

"Yes."

"The answer is no. And after this many days have passed, it's unlikely that the car will be found. Unless someone dumped it into the Cumberland River. Then we might find it the next time there's a drought and the river runs low."

"So this car just leaves Court Square, takes the bridge across the river into East Nashville and vanishes?"

"I don't have an explanation."

"My bodyguard radioed the East Precinct and they put out a neighborhood dragnet within a matter of minutes after the whole thing happened. Why couldn't they find that car?"

"Like I said, I don't have an explanation. And neither do the cops."

Gables sighed before changing the subject. "OK, back to the bodyguard situation. Have you given any thought to my suggestion that we increase the number of bodyguards I take with me to public events? I mean, I've got another news conference here in the next couple of hours."

"I think you're pretty safe today. Nobody would want to drive a getaway car when the streets are this icy. Plus, your news conference today is about the weather, which is pretty non-controversial. Unlike the plans for the arena."

"OK, but in general..."

"In general, you have to weigh your need for security against the perception traveling with a large contingent of bodyguards carries. Moving through neighborhoods circled by police will give some people – unfair though it may be – the impression that you're scared. Not a good perception for citizens to have about one of their elected leaders. Also, there's the cost. You and I both know there are reporters in this town who would love to do stories about how your security detail is keeping cops off the streets that could be used to improve public safety."

"So, no more bodyguards?"

"I didn't say that. I wouldn't say that because I wouldn't want to tell you not to increase your security detail, then have that on my conscience if something bad did happen later. I think you'll just have to use your best judgment."

"My best judgment? My best judgment is informed by your advice. So what do you think I should do, Horton?"

"Like I said, it's really kind of a personal decision…"

"What do you think I should do, Horton?"

"It was Silly String, sir."

Gables' eyes narrowed for just a minute, then he took another deep breath. "OK, for now, the size of the security detail remains unchanged. Although I think I would prefer to have a young patrolman accompany me instead of a…well, a more mature officer."

"Great. Sounds like a good decision to me."

"So you said you had bad news. What is it?"

"Actually, I have both bad and good news. Which would you like to hear first, Mayor?"

Another deep sigh. "Let's go with the bad news. You led with that, so something big must be on your mind."

"Well, sort of. Orlando has secured a spring training site."

"What? Where?"

"Just down the interstate a few miles, in Daytona Beach. Daytona's city leaders have been dreaming about hosting spring training for years. They've apparently promised to build a 10,000-seat stadium for spring training if Orlando gets a Major League team."

"I thought all of the spring training sites were further south. Daytona is in Central Florida. And unless I'm misinformed, it can still get chilly there in February and March."

"Chalk it up to global warming. Or Orlando's desire to have its spring training site only an hour away. Whatever the case, a deal has apparently been struck."

"And how do you know that, Horton?"

"I went to college with Daytona's city manager. He let me know before terms of the deal hit the media as a courtesy to me."

"Wonderful. So, to recap, Orlando already has a site, a dedicated funding source for stadium construction, a contractor to perform that construction and a now a willing partner for spring training. And we don't have any of those things locked down yet."

"We're close, Mayor."

"I'm afraid 'close' may be good enough to keep us as a minor league baseball city for another generation. I can't believe this! Orlando's so sure it's going to get that team that they're already making arrangements for spring training!"

"Well, about that..."

"Yes, Horton?"

"My friend, the Daytona City manager, said that he and I really needed to talk face-to-face. I think there's more to that deal that he didn't want to tell me over the phone."

"If you're asking my permission to go to Daytona, you've got it. Make it happen, as soon as the weather allows flights out of the airport."

"Will do, Mayor."

"But before you leave, Horton, you said you had some good news."

"Oh, right. Mayor, remember when you asked me to see if our computer folks could track down messages from the Anti-Arena Agitators? Well, the group posted another message yesterday and our folks were able to track its IP address."

"And?"

"The message came from a computer terminal at the main branch of the Orlando Public Library."

CHAPTER TWENTY-FIVE

Raymond Goldfarb was in a good mood. He was just coming out of a news conference about the way spring training was going.

And by all accounts, it was going great. So far, only the pitchers and catchers had reported; the rest of the players would join the workouts in March. But the pitchers and catchers seemed to be enjoying themselves and their practices were very energetic.

Two of the best pitchers in the league seemed to be fully recovered from offseason surgeries on their throwing arms, which was good news for the league.

And the media couldn't stop talking about the expansion plans. The plans to award a team to San Juan had captured the imagination of the working press – and there was endless speculation about which city would land the other franchise. Most media outlets were reporting that Orlando seemed to have the inside track.

Goldfarb had held the news conference on the field at Winter Haven's spring training facility. Although his was a job that could make a man unpopular in a hurry, Goldfarb still had the goodwill of the media as well as the rest of the baseball world.

And why not? He was a grandfather. A Methodist Sunday school teacher. The retired executive director of Ray of Hope, a well-regarded foundation that raised money for research of AIDS and other sexually transmitted diseases. And, most important of all, he had ruled fairly and justly since coming out of retirement to become Major League Baseball's commissioner.

Even the players and managers he disciplined generally had to admit that Goldfarb was a reasonable man. "Everybody loves Raymond," they joked about him.

So the media hadn't exactly roughed him up during the news conference. To the contrary, it was a session filled with light banter and jokes about when he planned to move to San Juan and run for mayor.

As Goldfarb retreated into the ballpark's clubhouse to get out of the Florida sun, he still wore a smile on his face. That smile disappeared as soon as his assistant handed him his cell phone. The voice he hated to hear was on the other end of the line.

How were things going with the expansion plans, the voice demanded to know.

Goldfarb assured him they were going fine.

What about the aggressive moves Orlando was making? What about this group, the Anti-Arena Agitators? Were they anything to worry about?

Goldfarb said no, they were not.

Was everything still going according to plan? That was the main question the caller wanted to know.

Yes, Goldfarb said, everything was proceeding according to plan.

Then the line went dead. Goldfarb continued to hold his phone to his ear for a few more seconds, breathing heavily. His stomach was hurting again.

Soon it would all be over. That was the only thing that helped Goldfarb cope with the situation.

Goldfarb finally slid the phone into his pocket. And he wondered if the beer concession stands in the ballpark would be stocked before the exhibition season had begun.

CHAPTER TWENTY-SIX

Against his better judgment, Horton Edison headed straight to the office from the airport after returning from his trip to Daytona Beach. When he arrived, Dr. Iris Moon was waiting outside his office. She did not look happy.

"Come on in, Dr. Moon," Edison said. "I can tell by the look on your face that you've got something on your mind."

Moon followed Edison into his office, then unfolded a copy of The Nashville Bulletin and laid it on his desk.

"Have you seen this yet?" Moon asked.

"If that's today's issue, I haven't," Edison admitted. He would have read the online version except he couldn't use his phone on the plane and he spent the cab ride back to City Hall trying to catch up on his e-mails.

"Check out the lead story," Moon said.

Edison did. The headline read: "One Nashville! Study Shows Baseball Team Would Have $5 Billion Economic Impact"

"Five billion dollars?" Edison said with disbelief.

At that, Moon suddenly sneezed.

"That number...is...ridiculous," she said, barely stifling another sneeze. "All...of...their...assumptions...are...flawed!"

"How so?"

Moon sneezed again.

"Do you need a tissue, Dr. Moon?" Edison offered.

"No, no, I'm fine. It's just that...in this 'study,' they counted all the spending at the ballpark as new spending."

"And you told us that it should only be considered new spending if it's money that comes in from outside the community. Spending by locals is just money that's moving from one place to another within the economy, right?"

"That's right. And they...they...used a multiplier of....five!" Moon said.

"What does that mean, exactly?"

"The multiplier is the number you use to calculate how money spent directly on the project flows through the community indirectly. So you spend X-amount in direct costs on salaries for construction workers. Then those construction workers go out and buy groceries, pay their bills and that sort of thing. That's the indirect spending. But it's crazy to multiply the indirect spending by five. Who can say...with any certainty...what happens...after money has changed hands...more than a couple of times..."

Edison slid a box of tissue across his desk just as Moon let loose another sneeze.

"OK, Dr. Moon, I think I get the picture. Without getting too technical with me, I'm assuming you're telling me that you think the One Nashville! study inflates the economic impact numbers?"

Moon nodded.

"And am I also safe in assuming that the numbers in your study are significantly lower than the numbers in the One Nashville! study?"

Moon nodded again.

"And the gap between their numbers and yours is..."

"About a factor of 10," Moon said.

"Oh. I see. That's a lot."

Edison sighed and stared at the ceiling.

"Did you, I mean, did the city order this study, Mr. Edison?"

"No. Absolutely not. We hired you and your firm, Underwood & Drake. That's the only study we commissioned."

"So why would the chamber put out a study like this?"

"One Nashville!" Edison corrected. "And I don't know. I find the timing very interesting, though."

"In what way?"

"Well, you were days away from giving us the results of your study, right?"

"Yes, I was. I wanted to go through my figures a couple more times, but..."

"And the numbers in the study by One Nashville! far exceed yours. Which makes them a better news story. More sensational."

"You don't think that..."

"I can't prove it, of course, but it looks to me like Rowan Atwell and his crew put their study out in a deliberate attempt to pre-empt your study."

"But why would they want to do that, Mr. Edison?"

"Please call me Horton."

"OK, why would they want to do that, Horton?"

"If you repeat this to anyone, Dr. Moon, I'll deny having said it. But this looks like pure politics to me."

"Please call me Iris. But how did they know what my study was likely to show and when it was likely to be released."

"Oh, I have an idea about that. But it doesn't matter."

"So what will you do?"

Edison sighed again and thought for a moment. "Well, as much as I hate to say it, we can't release your study now. Having two different economic impact studies with such different findings would only muddy the waters. I hate that you put in all that work and it won't see the light of day, but I'm trying to look at the big picture here."

Now it was Moon's turn to sigh. "I'm sorry, Horton. I never imagined anything like this could happen. I know this: It's probably not going to be any good for my career. I haven't been in the office since this story appeared, but Devin Underwood has a preliminary draft of my study. I wouldn't be surprised if he fires me the next time he sees me."

"I don't think that will happen. And if Underwood & Drake no longer requires your services, then I'm sure we can find a place for you in our budget department."

"Are you sure about that?"

"Yes, Iris, I am. As chief of staff, I am able to make a few things happen around here. And we could definitely use someone with your talents on our staff. Particularly while we're dealing with this push to get the baseball franchise."

"And Mayor Gables?"

"Mayor Gables and I don't see eye-to-eye on everything, but I'm confident I can make the case to him that you'd be a good hire."

"Oh." Moon paused for a second. "What if instead of being fired, I just quit? Would the city still be interested in hiring me then?"

"I believe we would."

"In that case, could you excuse me, Horton? I have a resignation letter to write."

Edison gave a low chuckle. "Well, come back and see me after you've taken care of that. But I do have another question: Have you come up with a financing plan for the stadium yet?"

"Yes, I have. We've talked about several different options – using sales tax revenues, using tax increment financing and setting up a tourism development zone. While I don't think any one of those sources would be reliable by itself, if we use all three, I think the plan would be pretty solid."

"Glad to hear it. And I like the way you said 'if WE use all three,' as opposed to 'If you use all three.' That has a nice ring to it."

Moon flashed a smile, something she rarely did. "I'll see you soon, Boss."

"You should still call me Horton!" Edison called after Moon as she left.

Edison was still chuckling as he reflected on the conversation he had just completed when his intercom buzzed. Mayor Gables wanted to see him.

Edison padded the few steps down to the mayor's office and silently slid into a chair across the desk from the mayor.

"Good trip to Daytona, Horton?"

"I would say so."

"What made it good?"

"Well, it's true that Daytona Beach officials have signed an agreement to serve as a spring training site if Orlando lands the new franchise. My friend, the city manager, made no secret of that."

"Wonderful," Mayor Gables said sarcastically.

"Maybe I should say that again: Daytona Beach officials have signed an agreement to serve as a spring training site IF Orlando lands the new franchise."

Gables looked puzzled.

"Mayor, the deal Daytona signed is contingent upon Orlando getting a team. It's not an exclusive agreement."

"Meaning?"

"Meaning, Daytona Beach really wants to be a spring training site for a Major League team. Any Major League team."

"Including one based in Nashville?"

"Yes, even one based in Nashville."

"So, do we have that in writing?"

"We will, Mayor. I asked the city manager if he would sign the same agreement with us, contingent upon Nashville getting the team, and he said yes. I faxed the agreement to our city attorney's office, they've signed off on it, and it's a go as long as you're comfortable with it."

"Oh, I'm comfortable, all right. Get me a copy and I'll sign it right away."

"I thought you would. I'll have my secretary bring it over as soon as we get done here."

Gables unleashed one of his best real estate salesman smiles. "Horton, I know I don't tell you this often enough, but I really appreciate everything you do for me."

"Glad to hear it, sir."

"So what other news do you have?"

"Well, I guess you've seen The Nashville Bulletin story about the One Nashville! economic impact study."

"I have. What does that mean for us?"

"Well...there's a study out there now. It's not our study, but it's a study. And I think having a second study that didn't line up with the first study would only tend to confuse people."

"We don't want that."

"No. And I understand our study is – would be – quite a bit more conservative than the One Nashville! study."

"So..."

"So I think we let the One Nashville! study stand on its own. In fact, it would be best if Underwood's firm never delivered its final product to us. That way, we wouldn't have to explain the differences between the two studies."

"Agreed. What else?"

"Well, I think we need to hire Dr Moon. I think she may be resigning from Underwood's firm and I think she would be a good addition to our budget staff. Particularly as we try to work through the issues related to this stadium construction project."

"If you think we need her..."

"I feel very strongly that we do."

"Then make it happen. You know I trust your judgment on personnel matters, Horton. Anything else?"

"Yes. I was checking through my e-mails on the way here from the airport. One was from our IT department. The Anti-Arena Agitators sent out another message about the, uh, Silly String incident. Also from a computer terminal at the Orlando Public Library."

"So maybe that weasley columnist Gilbert Wise was right for a change. Maybe the guy who hit the Jackhammer and I got into that car and headed straight back to Orlando. That would explain why our cops haven't been able to find the car anywhere around here."

"And I suppose it's out of the question to ask the city of Orlando for help in catching the guy who's responsible?"

"Out of the question. I'm not convinced that the city of Orlando isn't supporting what the guy is doing, either tacitly or actively. But I think the good news is, if he and his friends are in Orlando, they'll probably stay in Orlando. They would be taking too big a risk to come back here after what they've done. We'd have roadblocks up on I-24 east before they would know what hit them."

Edison shrugged noncommittally, then prepared to leave. "Oh, I almost forgot. Our soon-to-be employee, Dr. Moon, has come up with a financing plan for the new stadium."

"Now that's the best news I've heard all day!" Gables exclaimed, slapping his knee enthusiastically. "And you believe this financing plan is sound?"

"As sound as we're likely to get."

"Then do this for me, Horton: Fast track this. Let's get that financing plan to the Metro Council as soon as possible. We've been running this whole race behind Orlando. Now it's time to get caught up."

"I'll get on it, sir." With that, Edison stood up and started toward the door.

"Horton?" his boss called after him.

"Yes, Mayor?" Edison stopped at the doorway.

"We're going to win this, aren't we? We're really going to win this!"

CHAPTER TWENTY-SEVEN

Autumn Sunshine sat in the waiting room, at war with her thoughts.

On the plus side, the Anti-Arena Agitators movement seemed to be gaining traction. The group's online messages were being seen by a wide audience. And that audience was willing to respond to AAA's calls to action – at least, the vote in the baseball team naming contest seemed to bear that out.

The group had already received national publicity from the sporting press. And AAA's latest caper – the Silly Stringing of Mayor Gables and Wynn Hammerskal – had gone off without a hitch. The police had put out a plea through the local media for anyone who might have seen the getaway car to come forward. Thinking about that made it difficult for Autumn to suppress a laugh.

Yet, for all of AAA's successes, there was still cause for concern.

Yes, the group's Internet messages had a lot of followers. But Autumn knew from other grassroots campaigns she had worked on that Internet support tended to be a mile wide and an inch deep. There were lots of people who were willing to talk tough while they were safely cloaked in the anonymity of the Internet. But when it came time to taking action – action that required leaving the couch – that was a different story.

And while it was true that the group had received national media attention, much of it was derisive. Sports journalists treated AAA and its supporters as being horribly misguided, if not downright crazy.

And the Silly String incident didn't seem to have had much of an impact. City officials still seemed

217

determined to pursue the franchise in spite of what Autumn viewed as a strong political statement.

Autumn looked at her watch, then glanced across the room at the secretary who was staring at her. She was no more than 25 years old – tall, pretty and busty. And she was definitely giving Autumn the evil eye. In response, Autumn gave her a small smile and a wink. It was nice having someone so young feeling jealous of her, Autumn thought.

But what to do to take AAA to the next level?

Mucking up an Internet naming contest was one thing. Disrupting a news conference was another. Still, the group needed something to really change the conversation about this pursuit of the Major League baseball franchise and the seductive siren call of professional sports. Something that couldn't be dismissed as just another harmless prank. Well, that was the purpose of this meeting today, wasn't it?

The phone on the secretary's desk buzzed. She picked up the receiver, listened for a second, then said, "yes sir" and replaced the receiver on the handset.

"Mr. Blazen will see you now," the secretary said with a scowl.

Autumn popped out of her seat and headed toward Hunt Blazen's office. He met her at the door, a big smile on his face. Autumn smiled back.

Although it had only been a couple of days since they had last seen each other, they hugged each other as tightly as if they had been separated for years.

Autumn pulled her mouth close to Blazen's ear.

"How was your 'business trip' to Orlando?" she whispered.

The Nashville Bulletin, March 5, 2018

"Mayor Finally Steps to the Plate, Hits One Deep"
By Gilbert Wise, Sports Columnist

Have I mentioned lately what a superb job our mayor, Kent Gables, is doing? Last night, he convinced the Metro Nashville Council to support his financing plan to build a new stadium for our soon-to-be Major League baseball team. And you know what? In the end, despite some naysaying from various corners of our community, the vote wasn't even that close.

The ayes beat out the nays, 35-5. And the five 'no' votes were coming from the same council members who vote 'no' on everything that furthers the march of progress in Nashville. The mayor also dropped a couple of other bombshells at last night's meeting. For one, he and his crack staff have already agreed to terms with Grover James, a junkyard owner, on a purchase deal for the new stadium site along the Cumberland River. I realize he's being well compensated for his property, but I'd like to think Mr. James agreed to sell at least partly because he understands how important that team will be for this community.

Mayor Gables' other surprise was that the construction contract for the new stadium doesn't need to go out for bid. Remember how Orlando was able to circumvent the bidding process by hiring the contractor who had previously done renovations on the city's football stadium? Well, Mayor Gables stole a page out of the playbook of his Orlando counterpart by using the same firm that built Greer Stadium, our minor league ball field, all those years ago.

OK, the company that built Greer has been through several ownership changes and a couple of name changes since the 1970s. But they're still in the stadium construction business. And by agreeing to negotiate with that company, the city can avoid a cumbersome bidding process that would have added weeks or even months to the construction timeline. Which, with Orlando breathing down our necks, is time we couldn't afford to waste.

After yesterday's vote, Mayor Gables promised to deploy earthmoving equipment to the site by the end of the week to begin clearing and leveling the land to prepare it for construction. That will also save time while the architectural plans for the stadium are being finalized. OK, there are some in this community who have criticized our mayor for his seeming inaction in this pursuit of the Major League franchise. What those people don't understand is that quite often there are things going on behind the scenes that the public doesn't know about. Sometimes, it's best just to trust that our city leaders know what they're doing.

Mayor Gables is nobody's fool. He obviously gave great weight to the economic impact study prepared by One Nashville! about what Major League baseball could mean to our city. As far as I'm concerned, getting the team will cement Mayor Gables' place in history as one of the city's all-time great mayors.

Oh, getting the National Football League team was nice. But just about any town with more than two stoplights can get one big-time sports team. (Green Bay, Wisconsin, I'm looking at you.)
Getting the National Hockey League team was also nice. But there are a lot of medium-sized cities with two major league franchises. (New Orleans and Charlotte, this means you.)

But getting a third major league team - and a team that would represent us in our country's national pastime, no less - well, that would be a huge deal. If we get the baseball team, convincing the National Basketball Association to relocate the Memphis Grizzlies franchise to Nashville is all that would be left.

So, do I think it's too early to be talking about building a statue in Mayor Gables' honor? Not if we get the baseball team. I would be fine with one prominently displayed at the new stadium's entrance, reminding fans about what he was able to accomplish during his time as mayor.

OK, I know some wise guy is going to suggest that the mayors who recruited major businesses like Nissan or Dell Computers to build their headquarters here are more deserving of statues. But come on.

If you don't work for one of those companies, what impact do they really have on your lives? Are 40,000 people a night going to be willing to pay admission to watch Nissan's assembly line churn out cars? Nope. But they'll buy tickets to watch Nashville Stars baseball. I remain convinced that we're going to beat Orlando out for this team. Let's face it: Floridians don't have a history of supporting their professional sports teams. About 80 percent of them moved to Florida from somewhere else, so their loyalties lie with the Yankees, the Red Sox, the Cubs or some other team from some other God-forsaken place where the winters are awful. Most Floridians would prefer to spend their time laying out on the beach. Or visiting overpriced theme parks. Or drinking orange juice. Or whatever else it is that they do down there. It's been demonstrated in season after season that Florida's pro teams consistently have disappointing attendance figures.

And would Major League baseball be any different? No way. Baseball, after all, is a summer sport. And summers in Florida, the last I checked, are brutally hot and humid. Hey, I've been to spring training games down there where I've sweated through my undershorts. And that's in March! Imagine what it'll be like to sit out in the sun there for three hours in July.

So yes, I'm very optimistic about our chances for getting this team. Thanks to the good work of Mayor Gables and the Metro Nashville Council, our path is now clear. Our city's leaders have stepped up to the plate and delivered a home run.

And all of you out there who voted for them made a Wise choice.

CHAPTER TWENTY-EIGHT

Raymond Goldfarb laid the flowers on the grave gently, as if they might break if he wasn't careful enough with them. Yellow roses. Francine had always liked yellow roses.

Francine, oh, Francine, Goldfarb thought. *Why did you have to leave me so soon?*

He knew there was no easy answer to that question. That's just the way life worked. There was no fairness to it all, at least none that he could see.

There were some couples – couples he knew – that were so unhappy in their marriages that one spouse would have been relieved if the other spouse happened to die. He and Francine weren't like that at all.

They'd met at church, here in Des Moines, while they were both in junior high school. They were dating as soon as their parents would let them. And they had been together ever since. Until this date two years ago, when the cancer that had started in her lungs finally claimed the rest of her body.

Lung cancer. And she'd never smoked a day in her life. In fact, her lifestyle was everything an insurance company's actuary would want it to be. Not only was she a non-smoker, but she also abstained from drinking alcohol or caffeine. Her diet was healthy, too, mostly vegetables and white meat. Steak only on special occasions. And yet cancer had found her, anyway.

It wasn't as if Francine was someone who deserved such a cruel twist of fate. She was loved by everyone who knew her, including Raymond Goldfarb. She was a regular churchgoer who devoted herself to charitable causes. Rarely a weekend went by that she wasn't doing something to help the less fortunate.

She truly had a heart of gold. And it didn't hurt that she was also beautiful. Raymond Goldfarb had never regretted marrying her. Not for a single minute.

Which made it all the more agonizing to watch as cancer stole her life away, bit by bit. He could hardly bear to think about it even now, two years later. Goldfarb had decided that anyone who truly believed the saying that "time heals all wounds" had never experienced the loss of a loved one. Some wounds were just too deep.

Goldfarb sighed and looked around. Glendale Cemetery. Peaceful and pastoral. Located next to the Waveland Golf Course, which was also peaceful and pastoral. He and Francine had played golf together from time to time, when their busy schedules had allowed it. And of course they had played some of those rounds at Waveland.

Goldfarb's parents were buried at Glendale, as were Francine's. All in all, it wasn't a bad final resting place, Goldfarb had to admit to himself. If you had to go.

Goldfarb stared at the plot next to Francine's. The plot where he would be buried some day. Lush green grass with soft, sweet-smelling earth underneath. As Goldfarb reflected on the turn his life had taken, he thought about how nice it would be just to dig a hole there and lie down next to Francine. And sleep forever. Sleep was so hard for him to come by these days, so that didn't seem so bad, either.

But that's not what Francine would have wanted, he knew. She loved life so much and treated every single day as a special gift. She was one of those people who noticed life's small pleasures that often went overlooked: a warm breeze, singing birds, the smell of honeysuckle in bloom.

No, she would have wanted Goldfarb to keep living as long as he could. And to make the most of his life. But she couldn't have known how things had played out since her death. Would she have understood how melancholy he now felt?

He sighed again. She would have wanted him to keep going, to do whatever good he could do in his professional and personal lives. Would she understand how he had come to be in the predicament he now faced? Maybe. She had a heart of gold, but she was human.

Then again, so was he. He had a squeaky clean image that was mostly well deserved, but he wasn't infallible. He was reminded of that daily.

As if on cue, his cell phone started to ring. He looked at the incoming call number and frowned. The caller couldn't have worse timing.

Goldfarb was tempted not to take the call, to let it go to voice mail. But he knew the caller wouldn't leave a voice mail. Instead, there would just be call after call after call until Goldfarb finally answered the phone.

"Goldfarb here," he said brusquely into the phone. Usually, Goldfarb was friendly and mannerly with everyone he spoke with by phone, but this caller was testing the limits of his genteel manner.

"Where is here?" the caller asked.

"Des Moines, Iowa," Goldfarb replied.

"Des Moines. Well, better you than me." The caller probably didn't know how much those words would hurt, but he wouldn't have cared, either.

"It's my hometown," Goldfarb said.

"Well, everybody's got to be from somewhere, I guess," the caller said with an unkind laugh. "Although if I were from Des Moines, I would leave as soon as I could and never look back."

"How can I help you?" Goldfarb said. He was in no mood for small talk.

"Straight to business. I like that. What I need, Ray, is for you to make a statement about the competition for the new expansion team." Only close friends called Raymond Goldfarb "Ray." This caller certainly didn't qualify.

"What kind of statement? Haven't you already got what you wanted? Both Orlando and Nashville have financially committed to building new stadiums to accommodate the team. The die is cast..."

"'The die is cast.' What an appropriate expression, given the circumstances," the caller said. "But that's exactly why a statement is needed now."

"A statement saying what?"

"I want you to call a news conference and talk about how you would prefer any new stadiums built in Sun Belt cities to have retractable roofs."

"Retractable roofs? Why? We've never required that of any of the teams that currently have franchises in Sun Belt cities. Some have them, others don't."

"Right. But you wouldn't be requiring retractable roofs. Just saying that you would *prefer* that Sun Belt cities have them. For the comfort and safety of the fans. After all, heat stroke is serious business. And with global warming, one can never be too careful."

"Even if I don't say it's a requirement, Orlando and Nashville will perceive it that way."

"Well, they both want a Major League baseball team. So yes, if you say you'd 'prefer' a stadium with a retractable roof, that's probably what they're going to build."

"Neither city has a retractable roof in its stadium design plans. Changing those plans would probably cost them both quite a bit of money."

"So? Do you think city officials in either place are going to bat an eye at spending a little more taxpayer money to fatten the wallets of the project architects? No one cares about that stuff."

"I care."

"That's your problem, Ray. You need to stop caring so much."

"There's also extra expense in building a stadium with a retractable roof. Probably the most expensive type of stadium there is."

"Again, not your problem. Just call the news conference, say you think retractable roofs are really cool, then stand back and let nature take its course."

"You have no idea how much I hate this," Goldfarb said.

"I know you do. But this will all be over soon. Then you can go to your favorite bar in Des Moines and drown your sorrows. No one would think the less of you for that."

Raymond Goldfarb had always been a man who was slow to anger, but that last dig was too much for him to take.

"You've said what you want. I will think about it. Now leave me alone."

"Think about it all you like, but in the end, you and I both know you'll be calling that news conference and saying exactly what I want you to say. Right, Ray?"

Goldfarb angrily clicked his phone off. It wasn't like him to hang up on anybody, but he felt very justified in this situation.

When Goldfarb turned his eyes back toward his wife's grave, they were filled with tears.

Oh, Francine, he thought. *I miss you so much.*

CHAPTER TWENTY-NINE

It was the first Sunday night in April, and for the most part Nashville had quieted down in preparation for the workweek ahead.

As it almost always did, music and the sounds of revelry still blared from the downtown honkytonks, which were mostly populated by tourists and a few locals who either didn't have jobs or didn't care if they showed up for those jobs hung over the next day.

But along the East Nashville bank of the Cumberland River, the scene was much quieter. It usually was, except on game nights during the Tennessee Titans' football season.

The start of football season was, of course, still months away. In fact, Monday was opening day for the new Major League Baseball season. The Cincinnati Reds, in keeping with tradition, would play the first scheduled game of the day. In a break from tradition, they would be playing their cross-state rivals, the Cleveland Indians.

The matchup had been one of Raymond Goldfarb's ideas. Typically, National League and American League teams wouldn't face each other until later in the season, with the Reds and Indians among those interleague matchups. Goldfarb thought having a rivalry game would add some zing to opening day.

He was probably right, at least for baseball fans who lived in the Midwest. In Nashville, several hours south of Cincinnati by car, the buzz was all about the scheduled groundbreaking for the new baseball stadium on what had been a junkyard until a few weeks ago.

After the Nashville Metro Council had voted to approve the stadium financing plan, work had begun almost immediately to clear away the junkyard equipment and scraps and relocate them to a new site, paid for by the city, in the northern most-rural neighborhood of Joelton.

Now the soon-to-be construction site was encircled by a chain link fence and guarded by a very bored security guard sitting in a green and gold Ford Fusion with "Sleepwell Security" logos emblazed on both of the front doors and a green light bar on the roof.

A Metro police car pulled alongside the security patrol car and the drivers exchanged words for a few minutes. The Metro car then pulled away, heading east toward the residential areas farther away from downtown.

The Metro policeman and the security guard would talk like that every hour on the hour. It was a good way to help keep both of them alert. Sleepwell was a name chosen to suggest that the company's clients would have peace of mind. But without proper precautions, it could also describe the state of consciousness for the company's employees on uneventful night shifts.

Autumn Sunshine knew the routine well since she'd been casing the junkyard/stadium site for several days. She knew that the cop wouldn't be back for almost an hour since the far-flung boundaries of Metro Nashville stretched police patrol areas very thin. And she also knew that the security guard worked alone. After all, why should the city pay for more than one guard for a construction site of that size? Particularly since most of the building materials hadn't yet been shipped to the site.

Autumn took a deep breath to focus her concentration, just as she'd learned in yoga class, then walked toward the security patrol car. Not too fast, not too slow, and not too seductively.

"Hey there!" she called out as she got within earshot of the guard.

"How are you this evening, ma'am?" the guard replied.

"Not so good," Autumn said, with just a trace of a smile. No need to overdo it at this point. "My car ran out of gas a couple of blocks from here."

"I'm sorry to hear that," the guard said "I'll be happy to call you a tow truck."

"Oh, that's awfully sweet of you to offer!" Autumn said. "But that could take a while. You know how long tow trucks take to show up, particularly on weekends. I've got a gas can in my trunk. Would you mind driving me to my car to get the gas can, then to the service station so I can fill it up?"

"I wish I could, but I'm not really allowed to leave my post."

"Oh please?" Autumn stretched the word 'please' out to three syllables. In her experience, that one word, when said properly, could bend most men to her will. It didn't hurt that she was wearing tight jeans and an Oxford shirt with the top two buttons undone, either. "It really wouldn't take very long. My car is just a couple of blocks away and the nearest gas station is right around the corner. I almost made it there before the car conked out. It wouldn't take more than a few minutes to get the gas can, run me to the station and back to my car. I'm guessing maybe 15 minutes, tops."

"Believe me, I'd like to, but I could get into trouble."

"Really?" Autumn said, glancing around in disbelief. "It seems pretty quiet around here. Are you telling me you have to stay here all night? You never get to leave this spot?"

"I get a 30-minute dinner break."

"Well, there you go," Autumn said reasonably. "I'll tell you what, if you can help me out with my car, I'll buy your dinner. We can do both and be back here in 30 minutes."

"I'm not sure," the guard said, and the uncertainty in his voice showed. "I've never done anything like that before."

"Pretty please?" Autumn said, dragging out the 'please' again. "I really have to be at work early tomorrow. It'll be my first day on a new job. You would really be helping me out. And how often does a woman offer to buy you dinner?"

The guard grinned at that. Through the fog of late-night fatigue, it didn't occur to him to question his sudden good fortune too much.

"Oh, all right," he said. "I'll help you get gas and we can swing by a fast food place before I drop you back at your car. But I'll only do this on one condition: You've got to give me your number so we can get together and have a real dinner sometime when I'm off duty."

Autumn smiled much wider. Success. "Well, it sounds like I'll be getting the better end of the deal on both counts. But you're on."

The guard returned her smile and reached across to open the passenger side door of his patrol car. After Autumn climbed inside, they took off in the direction of the Kia Optima she'd left parked a few blocks away on Woodland Street.

She wouldn't remember exactly where the car was, of course, and it would take her twice as long to make the gas run and a trip to the closest burger joint as she'd promised. That would be more than enough time.

It was possible – probably even likely – that the guard would remember her well enough to provide a good description later. If he chose to admit to his superiors that he had allowed a pretty woman to lure him away from his post. And even if they could identify her, so what? It wasn't a crime to run out of gas or ask for help from a stranger.

And even if the guard had the presence of mind to take down the license plate of her Kia, it wouldn't matter. By daybreak, that car would be crushed flatter than a pancake at the junkyard in Joelton - just like the getaway car from the Silly String caper had been.

Hunt Blazen waited until the patrol car was safely out of sight before he made his move. The bolt cutters he lifted from a maintenance bay at one of his dealerships made quick work of the padlock on the gate leading into the construction site. Blazen and his two helpers were quickly inside and ready to proceed with their mission.

The groundbreaking ceremony was planned as a breakfast time event. The first media reports would go out before the opening day games began, allowing Nashville to claim its rightful place on the national stage on one of baseball's most celebrated days of the year.

That did require some advance preparations, though. The breakfast tables and chairs had already been set up under a large open-air canvas tent. The speaker's podium was next to the tent, with the ceremonial groundbreaking shovels already laid out next to a pre-plowed pile of dirt. A 15-foot-tall inflatable baseball player, with bat poised as if ready to swing, overlooked the scene. The inflatable was fed air from an electrical fan that led into the player's left foot. Since it would have taken a while to inflate the player to his full height, the fan had to be kept running through the night with an extension cord and a portable generator.

Three bulldozers were parked a few yards away from the ceremony's staging area. Other than the obligatory shots of VIPs wielding the gold spray-painted shovels to scoop up a few clods of dirt, the bulldozers were expected to provide the event's best visuals for the video and still photographers who would be present. The plan was to have construction workers begin grading work at the site as soon as the ceremony ended.

"You know what to do," Blazen whispered to the other two men. "Go!"

They all sprinted toward the bulldozers. As expected, they found the keys under the floor mats of each vehicle. After all, why bother hiding keys at a fenced and guarded construction site?

Within a few seconds, all three bulldozers had sputtered to life. Hunt Blazen and Autumn Sunshine had chosen their helpers well. Through the Internet, they had met many people who claimed to be sympathetic to the Anti-Arena Agitators' cause and willing to help. But finding two who were truly reliable took a bit of work.

Blazen had spent years on car lots, trying to determine which prospective buyers were serious and which weren't. Autumn Sunshine had spent years working for various causes, which helped her to separate the truly committed from the posers. So they were both good judges of the type of people they needed.

Blazen put his bulldozer into gear and it began rolling forward. After years of being in the automotive business, Blazen had driven just about everything with an internal combustion engine at one time or another. One of the two helpers was an unemployed construction worker and the other worked on his family's farm – so both of them also had experience operating heavy equipment.

As he drove, Blazen flashed back to all the memories he had that were associated with this piece of land. His father had frequently taken him on fishing trips along the riverbanks here, a small strip of nature on the edge of an old friend's junkyard. Those were some of the best days of Blazen's life. And also, one of his worst.

Like many fishermen, Blazen's father liked to take a nip or two while he was out fishing. Nothing major. He wasn't a drunk or anything like that. Just a guy who enjoyed the Great Outdoors a little more if he had a decent buzz going. He wasn't a big beer drinker, either, preferring good stiff mixed drinks – usually laced with vodka or whiskey.

One awful morning, like he had so many mornings before, Blazen's father had risen before dawn to mix a thermos filled with vodka and grape juice. Only in the dimly-lit kitchen, he had mistakenly picked up a bottle of Fabuloso cleaning fluid off the kitchen counter instead of the one containing grape juice. An easy mistake to make, but also a fatal one.

He'd died there on the banks of the Cumberland, right in front of Hunt Blazen's eyes. Foaming at the mouth, body half in and half out of the water until Mr. Grover had run up to help 12-year-old Hunt drag his father up on the bank.

Hunt's uncle ran the family business for eight years, until Hunt was ready to take charge himself.

But his father's death had haunted Hunt for years. He felt like there was nothing he could do to make something positive out of that tragedy. Until he had come up with the idea of building a charter school, with special emphasis on biological sciences, right on the site where he and his father had spent so many days enjoying nature.

That wasn't going to happen now; Blazen understood that. His dreams for the land were gone, along with his old friend's junkyard. Mr. Grover had told Blazen he couldn't fight City Hall. Well, maybe you couldn't beat City Hall, but you sure could fight. Blazen felt good about what he was about to do.

He steered his bulldozer close along one edge of the breakfast tent, snapping the ropes that anchored it to the ground like rubber bands as he went. Turning left, he broke the ties on another side of the tent, which caused it to collapse onto the tables beneath it.

Blazen smiled slightly, before turning toward the podium. The podium disintegrated as the bulldozer knocked it over, then slowly rolled across it. Next came the shovels, which crackled and popped like dry pine needles under the weight of the bulldozer's metal tracks.

Then Blazen turned to the inflatable baseball player. "Batter up," he muttered quietly to himself as he knocked loose the ropes anchoring the inflatable to the ground. When that was done, Blazen guided the bulldozer over the fan at the player's foot.

Freed from its anchors and with an opening now exposed at its foot, the inflatable baseball player shot into the air like a balloon that someone forgot to tie properly. It spun wildly around in circles, with the outstretched bat giving it the appearance of a helicopter with only one blade. In moments, the deflating figure was caught up in the trees along the riverbank.

Blazen stifled a laugh as he maneuvered the bulldozer toward a patch of open space. He lowered the bulldozer's scoop and dragged it in a straight line in one direction for a few yards before turning 150 degrees and repeating the process in a different direction. After completing those two lines, he lifted the scoop until he was in position to draw a line connecting the two other lines he had drawn in the dirt.

The letter "A." He repeated the same digging process two more times next to the first "A" before pointing his bulldozer in the same direction the other two bulldozers were already heading: The tree line at the steep bank leading down to the Cumberland River. All three drivers accelerated their vehicles and then jumped clear just before they tumbled over the precipice toward the swift-moving brown waters.

Blazen and his confederates were already running toward the gate as they heard the bulldozers splashing into the water.

CHAPTER THIRTY

Mayor Kent Gables was thoroughly wrung out by the time his meeting with the Hopewell Full Evangelical Church's ladies auxiliary had ended. He had been invited to speak to the group about how his faith informed his decisions at City Hall. A seemingly easy enough assignment. With religious groups, it was always easy for a skilled politician to figure out which buttons to push.

But between the time Gables had accepted the invitation and his speaking appearance, the ladies auxiliary had taken a field trip to Music Row, the heart of the city's thriving recording industry. Unfortunately for Mayor Gables, to get to Music Row their church bus had to travel through the Music Row Roundabout.

The roundabout's decorative centerpiece was called Musica, a sculpture featuring nine 14-foot-high bronze figures of people frolicking. Naked.

Apparently, this didn't sit too well with the ladies of Hopewell Evangelical. They couldn't understand why the mayor would allow such an abomination to be displayed in such a prominent location in their city.

Gables had tried to explain that the sculpture had been built and installed prior to his term as mayor and that it wasn't in violation of any municipal codes or ordinances. That answer didn't go over too well. Then Gables made it even worse when he pointed out that a lot of great sculptures, including Michelangelo's David, depicted people in the nude.

Gables had thought that reference would make him sound smart. But it would have been smarter to consider his audience. The ladies auxiliary didn't care much what they did across some ocean in Europe. The way they had it figured, they could get the best Italy had to offer at the Olive Garden near Rivergate Mall.

Nashville, they had told him in no uncertain terms, was the buckle of the Bible Belt. As mayor, he needed to be mindful of that. And if he couldn't, well, maybe he needed to spend a little less time reading the city codebook and a little more time reading the Good Book.

Gables had tried to backpedal as fast as he could, but it was obvious he had lost his audience. After one of the longest hours of his life, he was relieved to see Horton Edison waiting for him in the back of the church's cafeteria.

"Get me home, Horton," Gables said after glancing around to make sure he was out of earshot of the irate parishioners.

"Rough gig?" Edison said. He knew it had been. Although he had come in late, hearing the last 15 minutes told him all he needed to know.

"Yeah, you could say that," Gables said. "I thought this one was going to be easy. That was about as much fun as spending a weekend retreat with the Metro council members."

"Maybe you should have suggested that we could dress the statues up in Nashville Stars uniforms." Edison was only half kidding. Pranksters occasionally added clothing to the figures on special occasions – kilts on St. Patrick's Day, Predators uniforms when the hockey team was in the playoffs, etc. But Gables wasn't in the mood for jokes.

"Speaking of the Stars, did you get a chance to meet with the police chief?"

"I did."

"And what have they been able to find out?"

"Not a whole lot, I'm afraid. The vandals cut the lock on the fence and did their work while the security guard was away from his post."

"Why was he away from his post?"

"The story he told his supervisor is that he was on his dinner break when he spotted a woman whose car was broken down on the side of the road. He helped her get some gas and by the time he got back, the damage was done."

"Uh-huh. Wasn't someone supposed to relieve him while he was on his dinner break?"

"Actually, no. Our contract only calls for one officer on duty from dusk to dawn. And federal regulations don't allow us to keep someone on the clock more than eight hours without offering a meal break."

"We're going to fix that, right? We'll have two people on duty from now on so they can take their breaks at different times."

"Sure, we can do that. It'll cost a little extra…"

"For what we're going to be investing in this stadium, it'll be worth it."

"I'll speak to the security company about amending our contract with them."

"Good. What else have you got?"

"Nothing much. One of the three bulldozers actually made it all the way into the river. The other two got hung up in trees and underbrush on the way down. No fingerprints or other clues on any of them."

"And the fence? The lock?"

"Nothing. They must have been wearing gloves."

"Do the cops have any theories about who might have done this?"

"Well, the vandals dug the letters 'AAA' into the turf, so it seems pretty obvious it's either the Anti-Arena Agitators or someone who wants us to think it was the Anti-Arena Agitators."

"So that's it? No leads at all?"

"Well, Mayor, the chief thinks there's at least a possibility that the woman with the car trouble might have been in on it."

"Oh?"

"Yeah, we're talking about a pretty short window of time the guard was away from his post, even with stopping to help her. Now it could be that the vandals just timed everything perfectly – they just watched and waited until the guard left his post – but it could also be that the woman was supposed to slow the guard down to give them a few extra minutes, just in case they needed it."

"Hmmm. What kind of car was the woman driving? Was it the same one that was used in, uh..."

"The Silly String incident? No. The guard said it was some kind of Kia."

"Have the police been on the lookout for it? Have they put out an all-points bulletin?"

Edison tried not to laugh at how stilted the phrase 'all-points bulletin' sounded. "Yes, they've been on the lookout for the car. But they haven't found it yet, Mayor."

"So now we've got two cars they can't find. What is Nashville, the Bermuda Triangle for fugitives' cars?"

"Well, it's an awfully big city, Mayor, with an awful lot of cars and not an awful lot of cops."

"We need more cops, then."

"That's what the police union told you during last year's budget hearings. But we were trying to avoid a tax hike, remember?"

"I'll try to remember that next year."

Edison had his doubts about that. "So anyway, the police aren't sure this woman wasn't exactly what she claimed to be – a driver in distress. But they went ahead and got a description of her from the security guard."

"Well, that's something."

"It's not much of something, really. His description is a little hazy on some of the specifics. For example, he couldn't even remember her eye color. The police chief didn't come right out and say it, but he implied the guard's eyes may have been focused a few inches below the woman's face for a good portion of their time together."

"Wonderful. Not only does the guard miss a bunch of vandals trashing the one patch of land he's supposed to be watching, but he can't remember what this woman looks like. At least above her neckline."

"He did give a description, as best he could remember. The police sketch artist took it all down, just in case."

"OK, good. Let's go with that. Let's get the sketch out to the TV stations and see if that shakes anything loose."

"That would be a bit unusual, sir."

"Why is that, Horton?"

"Usually, we circulate police sketches when violent crimes have been committed, like murder or armed robbery. If we start asking for media help for every vandalism case in the city, that's about all they'll have time to talk about on the evening news. If they would even agree to run all those sketches. It might set a precedent, is what I'm saying."

"Set a precedent. So who cares? These guys, these 'Anti-Arena Agitators,'" Gables said while making an air quotes gesture, "they're doing everything they can to sabotage our stadium project. You can see that, can't you, Horton? Millions of dollars are at stake here. Not to mention the city's prestige. Stopping the Anti-Arena Agitators is a lot more important than worrying about whether we'll cut into the TV stations' time to air more video footage of piano-playing kittens."

"OK. I'll get it done."

"Anything else, Horton?"

"Yes, Mayor. The Anti-Arena Agitators have put out a couple more messages since the construction site got vandalized. I had our IT people track the origin of those messages."

"The public library in Orlando again?"

"No, sir. One message was sent from a Wi-Fi hot spot in the Atlanta airport. The other was sent from a Wi-Fi hot spot in the Charlotte airport. The messages were sent just a few minutes apart."

"So what can we can conclude from that?"

"I think we can conclude that the Anti-Arena Agitators have figured out that we might try to track them down that way so they're messing with us. Atlanta and Charlotte are major airline hubs. Lots of flights between Nashville and both cities. Somebody could fly out to either place, post a message online and catch the next flight back. If they took early enough flights, they could have been back to Nashville by lunchtime."

"So what does this tell us?"

"It tells us that these guys are at least smart enough not to caught because of our efforts to track their computer use."

"So we'll circulate the police sketch. What else should we be doing? Come on, Horton. You're my main guy for a reason. I want you to pull out all the stops on this one."

Edison thought about that for a second. "All the stops?"

"All the stops."

"Including those that might be...a little unconventional?"

"The less said about that, the better, Horton. But yes."

"I think I understand, Mayor."

Gables sighed deeply. "Well, all right, then," he said. "Is there anything else you need from me?"

Edison paused and looked at his surroundings.

"Well, I think the good people here at Hopewell Evangelical would tell you that now would be a really excellent time to start praying."

"Are We Living in the Keystone State? Seems
Like Our Cops Are"
By Gilbert Wise, Sports Columnist

Well, here we go again. Nashville's effort
to land a Major League Baseball franchise
is making national news again – and again,
for all the wrong reasons. This week's
Opening Day was supposed to be a coming out
party of sorts for our fair city. It was
supposed to be the day of the
groundbreaking ceremony for what will be
our new state-of-the-art baseball stadium.
That was ruined, of course, by the group
that calls itself the Anti-Arena Agitators.
The group's members stole into the
construction site like thieves in the
night, destroying construction equipment, a
tent, a podium and the ceremonial
groundbreaking shovels. And let's not
forget what happened to an inflatable
version of our beloved Nashville Stars
icon, who was ejected from the field in a
way no umpire ever would.

Is there any doubt that this was the work
of the Anti-Arena Agitators? Absolutely
none. The group scrawled its calling card –
the initials "AAA" – into the not-yet-built
stadium's turf. In case you haven't driven
by and seen the carnage firsthand, not to
worry: Scenes from the ruined construction
site have been displayed on national news
programs roughly every five minutes. And
again, as usual, our police department has
no solid leads.
You've got to wonder what kind of city
government Mayor Kent Gables is running
when this sort of abomination goes
unpunished.

It shouldn't come as a shocker, though,
after one of AAA's minions got away with

243

sliming Mayor Gables in broad daylight within spitting distance of his office at City Hall. His police are playing the equivalent of a 'prevent' defense that never prevents anything bad from happening. They say that the first 72 hours after a crime has been committed are critical to the investigation of that crime. Tick-tock, Mayor.

At this writing, Metro's finest hadn't made any arrests in the case. The only lead they have shared with us is a drawing of a woman who looks suspiciously like actress Connie Britton, who may or may not have had anything to do with what happened at the construction site. Come to think of it, I actually hope it was Connie Britton. Maybe if she were still working on scenes for "Nashville," the TV show's producers would reimburse us for the damage they did. If they do that and she agrees to sing the National Anthem on Opening Day of the Nashville Stars' first season, then we can call the whole thing even. But seriously, who does Mayor Gables have running this investigation? Inspector Clouseau from those moldy old "Pink Panther" movies?
Should the police department have any higher priorities right now than solving this case? AAA is making a laughingstock out of our city for all of North America to see.

If this had happened in Orlando, you can bet Mayor Skip Goodman's cops would be kicking down doors until the perpetrators were found and hung from a window in Mickey's castle.
Speaking of Orlando, guess what they've been doing while all this has been going on? Building a stadium, that's what. They're already several weeks ahead of us on that score. Photos in the local newspaper there show the steel girders are already up that constitute the stadium's skeleton. Pretty soon, they'll be putting

up the supports for the stadium's retractable roof. Could we start building here? Sure, if we can live with the thought that AAA's supporters might tear it all down as fast as we can put it up. So our only potential lead is this redheaded woman? Well, let's find her. In fact, let's round up every redhead in the city, if we have to. Really, can there be that many? Hey, if that woman from the Wendy's commercials is in town, even she's not above suspicion. You think I'm kidding? I read somewhere that the founder of Wendy's sent his daughter to the University of Florida, so it's easy to imagine where the loyalties of her TV doppelganger lie.

Am I starting to sound paranoid? OK, maybe a little bit.

But I'm firmly convinced that this baseball franchise is exactly what our city needs to truly be a player among the country's elite metro areas. And I'm equally convinced that the overwhelming majority of people who live in this community agree with me. Yet it only takes a few roaches to ruin a punch bowl. And that's what these people who claim allegiance to AAA are. They're just two-legged roaches.

Unfortunately, they're proving as tough to stomp out as their insect counterparts. Right now, instead of spraying insecticide to stop them, our police are spraying the equivalent of powdered sugar. AAA's supporters aren't dying off, they're getting stronger and bolder.

It's time for Mayor Gables to put on his big boy pants and tell his cops to start being more aggressive. Will that give some weed-smoking civil libertarians the willies? Probably. But again, we're talking about protecting the integrity of a project that's worth millions and millions and millions of dollars to Nashville.

When you think about it that way, there's really only one choice. The Wise choice.

CHAPTER THIRTY-ONE

Autumn Sunshine glanced at her watch as she waited at the rear entrance to the Blazen dealership's used car lot. Two in the morning.

A couple of minutes later, Hunt Blazen pulled up in a hot pink Chevrolet HHR. He killed the engine, stepped out and dropped the keys into Autumn's hand with a smile.

"Thank you, sir," Autumn said, returning his smile. "I even like the color."

Blazen chortled. "You know, somehow, I knew you would. That car has been sitting on the back of our lot for months. The car's in perfect working shape, so I'm convinced that the reason we weren't able to sell it was because of the color. It takes a bold woman to drive a car that pink."

"Or an even bolder man," Autumn replied.

"Thanks, but no thanks," Blazen replied. "This one is all yours."

"Well, thank you again. Anything I need to know about this car before I take off?"

"No, like I said, the car runs perfectly. I had been thinking about telling the body shop to paint it a different color. I'm sure we could have sold it then."

"Well, I hate to deprive you of a few more thousands of dollars of profit. I know it would help the Blazen family of dealerships' bottom line."

"Oh, more like hundreds in profit. But this will serve a higher purpose."

Blazen wrapped his arm around Autumn's waist and kissed her, gently and quickly at first and then longer and more passionately.

"Are you sure you have to go?" he asked.

She drew back a little bit and gave him a reassuring look. "We've discussed this. You know I do."

"Yes, we've discussed this. But I don't know that we ever decided it was absolutely necessary."

"Oh, come on, Hunt. That police sketch of me – or at least someone who looks vaguely like me – has been all over TV for the last couple of days. There's a chance somebody could recognize me from that."

"A chance. Not necessarily a good chance."

"But any chance represents a risk. And we've worked too hard, you and I, to take even a small risk of anyone picking up on that."

"So...if someone did recognize you and they arrested you...would you just turn informant and give me up just like that?"

"Oh, no! Well, not at first, anyway. But I would if they were going to waterboard me. I've got a real thing about water up my nose."

"Really? Hey, you've showed me the footage of the time you went skinny dipping in front of that whole crowd and all those TV cameras at Nashville Shores. You didn't seem to be worried about water up your nose that day."

"I was caught up in the heat of the moment. But that raises another good point. I've been on TV. If anybody who saw that footage put that together with the police sketch..."

"Speaking for all the men of Nashville, I would respectfully submit that no one who saw those TV news reports was looking at your face."

Autumn snorted in mock protest and punched Blazen playfully in the shoulder. "You're so bad. But, in all seriousness, if the cops pulled me over and arrested me tonight, they could interrogate me from now until the end of time and I'd never say a word about us or the

Anti-Arena Agitators. As you know, I've been in jail a few times before."

"That's right. I forgot I was dating a hardened criminal."

"And I'm dating a guy who wears a sheep head mask and sprays ball players and mayors for kicks."

"Oh, you don't think I enjoyed that, do you?" Blazen said with mock indignity.

Autumn held her thumb and forefinger about half an inch apart. "Just a little bit."

"OK, maybe a little bit. " Blazen chuckled again, then paused to think for a moment. "Autumn, do you think what we're doing is making a difference? I mean, any of it?"

"Hmm, what?" Autumn replied. "Are you kidding me? You *know* we're making a difference. When all of this started, people were ready to just accept that Nashville needed a baseball team – no matter what it cost, no matter what the consequences. But what we're doing, it's opened people's eyes! You've made them stop and think. You made them wonder, with so many other needs out there, does our city government need to be spending millions and millions of dollars on a ball field?"

"OK, OK. Maybe we've changed a few people's minds. But is it enough to really make a difference?"

"Of course! Do you know what's been going on all over this town, Hunt? People have been passing out bumper stickers at neighborhood meetings. Do you know what those bumper stickers say? 'I roll with the sheep man.' And they've got a big picture of a sheep on them. And people are actually putting them on their cars. I've seen two or three of them driving around East Nashville. And a friend of a friend told me that she saw someone from that downtown business owners' association sporting one on his Mercedes. So don't tell me that doesn't mean anything."

Blazen sighed. "OK, it means something. I'm still not sure it means enough. The mayor and council are still pushing pretty hard for this thing."

"And so are those people down in Orlando," Autumn said. "Have you read the papers? They've already got what they call the 'skeleton' of their stadium up. If they get their stadium building before we do, that could make a big difference on who gets the team, right? And thanks to your fine work, the people who want the team here haven't gotten very far on the construction work at all."

Blazen laughed at the memory. "It did feel good to bulldoze everything in sight."

"And you were so good at it! At least, from what I've heard on the news. I wasn't there."

"Right, right. I hope that security guard wasn't too disappointed that you gave him a fake number."

"Hey, 867-5309. It's in a song by Tommy Tutone. If he didn't pick up on that, he deserves to be disappointed."

They laughed together for a moment, then Autumn looked at her watch again.

"Well, it's late," she said. "I need to get on the road."

"So how far do you think you'll make it tonight?"

"I'll probably stop to crash somewhere in Missouri. Maybe Kansas, if I'm not too sleepy."

"And you expect to be in San Francisco...when, in three days?"

"That sounds about right. I can crash with a girlfriend of mine out there."

Blazen grabbed Autumn's hand and gave it a squeeze. "Are you sure this is the best place for you to go? San Francisco's a really big city. With millions and millions of people. All it takes is for one of them to spot you and turn you in."

Autumn laughed hard and squeezed Hunt's hand back hard. "Oh, come on, Hunt. They're not looking for a serial killer. Chances are, nobody outside of the range of the Nashville TV stations has even seen that police sketch. And if they did, so what? We're talking about a little vandalism here. California already has five Major League baseball teams, so nobody out there is going to even understand what all the fuss is about here in Nashville. Plus, big cities are a perfect place to hide. There are so many people and everybody's got so much going on in their own lives that they can't be bothered to notice what complete strangers are doing. Plus, after I hang with my girlfriend for a couple of days, I think I'll head over to an ashram I know about for a couple of days. I need to meditate and find my center again. That'll help me figure out what our next moves should be."

"And what if a cop sees you on the road?"

"First of all, this car doesn't exactly match the description of the one from the construction site, does it?" Autumn said, nodding at the HHR. "Having a car dealership – and having a friend with a junkyard – makes it easy to get and dispose of getaway cars whenever we need them, right?"

"Well, eventually we are going to run out of the slow-selling models..."

"Ha. Ha. Second of all, I'll be hundreds of miles from Nashville before I stop for the night. And third of all, what are the cops going to do if they do happen to see me while I'm driving? Pull me over for being red-headed? That's profiling. And if there's some kind of advocacy group for the redheaded people of the world – and I'm sure there is – then we might have a terrific class action lawsuit on our hands."

"OK, OK. You've made your point. So you'll call me when you get there?"

"Unless I pick up some hitchhiker who looks like Brad Pitt along the way."

Blazen's face went blank.

"Oh, come on, honey. What's Brad Pitt got on the Sheep Man? And I'd roll with you anywhere."

CHAPTER THIRTY-TWO

No part of the United States is immune from natural disasters. In California, there are earthquakes and mudslides. In the Rocky Mountain states, there are wildfires. Across the northern tier of states, the risk of blizzards. In the Midwest and Southeast, tornadoes. And Florida, of course, is known for its hurricanes.

For most Floridians, that isn't as bad as it sounds. After all, with all the advances in modern meteorology, Floridians typically learn about dangerous tropical weather while it's still somewhere off the coast of Africa. That gives them days to prepare for the worst. And more often than not, the worst never happens.

Hurricanes form, then fizzle out. Or they never make landfall. Or they hit some other spot along the North American coast. The unlucky Floridian might experience an actual hurricane once in his or her lifetime.

Which most would probably consider an acceptable risk in exchange for warm, sunny weather nearly year-round. Except hurricanes aren't the only natural disasters to plague Florida.

States such as Texas, Oklahoma, Kansas and Nebraska are generally considered to be part of what is called "Tornado Alley" – but in reality, in addition to the occasional hurricane, Florida is hit by more tornadoes per square mile than any other state in the country.

And, unlike the hurricanes, the tornadoes typically strike without much warning. That was the case with the tornadoes that rolled through the greater Orlando area in April of 2018.

Several of them hit well after midnight, covering an area of greater Orlando spanning the outlying suburbs "from Oviedo to Ocoee," as one of the TV stations would later report.

The twisters didn't discriminate. They leveled mobile home parks, rows of historic old bungalows, cheap cookie-cutter subdivisions and palatial estates. Some of the more poorly constructed homes would have come down if the Big Bad Wolf had started huffing and puffing. But even those built to state-of-the-art hurricane resistant standards were no match for 250 mile-per-hour winds.

It took the storms less than an hour to move through the area, but in that time, they managed to reduce large chunks of Central Florida to scattered piles of rubble. Including what had been a partially built baseball stadium.

The actual construction work hadn't gotten very far along, but many of the building materials had already been delivered and stacked at the site. The tornadoes had picked them up and redistributed them over a five-mile radius.

The Scorpions Den, Skip Goodman's legacy to the city of Orlando, was no more.

CHAPTER THIRTY-THREE

Hunt Blazen stared at his computer screen, uncertain what his next move should be. He was seated at one of the public computer terminals in the Nashville Public Library, checking e-mails sent to the Anti-Arena Agitators when one of them practically jumped off the screen at him.

It took a while to sift through the run-of-the-mill messages of support for AAA's efforts, which were sprinkled occasionally with a critical missive or two from sports lovers who claimed Blazen and his minions were trying to hold back Nashville's progress.

When he checked his inbox every couple of days, it wasn't unusual for Blazen to read messages from a few more people volunteering to help. A couple of them might actually be serious. After all, that's how Blazen had found the two guys who'd helped him take the bulldozers at the construction site out for a swim.

But this was something different. This could be a real game-changer. He read the message again.

BlueMoon: Mr. Sheepshead, I have inside information that I believe may be useful to you and the rest of the Anti-Arena Agitators. I have been directly involved in the city of Nashville's efforts to bring a Major League Baseball team here. Are you interested?

Blazen was. But he wasn't sure exactly how to proceed. He and Autumn Sunshine had grilled the two volunteers for the construction site extensively before agreeing to accept their help. They had to determine: A) If the men were serious; B) were they brave enough to participate in an illegal and risky operation; and C) were they actually able to drive bulldozers?

It turned out the answers to all of those questions had been yes. Blazen and Autumn had taken a risk and it had worked out. While Autumn was a fugitive – sort of – no one knew anything about Hunt or the volunteers who had been involved. Was this lead also worth the risk? Blazen wished Autumn were around to act as a sounding board. But they had both decided to keep their communications infrequent and low key for the time being.

Blazen took a deep breath and started typing under his login name. A box popped up indicating that BlueMoon was still online, so his response would appear as an instant message.

Sheepshead: I might be interested. Can you tell me more?

The cursor blinked for a few seconds, then a pen symbol popped up to indicate that BlueMoon was typing a response.

BlueMoon: Yes. I was hired to prepare some information on the financial feasibility of bringing a team to Nashville. Much of what I discovered during my work has gone ignored and unreported.

Sheepshead: A lot of us are unappreciated in our jobs.

BlueMoon: No doubt. But there's a lot more at stake than just that. We're talking about potentially millions of taxpayer dollars.

Sheepshead: Yes, we are. But why are you telling me this now?

BlueMoon: I've been conflicted about this project from the very beginning. You see, I'm not really much of a baseball fan myself. But I am a loyal Nashvillian. And I like to see our city's money spent wisely.

Sheepshead: OK, but again, why now? The Metro Council has already agreed to fund the stadium project. If your role with the city is what you say it is, you probably helped the mayor and council figure out how to pay for it. Isn't it a little late for a change of heart now?

BlueMoon: Not necessarily, thanks to your work at the construction site.

Blazen paused and stared at the ceiling for a second before typing his reply.

Sheepshead: What makes you think that I had anything to do with that? I'm just a guy who runs a website.

BlueMoon: Oh, please. I get that you don't want to come right out and admit you were involved, but I know you were.

Again Blazen hesitated.

Sheepshead: I'm not admitting to anything, but why do you think there's still a chance to stop this project?

BlueMoon: I think people were beginning to have a lot of second thoughts about the stadium deal before the council voted to approve the funding. At that point, opponents thought there was no point in fighting any more because it was a done deal. But after that incident at the construction site, I think they are emboldened again. After all, the city hasn't really passed the point of no return yet. The city doesn't have a signed contract with anyone to build this stadium – not with a group of team owners and not with the league. All of what they've done so far has been done on spec, with the hope that building a stadium would influence Major League Baseball to give Nashville a franchise. But the city could just walk away from the whole deal now, without any legal obligation to anybody.

Sheepshead: Still, why would the city do that? All that 'incident at the construction site' (as you called it) did was slow things down a little.

BlueMoon: Maybe. But part of the rush here has been the perception that Orlando is so far ahead of Nashville in its efforts to get a stadium built. Those tornadoes down in Orlando set their project back a lot. All the work they had already done was wiped out. And they lost a lot of money on the construction materials that were stored at the site. It will take a while to process the insurance claims to get reimbursement for what they lost to the storm down there. And it'll take more time to order new materials and get things re-started.

Sheepshead: And?

BlueMoon: And suddenly the time pressure isn't so great. Which means Nashville has a little more time to think about its next move. And usually more time translates into better decision making.

Another pause.

Sheepshead: Not always. In my line of work, I often find that people who take a long time to make decisions aren't really ready to make decisions at all.

BlueMoon: You're sort of making my point for me. The longer Nashville waits before taking definitive action, the less likely it's going to be that the city gets the new franchise, right?

Sheepshead: OK, so let's assume you're right. What's changed? Why would the city want to delay moving forward now?

BlueMoon: Well, I have some information that the Metro Council didn't know about when it made its decision to fund the stadium.

Sheepshead: Such as?

BlueMoon: You saw the economic impact report provided by One Nashville!

Sheepshead: Sure. It was in all the papers. So what?

BlueMoon: What if I told you that I had been hired to do an economic impact study on the city's behalf? And when I told them that study might not show as much of an impact as they were expecting, they didn't seem too thrilled about that.

Sheepshead: Interesting. So what happened?

BlueMoon: I did what they paid me to do, which was to keep working on the study. But then One Nashville!

came out with its study – which of course showed a huge economic impact if the city got a team. And suddenly, they weren't interested in my study any more. They had what they needed to justify building the stadium.

Sheepshead: So, why your sudden change of heart? As you say, you got paid to do a study. You were getting paid regardless, right?

BlueMoon: I was, until that happened. Then I got fired from my job.

Sheepshead: The city fired you?

BlueMoon: No, I wasn't a city employee. I worked for a private firm that was contracted to do the work. And they fired me because my boss thought the city wanted a study that showed a higher economic impact. Like the study One Nashville! did.

Sheepshead: You know, it wouldn't be too hard to verify that part of your story. The names of the contractors the city hires are a matter of public record. And so are the services they perform. It wouldn't take much for me to find out if the city hired a firm to do an economic impact study.

BlueMoon: No, it wouldn't. And if you asked about me by name at that firm, my boss could confirm that I'm no longer employed there.

Sheepshead: So what's your name?

BlueMoon: Iris Moon.

Sheepshead: And your boss is? Or was?

BlueMoon: Devin Underwood.

Sheepshead: Devin Underwood? He's a pretty big name in this town. If you're telling the truth, it shouldn't be hard to verify. I'll check this out.

BlueMoon: You do that. And after you've done that, I'd like to meet with you face-to-face.

Sheepshead: We'll see about that.

BlueMoon: What have you got to lose?

Sheepshead: You could be anyone. You could be a cop.

BlueMoon: Well, first of all, as you say, you haven't admitted to anything. And if I were a cop, I'm pretty sure that it would be entrapment for me to approach you the way I have. And I'm just offering you information. Last I checked, that's not illegal. What you do with that information once you have it is up to you. So what do you say?

Another long pause. Blazen tried to decide what Autumn would do, if she were here. Oh, who was he kidding? Autumn had stripped down naked and jumped into freezing water in front of a crowd of people because of a cause she believed in. Now he needed to take a plunge of a different sort.

Sheepshead: OK, OK. If what you've told me checks out, where do you want to meet?

BlueMoon: I'll give you the address of a place downtown. I'll be sitting alone at a table in the back row. I'll see you there at 10 p.m. the day after tomorrow.

CHAPTER THIRTY-FOUR

Raymond Goldfarb wasn't used to being kept waiting.

Not that he was an impatient man. In his previous life as executive director of Ray of Hope, he'd had to spend a great deal of his time raising funds to support the organization's research work. That involved a lot of waiting – and also a lot of indulging the egos of people whose egos really didn't need any further indulging.

As baseball commissioner, his life had changed. Now people waited on him, although he was too nice to keep them waiting any longer than he absolutely had to. Despite his busy schedule, he tried not to be late to his appointments. And when he was, he apologized profusely for it. It didn't matter if it was a group of Little League players or a multimillionaire team owner in his outer office. The way Goldfarb saw it, common courtesy was common courtesy.

But he knew not everyone shared his views. Some people in positions of importance seemed to delight in keeping others waiting. Goldfarb always saw that as a sign of insecurity.

Yet here he was, in the lobby of the most luxurious condominium high rise in Las Vegas, waiting for an audience with a man he really didn't want to see. Goldfarb's thoughts turned again to how he had gotten himself into this situation.

Yes, he'd made a mistake. A bad mistake. But everyone made mistakes. And most people didn't have to pay for them the way Goldfarb had. It hardly seemed fair. Then again, Goldfarb knew better than to expect life to be fair...

The phone at the concierge's desk buzzed, interrupting Goldfarb's thoughts. After a few moments of conversation, the concierge hung up the phone and turned to Goldfarb.

"Mr. Scales will see you now, sir," the concierge said. "He said that he would meet you at the rooftop pool. When you get into the elevator, just hit 'R.' Mr. Scales has unlocked the floor so you can ride all the way to the top."

Goldfarb nodded in thanks and followed those instructions. In less than a minute, he was walking out of the elevator onto a pool deck forty floors above the Las Vegas Strip. It was already warm on an April morning – and being closer to the sun didn't seem to help.

"Ray Goldfarb!" a man in a silk short-sleeved shirt and Bermuda shorts called out from a deck chair near the pool's nine-foot-high waterfall. "So good to see you again, my friend!"

"Mr. Scales," Goldfarb said stiffly. "Thank you for taking time to meet with me."

"Well sure, Ray, I'm always glad to see you. Come on over and have a seat. I'd offer you a bloody Mary or something, but I guess you're not drinking any more."

It was an unnecessary dig, but not at all out of character for Richard Scales. A person didn't become the owner of four of Sin City's largest casinos without having sharp elbows. And Scales tended to throw his elbows whether he needed to or not.

Goldfarb eased himself uncomfortably into a deck chair next to Scales'. They were facing the circular pool, which had an image of a $1,000 casino chip painted across its bottom. Scales was seated strategically close to a well-stocked tiki bar staffed by an attractive female bartender in a bikini. On the opposite side of the tiki bar was a jacuzzi, also circular, with a $100 casino chip painting on its bottom. Deck chairs and small tables were scattered at various spots around the pool. Most of them were empty – with the exception of two across from Scales and Goldfarb where a pair of very buxom brunettes were sunbathing.

Scales leaned across his chair to nudge Goldfarb on the shoulder, then nodded his head toward the two women.

"Not bad, huh?" Scales said. "Of course, I know you really prefer blondes..."

Yes, no doubt about it: Scales liked to throw his elbows.

"I want this to stop," Goldfarb said.

"You want what to stop, Mr. Commissioner?"

"What we've been doing."

"What we've been doing? Don't you mean what you've been doing? I haven't done anything yet."

"You know very well what I mean, Mr. Scales. This game we've been playing about the new franchise."

"Well, like I just said, I haven't done anything. And all you've done is announce that the league was looking to add another team. Which is your job. Everything that's happened since then in Nashville and Orlando has just been the result of free market forces at work. That's what happens in America. Don't you love America, Commissioner?"

Goldfarb ignored the taunt. *There are mistakes and then there are mistakes,* he thought to himself. Some mistakes a person makes do relatively little harm and are quickly forgotten. The one Goldfarb had made continued to haunt him.

He'd loved his wife Francine will all his heart. He couldn't remember what his life was like before he knew her.

She was a natural blond beauty who was a 4-H Queen who had participated in a pageant at the Iowa State Fair during her senior year of high school. She'd gotten her degree in public relations from Iowa State University.

They had been childhood friends, but that didn't make Francine any less impressed when Goldfarb had moved from working a couple of stints in administrative jobs at different nonprofit agencies to founding Ray of Hope at age 30.

She'd supported Ray of Hope's mission to help find treatments or outright cures for sexually transmitted diseases. Ray of Hope was a small operation at the time, but Francine could tell by the quietly confident way Goldfarb carried himself that her husband was going places.

And she went with him. Francine took a job on Ray of Hope's communications staff, then later moved into a position as an executive vice president. Her counsel helped Goldfarb grow Ray of Hope into a large and successful nonprofit.

Their marriage had lasted 30 years, when the awful news had come on their anniversary date. Francine had been to the doctor for a routine checkup a few days prior, but the call about her lab results came while she and Raymond were having their anniversary dinner. Francine had developed an aggressive form of lung cancer and had only a few months to live.

Raymond resigned from his post at Ray of Hope, turning the organization he'd built from scratch over to the board of directors, and stayed by his wife's side to the very end, doing the best he could to ease her suffering. Raymond had always been a strong man, practically unflappable in the face of the challenges he encountered throughout his career as a nonprofit administrator. But Francine's death caused a festering wound deep inside of him that would not go away.

He turned to alcohol to help him ease the pain, with only limited success. Getting sufficiently drunk would help him forget about Francine for a while, but the pain returned whenever he sobered up. He spent most of his time at loose ends, either drunk or hung over.

When Major League Baseball began searching for a new commissioner to help restore the integrity of the game, Raymond's friends had encouraged him to seek the position. He'd kept his drinking well hidden and was publicly known for his integrity and managerial efficiency. His friends had convinced him that a new job might help him cope with his grief in a more constructive fashion.

For the most part, it did. Raymond immersed himself in his new job as Major League Baseball's commissioner the same way he had for years with Ray of Hope. But there were times, particularly when he was all alone and his mind wasn't otherwise occupied, when the sadness slipped back into his life. And he continued to drink to help fight off those moments.

As the first anniversary of his wife's death approached, he knew that he couldn't spend that night alone. Although he wasn't much of a gambler, he decided to spend a few days in Las Vegas. He figured that Sin City's nonstop assault on the senses could help distract him.

He spent the anniversary night at a casino bar, where he had a few too many White Russians. Also in the bar that night was a pretty blond woman who bore a striking resemblance to Francine in her younger days. The woman was friendly – too friendly, Raymond realized in hindsight – and they had ended up in bed together that night in the casino's hotel.

The whole thing had been a setup. Richard Scales had spies everywhere, so he knew when the commissioner of Major League Baseball had arrived in his town. The woman was a prostitute whom Scales occasionally hired when he needed to provide female companionship for some of his business contacts.

Scales hadn't known about the prostitute's resemblance to Goldfarb's late wife; that was just a coincidence. But it was no coincidence that she'd been in the bar that night and seduced Goldfarb. The room she'd taken him to had been fitted with hidden cameras to film whatever took place there.

It wasn't long after Goldfarb had returned to New York that he received some photos in the mail. Most of them were stills taken of him and the woman in the throes of lovemaking. A couple were mug shots of the woman taken following her numerous arrests on prostitution charges.

Scales hadn't asked Goldfarb directly for money. In fact, he didn't make any demands initially. He just pointed out to Goldfarb that for someone with a squeaky clean image, the photos would not just be embarrassing, but ruinous to his career.

So Goldfarb had played along and done what Scales had asked him to do. Some of the things, like awarding the franchise to San Juan, weren't all that bad. Putting a Major League Baseball team in Puerto Rico made good business sense, even if he was doing it for the wrong reasons.

But when Goldfarb had, at Scales' urging, announced an open competition for the second new franchise, it had set up an arms race of sorts between Nashville and Orlando. Both cities were so anxious to get a team that their political leaders had agreed to commit millions and millions of dollars for new stadiums and the infrastructure needed to support them.

Goldfarb understood Scales' plans – and he knew that the endgame was close at hand. While Scales held leverage over him, Goldfarb didn't see an obvious way to thwart his plans. But Goldfarb had arranged this meeting with the hopes of accelerating the process to reach that endgame as soon as possible, to reduce the pain and disappointment it would cause for so many people involved.

It was for that reason that Goldfarb sat on the fancy condominium's pool deck next to a man he could hardly stand to be in the same room with and endured his stupid little insults.

"Listen, Mr. Scales," Goldfarb said quietly. "I've done everything you've asked. And this has unfolded pretty much the way you thought it would. Nashville and Orlando city governments have both committed to spending amounts necessary to build state-of-the-art baseball stadiums. Stadiums with retractable roofs, even. Although that's not a standard feature at stadiums in many of the league's cities."

"They have. So you've done your job well so far, Commissioner."

"But this charade has gone on long enough. Orlando already began construction on its stadium. And incurred what will probably turn out to be millions of dollars worth of expenses due to the tornado that destroyed what they had been building there."

"Well, you can't blame me for that. I may be a master planner, but I don't control the weather. And surely the city has adequate insurance to take care of those costs."

"Nevertheless," Goldfarb said, "those two cities have behaved as you predicted. You have got what you wanted. Now it's time to wrap this up."

Scales laughed and gestured for the bartender to bring him another drink. "Are you sure I can't order you one?" he said. "I won't tell anyone if you won't."

"Mr. Scales, I..."

"All right! All right! You want me to make my announcement that I'm interested in owning a Major League franchise here in Las Vegas, so I'll go ahead and do that. I'm anxious to tell the world about it, anyway. But I need you to do one more thing for me first."

"What's that?"

"Well, for years, professional sports have avoided Las Vegas because of the tie-ins to the gambling industry. Well, if you don't count boxing or the University of Nevada-Las Vegas Runnin' Rebels basketball teams of a couple of decades ago, that is. Now Las Vegas has a hockey team and will soon have a football team coming from Oakland. Meanwhile, people's views about gambling have changed. Casinos used to be considered seedy places run by people with mob ties. And sequestered in a few unapologetically decadent places like here and Atlantic City."

Scales accepted his drink from the bartender, dismissed her with a pat on the butt and took a long sip from his glass before continuing.

"Now gambling is everywhere. On Indian reservations and on these silly 'off-shore' places developers have built on stilts along rivers and lagoons all through the American heartland. God, you've got to love how people can compartmentalize their vices. They'll say gambling is so awful that they don't want it legalized in their towns. But a short walk down a gangplank to a place built on top of a few feet of muddy water? Well, sure, that's just fine. I'm surprised that people who want to legalize drug sales never tried to build shops out over the water. Apparently, anything goes there. And look at how the clientele at casinos has changed. It used to be a bunch of guys who looked like they would just as soon stab you as give you the time of day. Now casinos are filled with grandmas and grandpas who are intent on spending their final years on Earth pumping their children and grandchildren's inheritances into slot machines."

"I'm not sure I'm catching the segue, Mr. Scales."

"The segue, Mr. Commissioner, is that gambling casinos are no more threatening or undesirable to people these days than a Disney resort. Maybe less undesirable than resorts with parking lots packed with tour buses full of kids. So what I need you to do, Mr. Commissioner, is make a public statement that you're not concerned about gambling – when properly regulated and controlled – damaging the integrity of

Major League Baseball. In fact, you see no danger in having casinos and baseball stadiums share space on the same property."

"You can't be serious," Goldfarb said. "Don't you think that would be a little obvious, given that I haven't officially announced a decision to give the franchise to Las Vegas? Why would I just start talking about gambling out of the blue?"

"Oh, that's easy. You just need to call a news conference and we'll have a reporter or two there with planted questions. It will all seem very spontaneous. You're just answering some hypotheticals about gambling. Which will turn out to be less hypothetical when I announce my plans."

"So that's it then. You don't just want to build a stadium for a Major League team. You want to build another casino next to it."

"And a couple of restaurants and some other retail shops."

"That sounds like a pretty expensive proposition."

"Oh yes, it will be. But don't you see, Commissioner? That's why I needed you to put the bait out there for Orlando and Nashville. I needed a couple of cities – and I didn't necessarily know it would be those two, but I knew there would be some – that would start trying to outdo each other by committing to build fancier and fancier stadiums. In the gambling world, we call this bidding up the stakes."

"But by bidding up the stakes, you've increased the cost that you'll have to pay to get a project like that done."

"Not me. *I* won't have to pay the construction costs. Nashville and Orlando have set the standard by having their local governments pay stadium construction costs. When I make the announcement about my bid for the franchise in Las Vegas, I'll talk about my plans for a mixed-use development that includes both the casino and the stadium. It'll be a better bid than the stadium-only projects Orlando and Nashville have proposed. And officials from Las Vegas, Clark County and the state of Nevada will recognize that and fall all over themselves finding a way to publicly finance the deal."

"So then you'll have another casino. Plus a stadium with a Major League baseball team."

"That's the short view, yes."

"There's a long view?"

"Well, of course. I'll have the same people from my company that I've used to design and build my other casinos handle the development of this project. So once we've got this fancy stadium, casino and entertainment center built, it won't be long before teams in every other Major League city are going to want one of their own to keep pace. And guess which company will be the only one in the country with experience building a project like that? And the only one with experience running a casino attached to a stadium?"

"You're making a lot of assumptions that may or may not hold true," Goldfarb said.

"Hey, I'm from Las Vegas," Scales said cheerily. "Taking risks is what we do around here. But this isn't as big a risk as you might think. Once you've publicly declared that Major League Baseball doesn't have a problem with gambling and that Las Vegas will be getting the new franchise, the rest of the cards will fall into place. If you'll pardon the pun."

Goldfarb shook his head and silently stood up to leave. Before he could, Scales reached out to grab his wrist and whispered in a low voice.

"Don't feel too bad, Commissioner Goldfarb," he said. "You may have set some kind of record for the most expensive lay in the history of mankind."

CHAPTER THIRTY-FIVE

It took a few seconds for Hunt Blazen's eyes to adjust to the dim lighting in the bar. Most places in downtown Nashville were overrun by tourists this time of night, but this one seemed to cater more to the business crowd. Lots of guys and a few women in their business suits. About three out of every four were staring and poking at the screens of their smart phones. The rest were talking and laughing in really loud voices.

Over the din, Blazen could barely hear a band playing a fairly decent cover of Blue Oyster Cult's "The Reaper." He barely glanced that direction, though. He was looking toward the back of the room for the woman he was supposed to meet.

She wasn't hard to spot. She was seated alone at a table in the back of the room, just like she said she would be. She reminded Blazen of Bailey, the hot nerdy character on that old TV show, *WKRP in Cincinnati*. Only on the TV show, no one ever noticed Bailey because she was always being overshadowed by Loni Anderson's blond bombshell character.

No one was overshadowing this woman. In fact, it appeared she was in the process of fighting off the advances of two lawyerly-looking guys as Blazen made his way toward her.

"You don't have to be like *that!*" one of the men said as he and his friend tried to ease away from the woman's table as gracefully as possible.

"Bye!" Iris Moon called after them. "Don't forget to type up your account of this in your TPS reports!"

The men almost bumped into Blazen as they stumbled past him, muttering to each other about how crazy women could be. Blazen walked to the spot where the men had been standing a few moments before.

"Dr. Moon?" he said cautiously.

"Yes, that's right. And you're Hunt Blazen."

"How did you..."

"I recognized you from your TV commercials. You're the guy with the craaaaazy deals, right?"

"Um, that's right," Blazen said uncertainly. He wasn't sure exactly how to approach this conversation.

"Well, would you like to have a seat? If you don't, then other guys in this place will think you're just trying to hit on me. And if they don't see you sit down, they may think you're not getting anywhere with me. Which means some of them might come over and try to talk to me, too. Our private conversation wouldn't be so private if that happens. So, like I said, why don't you have a seat?"

Blazen did. In the background, the band was playing Kenny Loggins and Steve Perry's "Don't Fight It."

"How do I know I can trust you?" Blazen asked.

"You don't," Moon said. "It's really a leap of faith. But since you're here, it seems to me that you've already decided to take that leap. So I think you must really be interested in the information I have to share with you."

"OK, so I'm interested," Blazen said. "So what can you tell me?"

"What do you want to know?"

"What do I want to know? I want to know anything and everything that could possibly stop the city of Nashville from getting a Major League baseball team."

"I kind of figured that out from your website. But why do you care so much whether Nashville gets a team or not?"

"If you're asking me that question, then you haven't studied my website very carefully. I mean, come on. I'm a regular guy. And I like sports as much as the next guy. But do you think this is fair, the way this is happening? The city is commandeering property from private owners to build a stadium using public money – and don't try to tell me it's anything but public money – in the hope that a sports league that generates billions of dollars will give permission to a group of owners who have billions of dollars to use that publicly-funded stadium for a team to play a children's game?"

"So you're not buying the argument that the team, playing what you call a children's game, wouldn't bring economic benefits to the city?"

"The question is, as with almost anything in life, do those benefits outweigh the costs? And would the city still be able to get those benefits without giving up so much?"

"Well, the counter-argument there is that if Nashville wasn't willing to spend what it takes to get a team, then other cities would. Like Orlando, for example."

"Right, right. It's a vicious cycle. Cities pitted against each other in an economic arms race. Nobody dares not to play the game. But what if...all those cities got together at the same time and decided not to play the game? What if they told all those sports leagues and prospective team owners out there that they were welcome to have teams play in their cities, but the teams would have to be financially self-sustaining? And by the way, those teams already *are* self-sustaining. They make plenty of money just doing what they do. But they're not going to turn down free stadiums or whatever other perks cities desperate for some sort of validation are willing to give them. Is any of this making sense?"

Blazen was so intent on the conversation that he hadn't noticed that the band had stopped playing and apparently gone on a break.

"I think I understand where you're coming from," Dr. Moon said, appearing a bit distracted.

"So what's your story, Dr. Moon? Why are you willing to betray the trust that the city has put in you as its economic advisor?"

"Who says I have?"

As she said that, Hunt Blazen noticed there was a man standing beside him. He assumed it was another one of Iris Moon's admirers. He turned his eyes toward the man, planning to say something intended to shoo him away. And then he recognized the mayor's chief of staff.

"Hunt Blazen. I must say I'm a little bit surprised," Horton Edison said. "Or should I call you 'Sheepshead'? That's the nickname everyone seems to be using for your alter ego these days."

Blazen lurched out of his seat, preparing to bolt out the door. Edison stopped him by putting his hand against Blazen's chest – lightly, not forcefully.

"So what do you think happens next, Hunt? You want to run out into the streets and have a dramatic foot chase scene, just like in the movies? Maybe one where we somehow end up jumping from rooftop to rooftop? Or in your line of work, I'm guessing a car chase would be more your speed, if you'll pardon the pun. And speaking of cars, I'm betting it wouldn't be too hard for me to place a call to the police chief and get him to call a judge to get a warrant to search your car dealerships. And I bet if we had someone check over your inventory lists, they would discover that you've got at least a couple of vehicles missing that haven't been sold or reported stolen. Maybe cars that match the description of those used in crimes committed by the Anti-Arena Agitators. A group that you clearly belong to since you responded to Dr. Moon's messages. So maybe instead of running out of here like a kid who just egged the teacher's house, why don't we sit down and have a little talk?"

Reluctantly, Blazen sat back down. Edison joined him at the table.

"You know, I can't say I'm *totally* surprised," Edison said. "The mayor told me you were pretty upset when you found out that the stadium was going to be built on that property you were interested in. Then again, this whole deal with the team and the stadium has upset a lot of people around town. Melvin and Ingrid Swift of that Clean & Green neighborhood group haven't been happy because they feel like the mayor's been paying too much attention to downtown at the expense of other parts of town. They made sense as potential suspects because we knew Sheepshead had a female accomplice. However, I've met Ingrid Swift on numerous occasions. And I saw the description the security guard gave police of the woman he helped the night the bulldozers at the stadium construction site all decided to go for a midnight swim. And, trust me, Ingrid Swift doesn't match that description."

Edison paused and glanced at Blazen, who said nothing.

"Thor Jantsen of the Convention & Visitors Bureau was a possible suspect, too," Edison continued. "Thor doesn't like the idea of spending a good chunk of the tax money collected downtown on the stadium when there are other things it could be paying for. But I have to admit that my money was on Big Paul, at least based on motive. I know he was incensed when he found out the mayor was going to try to get a Major League team without even giving him the courtesy of telling him first. Then again, the guy in the sheepshead mask on the Internet had a slightly slimmer physique than Big Paul. And I'd have a hard time imagining him creeping around construction sites at night, at least not without being able to load up on carbs at a nearby food truck. But you, well, you've kept yourself in pretty good shape, Hunt."

"I'm not sure I know what you're talking about, Horton." Blazen was scowling, although he was trying to keep his voice calm.

"Let's don't play games here, Hunt. Do you think you're Bruce Wayne or something? As much as we'd all like to, we don't get the luxury of having alter egos."

"Again, I'm not sure I'm following you, Horton."

"If you were trying to sell me a car, I believe you might be able to snow me, Hunt. But let's look at the situation: Dr. Moon reached out to you at the Anti-Arena Agitators website. She set up a clandestine meeting. And now you're here."

"You can't prove anything." The scowl deepened.

"Oh, you just happened to show up here at Capital Indiscretions tonight, came over to see Dr. Moon, who you don't know, and just happened to strike up a conversation about the stadium project. Because that always makes such a good icebreaker when you've just met someone."

"This wouldn't stand up in court. It's entrapment or something." Blazen was turning red and beads of sweat were popping up on his forehead. Edison couldn't help but think about all the car buyers who had been forced to sit in uncomfortably hot sales offices at Blazen's dealerships through the years.

"You're looking at this all wrong, Hunt. We didn't set up this meeting to slap the cuffs on you and haul you off to jail. I'm not a cop. Are you a cop, Dr. Moon?"

"No, I'm not," Moon said.

"And if we wanted to do that, as I just mentioned, we could get the police involved and they could probably find enough evidence to keep you locked up for a long time," Edison said. "Long enough that you wouldn't be able to bother us until a decision has been made about which city gets the team, anyway."

"OK, so where does that leave us?" Blazen asked.

"Well, Hunt, since this is what I consider to be an off-the-record meeting, I'm going to be real honest with you," Edison said. "More honest than I would be if we were on the record. The truth is, I can see where you're coming from. I personally never thought the idea of getting a baseball team was as big a deal as my boss does. And from what I've learned from Dr. Moon, the economic benefits of having a team aren't all they are cracked up to be. Correct, Dr. Moon?"

"That's right," Moon said. "Looking at the economic benefits of a baseball team – or any other pro sports franchise – is a little bit like taking an inkblot test. People tend to see whatever they want to see."

"But you're still helping your boss get a team," Blazen said.

"Yes, I am," Edison said. "That's my job. And I'm pretty good at my job."

"So where does that leave us?" Blazen asked.

Edison paused for a moment, casting his eyes to the ceiling for a second before looking back at Blazen.

"Here's what I'd like, Hunt," Edison said. "I would like to go back to doing what I've been doing. Which is help the mayor and, by extension, the citizens he serves. That covers a lot of responsibilities, including making a good faith effort to get a Major League Baseball team. No matter what my personal feelings about it might be. I would also like Dr. Moon to keep doing what she's been doing, which is helping me to help the mayor. And I would like you to go back to what you were doing before you decided to put on a sheep head mask and start acting like a clown."

"Or else?"

"Or else you can preach your righteous indignation about the evils of pro sports to your cell mate."

A long pause from Blazen as he weighed his options.

"OK, Horton. I guess you've got me."

"Thanks for being so understanding, Hunt," Edison said. "So why does that land at the junkyard site mean so much to you, anyway? I understand you want to open a charter school, but there are a lot of places you could do that."

"None of those other places are the property where I watched my dad die."

"I didn't know about that," Edison said. "I'm very sorry for your loss, Hunt. I really am. And maybe there's a way we can make this up to you, whether Nashville gets the team or not."

"I'm not sure how you could do that," Blazen said.

"Off the top of my head, I'm not sure, either," Edison said. "But I'll give it some thought. But now I've got to be going. My band's break is almost over."

"And They Call the Winter Months Baseball's Silly Season"
By Gilbert Wise, Sports Columnist

Happy Tax Day, everyone! I know some of you may have been so busy yesterday finishing up (or starting) your tax returns that you didn't get a chance to catch Major League Baseball Commissioner Raymond Goldfarb's press conference. Which is OK, because it got a little weird. Goldfarb's office called the press conference to make what was billed as a "major announcement" about the new baseball franchise. OK, that sounded pretty good. To me, a "major" announcement would be one in which the winner of the new franchise is unveiled. I mean, what are we waiting for at this point?

Nashville and Orlando have both made their best pitches, so to speak. Both cities have agreed to build top-of-the-line stadiums. And their respective local governments have committed to spend the money needed to pay for them. We all know what attributes each of the cities has. Nashville is the "It City" – the New York Times even told us so – that's booming economically, culturally and socially. Orlando's an OK place to visit if you don't mind traffic, sunburn and waiting in line at overpriced theme parks. There isn't a lot of new information that the sleuths at Major League Baseball could hope to learn about either place. The cards are on the table.

Speaking of cards on the table, the press conference took a really odd turn when straight out of the box, some reporter I'd never seen before – I suspect he's one of those freelance writers who are taking work away from hard-working full-time journalists everywhere - asks Commissioner Goldfarb for his thoughts about gambling. Goldfarb, ever the diplomat, dutifully answered that he doesn't have a problem with gambling per se. But really, who cares? What does that have to do with anything? But this guy kept pressing Goldfarb, who kept giving hypothetical answers to hypothetical questions. None of which had anything to do with the issue of which city is going to get the new franchise. You have to drive a good three hours to find the closest legal gambling establishment to Nashville. Orlando has some gambling nearby, I think - places where they race skinny dogs and guys play a strange game with equipment that looks like that Trac Ball set you bought for your kids that's been laying on the neighbors' lawn for the last two years.

That shouldn't be any kind of factor in determining which city gets the Major League team. If anything, people are going to be less likely to visit those seedy gambling halls when they could spend their hard-earned money on three hours of high quality baseball.

Goldfarb looked extremely uncomfortable during that part of the press conference. In fact, everyone in attendance seemed to be, except that doofus who was asking all the stupid questions.

Finally, another reporter did get around to asking the only question that's pertinent at this point: Which city is going to get the new franchise? Well, Goldfarb didn't say. And he certainly didn't tip his hand to which way he's leaning. In fact, to use one more gambling analogy, he showed us all his best poker face. So when will a decision about the new franchise be announced? That was the next question asked when it became painfully clear that Goldfarb wasn't going to give us the information we really wanted to know.

And Goldfarb answered that one. Sort of. He said a decision will be made "sometime before Memorial Day." Which is still a month and a half away. Why so long? What could he possibly hope to learn between now and then? He didn't say.

So, we wait. We continue to wait. This is like one of those stoppages in a baseball game where a manager meeting with his pitcher and catcher lasts through about three or four songs played on the stadium's PA system. My best advice, though, is to just be patient. Nashville is going to get this franchise. To quote Darth Vader from one of the good Star Wars movies, it is our destiny. Surely, when all the pros and cons are weighed, Major League Baseball is going to make a Wise choice.

CHAPTER THIRTY-SIX

Horton Edison and Kent Gables sat in front of the television in the mayor's conference room, preparing for what had become a regular afternoon ritual. Ever since they had begun their campaign to bring the new baseball franchise to town, they had found it helpful to see what was happening on Wanda Fong's "Clubhouse Chatter" program.

Wanda didn't talk about the expansion race every day, but Edison and Gables didn't want to run the risk of missing something if she did.

"Good afternoon, everyone. I'm Wanda Fong and this is Clubhouse Chatter. We had a special program planned for you today, with Major League Baseball Commissioner Raymond Goldfarb scheduled to talk about plans to add another expansion team..."

"Well, this should be a good use of our time," Gables said.

"Unfortunately, we're told Commissioner Goldfarb is a bit under the weather today and wasn't able to make it. So instead of hearing his views on expansion, we'd like to hear what you think. So for the next half hour, we'll be taking your calls. In fact, we have a caller on the line already! It's Skip Goodman, the mayor of Orlando..."

"Oh, you have got to be kidding," Gables said more to the television screen than to Edison.

"Mayor Goodman, thank you for calling in to our program today. We're glad you found time in your busy schedule to spend a few minutes with us..."

"Busy schedule!" Gables said. "Yeah, right. I bet this is really cutting into his post-lunch nap time."

"Well, I'm always glad to talk with you, Wanda. I love the work that you're doing here on 'Clubhouse Chatter.' You're doing a great job of keeping people informed about what's happening with these expansion teams."

"Thank you very much, Mayor Goodman! Before we get into that, though, let me first express my sympathy for the tragedy your city recently endured..."

"Tragedy? Have you heard some news from the commissioner's office that I haven't?"

"No, Mayor. I mean the tornado that recently hit your city. How are people down there making out?"

"Oh, right. We're all doing the best we can, Wanda. Of course it's a difficult time for all of us, but we'll pull through together as a city. You know the fairy tale about the big, bad wolf who huffed and puffed and blew down two of the little pigs' houses?"

"Can't say I've heard that one, Mayor. It must be a generational thing."

"Well, in the story, those two pigs take refuge in the sturdy brick house made by their friend, the third little pig. Which the wolf can't blow down. The city of Orlando is like that sturdy brick house. The wind can huff and puff, but it can't blow us down."

"Can you believe this, Horton? This guy is talking about pigs on TV. Pigs building houses. Have you ever heard something so stupid?"

Edison thought about the question for a second, but decided not to answer.

"That's really wonderful news, Mayor. Speaking for all of us here at the network, we're so glad that your city is on the mend..."

"Thank you, Wanda. That really means a lot to all of us. But I know your viewers are tuned in today because they want to know more about Major League Baseball's expansion plans. And I believe there is something that disaster can teach us about why Orlando should get that new team. The way we've responded shows our city's resiliency, the can-do spirit of our people..."

"This is unbelievable!" Gables sputtered. "He's using that tornado to try to win support for the city's expansion bid. Have you ever heard of anything more crass? I mean, you don't hear me playing up the fact that our construction site got attacked by a bunch of vandals! We're victims of domestic terrorism! Shouldn't that count for something?"

Again, Edison knew a rhetorical question when he heard one, so he said nothing.

"I'm not going to stand any more of this," Gables fumed, leaping to his feet. "I'm calling in to that program right now!"

Gables pulled out his smart phone and began dialing the number that had been scrolling across the screen since the program began. Edison was tempted to tackle his boss and wrestle the phone from his hands. Instead, he sighed heavily and put his head between his hands on the conference room table.

Gables was pacing the room now, cursing Goodman and gesturing wildly at the TV. After a few seconds, someone picked up on the other end of the line.

"Hello, this is Kent Gables, mayor of the city of Nashville, and I'd like to get patched onto the program right now! No, I'm not kidding. Kent Gables! How can I prove I am who I say I am? I don't know – did anyone ask Skip Goodman for any proof of who he was before you let him get on there and start spewing his propaganda?"

Edison raised his head from the table. "Please don't do this, Mr. Mayor," he said quietly. Gables was too intent on the call to pay him any attention.

The call screener was suggesting that Gables hold the line until the next segment, after Goodman had finished his call.

"No! No! No!" Gables was shouting. "That's completely unacceptable. You're letting the mayor of Orlando go on your program and lobby for an expansion team and I have a right to state my case and rebut the arguments he's making. This is a question of providing equal time to opposing viewpoints. And if you don't put me on there during this segment, I'm going to report this to the Federal Communications Commission. Do you want to be the one who's held responsible for getting the program fined by the FCC?"

Edison wasn't sure the FCC's equal time provision applied to debates about sports teams, but he wasn't going to argue that point. He tried one more time.

"Please, Mayor. You need to stop and catch your breath here. You know we've talked before about how you shouldn't go on TV when you're angry."

Gables put up his hand to silence his chief of staff. "OK, that's good," he was telling the call screener. "That's a wise decision on your part. Yes, I'll hold..."

Edison gave in and put his head down on the desk again. He knew this was going to be too painful to watch. He didn't even really want to listen, but he felt he had to.

On TV, Goodman was continuing his speech about the many virtues of Orlando's residents when Wanda Fong interrupted him.

"Excuse me, Mayor Goodman, but I understand we have your counterpart from Nashville, Mayor Kent Gables, on

the line with us now, too. Welcome to the program, Mayor Gables. I understand that you might want to take issue with some of the things Mayor Goodman has been telling us."

"You bet I'd like to take issue with what he's been telling you because he's feeding your viewers a line of bull!"

"Wanda, I'm not sure what Kent wants to say, but I think he ought to wait his turn until I finish..."

"I understand your position, Mayor Goodman. But I think our viewers would really like to hear what Mayor Gables has to say."

"Thank you, Wanda. I just want to say that Skip is really insulting your viewers' intelligence by trying to use that tornado to help his team's chances of getting the baseball team. I mean, we all live in communities that have tornadoes from time to time. We've had them here in Nashville. I bet they have them up where you are too, Wanda."

"I really couldn't say if we've had a tornado here in Bristol, Connecticut. There's hasn't been one since I lived here, anyway..."

"OK, maybe not everywhere gets tornadoes. But a lot of places in the U.S. do. And every community experiences some type of natural disaster from time to time."

"As usual, you're missing the point, Kent," Goodman said. *"I was describing how good the people of Orlando are at pulling together in a crisis..."*

"Ah, Skip, you make it sound like people in Orlando were cut out of a perfect mold in some factory somewhere, with all these great qualities you describe. Basically, Orlando is just a gathering place where a bunch of wanderers from all over the country have settled because they want to be someplace warm and apparently don't mind the stifling humidity. You can't just describe them all like they're one person."

"Don't tell me you don't do the same thing when you make speeches about Nashvillians, Kent."

"That's different. We actually do have people whose families who have lived in Nashville for generations. Your earliest settlers arrived in air-conditioned cars, not stagecoaches, when they showed up in the early 1960s. Waiting for the loans on their bland suburban homes to clear escrow was the only hardship they ever experienced."

"If you believe Orlando is such a Johnny-come-lately, Kent, then it must sting a little to know that we have left your town in the dust in such a short period of time."

Wanda Fong shifted in her seat uncomfortably, but didn't try to intervene.

"You haven't left us in the dust! Nashville is still a city on the rise. Orlando peaked about the time construction workers topped out the castle in the Magic Kingdom."

"Always with the jokes about the theme parks, right, Kent? You used to tell them when you gave speeches down here for the realtors association. And you know what? They weren't funny back then, either."

The mention of the realtors association seemed to strike a nerve with Gables, who screwed up his face and squeezed his phone tightly.

"You know what would be funny, Skip? You trying to debate me about this new expansion team."

"What are we doing right now, Kent? Seems like this is a debate."

"I mean, face-to-face. Unless you're scared."

Edison looked up again momentarily and shook his head.

"Just tell me when and where, Kent."

"How about right here on this program? How does that sound to you, Wanda? You think you could make some time for us to hash this out with you and your viewers in person?"

"Yes, I think we could do that. Does that sound OK to you, Mayor Goodman?"

"It's more than OK with me, Wanda. Just tell me when and where."

"Tomorrow would be soon enough for me, Wanda. I can catch a flight out early in the morning. Unless Skip can't make it. I know he's probably about to tell us how busy he'll be tomorrow."

Edison couldn't help but emit a small groan.

"No, I can make time for this. Getting this baseball team is our city's number one priority right now. Can we get on tomorrow's program, Wanda?"

"We'll have to move some of our other scheduled segments around, but yes, I think we can do that. Could you gentlemen please hold the line so our staff members can discuss the logistics with you?"

"That's fine by me."

"I can do that, too. Just have a back-up ready in case the Mayor of Mousetown suddenly discovers he's got a scheduling conflict."

With that, the audio feeds from both Goodman and Gables were silenced. Wanda turned to look directly into the camera and smiled.

"Viewers, it sounds like we're in for an epic battle royal tomorrow. Right here on this program, we'll have both Nashville Mayor Kent Gables and Orlando Mayor Skip Goodman defending their cities' honor on 'Clubhouse Chatter.' If you care anything about baseball, this is must-see TV. I'm Wanda Fong and I'll see you all right back here tomorrow. Until then, try to keep 'em between the foul lines."

Gables, still on the phone with a staffer from the Bristol studio, turned to Edison.

"It's time to get packed, Horton. Tell my secretary on your way out that she needs to make arrangements for both of us to catch the first flight out tomorrow morning."

Edison rose and slowly headed toward the door.

There's always hope, he thought to himself. *Maybe the plane will crash before we get there.*

CHAPTER THIRTY-SEVEN

"Please don't do this, Mr. Mayor," Horton Edison said to his boss as they were waiting backstage behind the set of "Clubhouse Chatter."

"Horton, will you give it a rest?" Gables said. Even though he was coated with the heavy copper-coated foundation favored by TV makeup artists, the redness in his face and neck still shone through. "We talked about all of last night. We talked about it on the plane from Nashville to New York. And we talked about it on the cab ride from New York to here. When are you going to understand that this is just something I have to do? It's long past time for me to put that little twerp from Orlando in his place."

"There will be other opportunities for that," Edison said, not really sure if he was telling the truth or not. He was really trying to stall for time. Even if he couldn't talk Gables out of appearing on the TV show, giving his boss even a couple of days to cool off might help. "Winning a debate with this guy isn't going to make a difference, anyway. The real goal is to make sure Nashville gets a franchise instead of Orlando, right?"

"Yes, of course we want the franchise. But don't you see that this could help us get it? Who knows what criteria the commissioner is looking at to determine which city is better? If I go on national TV and humiliate this twerp, then it might be the final straw that turns the decision in our favor."

"I hope you're not planning to use the word 'twerp' when you're on the air, Mayor."

"And what if I do, Horton? You don't know him like I do, but that's exactly what he is."

"You don't think it sounds a little childish for a mayor of one of the country's 25 largest cities to resort to name-calling one of his rivals?"

"No, I don't. Why, do you?"

"Mayor, you do understand that I'm here to help you, right? And sometimes that means telling you things you really don't want to hear."

"What I don't want to hear?"

"Yes, Mayor. Remember how you reacted last night when I told you about the backlash on social media when you referred to Orlando as 'Mousetown'? You told me I was just being negative."

"You were. And you are. I'm not going to let Twitter guide my decisions about what's best for my city. I wish you could be more positive. Here I am, about to go on national TV, and you're bringing me down. I don't need this negative energy right now, Horton."

Edison was about to respond when one of the stagehands motioned for Gables to follow him. Skip Goodman had already been introduced and was seated to Wanda Fong's right.

Gables and Goodman had refused to walk onto the set together. Goodman had been introduced first after a coin flip was decided in his favor. But now Gables was being introduced, and from backstage Edison watched his boss take his seat on Wanda Fong's left on a stage that looked like a sports locker room.

"Good afternoon, everyone!" Wanda Fong said with a cheerful smile. "Welcome again to 'Clubhouse Chatter.' I'm Wanda Fong – and today's program will feature – well, let's call it a 'spirited discussion' – between the mayor of Nashville and the mayor of Orlando over which of their cities should get the new Major League Baseball franchise. So let's welcome them. On my right, we have Skip Goodman, the mayor of Orlando."

"Thanks, Wanda," Goodman said. "It's great to be here again."

"And on my left, we have Kent Gables, mayor of the city of Nashville."

"Thank you, Wanda. I'm glad to have the opportunity to help your viewers understand why Nashville is the logical choice for the new franchise."

"OK," Wanda Fong said. "With that, let's get started. Now, as our viewers from yesterday's program will remember, the two of you got started on this spirited discussion by telephone on yesterday's program."

"That's right, Wanda," Goodman said. "A discussion that began when Kent here decided to interrupt the conversation that you and I were having."

"I interrupted," Gables said, "because you were trying to manipulate this program's viewers by tugging at their heartstrings about the tornado that hit your town."

"I wasn't trying to do any such thing, Kent. Wanda asked me a question about how people in our town were coping after the tornado and I just answered that question honestly."

"Oh, give it a rest, Skip. You and the word 'honestly' don't belong in the same room together."

Offstage, Edison put his hand to his chest, where he could feel a small knot starting to form.

"You're disputing that we had a tornado, Kent? Because we did. It was on TV and the Internet and everything."

"I'm not saying you didn't have a tornado. I'm just saying that now you're trying to use it as a chunk of political capital to get what you want."

"Wow, that's a strong charge," Wanda interjected. ""Mayor Goodman, how do you respond to that?"

"By not dignifying it with a response," Goodman said. "I guess Mayor Gables wants us to pretend like that tornado never happened, just so it won't help our chances of getting the team."

"Oh, like your city is the first one to ever experience any kind of setback," Gables said. "You had a tornado.

It caused a lot of damage and disrupted a lot of people's lives. I get it. But we've had to work through our share of adversity in Nashville recently, too."

"Could you please elaborate on that, Mayor Gables?" Wanda Fong said, unnecessarily. The truth was, she realized she could say nothing at all for the next half hour and these two would argue right to and past the show's closing credits. But she felt like she needed to say something every now and then to remind viewers that this was her show.

"Yes, I can, Wanda. Since we began our efforts to bring a Major League Baseball team to our city, we've been hounded by a group of domestic terrorists known as the Anti-Arena Agitators. Most recently, this group vandalized the construction site where our new stadium will be built."

"Domestic terrorists?" Wanda Fong said.

"Yes, we don't think there's a better way to describe them," Gables said.

Edison, with images of Hunt Blazen and his goofy car commercials flashing through his mind, could think of several better ways. But Gables had already invoked the t-word. And Edison suspected Goodman was about to pounce on the mistake.

"Domestic terrorists?" Goodman said. "Is that what you're calling them? Because if what I read in your newspapers is correct, then the group's two 'attacks' prior to the vandalism incident involved spraying you with Silly String and rigging a stupid Internet naming contest. That hardly puts them in the same league as ISIS or al-Qaeda."

"Skip, just a minute ago, you were accusing me of minimizing the seriousness of the tornado that hit Orlando..." Gables said.

"You did," Goodman shot back.

"But now you're trying to make it sound like deliberate attempts to sabotage our bid for the team are no big deal."

"A tornado and a few pranks aren't in the same ballpark. If you'll pardon the expression, Wanda."

Wanda Fong acknowledged the comment with a smile that came across almost as a wince. She knew that putting these two men who obviously had bad blood between them on her program would be a ratings bonanza. There had been plenty of media coverage of the mayors' telephone exchange from yesterday. But, like Edison, she was starting to get an uneasy feeling about how things were unfolding.

"A few pranks? It's funny that you dismiss them so easily, Skip. Because we have evidence that someone in Orlando was behind these attacks. Someone operating on property owned by the city of Orlando."

"That's outrageous!" Goodman shouted.

"Mayor Gables, that is a strong claim," Wanda Fong said. "Can you share that evidence with us today?"

"Sure I can, Wanda. You see, this group, the Anti-Arena Agitators, has been sending out messages to its followers over the Internet. And we've been able to track the origin of these messages. Wanda, would it surprise you to know that many of them originated from the Orlando Public Library?"

Edison now felt weak in the knees. Of course, he now knew that Hunt Blazen was the mastermind, if one could use that term, behind the Anti-Arena Agitators. Although Edison hadn't shared that particular piece of information with Gables, he had told him that many of the AAA messages came from WiFi hookups in airports that were all hub cities with direct flights to Nashville.

So Gables knew there was a high probability that the first messages were sent from Orlando as a red herring, to throw Nashville officials off the trail. And there was absolutely no evidence to suggest that Goodman or anyone else in Orlando's city government had anything to do with those messages. But by saying some of those messages had come from "Orlando city property," Gables was strongly inferring that Orlando's leaders, particularly Goodman, had sent them.

"Kent, I believe you have completely lost your mind!" Goodman said. "It's absolutely crazy to suggest that me or anyone else in Orlando had anything to do with that."

"I'm just telling this program's viewers what the evidence suggests," Gables replied.

"Your so-called evidence, if it even exists, doesn't prove anything," Goodman said. "Maybe you could get away with misleading and deceptive practices when you were hocking real estate, Kent, but we're in the big leagues now, buddy. You've got to do better than that."

At the mention of Gables' real estate career, Edison could see the skin under his boss' makeup take on a darker shade of red. Edison recalled that Gables had a similar reaction on the phone yesterday when Goodman had something about the realtors association. Edison didn't know exactly what the subtext to these references was, but he knew it wasn't good.

Gables, on the other hand, understood perfectly well what Goodman was doing. Gables had been a rising star in the real estate profession before he entered politics. He was well known and respected by his colleagues throughout the Nashville area. Which led them to nominate him for the job as treasurer of the Tennessee chapter of the National Association of Realtors.

A few years later, Gables was elected president of the Tennessee chapter. And then a few years after that, he was elected to a one-year term as president of the entire association. It was a part-time job, but it was a great accomplishment for anyone working in the real estate business. It should have been one of the highlights of Gables' career. Until Ellen Atwater happened.

Ellen Atwater was also a rising star in the real estate business in her home state of Maine. Like Gables, she had risen through the ranks of leadership in the Maine chapter of the realtors association. She and Gables had become friends when they saw each other at the national association's annual meetings. Then, when Atwater was elected as the association's vice president the same year Gables was elected president, they became more than friends.

As the two of them got together to plan for the association's annual meeting that would cap their terms in office, they began a steamy love affair. Although the affair was never made public, it had ultimately ended Gables' marriage. And it might have eventually led to a marriage between Gables and Atwater.

Unfortunately for Gables, he had delegated to Atwater the task of working out logistics with the meeting's host city. Which was Orlando, a city led by a charming and slick-talking mayor named Skip Goodman. Goodman and Atwater began a love affair of their own. Faced with a choice between Goodman, who was single, and Gables, who was going through a messy and emotionally taxing divorce, Atwater had chosen Goodman.

Atwater's relationship with Goodman hadn't lasted, either, but by the time they broke up, Gables' personal life was ruined. But not his professional life. To help him forget about his troubles, Gables threw himself into his real estate work, then when that didn't work, his political career. After Gables was elected mayor of Nashville, he had seen Goodman at various professional functions. Each knew about the other's history with Atwater, which had ignited a long-running private feud between them.

So when Goodman made reference to the realtors association or Gables' real estate career, he knew exactly what he was doing. Goodman was ripping the scabs off old wounds to make Gables furious. As they argued on the 'Clubhouse Chatter' set in front of a national television audience, the taunts were working.

"Oh, Orlando is the big leagues, Skippy? Lousy food, watered-down drinks and crowds of pushy tourists everywhere you go. To me, it's like a big cruise ship without the water."

"Sorry to hear you don't like our town, Kent, but a lot of people do. At least one of whom we both know pretty well."

"You'd better watch yourself now, Skippy." Gables was clenching and unclenching his fists as he talked.

Wanda Fong shifted uncomfortably in her chair again. She looked like she wanted to say something, but didn't know what. Edison's guts were churning so bad that he had his hands on his knees. At that moment, he would have preferred to have been Nixon's advisor before his ill-fated debate with JFK.

"Some people like Orlando so much that they scream for joy when they're in town, Kent."

"This is your last warning," Gables said, his body tensed in his seat.

"And as for Orlando being like a cruise ship without water, that's not true," Goodman said, fixing a wicked grin at Gables. "We've got plenty of water in Central Florida. I personally have spent a lot of time AT WATER!"

Gables could take it no longer. With a guttural sound he leaped out of his chair and launched himself at Goodman. Fong, who'd been a college gymnast before starting her career in broadcasting, deftly managed to dodge Gables as he flew past her.

Gables tackled Goodman just as he was rising from his chair. The two men fell together into the faux lockers at the back of the set, knocking them over. Wanda Fong stood paralyzed, a look of horror on her beautiful face, as the mayors of two major cities rolled around at her feet, pulling each other's hair and trying to gouge each other's eyes out. Since they were equipped with wireless microphones, the TV audience could still hear what the men were saying as they fought.

"She never loved you!" Gables snarled.

"Well, she definitely never loved you," Goodman replied through gritted teeth. "And she told me I was better."

"When she was with you, she was in Orlando," Gables said. "There were limited entertainment options unless you've got $100 for a theme park day pass that doesn't even include parking!"

"When she was with you, she was in Nashville. And she was with you!" Goodman hissed. "You didn't set the bar very high for me!"

Finally, Wanda Fong got her composure back. "Well, obviously, this has taken an unexpected turn for the worse. I apologize to our viewers who might be upset by what they've seen on today's program. I hope you'll all join us tomorrow when I'll be back to sort out these latest...developments. Have a great afternoon, everyone!"

Wanda Fong waited until the red lights on the studio cameras went out, indicating that they were off the air. Then she turned to her producer offstage and mouthed the words: *Who's 'she'?*

Edison watched Gables and his archenemy writhing on the floor for a few more seconds, then headed for the Coke machines for something to wash down an aspirin or five.

The Nashville Bulletin, April 18, 2018

"A Catfight in the Clubhouse - and Where We Go from Here"
By Gilbert Wise, Sports Columnist

Why is this happening to us? Nashville was close to having its own Major League Baseball franchise. So close that there were rumors that people around town were brushing up on the lost art of how to fill out a scorecard. Score last night's outing for the city as a 'K.' A strikeout. A complete and utter whiff.

For those of you who missed it live or any of the 3,654 replays shown on TV and the Internet, Kent Gables, Nashville's alleged leader, just made a complete fool out of himself in front of a national audience.

Appearing on "Clubhouse Chatter," one of the finest programs in all of television, Gables got into a silly and somewhat mystifying argument with his counterpart from the city of Orlando. I mean, really, does anybody know what those guys were talking about at the end of that exchange? Then the argument devolved into a fight. And not even a very manly fight at that. These guys didn't duke it out like Ali and Frazier. Or even Tyson-Douglas. This was more the type of pugilism you'd expect to see between Ron Burgundy and Wes Mantooth in the next installment of the "Anchorman" movies.

No truth to the rumor that Nashville has hired mixed martial artist Ronda Rousey to give our mayor a few pointers on how to defend himself without resorting to scratching and hair pulling. I make jokes because if you can't laugh at a situation like this, you have to cry. You can only imagine what was going through Major League

Baseball Commissioner Raymond Goldfarb's mind as he watched that spectacle unfold.

Put yourself in his position for a minute. You're trying to decide which of two up-and-coming southern cities to give the keys to the golden kingdom. Those cities are supposed to be putting their best feet forward, for him and the rest of the baseball-watching world.

Instead, we get an episode of "The Jerry Springer Show." You know people in the established top-tier northern cities are laughing up their sleeves as the rubes from south of the Mason-Dixon line show, once again, that they're not quite ready for prime time.

Which city came out looking worse, Nashville or Orlando? Maybe Nashville. After all, Gables clearly was the aggressor in the fight, if I may use the words 'aggressor' and 'fight' very loosely. Orlando Mayor Skip Goodman was right there, too, showing he could knee to the groin with the best of them. But it was Gables who melted down first.

In this sort of race, one gaffe – again, using the word 'gaffe' very charitably – might be enough to tilt the scales in Orlando's favor. Baseball, it's been said, is a game of inches. And getting a Major League Baseball franchise truly is.

Nashville had a nice run. For a while there, all the national media were talking up Nashville's chances. At least from outward appearances, the city was being taken seriously. It was never a slam dunk that the Music City would beat out Orlando for the team, but it certainly didn't seem impossible.

Now, well…

Could it be that Nashville tries just a little too hard?

We can't claim Chicago-style pizza or Philly cheese steaks, so we dump a bunch of cayenne pepper on fried chicken and call that our signature food.

We don't have an Empire State Building or a Sears Tower, so we build a skyscraper shaped like Batman's cowl. We don't have a Metropolitan Opera House or a Faneuil Hall, so we build a convention center that's shaped like a giant guitar.

Do you see my point here? Nashville is the new student at school who tries to impress the cool kids by pointing out how great he was in choir at his old school. Which is fine, if you like wedgies and being stuffed inside your own locker a lot.

Orlando seems more comfortable in its civic skin. It's long been America's vacation spot, at least for people who live east of the Mississippi River. And after people visit there, a lot of them want to live there. And not just wannabe country singers who come to town with big dreams in their hearts and guitars slung over their shoulders. Those people do a great job of holding Nashville's food service and bartending industries together. By contrast, Orlando attracts people who are capable of holding down real jobs. And earn real money. So they can afford to buy real tickets to Major League Baseball games.

Right now, Orlando does a lot better than Nashville in the "eyeball test." That is, it's a lot easier to imagine a Major League team in Orlando than in a city that elects a mayor who should come with his own laugh track.

I'm not a native Nashvillian, but if I were, I'd be feeling pretty embarrassed right now. When I moved here 10 years ago, I was assured that the city's days as a "Dukes of Hazzard" set were over. The jokes about banjos and corn cob pipes were supposed to be a thing of the past.

I thought I was moving to a city that was becoming more modern and progressive. Now I'm seeing a different side to Nashville, which suggests that the backwater is back. The farmer's overalls may be in the closet, but they haven't been thrown away. Nashvillians may be wearing collared shirts now, but that still doesn't mean the necks underneath them aren't red.

I know that I'll get a flood of angry calls and e-mails, asking why I live here if I don't like it here.

The truth be told, I moved here because of the work. I had an opportunity to become a sports columnist in what I thought could be the next sports boom town. Now, in hindsight, I'm starting to think that I didn't make a Wise choice.

CHAPTER THIRTY-EIGHT

The drive from Bristol, Connecticut to New York City wasn't a short one at any time of day or night, but it seemed particularly long as Horton Edison made the trip the night after his boss' ill-fated appearance on "Clubhouse Chatter."

Edison asked the Uber driver to drop him off a few blocks up Mulberry Street from the restaurant in Little Italy where he was supposed to meet Major League Baseball Commissioner Raymond Goldfarb.

Edison wanted to walk those last blocks to give himself a little more time to think. Time to think of what to say. Even though nothing had come to him in the last 24 hours since the most talked-about episode in the TV program's history had aired. Whenever "Clubhouse Chatter" went off the air – whether it was next week or 20 years from now – the program featuring the fighting mayors was sure to make the highlight reel.

So now Edison had some explaining to do.

His job required him to be a master of political spin. But when millions of people watch your boss, a full-grown man, writhing around on the floor with another grown man while a perky ex-gymnast skips back and forth to avoid being tripped by their flailing legs, it's hard to say anything remotely mayoral was occurring at that point in time.

Still, it fell to Edison to try to make the best of this situation. He'd called Goldfarb's office the first thing that morning, after he'd put a physically bruised and emotionally subdued Kent Gables on a plane back to Nashville. Although Goldfarb's meeting calendar for the day was already booked, he'd generously agreed to a dinner meeting with Edison.

Edison almost wished Goldfarb hadn't been able to make time available for this meeting. It was no fun being the janitor who had to clean up the messes made by someone else's emotional outbursts.

From the very beginning, Edison had his doubts about Mayor Gables' grand plan to go after a Major League Baseball franchise. It was clearly a high-risk, high-reward enterprise. But did the risks outweigh the rewards?

Despite the substantial amounts of time, money and other resources Edison and others at City Hall had devoted to this project, they had nothing to show for their work. After what happened last night, they probably never would.

And could anyone say the pursuit of the franchise had done anything but damage Gables' political stock? It was one thing to make a noble attempt to land a franchise, but come up short to some other worthy city. It was something else to come so completely unglued that media wags were already calling Gables "Mayor Meltdown."

The media hadn't gone after a mayor so gleefully and viciously since Toronto residents were deprived of the services of their crack-smoking chief executive Rob Ford a few years earlier.

Edison didn't know Goldfarb personally, so he had no idea how the commissioner would react to what he had seen. Would he lecture Edison about the need to show proper decorum to protect the integrity of the American national pastime? Would he suggest that Nashville immediately withdraw its bid for the team?

The latter certainly seemed like the worst-case scenario. So, Edison thought to himself, maybe avoiding that fate would be a victory of sorts. If he could somehow convince Goldfarb not to immediately disqualify Nashville, then that would save some political face. At least temporarily.

Surely, Nashville's chances of being selected as the franchise's new host city were now toast. Still, if Nashville stayed in the race - at least officially - and the process played out over a few more months, and then Orlando was selected, that wouldn't be so bad. That would at least give people time to forget about the "Clubhouse Chatter" incident.

Edison wasn't sure he completely believed that. A few months, or even a few years, might not be enough time to restore the city's reputation – or Gables'. People hadn't completely forgotten the time a sitting Nashville mayor went on a national morning talk show to showcase his mistress' dubious country musical talents – and that happened more than 30 years ago.

Which made more embarrassing national television - professing one's illicit love to a woman who sang like a wounded alley cat or treating a professional colleague to a bout of schoolyard justice? Edison wasn't sure he could answer that honestly.

So out of a range of bad-to-awful possibilities, convincing Goldfarb not to deep six Nashville's bid right away seemed like the least bad option. So that's what Edison would try to do.

Before Edison really had a chance to work out a game plan for how to do that, he reached the restaurant where Goldfarb was seated at a table on the patio outside. Edison recognized Goldfarb immediately from seeing him on his numerous television appearances, although the commissioner looked older and more tired in person.

"Commissioner Goldfarb?" Edison said. "I'm Horton Edison."

Goldfarb looked up at Edison through bleary eyes, then wordlessly motioned for Edison to take a seat. As he did, Edison noticed that Goldfarb had apparently been at the restaurant for a while. Two empty bottles and a nearly empty bottle of a super Tuscan wine were already on the table. Goldfarb topped off his glass, poured the remainder of the bottle into the glass at Edison's place setting, then signaled for the waiter to bring another bottle.

"Nice to meet you, Mr. Edison," Goldfarb said, extending his hand for a limp handshake. "I've heard a lot of good things about you."

Edison wondered if that could really be true. A handful of mayors achieved national name recognition, usually when their cities were in the news for some awful crises. Chiefs of staff tended to be unknown to just about everybody outside of those who regularly worked with city government.

"Commissioner, I want to thank you for agreeing to see me on such short notice," Edison said. "I know your schedule is very hectic. But after what happened last night, I wanted the opportunity to speak with you as soon as possible. And since I was already in the area, I thought it would be best to do that before I headed back to Nashville."

"What happened last night..." Goldfarb said, his voice trailing off.

"Yes sir," Edison said. "I'm sure you saw, either live or on a replay, last night's episode of 'Clubhouse Chatter.' And I want to assure you that what you saw isn't typical behavior for Mayor Gables, the man I represent."

"He's a lover, not a fighter?" Goldfarb said. He had just a hint of a smile, but it seemed to be a gesture of kindness rather than mockery.

"He's usually very mild mannered," Edison said. "What happened last night was totally out of character for him. I think it's just that he's been under an enormous amount of pressure lately. Not just because of this competition to get the new baseball franchise, but all his other duties as mayor, too."

"It sounded to me like he and Mayor Goodman were fighting over a woman," Goldfarb said flatly.

Edison didn't know how to respond to that. Based on what the clip-on microphones had picked up during the scuffle, it certainly did seem as if the fight had as much or more to do with personal reasons as it did with professional ones. Edison was sure there was more to the story than Gables had told him yet. But Edison didn't know the full story and he wasn't inclined to make one up.

"To be truthful, Commissioner, I don't know exactly why that happened the way it did last night," Edison admitted. "I haven't really had a chance to sit down with my boss yet and talk all of this through. I can only hope he'll have a reasonable explanation for losing his temper the way he did. And when he shares that with me, I'll be happy to share it with you."

"I appreciate your candor, Horton," Goldfarb replied. "I hope you don't mind if I call you Horton. And I wish you would call me Ray. This meeting is about as informal and unofficial as any of my meetings ever get."

"Please call me Horton, Ray."

"Good deal, Horton. You know, in my line of work, I get to know a lot about a lot of different people in cities all over North America. It truly is one of the perks of the job. And the people I know who also know you speak very highly of you."

Goldfarb paused to take a generous sip of his wine before continuing.

"I'm glad to hear that, Commissioner, er, Ray. And of course your reputation precedes you everywhere you go. Even to the media, who seem to be able to find fault with anyone, you seem to be beyond reproach."

"Beyond reproach," Goldfarb said quietly, shaking his head.

"I'm not saying that just to try to flatter you, Ray, I really mean it. And, even if I were, I wouldn't insult your

309

intelligence by acting as if flattery is going to be enough to fix this situation."

"Oh, I know that, Horton. The main thing I've heard about you is that you're a straight shooter. You tend to tell it like it is, even if there's a vision of puppies-and-rainbows that would be a lot easier to tell than the truth."

"Sometimes that works to my detriment."

Goldfarb laughed, again not unkindly. "Yes, Horton, I bet it does. We may be in different lines of work, but politics is as much a part of my world as it is yours. And we both know that in politics, truth, common sense and wisdom don't always carry the day. Sometimes it all comes down to what the slickest talker in the room can sell to the person in charge. The people who are best at 'winning the meetings' are usually the ones who most need to be locked in a closet when important business is being decided."

Edison laughed, too. In spite of the unpleasantness of the subject matter Edison had come to discuss, Goldfarb had a way of putting him at ease.

"No argument here," Edison said. "I think these people who are always trying to come up with new technology to improve the workplace ought to look into a mute button for BS-artists."

Goldfarb chuckled and finished his glass of wine as the waiter approached, uncorked the new bottle and refilled his glass. Edison took a small sip of his own wine, but waived off the waiter's offer to top off the glass. When the waiter asked if they were ready to order, both men said they needed more time.

"Sometimes a mute button would even come in handy for bosses. Right, Horton?"

"Well, like I said, I'm not sure what happened..."

"And I said it sounded like a fight over a woman," Goldfarb said, taking another gulp of wine. "Which would be understandable."

"I'm not sure I follow you, Ray."

"Sure you do, Horton. We're men. And I believe that at some point or another, all men lose their minds and do stupid things because of women."

"OK, that's probably true. But even if it is true, I hope that whatever issues Mayor Gables is working through won't ruin things for the citizens of Nashville."

"With the franchise, you mean?"

"Yes, with the franchise. I know what happened last night didn't help our chances of getting it. But I hope it didn't kill our chances, either. Because this affects a lot more people than me or my boss. I don't have to tell you about the benefits a baseball franchise can bring. Entertainment. Jobs. Tax revenues. Even pride."

"Oh, yes, the civic pride argument," Goldfarb said between sips. "I've heard that one a lot in this job. And I believe it. I really believe there are a lot of people who live in cities that have major league sports that take great joy in that. But having a major league sports team isn't the be-all and end-all of a city's existence. I'm saying that unofficially, of course. But I grew up in Des Moines. We didn't and still don't have major league sports there – and probably never will. But it was a great place to grow up. And it still is a great place to live. And Nashville and Orlando are great places to live. And they still will be, no matter what."

"Agreed. I understand that and you understand that, Ray. But my job is to advocate for my city, which is Nashville. So that's what I'm here to do. Call it damage control or whatever you want to call it, but I hope what happened on that TV program isn't going to be the deciding factor regarding which city gets the new franchise."

Goldfarb drained his glass, stared up at the night sky for a second, then sighed deeply.

"It won't be the deciding factor, Horton."

"I'm glad to hear that, Ray. Because there are so many other things that ought to be taken into consideration..."

"The considerations are all over."

"I'm not sure I follow you, Ray."

"Nashville isn't going to lose the franchise because of what your mayor did last night. That decision has already been made."

"It has?" Edison shot Goldfarb a puzzled look.

"It has." The commissioner refilled both of their wine glasses. "And against my better judgment and totally off the record, I'm going to tell you why neither Nashville nor Orlando is going to get that franchise. So you might as well drink your wine. This is kind of a long story and you've got some catching up to do."

CHAPTER THIRTY-NINE

Horton Edison met up with his boss on a hiking trail beside Radnor Lake, not far from the mayor's home.

After his return from Bristol, Gables had told his staff that he would be working from home all week. Edison hadn't suggested that strategy, but it made sense. Having Gables around the office would only serve as an additional distraction for anyone trying to get work done around City Hall.

As it was, the mayor's office was flooded with media interview requests, by phone and by e-mail. There were also quite a few reporters who were camped out in the reception area outside the office, hoping to catch Gables coming or going for a quick ambush interview.

Edison had avoided them on the way into work by arriving early in the morning, well before most journalists thought about reporting for duty. He slipped out in mid-afternoon by sending out the city attorney ahead of him as a decoy. As the reporters chased the city attorney to the elevators, dutifully recording the words "no comment" at least seven different times, Edison had quietly slipped down the stairs to the parking garage and the safety of his car.

Rather than risk drawing attention by parking at the mayor's house, Edison had instead used one of the public parking spaces set aside for visitors to the Radnor Lake wilderness area and walked to the meeting spot. It was a pleasantly warm April afternoon, but still too early in the day to attract the large number of hikers and runners who would be out after they got home from work.

Edison found Gables staring out across the water, wearing sunglasses that only partially concealed the bruises and scratches left over from his fight with Skip Goodman.

"Good afternoon, Mayor," Edison said, trying to keep his tone as neutral as he could.

"Hey there, Horton," Gables replied. "How were things at the office today?"

"They were OK."

"OK? They were really OK?"

Edison paused before answering. "Well, Mayor, I remember you telling me in one of our recent conversations that I could be too negative at times. So I'm trying to put the best face on this that I can."

Gables offered a thin smile. "You were right. Is that what you want me to say, that you were right?"

"Right about what, Mayor?"

"You were right about it being a mistake for me to call in to 'Clubhouse Chatter.' You were right when you told me it was a mistake to agree to an on-camera interview on the program. And you were right when you told me that if I did an on-camera interview, I should have waited until I cooled down and collected my thoughts a little bit."

"I know you're not going to believe this, Mayor, but it gives me no great pleasure to hear you say that."

"It doesn't?"

"No, not really. It doesn't do much good to hear that now."

"No, I suppose you're right," Gables said with a half-hearted chuckle. "It's like realizing you should have taken the pitcher out of the game right after he gives up the game-winning home run."

"Well, I wouldn't have used a baseball analogy under these circumstances, but that one is pretty much on the nose."

"I wish I could explain to you why all of this happened, Horton, I really do. But I don't think I can relive it all right now."

"You mean the part about you, Mayor Goodman and Ellen Atwater?"

Gables shot Edison a surprised look. After watching Gables and Goodman go at each other's throats on the TV program, it had only taken Edison a few discreet phone calls to find out that the Gables-Atwater-Goodman love triangle had been an open secret around Orlando during the months leading up to the realtors' convention.

"Horton, I really don't know what to say. If you've never been in that sort of situation, you just can't understand the kind of pain it can bring. For everyone involved. And that kind of pain can make a person do things he wouldn't normally do. Crazy things."

Edison picked up a small stone and skipped it across the lake. It hopped three or four times before finally dropping below the surface.

"I can't say that I've been in exactly that kind of situation," Edison admitted. "But I can relate to what it's like to have woman troubles."

"Really? I never see that side of your life, Horton."

"It's a little bit different for me. You're the mayor of a major city. I'm not. Your life is always in the spotlight. Mine isn't. So while your problems seldom slip under the radar, mine usually do."

"I guess that makes me feel a little better. If you're telling me the truth."

"Telling you the truth is what sometimes gets me into trouble, Mayor."

Gables chuckled again. "No, I hope you don't really think that, Horton. I appreciate all of your advice. I may not realize it when I first hear it, but eventually it sinks in."

For Edison, these were words he had never heard before from Gables. Although they gave him some measure of satisfaction, he also realized that he was catching his boss at a very weak moment. Then again, last night he had caught Raymond Goldfarb at a very weak moment. But that didn't make what the baseball commissioner had told him any less true.

Edison was trying to think of the best way to tell Gables what Goldfarb had told him when the mayor spoke again.

"You realize my political career is over, right, Horton?"

"Not necessarily. I would say that it's taken an unusual detour, but it's not necessarily over."

Now Gables snorted. "If you're saying that to avoid sounding negative, you're overcompensating. I know I screwed up. You don't have to be afraid to say it."

"OK, in that case, I'm not going to be. The TV program could have gone better," Edison said. He wasn't going to ignore an invitation like that from his boss. "But it's not the end of the world. Politicians have come back from worse offenses than what you've done."

"Like who?"

"Remember Marion Barry, the mayor of Washington D.C. who got caught smoking crack? On videotape? That wasn't the end of his political career."

"Drug use isn't a violent crime. I got caught on video assaulting a fellow public official."

And slandering him, Edison wanted to say. But this didn't seem like the right time to bring up what he had learned about Hunt Blazen and the Anti-Arena Agitators. The website, www.dontgetfleeced.com, had gone inactive, which was Edison's main interest in that regard.

"Mayor, I really don't think Skip Goodman is going to file assault charges. You may have initiated the attack, but he didn't come out of this looking particularly good, either. The publicity criminal charges would bring aren't going to help his political career. Or his city's chances of getting a Major League team."

"The Major League team..." Gables' voice trailed off as he stared across the water. It was like he was watching a particularly beautiful cloud drift away. A cloud he would never see again.

The look made Edison a little sad. He knew how much getting a Major League team had meant to Gables. He wanted to tell Gables what Goldfarb had told him. That is, that it wouldn't have mattered if Gables and Goodman had never gotten into a hissy fight on national television. Neither Nashville nor Orlando would have gotten the team even if that had never happened. Because the game was rigged. Rigged in a way no one in either city suspected.

On the other hand, Edison had to admit that there might be some benefits to having Gables believe that not getting the team was a direct consequence of his actions. If Gables felt a sense of loss because of what he'd done, then maybe that was all part of the karmic balance of the universe.

"You know, Mayor, this might not be as bad for your political career as you think."

"Come on, Horton. I feel like you're overcompensating again."

"No, not really. Look at where you are now and where you might want to go in the future. After serving as mayor of Nashville, your next most logical move would be to run for statewide office. For governor. Or maybe a U.S. Senate seat."

"OK, so?"

"So Nashville may be establishing itself as a genteel island of modernism and culture in the New South, but it's surrounded by an ocean of good old boys. And to those good old boys, having a political leader who isn't afraid to whup a rival's butt might not be such a bad thing."

Gables cracked another smile. "'Governor Gables' does have a nice ring to it."

"Governor 'No Guff' Gables."

"I like the sound of it, Horton. OK, maybe I can buy what you're selling. But how to we get from here to there? It's going to be hard to make people forget about what happened on 'Clubhouse Chatter.'"

Now it was Edison's turn to crack a slight smile. "Maybe it will be, and maybe it won't be. But I do have a plan."

CHAPTER FORTY

Wynn "The Jackhammer" Hammerskal was late to the meeting, as usual. Horton Edison and Iris Moon were both on their second cups of coffee when the former baseball player stepped off the elevator into the foyer of the Nashville Skyline Club.

The Skyline Club, located on the top floor of one of the city's tallest office buildings, was one of Nashville's premiere spots for power lunches. Or power breakfasts, if that was your thing.

But the Skyline Club wasn't open to just anyone. Only members and their guests were allowed to eat there. And you couldn't become a member by filling out an application or even by bribing the right people. You had to be approached and invited by someone else who was already a member.

Horton Edison had been invited not long after he became a mayoral chief of staff. But he rarely ever took advantage of his membership. Places like the Skyline Club were too elitist for his tastes.

There was one distinct advantage of dining at the Skyline Club: The staff and the other members all understood the value of discretion. If you were planning to meet with a high-profile athlete a couple of days after your boss had a meltdown on national TV, there was no more private place to be.

As usual, Hammerskal was yakking on his cell phone as he approached the table where Edison and Moon were seated.

"Yeah, yeah, we're almost ready to go into production with it," Hammerskal was telling someone. "Oh yeah, it's going to be better than any other games on the market.

Don't worry about that. You know what I say: Go big or…"

Hammerskal paused because Edison had wordlessly risen from the table and was reaching for his phone. Gently but firmly, Edison took the phone from Hammerskal's hand and held it to his own ear.

"He'll call you back," Edison said. "He's got more important business right now."

"I don't know who you think you are," Hammerskal said as Edison handed the dead phone back to him. "I'm just going to call him right back."

"No, you'll call him back when this conversation is over," Edison said calmly. "Because what we're going to tell you, we're only going to tell you one time. And that time is right now."

"What's gotten into you, Horton?" Hammerskal said. "I don't think your boss, the mayor, would appreciate your manners."

"Well, he's a little busy these days. So I've asked Dr. Moon to sit in on this meeting with us instead. As far as manners go, I wonder if there's a book on etiquette somewhere that says the person on the phone is always more important than the person standing right in front of you. Because it seems like everybody's default position these days is that the person on the phone is so much more important. Even if it's just the dentist's office confirming tomorrow's teeth cleaning appointment."

Hammerskal sat down heavily at the table. He pulled a baseball from his pocket and absentmindedly began tossing it into the air. A waiter approached, filled a cup of coffee for him, then quickly retreated. Hammerskal glanced over at Dr. Moon and his humor seemed to improve a little.

"How are you doing this morning, darling?" Hammerskal asked her as Edison retook his own seat.

"Pretty fair," Moon said, rubbing her nose furiously. "But I'm not sure you'll be saying the same a few minutes from now."

Hammerskal laughed. "Man, you two are a real couple of buzz kills, you know it? Who took a whizz in your corn flakes, anyway? Don't tell me you're all bent out of shape because of what happened with Mayor Gables on 'Clubhouse Chatter' the other night. Because that was awesome! I could have sworn you guys must have planned all that out."

"No, we didn't," Edison said.

"Really? Because I loved it! It was just like the pro wrestling I used to watch when I was growing up. Our guy didn't take anything off of that Orlando mayor, did he?"

"And didn't think that was just a little bit immature and undignified?" Moon asked.

The smile vanished from Hammerskal's face. "Well, maybe a little bit. But come on, now. I don't really think the mayor did anything to hurt our chances. This isn't a competition to see which city gets to host the summer philharmonic symphony series. It's baseball. It's supposed to be a little bit rough and tumble. If you don't get dirty playing baseball, you're not doing it right. So if you want to get a baseball team, getting dirty isn't a bad thing, is it?"

Edison chuckled and glanced out the window for a second. The Skyline Club used to have a great view that extended miles in all directions, all the way to the city's distant suburbs. Since the city began growing, though, all its patrons could see were the tops of other skyscrapers. Edison turned his eyes back to Hammerskal. "We'll never know, I guess."

"What do you mean, we'll never know?" Hammerskal said. "We'll know when there's an announcement about whether or not we get the franchise, right?"

"We're not getting the franchise, Wynn," Edison said.

"Oh, you don't know that. We can't be sure of anything yet."

"Yes, we can," Moon said. Her eyes locked with Hammerskal's for a second or two.

"What...what makes you so sure?" Hammerskal said.

"The decision about the new franchise has already been made," Edison said.

"And how do you know that?" Hammerskal said, a look of confusion filling his face.

"That's not important. But we know."

Hammerskal shifted uncomfortably in his seat. "Say, wasn't Julius Malfair supposed to be here for this meeting? He should really be hearing this."

"Well, I told Julius we were meeting today," Edison said. "I might or might not have told him the correct location of where we were meeting. Anyway, you can fill him in later, if you decide that's what you want to do. I wanted you to hear what we have to say first."

"OK, then, spill it," Hammerskal said, shrugging his shoulders theatrically. "Are you telling me we won't get the team because you want to renegotiate the agreement about the stadium construction? Because Malfair will definitely need to be here if that's what you're after."

"No, we're not trying to renegotiate the agreement," Edison said. "We're not getting the team."

"And Orlando is?" Hammerskal said.

"No, not Orlando. Las Vegas," Edison said.

Hammerskal, who'd been doing a good job of tossing and catching the baseball while he'd been following the conversation finally lost his concentration. The ball fell to the floor and rolled under a nearby table.

"Las Vegas?" Hammerskal said. "Since when were they ever in the running?"

"Strictly speaking, I don't know that they ever were 'in the running,'" Edison said. "But they are now standing at the finish line, having a cold beer while Nashville and

Orlando fight it out for second. Which, as you know, in this race gets you nothing."

Edison had seen the look on Hammerskal's face before, the time he'd been sprayed with Silly String at the news conference.

"I don't understand this," Hammerskal said. "What did we do wrong?"

"As far as I can tell, we didn't do anything wrong," Edison said. "We just got outplayed."

"Outplayed?"

"Yes. You know how pitchers in baseball sometimes put Vaseline or other illegal substances on the ball to give themselves an edge? Not that you ever did anything like that, Wynn, but you're aware that the practice goes on?"

"Sure, but I don't see what..."

"Let's just say Las Vegas did something very similar to us."

"Well, OK, so we'll appeal to the umpire," Hammerskal said anxiously. "If Las Vegas cheated, then we've got to tell somebody."

"Sorry, Wynn, but in this case, the umpire has been compromised," Edison said. "I think this is one we'll just have to chalk up in the loss column."

Hammerskal started to say something, then caught himself. He dropped his head to his chin as if deep in thought. Finally he spoke again, very quietly.

"All I ever wanted was a baseball team for Nashville. Was that so wrong?"

"Wanting a team is one thing," Moon interjected. "But understanding the sacrifices is another."

"What sacrifices? I keep hearing all this noise from all these naysayers who make it sound like having a team here would be a bad thing. Don't they know that baseball is America's..."

"National pastime," Moon said. "Yes, we've all heard that one before. But you know what, Mr. Hammerskal?

It may come as a big shock to you, but not everyone in this town is a baseball fan. Some people don't like sports at all. And some of them resent it when they see their city government bending over backwards to find ways to pay for a stadium to cater to the whims of a limited audience when there are so many other needs out there."

"But this team would have been great for Nashville," Hammerskal said. "Baseball is great family entertainment. For families with little kids."

"Right, the 'do it for the kids' argument," Moon said.

"Always popular with school boards," Edison muttered, half under his breath.

"Mr. Hammerskal, did you know that the average cost for a family of four to attend a Major League Baseball game is $210.46?" Moon continued. "That's a lot more expensive than renting a movie on Netflix and ordering a pizza."

Hammerskal frowned, but said nothing.

"And that's what a Major League game costs now. Players' salaries keep going up and up – something I'm sure you're familiar with. So the cost of tickets, concessions, parking and everything else is going to keep going up, too. So spectators are asked to keep paying more and more to see baseball games. To justify the higher costs, team officials tell cities that stadiums need to be renovated. Then expanded. Then finally, the stadium that was brand new a decade ago is suddenly obsolete. Then the team owners say they'll move the team somewhere else unless they can get a new stadium that's ten times fancier than the one they already have. So city officials try to keep the team owners happy by giving them what they want."

"We do," Edison interjected again. "Sort of a collective weakness we have."

"So cities keep pouring more and more resources into these stadiums requested by sports teams, which are private businesses – make that private businesses that do very well for themselves. It may not be a one-to-one correlation, but cities end up spending less money on expenses like social services, economic development and education as a result. So now let's think about the two kids in this hypothetical family of four that's paying $210.46 to attend games now. How much will that cost be when they're old enough to take their kids to baseball games? $400? $500? More? So those kids will need to be pretty well educated and have pretty good jobs to afford those high prices, right? But maybe they won't have the education they need to get those good jobs to pay those high ticket prices because their city government thought subsidizing multimillion-dollar businesses was more important than educating its young people."

Moon punctuated her speech with a fit of three violent sneezes while Hammerskal stared blankly at her.

"Man, that's harsh," Hammerskal finally said.

"Yes, it is harsh," Moon agreed. "It's a rough world out there. The question is, what – if anything - are you willing to do about it?"

CHAPTER FORTY-ONE

Wynn Hammerskal took a sip of his mint julep, then nodded his approval. The first one the bartender had mixed was too sweet, but he had followed Hammerskal's advice to cut back on the sugar and increase the Jack Daniels. It was hard to get anyone who wasn't actually a Southerner to properly mix a mint julep, Hammerskal had decided.

He was sitting in the Jacuzzi next to a strikingly beautiful brunette. Across from him sat casino mogul Richard Scales, who was flanked by another gorgeous brunette.

The Jacuzzi was on the roof of Scales' luxury condominium building, one floor up from his penthouse. Although Hammerskal had always thought of Las Vegas as an unbearably hot place most of the year, it was actually cool at night and so the warm bubbling waters felt comfortable. After a few drinks, Hammerskal felt very comfortable.

"So we're agreed on this?" Scales said.

"Oh, yeah, we're agreed," Hammerskal said. "From what I've heard, you've come up with a winning game plan."

"I'm glad to hear you think so, Wynn," Scales said, signaling for the bartender to bring another round of margaritas for himself and his date. "Since you're from Tennessee, I thought you might be locked into sticking with Nashville's bid."

"Hey, don't get me wrong, I love Nashville and I love Tennessee," Hammerskal said, taking another sip of his drink. "But one thing you should know about me if you followed my baseball career is that I like to win."

"And baseball is a business."

"That's right," Hammerskal said. "It's a business. You go where you think you can have the most results, whether it's close to home or not. Why do you think I asked to be traded to the Yankees at the end of my career?"

Scales chuckled. "Good point. From what I know, you and the word 'yankee' wouldn't usually come up in the same sentence."

"It took a while for me to get my head around it," Hammerskal said. "Being called a New York Yankee just didn't feel right at first."

"But you got over it."

"I got over it."

"Being part of the sport's all-time winningest franchise will do that for you, I'm guessing."

"That's right, Rick." Hammerskal had begun the night calling his companion 'Mr. Scales. ' As the night progressed and their win streaks at the roulette tables grew, that quickly changed to 'Richard' and then finally 'Rick' – at Rick's insistence. "Life's too short to play on losing teams any longer than I have to. And after sizing up the situation in Nashville after that fiasco with the mayor on 'Clubhouse Chatter,' I needed to find a better deal. And it sounds like you've got one."

"I do, Wynn. You did the right thing. I'm still curious about how you knew to seek me out, though."

"Well," Hammerskal said, winking at his companion, "it's hard to keep a lid on something as big as what you're planning. People talk. I listened."

Another chuckle. "You know, you're right about that, Wynn. You know that saying that there's no way three people can keep a secret unless two of them are dead. Well, that's true when you've got as many people working around you as I have."

Scales nodded toward the bartender, standing a short distance away at the tiki bar. "For all I know," Scales said, "that guy has been leaking information to the outside world to make a few extra dollars on the side. Or maybe even these young ladies. While we're enjoying their company, they could be mentally taking notes on our conversation."

Hammerskal's date giggled and Scales' date feigned an expression of mock indignation.

"They could even have microphones hidden in their bikinis," Hammerskal said.

"Well, with any luck, we'll be able to strip search them later tonight," Scales said, prompting both women to start splashing at the men playfully. After a few seconds of roughhousing, they all took a break to sip their drinks.

"But, you know, Wynn, that does make me think," Scales said. "I'm sure you've got inside sources that are as good as anybody's in baseball. But if you heard about my plans, that means other people could have, too. Now, I'm not worried about other people finding out because I have inside sources, too, and they assure me that I'm going to get the new franchise. But on something this big, I think it's important to get out in front of it and manage the story in the media. So I think it's probably best to go ahead and have a news conference announcing my plans sooner rather than later."

"Whatever you think, Rick. Just tell me what you need me to do."

"If we're going to do a news conference in Las Vegas, it has to be fancy," Scales said. "But not too fancy. We'll have it in the grand ballroom of my casino, of course. We'll have an orchestra, a few showgirls and a guy wearing the mascot's costume."

"Mascot?"

"Yeah, we're going to call this team the 'High Rollers.' So the mascot will be an angry pit boss. I've already had the costume custom made. It's fantastic! Big burly guy, with a cigar and one of those unibrows that stretches all the way across his forehead. Clipboard in one hand and a green eyeshade on the top of his head. I modeled the costume after a guy who actually works as a pit boss in my casino."

Hammerskal held up his glass in a salute, then took another swig of mint julep. "Sounds good," he said.

"So anyway, I'll take the stage first, but only long enough to introduce you as one of the part-owners of the Las Vegas High Rollers. You'll come up to the mic and talk a little bit about your baseball career and how much the sport means to you. Give the crowd a taste of that thing you do – the Jackhammer Jump – and I guarantee they'll go nuts."

"I can do that," Hammerskal said. "No problem at all."

"I know you'll do a great job with that, Wynn. I've seen you work a news conference before. So you wrap up your speech, then I talk about the details of the proposal to put the new team in Vegas and my plans to build a huge development that will include a new baseball stadium, a casino and restaurants and shops. While all that is sinking in, I'll cue the orchestra and the showgirls and they'll play and dance us to a big finish. Sound like a plan?"

"It's a plan all right. I just want to be sure that besides making me a part owner of the new team, you'll also back me in my plans to develop a new baseball videogame."

"Sure, why not?" Scales said. Actually, he thought the idea was kind of juvenile. But if that's what it took to get this hayseed in his corner, it was a small price to pay. Who knew? Maybe Scales could develop some kind of tie in to online gambling so he could monetize that part of this operation, too.

"That's awesome," Hammerskal said. "And you're sure you'll be able to get the franchise? I don't want to get hitched up with another loser, you know."

"Trust me, Wynn, if there's anything that I am sure of, it's that I'm going to get that franchise. And the public backing I need to pay for that development project. Pretty soon, you and I will be raking in so much money that there won't be enough cigars in the world to light with all the hundred dollar bills we'll have."

Hammerskal laughed and pulled his date a little closer to him. "That's all I ever wanted," he said.

CHAPTER FORTY-TWO

As was usually the case in Rick Scales' world, everything was going according to plan.

The reporters had begun filing into the casino's grand ballroom following the reception where they had been plied with plenty of finger foods and booze. There they were joined by enough of Scales' friends and supporters to make sure there were no empty seats. Scales had learned long ago that one of the many perks of being rich was that it wasn't hard to find friends and supporters when you were throwing a party.

And that's how Scales wanted the whole country to perceive this event – as a big party. A party in which he would unveil his grand plans to merge the worlds of professional baseball and casino gambling. His public relations staff had done a great job of making sure representatives from all of the important national media outlets were here. And just for good measure, the news conference was also being streamed live on the casino's website.

As the guests began taking their seats, the orchestra struck up a big band rendition of Kenny Rogers' hit song "The Gambler." Scales knew it was a little obvious, but it fit the occasion.

Joining him onstage were Wynn Hammerskal, a guy in the pit boss costume and six lovely showgirls dressed in glittery costumes and feathered headdresses. That, too, was a little obvious. But this was Las Vegas, and Scales knew that's what people expected.

Scales and Hammerskal took their positions to the right of the podium decorated with a banner bearing the casino's logo, which showed what appeared to be a pair of lions playing craps under the lettering "RS Casinos, Inc." Underneath that banner was a second banner bearing a logo for the Las Vegas High Rollers, a baseball player with a dollar sign instead of a number across the front of his jersey and a dice-retrieving wand in his hands instead of a bat.

Scales was planning to drop the casino banner and unveil the team banner at the end of the news conference, while the balloons, confetti and indoor fireworks were cascading from the ceiling and the showgirls were dancing to the orchestra's take on John Fogerty's "Centerfield." There was no sense doing anything in Las Vegas unless you did it big.

The team logo hadn't been approved by Major League Baseball's league office. Nor had the team, officially. But Rick Scales had Raymond Goldfarb in his back pocket, so those were just formalities.

Beside the exits in the back of the room, casino employees were prepared to hand each person in the audience a complimentary $20 chip for use in the casino after the show was over. That was expensive, but Scales expected a big payoff. Some of the reporters would decline their chips for ethical reasons, but even they would be impressed by the gesture. The others would end up spending the $20, plus a lot more, before or immediately after they filed their stories. Despite his initial outlay, Scales expected to come out ahead financially before the evening was over. After all, what was it they said in the "Ocean's Eleven" movie? The house always wins.

Based on his life experiences, Scales knew no other outcome. He'd been a winner throughout his business career. And he'd be a winner again today. A winner with a plan to monopolize the stadium/casino construction business for decades to come.

As Scales approached the podium covered with an array of microphones, the showgirls took their positions in a straight line to the left of the speakers. The guy in the pit boss costume milled around behind the others, brandishing an oversized prop cigar.

"Welcome to Las Vegas, ladies and gentlemen!" he intoned with a broad grin. "Are you feeling lucky today?"

Many in the audience answered with approving shouts and applause.

"I think you are lucky today," Scales continued. "Although let's hope, for my sake, that you're not *too* lucky."

The audience responded with laughter.

"You know, I'm feeling pretty lucky today myself," Scales said. "I've invited you all here today because we have a very big announcement for you. An announcement that will change the face of sports – and wagering on sports – forever."

A hushed murmur from the crowd.

"I'm going to get into the details about that announcement in just a minute. But first, I would like to introduce you to someone I'm proud to call a partner in my latest business venture. He's been called a reincarnation of Dizzy Dean, one of the greatest pitchers in Major League Baseball during the 1930s. Almost a century later, he was one of the greatest pitchers of his time. He's a man who doesn't conform to the rules of others; he's always charted his own course throughout his career. I love that about him, because together he and I are going to chart a new course for professional baseball. You know him, you love him, ladies and gentlemen, let's give a big Las Vegas welcome to Wynn...'The Jackhammer...Hammerskal!"

The crowd erupted into thunderous applause as Hammerskal hopped to the podium doing his trademark Jackhammer jump, which the pit boss mascot was mimicking in the background. Some of the spectators rose to their feet and joined them, shaking and bobbing their heads up and down until Hammerskal waved his hands to signal for quiet. Scales, hands behind his back and chin tucked slightly downward, strode theatrically past the showgirls to the other side of the stage to give his warm-up act a chance to do his bit.

"Wow, I just can't tell you how excited I am to be in Las Vegas tonight," Hammerskal beamed. "I'm here today to do something I've never done before. And for those of you who've followed my life and career know, there aren't too many things that The Jackhammer can say he's never done before."

The crowd hooted with laughter.

"I think most of you know that for the last several months, I've been working with some people in Nashville to try to get a Major League Baseball franchise located there. And you know, before all that started, I didn't think there was anything you could tell me about baseball that I didn't already know. I've loved baseball ever since I was a little kid. I got to live my dream of playing in the Major Leagues, where I'd still be today if not for a very unfortunate accident that ended my career."

A few knowing chuckles from the crowd.

"Well, I thought I knew a lot about baseball, but this whole process has been an education for me. I knew a lot about what happened between the lines on a baseball field, but I didn't know anything at all about the business side of baseball."

Hammerskal had been grinning, but his expression suddenly turned serious.

"I learned that there are a whole lot of people out there in our great country, young and old, who love baseball the same way I always have. People who would love to see the greatest players in the game, playing right in their hometowns. And there's nothing wrong with that. I still believe that baseball is the greatest game there is."

A small smattering of applause. The tension in the room seemed to have intensified during the last few seconds of Hammerskal's speech.

"But what is wrong is that there are also a lot of people out there who take advantage of the people who really love the game. And let me just tell it to you plain – these people, the ones who take advantage, are the Major League team owners."

Now there was a confused muttering among the crowd. They couldn't tell if Hammerskal was being serious or if this was just the set-up to another one of his punch lines. Scales was wondering the same thing.

"These owners, they make millions of dollars from their teams, on top of the millions and millions they already had before they ever got into the baseball business. But they know how badly cities want the product they are selling. Every city would love to have a Major League Baseball team. But not every city can have one. And these owners know this. So they make cities build their stadiums for them, even though the baseball teams have plenty of money to build stadiums on their own. Cities build roads, electrical lines and water and sewer lines to serve those stadiums. They give the team owners tax breaks and other incentives. And they do all this at the expense of the cities' taxpayers – including all the other businesses in town that play by the rules and pay their own expenses."

Scales had listened to Hammerskal veer off message in stunned silence. For a minute there, Scales had thought Hammerskal was about to make some point that would end up disparaging Nashville and Orlando, but he had gone too far. After all, Scales was expecting a taxpayer-funded stadium/casino development and whatever other incentives he could wrangle out of Las Vegas city leaders.

"Wynn, I think we've gotten away from the main point here," Scales said, off-microphone. "Let's bring this one home."

"You know what happens, though?" Hammerskal continued. "These owners are never satisfied for the free stadiums they get for very long. Pretty soon, they want brand new stadiums that are even fancier than the ones they already have. And if the cities they're in aren't willing to pay for new stadiums, then they threaten to go to some other cities that will. And so all these cities keep trying to outdo each other, which ends up costing them and their taxpayers more and more in the long run."

Scales took a step back toward the podium. "I'm going to have to put a stop to this," he growled.

Just then, a voice called out from under the headdress of the showgirl on the end of the line closest to the podium. "Are you ready, girls?" called Autumn Sunshine.

"We're ready!" answered Dr. Iris Moon from the other end of the line. The women locked arms and pivoted so they were facing Scales, blocking his access to the podium. Moon snapped a finger of her free hand toward the orchestra, which began playing the Broadway musical favorite, "One."

The women shuffled back and forth, kicking their legs out high and across their bodies in unison each time the orchestra hit the first note for a new line of the song.

"So let's call this what it really is," Hammerskal continued, raising his voice to be heard over the music and the increasingly loud mutterings from the crowd. "It's blackmail. These team owners are blackmailing cities! And it's all legal!"

Hammerskal shot a meaningful look over the heads of the showgirls toward Scales. "Well, not all of it is legal. Some of it is just the plain old type of illegal blackmail that a person should be put in jail for."

Scales had seen and heard enough. He lunged toward the podium, planning to wrestle control of the microphones – and control of his event – from Hammerskal. Then he heard the crack and felt himself falling. He landed on his side, still conscious but too stunned to move. He'd planned to mow right through the line of showgirls on his way to the podium, but he'd dropped his head just as they were executing another one of their kicks. The stiletto heel of the woman on the far end of the line – the one who'd spoken first – had caught him squarely in the jaw.

From where he lay, he could still see what was happening at the podium between the legs of the still dancing showgirls, but he could neither hear nor speak. And his addled brain could only come up with two questions:

Why was Connie Britton in his chorus line and why had she kicked him in the face?

At Hammerskal's signal, the orchestra stopped playing and the showgirls stopped dancing, although they still stood in formation between Scales' prone form and the podium.

"I will be happy to tell all of you reporters the rest of what I know in private interviews after we're done here," Hammerskal said. Then, glancing down toward Scales, he added: "Well, maybe not everything. I think our host is going to agree with me that sometimes that old expression, 'What happens in Vegas, stays in Vegas,' makes an awful lot of sense. Now before I leave, I'd like to introduce you to someone else who'd like to say a few words that I think you might like to hear."

The crowd went silent as the man in the pit boss costume walked to the podium and removed his giant pit boss head.

"Hello, everyone. My name is Kent Gables and some of you may recognize me as the mayor of Nashville."

Another gasp from the crowd was quickly swallowed by more silence.

"I'm one of those city leaders Mr. Hammerskal was just talking about a minute ago," Gables continued. "Like him, I really love baseball and always have. And I really wanted to bring a Major League team to my city. In fact, I wanted that so bad that I lost perspective on some very important things. I was willing to make some concessions in order to get a team that may not have been in the best interests of the taxpayers I was elected to represent. I own up to that mistake. Also, as many of you know, I recently made a fool of myself on national television by getting into a fight with the mayor of Orlando over this competition to get a team. Well, it was about that and also some other things that I don't want to go into, but that, too, was a mistake. And Skip Goodman, if you're listening live or you see any of the news accounts about this event, I want you to know that I apologize."

Gables paused for a moment to let his words sink in before continuing.

"What I won't apologize for – what I'll never apologize for – is wanting the best for my city. And that's not limited to sports or any other form of entertainment. I want our city to be recognized as one of the country's greatest, but not just because we're home to a bunch of athletes who can hit baseballs a long way. You know, people talk about how the group of Major League cities is so elite. But there are more than 30 of them already, and counting. I want to be known as a mayor who's done something for his city that no other mayor has ever done before. That's why today I'm announcing my plans to establish a new system of public schools – really a system within a system – that are dedicated to training our young people to excel in the kind of math and science skills they'll need to compete for the best jobs in the global economy. We've got a local businessman, a man named Hunt Blazen, who I plan to appoint as superintendent of this special school system. He's got the passion and the drive to make these schools succeed. These schools, covering all the grades from kindergarten to high school, will need funding, of course. But I've spoken with the leaders of our local chamber of commerce and other economic development groups. They understand the value of having a highly educated workforce that will give our city the ability to compete with countries all over the world for the best jobs in the best industries. So these groups have agreed to support my recommendation to our city council that we go ahead and establish the special taxing district we were planning to put in place to finance a stadium. But instead of building a place to play, that money will be used to make our city's school system one of the nation's elite. And if Major League Baseball wants to put a team in that kind of city, we'll be OK with that. But if they don't, we'll still be guaranteeing that our citizens go out winners. And that's a challenge I'd like to make to all the other cities around the country: Instead of using up valuable resources competing amongst ourselves for sports teams, let's instead devote our time and money to make our schools and all the other municipal services the best they can possibly be. If we do that, in the long run, it'll mean a lot more than a World Series ring. Thanks for your time."

With that, Gables, Autumn, Iris and the other showgirls walked off the stage. Hammerskal did, too, pausing only long enough to sweep both his hands in a circular motion, ending up pointing to the ceiling. That was the signal that brought down the balloons, confetti and fireworks as the ballroom descended into chaos...

...At a small diner a few blocks away from the Las Vegas strip, Horton Edison closed his laptop as the live feed of the casino news conference ended. As he rose and prepared to pay his bill, he was smiling.

CHAPTER FORTY-THREE

The Uber driver dropped Julius C. Malfair off at the curb of a busy street in The Gulch. The Gulch was one of the city's newest neighborhoods, built on the grounds of what had once been a huge railroad switching yard just west of downtown.

What had once been a dingy area frequented by vagrants was now the home to trendy restaurants, bars and ultra-modern high-rise condominiums. Malfair made his way slowly along the sidewalk, eyes downcast.

As he walked past a brewpub, a sushi smorgasbord and a place that specialized in American South/Korean fusion cuisine, he could hear the muffled sounds of laughter and cheerful banter inside. Malfair was not at all cheerful.

He'd been so close. He had almost delivered a multi-million dollar prize, a Major League Baseball franchise, into his clients' hands. It was the kind of deal that made the career of a lawyer like him.

Unless it broke his career instead. None of what had happened was Malfair's fault. He'd done everything his clients had asked. He'd taken their stooge, Wynn Hammerskal, and turned him into the perfect pitchman for their cause.

Everybody knew Hammerskal was a little crazy; that was his reputation. But who could have predicted what he was going to do out in Las Vegas? Or even that he'd be in Las Vegas?

That stupid mayor Kent Gables hadn't helped matters, either. One nationally-televised meltdown was more than enough for anyone's lifetime. Gables had two in the span of only a couple of weeks. Fighting with another mayor on a talk show. Crashing a press conference in a mascot's costume.

But it was Hammerskal's speech that had really driven the final nail into the coffin. All that touchy-feely hooey about how baseball team owners always had their hands out, looking for corporate welfare. So what if it was true? That wasn't the truth he was supposed to be telling as a part owner and media spokesman for the Nashville Stars baseball team.

Oh, Hammerskal knew how to give a good speech. It was so good that it had inspired a consortium of West Coast web application developers to pool their resources and privately finance a stadium to support an expansion team in Portland.

Privately finance their own stadium! Those idiots had more money than sense. But they had apparently made an impression on Raymond Goldfarb. The commissioner of Major League Baseball had recommended that the league owners accept Portland's bid for the team – and the team owners had accepted that recommendation. If there was one thing the league's other owners respected, it was someone who could bring a lot of cash – and the promise of even more cash – to the table.

So Portland and San Juan were getting the new teams. Nashville and Orlando were not. Media pundits across the country were already praising the geographic symmetry of admitting one team from the Caribbean and another from the Pacific Northwest.

So as Malfair turned and entered the lobby of the 25-story condominium complex, he knew what was waiting for him. One of The Cabal's members kept a condo on the top floor as a second home for the times he worked too late to commute back to his elegant house in the suburbs. The rest of The Cabal's members were joining him there for today's meeting. And Malfair had been invited as their guest of honor and the topic of today's agenda.

Malfair had made his reputation by delivering results. He knew he wasn't an easy person to get along with. And he did things on his clients' behalf that they often didn't approve of. But as long as he was winning, the end always justified the means.

But he hadn't won this time. He'd been hired to deliver one result: A Major League baseball team for Nashville. That wasn't going to be happening. And he had no illusions that his charm or personality would be able to bail him out of this.

Malfair had always relied on word-of-mouth for his client base. He never needed to advertise. He didn't even need a showy office near the courthouse. All he needed was a network of contacts that spread the word about his ability to deliver the goods.

Now, he'd let down a group of the city's most powerful business people. Business people whose reach extended throughout Nashville and to places far beyond the city limits. Although Malfair had always worked in the shadows, never in the spotlight, it wouldn't take long for his defeat in this venture to be broadcast as effectively as if he'd sent out a news release.

Malfair paused at the lobby's elevator bank to collect his thoughts. He couldn't help but think about how Abe Vigoda's character in "The Godfather" must have felt when he was lead away to be executed.

As Malfair punched the elevator button and waited for the doors to open, he wondered to himself how much those personal injury lawyers had to pay for their TV ads.

"Start Spreading the News - I'm Leaving Today"
By Gilbert Wise, Sports Columnist

Well, this is it, Nashville: I am outta here! As my loyal followers on social media already know, I gave my notice here at the Bulletin yesterday. By the time you read this, I'll be on my way to my new job in New York City. That's right, I'm off to the City that Never Sleeps. Where soon I'll be A-Number One, Top of the Heap…well, you get the picture. I'm not going to lie to you - it was fun while it lasted. I feel like I had a pretty good run in the Music City. I did my very best to elevate the quality of journalism in this little town. And I'm sorry to say, Nashville, but that's just what you are: A little town. The proof came when you had the chance to land your very own Major League Baseball franchise…and you booted it. It was all within your grasp. You could have had all the prestige of being in the same exclusive club as Los Angeles, Boston, Philadelphia and even New York. But when it mattered most, you showed that you didn't quite have what it takes.

We could point the finger of blame in a lot of places. There's Kent Gables, the mayor who showed he's not quite ready for prime time. There's Wynn "The Jerkhammer" Hammerskal, who showed he's no better at closing a deal than he was at driving a bullpen car. And there's all the whiny naysayers, led by the nutjob Anti-Arena Agitators, who didn't know when to shut up and let nature run its course.

So what happened? You let a city from the Pacific Northwest eat your lunch. You let Portland-freaking-Oregon eat your lunch. A place that would be nothing but a haven for lumberjacks and hippies if it didn't have such a good marketing campaign. But you've got to hand it to Portland: They had the will, so they found a way. As its citizens shiver through those dreary, rainy winters, at least they know they'll have something to look forward to when spring arrives. So now they've got the Trailblazers, a National Basketball Association team. They've also got a Major League soccer team, whose name escapes me at the moment. And now they've got a Major League baseball team.

I'd call them a two-and-a-half team town, but I don't like wasting time reading hate mail from all those goofballs who like soccer. So let's be charitable and call them a three-team town. That's what Nashville could have been. Looking back on it, though, it all seems so improbable now.

During the time I lived here, I noticed that Nashvillians spend a lot of time talking about how far their city has come. How progressive they are. How they've shed their backwater roots and become a cultural melting pot. How they're expecting 1 million new residents in their metro area over the next decade.

You know what? It all seems like Nashvillians protest too much. Deep down, they're still a bunch of farm hands who took their monthly baths, put on their best Sunday clothes and drove their pickup trucks into town for the big barn dance.

But while they're all gussied up, they're still all nervous and fidgety. Because they realize that if anybody looks at them too closely, they'll see the necks under those sun-dried shirt collars are still plenty red. Hey, I'm not bitter. Different strokes for different folks, as they say.

I'm headed to a real city where the people don't have to waste their time convincing everyone else that they're cool. National Football League teams? National Basketball Association teams? National Hockey League teams? And yes, Major League Baseball teams? New York has two of each. Plus enough soccer teams, indoor football teams and lacrosse teams to keep all the nonconformists happy. In short, it's a dream gig for a sports columnist like myself. No, I realize that I won't be the only sports columnist in town. In fact, there are probably enough of us to start our own borough.

But the cream always rises to the top. Which is what I plan to do. I know that if I can make it there, I can make it anywhere.
So go ahead, Nashville. Keep enjoying your moon pies and your way-too-sweet iced teas. I've made my big career move. And I know that I've made a Wise choice.

Chapter Forty-Four

It was a typically light crowd for a Wednesday night at Capital Indiscretions as The Chronies were wrapping up their second-to-last set with their rendition of Tom Petty's "Breakdown."

As his eyes drifted to the back of the room, Horton Edison spotted an extremely attractive woman fending off the advances of some kid in a Vanderbilt baseball t-shirt. As Iris Moon caught sight of Edison, she waved.

Edison put his hand over his microphone and muttered a few words to his band mates. They all laughed at the same time, then joined Edison in the first few lines of "One."

"We're going to take a short break now everybody," Edison announced to a smattering of applause and a couple of enthusiastic whoops from the patrons who'd had a few too many. "We'll see you back on stage in just a few."

Edison walked back to Moon's table and sat down.

"Well, hello, Dr. Moon," Edison said. "I haven't seen you in a while."

"Yeah, after all that happened, I needed a little time off," Moon said.

"I seem to remember signing your leave request," Edison said. "And I've taken a little time off myself. After I took time to clean up a few loose ends."

"So everything's going to be OK, then?" Moon asked.

"Well, other than the fact that we didn't get a Major League Baseball team, I think things are going to be OK."

"They don't have warrants for our arrest back in Nevada or anything, do they?"

"Arrests for what?" Edison said. "About the only charge Rick Scales could file would be against Autumn for assault. Thanks to the magic of the Internet, millions of people saw that ding-a-ling run right into her foot. Clearly, it was an accident."

Edison gave Moon a look. "It *was* an accident, right?"

Moon laughed and took a sip of her beer. "Yes, an accident. As far as you know."

"So is Autumn going to be OK?"

"Oh, yeah! After the incident at the casino, she told me that for the first time in her life, she felt 'empowered' by her activism. And I'm sure if Hunt Blazen gets the job managing those new schools, he'll find a place for her. The two of them seem to be getting along very well."

"I hope that works out all right," Edison said. "My boss and I still have a lot of work to do. We still have to convince the school board that this is a good idea. Which I don't think will be too tough of a sell. After all, it's not like it would be taking away public money and giving it to charter schools, which public school boards hate. Instead, this would be a set of high-performing schools that could boost the district's test scores, which school board members love, while maintaining some autonomy from the rest of the school system. Another concern will be about which students will be able to attend these special schools. But having a bunch of parents and students clamoring to get into public schools is a problem that most education administrators would love to have."

"What about the business community? It couldn't have been easy on the idea of them paying more in sales taxes to support the community's education system."

"Rowan Atwell and his bunch were skeptical at first, but they came around fairly quickly. I told them that if they are truly concerned about economic development in Nashville, their first priority should be a top-notch school system. Plus, the mayor sort of challenged them

– and actually elected officials across the country – to put their money where their mouths are about supporting education."

"Ah, yes. Your boss, the mayor. What will happen to him?"

"Politically speaking, this could be the best thing that's ever happened to him. He's got people convinced that he's tough and maybe a little crazy, but still smart enough to come up with ideas of substance. That could be a winning combination. He might run for governor. Or maybe he'll cut a deal with someone else who wants to be governor and would be willing to find him a good job in the state Department of Education. Who knows? Someone might even find a spot for him in Washington. You know those D.C. talk show hosts would be salivating at the prospect that he might go after somebody else on one of their programs."

Moon laughed. "He has developed a sort of macho reputation, hasn't he?"

"Definitely. And let me tell you that before this happened, the only way Kent Gables ever intimidated anybody was when he was sitting at a desk, pushing a bunch of house closing documents at them."

"What about Raymond Goldfarb, though? Do you think that there's any chance Scales will follow through on his threat to blackmail him?"

"No, for several reasons. First of all, anything he could say at this point would be sour grapes, since everybody now knows that he wanted a franchise, but didn't get one. Second, we found the prostitute he was with that night..."

"Wait, you found the prostitute? How did you do that?"

Edison cracked a sly smile. "Dr. Moon, I'm a political fixer. That's what I do."

"OK, so you found the prostitute."

"Yes, we found the prostitute. And it turns out she was never in on what Scales was doing. He paid her $5,000 to seduce Goldfarb and, unknown to her, Scales was going to parade her arrest record and her reputation all over national TV if the story broke."

"Wow."

"Anyway, she got a much better offer. Wynn Hammerskal paid her $10,000 to do one thing if Scales ever went to the media – which is tell the truth. The truth is that she went to a bar and seduced a widowed man into having what he thought was consensual free sex with her. If it's a crime for a red-blooded and lonely man to fall for that, then they're going to have to build a lot more prisons all over America."

"So he's staying in his job as Major League Baseball's commissioner?"

"Only through the expansion process and the new teams' first seasons. After that, he's already given notice that he's resigning."

"What will he do then?"

"He's told me that he spoke with the board of directors at Ray of Hope, his old organization, so he can become a consultant for them. That's his true passion, anyway. The only reason he left in the first place was because he hit a very low patch after his wife's death. Now he's ready to get back in there and do what he does best."

"Hammerskal really stepped up to the plate, so to speak, when you asked him for his help with your plan."

"I haven't even told you the best part: Wynn Hammerskal gave the prostitute a small business loan so she could get out of the life and open a hot yoga studio back in her hometown of Santa Fe."

"So he spent all that money converting a prostitute into a hot yoga instructor, plus what he paid to bribe the orchestra, the chorus girls, the stage manager and the guy who was supposed to wear the mascot costume."

"Ah, he just slipped them a few extra dollars to make the news conference a little more fun. It wasn't any big deal to them, particularly since they thought he was working for Scales at the time."

"Still, it was pretty generous on his part."

"Yes, it's nice to see some of the exorbitant amounts of money the New York Yankees spend on player salaries put to some good use. In fact, since he's pretty much through with baseball at this point, I fully expect him to become the Jackhammer of the Philanthropy World."

"He'll drill the contributions right out of donors," Moon said, with a giggle. "You must have made quite an impression on him."

"No, *we* made quite an impression on him. Why do you think I wanted you there when I laid out what was happening with the Las Vegas deal? He's quite smitten by you. Jocks like him love beautiful women. But you show them a beautiful woman with a brain, and they go nuts. Or at least he did."

"It seems like you really delivered big on all counts," Moon said. "Doesn't this whole thing improve your political prospects? You could take your old boss's place as mayor."

"My political prospects? No one but a few insiders know I had anything at all to do this," Edison said. "Remember, while Mayor Gables and Hammerskal were giving speeches and you women were using Rick Scales like a soccer ball, I was nowhere near the casino. I've always been a behind-the-scenes guy. I think that's where I can get the most work accomplished. So with any luck, the next mayor will see fit to keep me around. At least until some record producer discovers how great The Chronies really are."

"So, if you're staying at City Hall..."

"I think there will be a place for you there in the mayor's budget office, regardless of whether I'm around or not. And that, too, is a behind-the-scenes job where the right person can do a lot of good."

"I think I'd like that," Moon said as she took another sip of beer.

"You'd be great at it. In a couple of years, *you* could probably run for mayor yourself. Just something to think about."

"So I'll think about it."

Edison gave Moon a long look, then a smile traced across his lips. "Listen, there will be plenty of time for us to talk about all this, but I need to get back up there onstage."

"Do what you've got to do," Moon said. "Hitting it big with The Chronies sounds like a great retirement plan for a long-serving public official."

Edison got up and prepared to leave, then glanced back at Moon. "One last request: If I could bribe the band into playing 'One' again, would you like to join us onstage and wow the audience with some of your dance moves?"

"No, thanks," Moon said, with a dismissive wave. "Whatever I do from here, I know that my career as a showgirl is officially over."